S. R. Masters grew up around Birmingham in the UK. After receiving a Philosophy degree from Cambridge University, he moved to Oxford to study public health. He's worked across a variety of areas in the health service, including clinical trials.

His short fiction and novels have been published internationally. Labelled as "a writer to watch" by Publishers Weekly, he is also the author of *The Killer You Know*.

www.sr-masters.com

twitter.com/SRMastersAuthor

instagram.com/SRMastersAuthor

D1328668

THE TRIAL

S. R. MASTERS

Also by S. R. Masters

The Killer You Know

One More Chapter
a division of HarperCollins*Publishers* Ltd
1 London Bridge Street
London SE1 9GF
www.harpercollins.co.uk
HarperCollins*Publishers*
1st Floor, Watermarque Building, Ringsend Road
Dublin 4, Ireland

This paperback edition 2022
1
First published in Great Britain in ebook format
by HarperCollins*Publishers* 2022

A catalogue record of this book is available from the British Library

ISBN: 978-0-00-852012-0

This novel is entirely a work of fiction. The names, characters and incidents
portrayed in it are the work of the author's imagination. Any resemblance to
actual persons, living or dead, events or localities is entirely coincidental.

Printed and bound in the UK using 100% Renewable Electricity
by CPI Group (UK) Ltd

For Joe and Alice

PATIENT 3

Please use this diary to record how you have felt during the day, thinking of your physical health, mental health and overall wellbeing.

Day 14

This morning, when the pretty doctor gave me today's pill with that patronising little smile of hers, I was caught between an urge to run far away from her, to protect her, and an urge to smash her face into pieces so you would send me home.

    Does that help you? Is this the sort of thing you want to hear about?
    You definitely should hear about this stuff.
    Because it's your pills doing this to me.
    I wasn't certain at first, partly because of the headaches, which have left me feeling weak and unsure of myself, but also because of the whole

opulent package. The private jet, the island setting, the beautiful room with the sea view in front of me now…It beguiled me. Surely anyone with this much money must know what they're doing. They wouldn't be giving people a drug with side-effects this bad?

But I can't stop these thoughts, these alien thoughts, which worm into my head every day. New perspectives. New connections. New opinions. Like how I felt about the doctor this morning when she gave me my pill. And this maddening disorientation I feel when I consider what I've been doing with my life.

It's making me want to do things that I'd never do.

And the headaches aren't getting better. You promised they would, but they're getting worse. So much worse.

How am I then, you ask? Let me be honest with you. Let me really help your research and earn my fee.

You want to know about my physical health? How about: it's like I have another person inside here with me. An awful, animal person, with weak, animal appetites, and they're taking over my body.

And my mental health? Well, I want to run around your fancy complex scratching a warning into every surface so that any other idiot who comes here won't believe you when you tell them they won't feel a thing.

I want to warn them that you're going to take their souls.

And how about my overall wellbeing? It feels like you've opened a door in my head that can never be closed. That I've seen the world in a way that I can't ever unsee. And the worst part is, I want to run headlong into this new darkness. Because I know once it consumes me, the light I'm running from won't matter.

Yet right now I'm in the doorway, being yanked both ways by two powerful opposites.

In the last few days I've found myself on my balcony here, or on the patio high above the beach, and I think about how the damage might already be permanent. And I think about falling. Obliterating myself beneath this blazing sun to spite the darkness.

The Trial

And there have been times where I've wanted to go to the kitchen, find myself a knife, and stain your white coats red. Then I'd gather up those pills of yours, take them out to the cliffs, and cast them into the sea before burning this place to the ground.

Part One

Recruitment

Chapter One

1

Elle pretended to be absorbed by the glossy holiday brochure open on her lap below the reception desk while just metres away a giant man paced in the lobby muttering to himself and kicking the chocolate-coloured sofas.

'I told them,' he said to the vending machine on the back wall, 'you have to watch closely.'

He returned to the sofa. *Smack. Smack.*

Terry was one of the regulars. It had been weeks since she'd seen him around the hospital, and she'd been worried about what might have happened to him. Now, with every *sock* of the leather upholstery, Elle flinched. She wanted to push her chair away from the desk and into the back office, where she could escape upstairs and get help. But she didn't want to draw his attention. So instead, she looked at her holiday brochure and tried to keep still. Palm trees. White sand. A crimson cocktail.

'Do they listen though? *Do they?*'

Smack. Smack. Smack.

Terry mostly appeared at reception to access the hospital Contemplation Room, a space set aside for patients' spiritual needs. Elle would push the little red button on the wall to let him through and he always thanked her. Quiet and shy, something of the local ale uncle about him, he could barely make eye contact, let alone trouble.

Elle wasn't privy to the details of his mental health history – her job was strictly non-clinical – but Terry had been doing well enough to walk around without a chaperone. A common story at Parkwood, though, was patients being discharged too early – especially since Core Solutions took over some of the NHS contracts two years ago. They struggled, and sometimes returned unannounced – often in a bad way. She'd had two incidents in the last six months, one of which had needed police involvement because there was no longer any on-site security.

Something clattered in the lobby. Terry was shaking the vending machine.

She couldn't ignore it now. He was going to hurt himself. Elle stood, leaned over the desk, and called through the open glass hatch. 'Terry, are you okay? Do you need me to call anyone for you?'

He turned to look at her, recognition briefly in his eyes. Then he yelled, 'They look at you like goats. You want to watch out.' He kicked one sofa hard enough to lift it from the ground.

'Okay, Terry,' she said, 'I'll get someone to help you. Just wait there, okay?'

She slid the glass window closed, locked it, and turned to the phone. After the second incident she'd asked for more training and guidance from Core Solutions. Nothing had been forthcoming, so recently she'd invented her own protocol: Ward, PCSO, police.

Guessing Terry wasn't likely to be under hospital care anymore, she called the neighbourhood PCSO. It went to voicemail.

Elle glanced up to check the lobby again and startled. Terry stood just centimetres from the glass. Despite the November cold, he wore only a food-stained Iron Man T-shirt tucked into a pair of shorts. He slammed his palms against the glass, which shook in its rails.

'Can I get through? I need to get upstairs.'

Elle took a step back. 'Okay, let me get you help, Terry.' She tried sounding assertive yet compassionate. She didn't want to agitate him further.

He palmed the glass twice again. 'I need to see him.'

Elle could see the illness at work on the surface, his tense posture and dancing eyes. Yet it was in those eyes she could see the other Terry, too, imprisoned and afraid, and almost apologetic.

Terry spat on the glass. He yelled. He struck again, harder. Then seemingly defeated, he walked away muttering.

Elle took a deep breath, reached for the phone and tried the number for the PCSO again.

The reception window shattered, and Elle covered her face as glass shards rained around her. A round coffee table struck the desk, briefly lodging in the hatch before the weight of its legs pulled it back out. The remaining frame of jagged glass didn't stop Terry from attempting to climb through, and Elle darted into the back office, footsteps crunching. She turned, ready to shut herself in.

Terry had one bleeding knee on the desk and was stretching for the red button on the wall. If he pressed the one for the conference facility door he would be free to walk around amongst the fifty or so guests on site. Elle thrust out her arm and got there first, pulling the plastic lever below the switch to disable it. His hand swatted the button a moment after. He didn't know what she'd done, and retreated through the opening to try the double doors. Elle stepped back and slammed the door.

On the other side of the wall Terry began to kick out again.

'Terry, please calm down.' Her voice was so weak he probably couldn't hear it.

Elle looked down at the lock. The key wasn't there. It was in the reception drawer.

She grabbed the handle again; she could retrieve the key if she was quick. But the thumping ceased. His frustrated grumbling grew louder, followed by the sound of glass and other objects tumbling to the floor. He was entering the reception again.

Elle turned to flee. Once out in the corridor she could lock him inside, stop him getting upstairs. But at the back door she hesitated. What if he hurt himself in the office? She scanned the room. The stapler, the guillotine, a letter opener.

Terry kicked the door between reception and the office; he hadn't yet realised it was unlocked. The thin partition walls shook.

Was there time to clear the danger? She wouldn't be able to live with herself if—

The handle of the reception door squeaked and moved downwards. Before Elle could get out Terry stepped inside, shoulders heaving, a bull about to charge.

'Terry, you shouldn't be in here.'

'I need to see him.'

The people upstairs today were on a local authority training course, not clinicians experienced with seriously unwell patients. She had no idea what Terry would do, given his aggressive state, and she was the last line of defence.

He came towards her, and because the door swung inward

she would have to step into him to open it. So instead she stepped away, moving deeper into the office. Only Terry wasn't interested in the door. He changed his direction and came for her instead.

Panicking, she grabbed one of the fire extinguishers on the wall, snapped out the safety plastic and pointed the nozzle at him.

Embarrassed and scared, she said, 'Terry, please step back. I don't want to hurt you.'

He kept coming, shaking his head, muttering about how she didn't understand. His eyes were so very sad. She ordered herself to squeeze the handle, but…she couldn't do it. He was unwell. He didn't deserve to be assaulted.

She threw the extinguisher at his feet to put it between them, turned, and yanked open the door to the stationery cupboard. She shut herself in, darkness blanketing her. She snapped a lock that she'd only half-believed might be there and reached for the light switch, finding only cool brickwork. The stupid thing was on the outside wall, wasn't it? Now her only illumination poked beneath the crack at the base.

She sat with her back pressed to the door, trying to catch her breath. Trying to stop shaking.

'Terry, listen to me—'

Kick.

The force jostled her.

'Terry—'

Kick.

She tapped the pocket of her trousers. Her phone was still in her bag under the table.

'You need to go outside before I call the police. I'm frightened, Terry.'

The kicking stopped. Elle waited, listening intently, her eyes teary and her head involuntarily shaking from side to side.

'Terry,' she said.

After five minutes which felt more like an hour, she heard rustling at the door's base and scooted away. Her brochure, picked up that morning from an *actual* travel agent's as she cycled to work, slid into the cupboard with her.

A moment later the light came on.

She breathed. She listened. Outside a door opened and closed. Silence.

She stared at the brochure. Huffed a bitter laugh.

On the cover a sun-kissed couple held hands on a white sand beach, gazing at one another like they'd just been granted immortality in paradise. God, she really needed a holiday.

2

Elle's manager insisted she go home. The Learning and Development Centre had been closed for repair and cleaning anyway, and Elle needed time to recover. But Terry was now over at Marlstone Hospital having suffered deep lacerations on his arms and legs, and Elle wanted to stick around for updates. She'd been right about Terry's recent discharge, and those in the know confirmed he'd suffered a psychotic episode having abandoned his medication. She wouldn't be able to sleep tonight if she didn't know he was going to be okay.

She found a desk in the staff library, motes of dust soaring above her in the light from the high windows. Mostly she had the room to herself, but each time a visitor entered she startled. Her hands shook when she raised them to the keyboard, and she struggled to pay attention to the incident report on her screen. What happened was replaying once again in her mind when a soft voice to her right said, 'What are you still doing here?'

It was the head librarian, Winston, a greying man with

striking blue eyes and a penchant for attractive waistcoats. He was one of her few work friends – largely down to their shared interest in books. He'd brought Patricia Highsmith and James M. Cain into her life, while into his she'd bought Gillian Flynn and Anne Tyler. He'd heard about what happened downstairs, and looked at her with the pity usually reserved for a sick relative.

'Cup of tea?'

She nodded, and in his office she recounted her version of events while the kettle boiled.

'I should have handled it better,' she concluded, her cheeks hot with shame. 'I probably aggravated him.'

Winston looked amused. 'Is this you being serious? It sounds like you handled everything extremely well under a lot of pressure.'

'I shouldn't have engaged him. It was stupid, sticking my head out and telling him off. I should have just run for help.'

'And what would you be saying now, had he tipped that machine on himself?' He handed her a tea and they sat across from one another at Winston's desk. 'Or if a visitor had been hurt in the reception? Terry'll get the support he needs now, he'll be okay. Now, what about you? How are *you* feeling?'

'Guilty.' She sipped her drink. 'I pointed a fire extinguisher at him, Winston. I nearly fired it. I could have really—'

'Soaked him? Elle…you didn't know what was happening. He was in an aggressive and violent state.'

'He probably wouldn't have hurt me. And what if he'd bled to death?'

'That front hatch should have been upgraded to shatter-proof glass a decade ago.'

'If I'd stayed quiet in the first place, he might have just… walked off.'

'You think?'

Elle didn't know. It certainly hadn't felt like he was close to walking away at any point. 'Well…I just hope he's okay.'

Winston shook his head and his expression darkened. 'Why do I feel like we've had this conversation before?'

'What do you mean?'

'You're very charitable, Elle.'

'Thank you.'

'Well… I didn't entirely mean it as a compliment.'

She formed her mouth into an exaggerated O. 'I didn't realise.'

He laughed. 'Don't take this the wrong way… But do you remember I told you about that gentleman on Ash Ward I befriended, the bookworm?'

'The psychopath?'

'Not officially, they didn't like to use that term. But they ran the diagnostic checklist off-books and…well, yes. And you remember, he seemed nice face-to-face, very charming. But he'd actually done all these terrible things, and had not a jot of remorse about them. In fact, he was pathologically predisposed to blaming other people for his crimes. He beat a man to death for laughing at his jacket, and when the police asked him about it he calmly explained it was the victim's fault because he shouldn't have wound him up. That sort of thing.'

'I remember. But Terry wasn't psychopathic.'

'No. No, I'm talking about you still. You're also pathologically prone to blaming the wrong person. But in your case, you always blame yourself instead of the actual culprit. You and he are almost perfect opposites in that respect.'

She appraised him sceptically. 'I don't think that's true.'

'Elle… I watched you apologise to that oaf who knocked your laptop off the desk the other week. You even said you shouldn't have put it so close to the edge.'

'Oh, come on. I was just being polite. And maybe I should have been more…aware of him.'

'It was his fault. I saw the whole thing. He was too busy fiddling with his phone.'

Unable to hold his gaze, Elle turned to the print on the wall behind Winston, Chagall's *A Midsummer Night's Dream*. The two of them talked often, so his candour wasn't inappropriate. But still, how could it be wrong to be considerate? You *had* to think hard about the people around you. Because deep down we were all the same, weren't we? Not identical, of course, but on the Venn diagram of humanity all the circles would almost entirely overlap. Even the largest differences were still slight when compared with the similarities. Quirks of the environment, maybe, or perhaps one or two genetic switches flicked the other way. That underpinned 'Do unto others', the golden rule.

In fact, you *needed* to believe it. Because how else could you cope in the vast, mostly empty stadium of space, unless you had a team? A team meant you could find a consensus, and build things according to your shared needs and wants, your shared values. Without those, well, you might as well just not bother with anything and follow every selfish impulse you had. Forget about caring for others. Forget about the vulnerable, like those they both saw day in and day out at the hospital. Forget everyone, in fact, because for all you knew, their wants, needs and values were as different from yours as…as a goat's.

She said none of this to Winston, though. Instead, she sighed and said, 'Well… I don't think there's anything wrong with trying to put yourself in other people's shoes.'

'No, there's not,' Winston said, his voice softening. 'Just don't forget to put on your own. Your feet'll get cut.'

She paused. 'So you think I need to…what, embrace my inner psychopath?'

'The world would be a wonderful place if more people were like you. But there'd be a lot of martyrs, too, burning in other people's fires.' His smile was gentle. 'Just look after yourself, Elle, as well as everyone else. Sometimes in life, you know, you have to shoot a fire extinguisher at someone.'

She knew he meant well, but they'd have to agree to disagree. She was about to say something else but stopped herself, realising the whole conversation had been entirely about her. Core Solutions had put Winston's whole library service in review, as they didn't understand why staff needed a library in the digital age. His actual job was at stake, and here she was, bending his ear with her insignificant problems.

'So,' she said, leaning forward, 'never mind me. How are you?'

Winston broke into laughter.

3

At home Mum sat at the desktop computer in the lounge, her back to the front door.

'Hi, sweetheart,' she said, without turning around. She was scrolling Facebook, an activity which took up a good few hours of her day when she wasn't watching television. Their tenancy forbade smoking in the house, yet the air was redolent with another skirmish between incense and cigarettes. 'You're back early.'

'There was an incident at work. They sent me home.'

'Yeah?' She spun on the office chair to face Elle. Her nails were done, and she was in full make-up and lipstick. It had just gone 4 p.m., and she was still wearing her dressing gown and slippers. 'You'll never guess what, Elle.'

'What?'

'That bloke I saw last week.'

'Mike?'

'No, not him. That was just a likkle drink. No, I mean Phil.'

'Oh, yeah. What about him?'

'Turns out his brother's wife's nephew, right, well, his mate is the brother of that bloke from *Love Island* last year, the tiny one. Can you get your head around that? *Love Island*.'

Elle set her expression to impressed. 'How weird is that?'

'Weird. Like, I'm actually connected to *Love Island* now.'

'Six degrees of Deborah Ronson.'

'You what?'

'Nothing, Mum. Do you want a cup of tea?'

'Oooh, yeppies.'

Last night Elle had cleaned the kitchen while Mum was out. Now, the surfaces were cluttered with her breakfast detritus. Trails of tea droplets scored the floor tiles between the bin and the kettle. The milk sat out warm in a beam of low winter sun.

Elle tidied and cleaned again, made Mum her tea, and hid from the ever-blaring telly in her room. She lay on her bed, flicking through the collection of holiday brochures she'd been collecting over the last year. The travel agent had looked puzzled when she'd requested one that morning, as usually only the older customers liked them. But Elle liked physical objects.

She'd be thirty next year, and was of an age where the vestigial traces of the analogue past had still ornamented her youth. Cassette players, VHS tapes, filing cabinets: these things all carried warm associations with better times and places, specifically Granny Alice's villa in Spain during her late teens. They were bridges across time and space, and with the right object you could travel anywhere.

Where the brochures were concerned, they were bridges to some vague future where she'd finally have time to crack all the uncreased spines glaring down at her from the bookshelf. Be able to eat a meal she hadn't cooked to Mum's specific taste requirements. Have access to some sun. Some vitamin D.

Only it was a fantasy, wasn't it? Because she couldn't really abandon Mum for three weeks. There'd be too many questions, and God knew what she might get up to in Elle's absence. Plus she'd have to take money out of her secret savings pot, the one that she was filling to eventually buy a place of her own. Mum would become suspicious, want to know where the cash had come from.

Then again, if she didn't go now, especially after what happened today, when would she do it? In late January she was due to start the first few modules of a part-time forensic psychology Masters – her way out of the menial world of learning and development administration. Working *and* studying. She barely had any time now. After that there would be the early years of an actual career, scrapping it out in a competitive field to prove her worth. Between now and Christmas was really the closest thing she would ever have to free time.

She turned to the page in the brochure with a particular all-inclusive package deal in the Canary Islands. She liked the hotel in the picture, poking out into the sea on stilts and reminiscent of a cruise ship. It brought to mind Agatha Christie, *Death on the Nile*. She liked the look of the male model in the beach photo, his unusually pointy nose, and that his arms and legs weren't shaved like the other models'. Mostly she liked the guarantee of sun in the winter and the relatively short flight.

Elle picked up her phone and stared at the number at the bottom of the page.

She could have been killed today. Or at least seriously injured. Didn't Winston have a point about her needing to look after herself sometimes? And it wasn't as if she threw money around the place. Her last real holiday had been in her early twenties, a trip to Robin Hood's Bay with some old uni friends who had long since moved on to bigger and better things. High-powered jobs in big cities. Marriages and kids. And the last time she'd been on a plane was to Granny Alice's funeral almost a decade ago. Ever since finishing her English degree, she'd been working to keep herself and Mum afloat, putting right their many setbacks, trying to get her own life started. Really she hadn't had a moment just to take a step back and think.

'Elle,' Mum yelled above the television. 'Have you moved my fucking cigarettes again?' Her footsteps thumped through the flat.

Elle typed the number into the phone and didn't reply. Eventually, the front door slammed. She was convinced Elle hid them, but would always find them where she left them in the end.

Her finger hovered over the green call button. Her plan had always been to spend hours researching the cheapest deals and best destinations online should it ever get to this point; the brochure had just been about layering her fantasy. But now she wanted to plunge not glide. And it felt good helping a bricks-and-mortar business, the sort of thing Granny Alice would do if she were still alive. Like only eating Fair Trade chocolate and buying her eggs from a local farm.

She made the call in a nervous fever, cold and slightly out of breath. She spoke quickly, never giving herself a chance to change her mind. And when it was over, she threw the phone down on the bed and covered her mouth. She'd done it. Three weeks in Fuerteventura. Three bloody weeks in the bloody Canary Islands.

When she came into the lounge to retrieve her bag, Mum was back at the computer, the smell of smoke still about her. She flicked from Plenty of Fish to Facebook on her tabs. 'Who you been talking to?'

Not wanting her to know just yet, Elle said, 'Just work stuff,' and turned her face to hide her smile.

All-inclusive. Five-stars. The bloody Canaries.

4

After a second day spent in the staff library, the reception repair work underway, Elle came home to find a letter from the travel company sitting prominently on the kitchen counter. She froze. The logo and company name had been printed in red on the front. She'd asked for an email confirmation. Why was this even here? Mum sat at the computer, guiltily closing tabs before turning to beam at Elle.

'Nice day, sweetheart?'

'Yes, thanks.'

Mum stood and joined Elle at the counter. 'You going on holiday, love?' She nodded at the letter.

Elle's mouth dried up. She suspected Mum had opened her post in the past, which meant if this was a confirmation letter, and she'd read it, Elle couldn't lie. 'I was thinking about it.'

Mum nodded and narrowed her eyes. 'Good for you.'

'Would you be okay with it, do you think?'

'Crack on, love,' she said with a shrug, 'you fill your boots. They're expensive though, them lot, aren't they?'

Wary of Mum's reaction, Elle said, 'Well, I'm usually pretty frugal. And I have some money I always keep for emergencies. You know.'

'A holiday emergency. Very nice.'

Mum didn't break eye contact, and Elle's heart began to race. 'I didn't think it would be your sort of thing. You could have the place to yourself for once.' Mum said nothing, and Elle felt the full force of her silence. 'But if you did want to—'

'Would have been nice to have been invited, but we all need our space.'

Elle didn't know how to respond now. Whether Mum was cross or being cool. 'Nothing's set yet, if you want to do something together—'

'No, I think it'll be good for you. You're a good girl, Elle. Don't I always tell you? You deserve a treat.'

Elle wanted to believe her, and smiled with shaky gratitude. Yet she couldn't break Mum's gaze. It pinned her like a lab frog.

5

Her doubts about spending the money, about her mortgage fund and Mum, mattered little ultimately. The universe had its own brutal way of settling life's difficult moral conundrums.

'Oh, darling,' Mum said, as soon as Elle had walked through the door three nights after booking her trip. 'I'm in such a state. Listen to this.'

She held up her mobile phone, already on loud speaker.

'I want my fucking money,' said a male voice. 'You get it me this week, Deb, or I'm coming to get it from you.'

'Who's that?' Elle said.

'That Mike I've been seeing. He's saying I owe him this money, and now he's properly lost it with me.'

She pressed Play on the message again, dropping her face into her free hand.

'Hey,' Elle said, crossing the room and crouching to hug her. 'We'll sort it. We'll sort it.'

It wasn't what she wanted to say. What she wanted to say was, 'Not again.' What she wanted to say was, 'Why do you fall in with these people?'

She rubbed Mum's back and felt the rise and fall of her shoulders. 'We'll sort it, Mum.'

'Yeah?' Mum looked up, hopeful. She had a funny way of crying without tears, and her make-up remained untroubled by her sadness.

'What happened? Why does he need money?'

'He offered it me. Gave me a few grand to get the car mended. You know, because of the engine.'

'What happened to the engine?'

'And it costs that much to get it done, and he said not to worry. I didn't think he wanted it back?'

'I didn't know the car was broken.'

'I didn't want you offering to help. I know what you're like.'

'Oh, Mum,' she said, sadness building already about the inevitability of this conversation. Knowing how difficult Mum found it to get work and earn money due to her many issues – her bad back, her spells of fatigue, her mounting lack of confidence. Knowing how many times she'd had to help Mum out in the past, often with very large sums. 'How much does he want?'

'Three grand,' she said. Something must have shown on her face, because Mum added, 'But I think two would be enough to get rid of him. It's because I broke it off with him, Elle. He didn't take it well.'

Elle nodded. It was just over the amount she had spent on the holiday. 'Do you think we should just call the police, maybe?'

Mum shook her head, widening her eyes. 'I can't do that, love. He's one of those people that's *got* people, you know? He was in prison before. And, besides, I'm not like that. I can't grass. No, I'll just have to take what's coming, won't I? I shouldn't have been so stupid. It's not like either of us have that sort of money.'

Elle swallowed. She already knew what was being asked of her. 'Mum—' She was about to tell her that she'd already bought the holiday. That she couldn't help her even if she wanted to, which she really did. She always did. Mum had never had it easy, especially having lost Dad when Elle was so young. But she couldn't lie. Hadn't she known the holiday was excessive, really? This was just the universe restorIng balance.

'I've got savings,' she said. 'We can use that, if you really think it'll make him go away.'

'No, Elle, not your holiday money.'

Elle hugged her again. She didn't necessarily have to use the holiday pot. She could dip into her house-deposit pot instead… The problem there was that Mum would then know that it existed. And even though deceit didn't sit well with her, she didn't ever want Mum to know about it. Not only because Mum would be upset by her plans to one day leave. No, that was part of it, but, if she was honest, it was also because Mum had a tendency to spend money when she knew it was there. That was just her nature, nothing good or bad about it inher-ently. But it needed managing. And given Elle already paid the rent, most of the bills, and bought the shopping – which was only fair because she was the one with the degree, the one who *could* find work – Mum's ignorance really helped them both. Mum had lost track of the cost of living.

'I haven't booked the holiday yet,' Elle said. 'So…let's just give him what he wants. Get him off your back and worry about the rest later.'

'Oh, sweetheart.' Mum grabbed Elle and pushed her face to her chest. 'I can't ask you to do that. No.'

'It's fine, Mum,' she said. 'You haven't asked. I offered.'

6

The travel agent sounded upset when Elle cancelled. Had she sensed Elle's heartbreak, or was she just on commission? Afterwards, Elle took out the cash from the bank, and that night Mike, a tattooed brick wall who insisted on doing the swap in person, took the money from Elle at the front door while Mum hid in her bedroom.

After he'd gone, Mum kissed her and went to the pub to drown her sorrows. 'Going to The Bull' was one of the few joys in Mum's life, so Elle couldn't question the decision – even if she did worry that Mum might run into Mike there so soon after he'd been in the area. After all, it was where they'd met.

Alone in the flat, Elle watched television and flicked to her favourite page in the brochure. She traced her finger idly around the shape of the island in the photograph, taken from out at sea. She'd spent a year amassing her holiday pot while still having enough to put aside in the other pot. A whole year.

Still, maybe it wasn't such a disaster. What if she got a second weekend job over Christmas? Maybe this setback could spur her on to do that, and she could use that extra money to go away somewhere cheaper. A little DIY thing on Airbnb, perhaps. She didn't need a fancy hotel and champagne breakfast anyway. She wasn't the flipping Queen. There might be time in the last week of December or early January before her course started.

On her phone she checked out prices in the Canary Islands, but the battery died. She sat down at Mum's desktop, clearing the screen saver with a swipe of the mouse. Mum's Facebook page was up, and staring back at her was a picture of Mike and Mum, their cheeks pressed together, posted two weeks ago.

She opened a new tab, which joined the other ten, and typed 'Canary Island home rentals' into the search bar.

The first hit was a sponsored link, and on reading it Elle cocked her head.

18–40? PAID CLINICAL TRIAL IN THE CANARY ISLANDS – UP TO £20,000 TAX FREE

She hovered the cursor over it, but didn't click. Too good to be true, surely?

Take part in our drug trial! Benefits: healthy financial package and month-long all-inclusive island break. Become a volunteer. Apply online. Steps: Application, Eligibility Questionnaire, Screening, Consultation, The Trial.

Elle shook her head. She didn't know how advertising algorithms worked, but if they'd worked out the precarious state of their home finances, it could well be a scam. She had heard about clinical trials paying good money, though, and had even seen them advertised around the hospital. But she hadn't realised the amounts involved could be so enormous. Was that even ethical? Maybe it was a typo.

She mentally bookmarked the advert, despite not clicking on it. And she was surprised a little later that night when, unable to sleep, she entered the same search on her phone and couldn't find it. She tried other combinations of words, actually searched for 'clinical trials in the Canary Islands', but the only adverts that appeared on her phone were for flu trials or Canary Island holidays.

Exhausted but curious, she tried Mum's computer again, typing in 'Canary Island home rentals' as she had done earlier.

The advert appeared. This time, she clicked it, cut out a lengthy web address that looked like someone had fallen asleep on the keyboard, and emailed it to herself, intending nothing more than to see if it worked on her phone.

But she didn't leave the computer. Instead, she examined the landing page. If it was a scam, it was a slick-looking one. The backdrop wasn't unlike a brochure photograph. A glittering swimming pool surrounded by empty sun loungers. The copy was identical to what she'd seen on the advert. But here there was a mission statement too:

We are Apollo Wellbeing, a biopharmaceutical start-up developing innovative solutions in the field of medicine. Our view is that health is a state of complete physical, mental and social wellbeing, and not merely the absence of disease or infirmity.

The last line had been stolen. Elle recognised it from her degree pre-reading: it was the World Health Organisation's definition of health. Which was interesting, because modern drug companies didn't usually acknowledge the existence of non-clinical models of care in such an up-front way. What was this trial then?

Elle clicked a large green box marked APPLY.

The screen turned white, and shortly black text faded into view.

PLEASE CLICK AN ANSWER FOR EACH OF THE FOLLOWING STATEMENTS AS THEY APPLY TO YOU.

The statement faded away, and was replaced by a question:
I have robbed someone.

Elle laughed. Four option boxes appeared: True, A Little True, A Little False, False. She clicked False.

'Can something be a little true?' she said.

This question faded and was replaced by another:

I don't mind queuing.

Well, no one really liked queuing, but Elle didn't get irritated the way she'd seen some people do. A Little True, then.

Next up was:

Honesty is the best policy.

Which of course, it was.

She answered forty questions in total, each one seeming to mine her personality and values, and, after twenty minutes she was finally asked to enter her email address and name. If she had to guess, the questions were likely designed to weed out the sort of people you wouldn't want to have on a month-long clinical trial on an island, and based on her answers she suspected she had a good chance of at least making the next stage.

After the site thanked her, the browser closed itself down. Curious. She opened it again, and looked for the site in her mum's internet history. It wasn't there. Elle entered the search again to bring up the advert, only now it was showing exactly what she'd seen on her phone the other night.

Before she could investigate further, her phone chimed. She opened her lock screen and the entire text of the email she'd just been sent was visible.

Dear Elle Ronson,

Thank you for applying to join one of our clinical trials. We are extremely grateful that you took the time to complete our questionnaire. However, on this occasion you have been unsuccessful.

'Oh,' Elle said, the small amount of hope that had built in the last ten minutes forcibly displaced.

That was that then – never mind. She put her phone away, poured herself a large glass of white wine, and read a book until her eyes grew heavy. And for a week at least, the trial never entered her head.

7

Saturday morning a parcel arrived for Mum. She was still out from the night before, so Elle signed for it, noticing the New Look logo – one of Mum's favourites.

Later, Mum found the package and said, 'Great, my prezzies have arrived.'

'Prezzies?'

'Yeah. Just some stuff I've got for friends. Birthday things.'

Perhaps if Mum hadn't taken the trouble to explain that, Elle might have been able to ignore the brand-new dress Mum stepped out in that night.

But then came a new car a week later, a neat little box Mum claimed she'd part-exed for her rusty Ka with a mate down the pub.

'Honestly, babe, I couldn't turn him down. It was too good an opportunity to miss.'

Mum wasn't averse to wheeling and dealing; she had form. But the timing… Mixed with the unshakeable disappointment from her cancelled holiday, it was poison. Elle, so practised at rationalising and absorbing Mum's lies, didn't believe her.

When Mum went out to the pub on Friday night, Elle went out for a walk. The local area wasn't exactly the most scenic – never mind safe – place to get some air. And more often than not, a Friday-night jaunt meant enduring at least a wolf whistle, if not a full-on verbal assault. White-shirted aftershave clouds, drunk before even getting the bus to town, lurked at bus stops and against pub walls. But Elle needed to move, was possessed by a desire to get out and make something happen.

And was she really that surprised when she ended up passing The Bull, and, just on the off chance Mum might want a pint with her, walked inside?

She was there, of course, because outside of the basics, like food, shelter, and sex, Mum craved the novelty of company on offer at The Bull. You could usually count on a mix of regulars and passing strangers most nights. She was sitting in the far corner on a table with six other people, many of them as young as Mum liked to pretend she was on her Plenty of Fish profile. Laughing her head off, wine glass in hand, free arm around of all people, Mike. Mike the voice-message violator. Leaning over now and kissing Mum on the head. The two of them laughing together. Laughing at Elle, even though they hadn't seen her yet.

'You alright, love?' a man behind the bar asked.

Elle turned, close to tears, and ran home.

8

She ambled around the flat getting drunk, piecing all the evidence together. Had Mum made Mike say those things on the phone to convince Elle? Made up a threat to her life to steal from her own daughter? Elle ran to the toilet and threw up. She mopped her mouth on a damp towel and went back to finish her wine.

Even for Mum, this was a new low. And she'd just let it happen again, like she always did. Like the time Mum used Elle's credit card for three months without telling her. Or when she borrowed a chunk of Elle's savings to go on a 'sciatica retreat' that turned out to be a spa holiday. She'd lost count of the times Mum forged her identity to take out various loans.

And she'd just let it go each time. Found a way to see it from Mum's perspective, forgive her and move on.

Then there had been the ordeal with the will, when Granny Alice had left Mum's share entirely to Elle. Granny Alice had explained her reasoning in Spain during the final weeks of her life. She'd leaned over from her hospital bed, and in a hushed voice told her Mum was broken in some fundamental way, and that Elle would need every penny of the money to stand half a chance against her.

'I believe honesty is the best policy,' Granny Alice said, 'and you need to understand she's not like you and me. Don't let her ruin you. Because she will if you let her.'

To be left something hadn't been such a shock. After all, Granny Alice had occupied much of the parental space left by her late father, not to mention, if she were being truthful, a fair chunk of motherly territory, too. In her childhood, Elle spent the greater portion of most weeks at Granny Alice's terrace in the outer suburbs of Birmingham – sometimes spending months there without ever seeing Mum. But cutting out Mum entirely, and in such a cold fashion, left Elle upset and shocked at a woman she practically worshipped.

Even though she knew then, at just nineteen, that Mum wasn't perfect, the sorrow she felt for Mum at having her own mother say such things made her want to help Mum even more than she'd already been trying to do. Mum hadn't had it easy since Dad died, and she found the basics of life – friendships, work, love –difficult. Was it any wonder when her own mother spoke about her so coldly?

After she passed, Elle decided to use Granny Alice's money to better Mum's situation. She transferred the whole amount to her, on the promise it would be used to build a new life for them both. Mum had cried. Promised things would be different. She'd buy a new house. Get some qualifications, start a career. Maybe buy a holiday for them both.

'You really are my angel,' she'd said.

But Granny Alice had been right. Mum burned through the money in three years of long-haul travelling and high-end living – all behind Elle's back while she was at university. Once she'd been given access to the money, she was unstoppable. And due to Mum technically being rich during her university application, Elle had ended up paying a much larger proportion of her fees at university, and came home with debts that could no longer be settled.

Elle opened a second bottle of wine and looked around the flat. She was a captive here, a hostage for Mum's ends. And the more she drank the more that revelation felt like a secret power that could see through walls and break down doors. All this time she'd assumed that deep down Mum was like her, and just needed her love to correct the course her life had taken. What rubbish. What shit. Just because there hadn't been any 'incidents' in the past year didn't mean Mum was getting better. That she was slowly learning the value of being an honest person, or, at the very least, coming to respect Elle enough not to exploit her.

No, she was just getting better at hiding her deceit. And Elle just kept gobbling it all up. Well, no more. She had to get out of this flat, out of her Mum's life. This time had to be the last.

She found herself sitting at Mum's computer, staring at the picture of Mike and Mum on Facebook. Her rage burned with thrilling intensity, yet close by prowled a smothering sadness. Because Elle knew herself well enough to realise that by morning, when she'd sobered up, all this anger would have diminished. Simmered down by reasonableness into bitter, manageable crystals that would lodge in her cells and form a life-ending tumour some time in her future. So while she had this power, she would nourish it. Keep the drink coming, journey far past the point of regret, and into a realm where even memory couldn't reach.

9

She awoke slumped on the beanbag in her room. A hangover pinched her head and neck in a hot vice, and Elle squinted at the bright sunlight coming in through the window. She gradually rose to her feet, drew the curtains and lay on her bed, flattening her goose bumps beneath the duvet.

What time was it? Her phone was on the bedside table. She reached over, but it was beyond her grasp. With a feat of Olympian heroism she rolled onto her side, the room swimming with the effort, and managed to wrap her hand around it.

It was only 10:30 a.m. Her condition required at least another five hours in bed. She couldn't remember what time she'd even fallen asleep, nor what she'd done after opening a third bottle of wine during a binge-watch of *Friends*. But there on her phone screen was a clue, and with half-open eyes Elle re-read the start of an email sent to the secondary address she used for her YouTube account. She clicked to open the message, and sat up.

Dear Elle Ronson,

Thank you for applying to join our clinical trial. We're pleased to inform you that we would like you to undertake a further application and screening questionnaire, with a view to you joining us in the Canary Islands. The link can be found below, and must be completed in the next 24 hours to be eligible.

Yours sincerely,

The Apollo Wellbeing Team

It came back to her then, that she'd tried to beat their questionnaire last night. She groaned. Obviously she'd succeeded, but how? A vague memory of answering the first statement came to her. *Have you ever robbed someone?*

Yes. She'd put yes, hadn't she? She couldn't recall much more than that, but she knew that much with certainty. Because she recalled telling herself it's what Mum would have put if she were answering. Had sort of put on a Mum character as part of a cathartic mickey take. She grimaced at the memory. Thank God she'd been alone. Was it possible, then, that she'd lied on the other questions, too?

She let out another groan, pushing her face into the pillow. And if it hadn't risked aggravating her hangover, she would have laughed.

10

By the time she felt well enough to get out of bed she'd received another email reminding her to fill in the second questionnaire. Reminding her that a free holiday and up to £20,000 was potentially hers. They were really laying the holiday stuff on thick, with the trial itself more of an afterthought.

Had the emails contained contact details beyond the bafflingly long no-reply address, she would have told them there'd been a mistake. That she'd just been playing around to see how far she could get. But there was no way to get in touch with Apollo Wellbeing, despite her looking online. Other than the advert, their web presence was non-existent. So the best she could do was try to forget the whole thing. It had probably just been a scam anyway.

Over a tea-time bowl of cereal, followed by paracetamol and ibuprofen, Elle tried to decide what to do about Mum.

Confronting her never went well. Mum was built with the emotional equivalent of a crumple zone, and could take the most withering criticisms without it even touching her core. She would apologise, maybe even cry, and days, weeks, sometimes months later, she'd return to her usual self.

And to what end such a confrontation? She couldn't kick Mum out. For a start, she simply wouldn't leave. Elle would have to be the one to move, and right now, where would she go, exactly? She was the last of her childhood friendship group still in the West Midlands, her uni friends were more like acquaintances these days, and the Mum-shaped sun at the centre of her life had been too hot for the few meaningful romances she'd had since uni to flourish. Winston, then?

The idea made her laugh out loud. Besides, she had no idea how Mum would cope without someone organising her life. Once Granny Alice moved to Spain, Elle had gradually taken over that role. There was a chance Mum might end up homeless? Or turning to one of the more undesirable types that frequented The Bull for help. As angry as Elle was, she still loved Mum. She could never truly abandon her.

Which was the problem with 'that's it' moments: they were only as powerful as your range of alternatives. And while she'd put aside all that money to one day move out, she'd never really put her imagination to the task of detailing how that might work. Was she going to keep paying for Mum's rent and living costs while also having her own place? That didn't seem sensible or possible. So what then?

What she needed was simply space. A break from Mum to rest her mind and get a fresh perspective. Perhaps, just perhaps, something might come to her, a way out that wouldn't destroy Mum. Something she couldn't see for all the other things competing for her attention. But now she was back to square one, because hadn't her holiday been about doing just that?

She opened her email on her phone and re-read the invitation from Apollo Wellbeing. She shook her head. It was really no better than buying a lottery ticket or putting on a bet. Even if she did fill out the second questionnaire, they would weed her out eventually, and she'd be back where she started, time poorer and still stuck with Mum.

Anyway, lying to get on a trial was wrong. It would skew all the results, render them worthless. Assuming it was a small trial, of course. It might not actually make much difference to a larger one, would it? And that was assuming she had lied. Last night was a bit unclear.

Wasn't it theoretically possible that the answers she'd given initially had nothing to do with why she'd been turned down? Might it have been a gatekeeping device to make sure she wasn't a robot? Her rejection could have been the result of bad timing, Elle victim to a random-selection algorithm. Might it even have been a glitch? Surely the second questionnaire, and any afterwards, would know if she wasn't a good fit?

That didn't feel right. Felt like the sort of slippery reasoning that got you into trouble.

It didn't feel *entirely* wrong either. It felt sort of like something Anne Shirley might do if Green Gables had Wi-Fi. More scampish than malicious. Suppose she did end up getting through and getting paid £20,000. Or even half of that. Added to her savings, she'd be in a position to buy next year. She could graduate and start looking for work outside the West Midlands straight away. She'd definitely be able to afford to keep paying for the flat, give Mum time to adjust and find an alternative.

Moreover, would a pharma company *really* miss the money when it came to it? Would science *really* suffer that much based on one participant being able to trick a weak recruitment tool?

That notion didn't feel quite as scampish, and so again she

tried to recall any other lies she'd told on the questionnaire last night, and, coming up short, she nodded, confident that it was possible she *might* have told the truth on the remaining questions.

Voices drifted from down the hall outside the flat, one of them Mum's. She didn't want a run-in with her yet, so she gathered her things to return to her room. But the key turned in the lock and Mum was inside before Elle could scurry away. And she'd brought company.

'Oh hello, lazy bones,' Mum said, 'have a good one last night, did we? Don't mind us, just grabbing that little charger thingy for the car. You remember Mike?'

Elle gawped. 'Hi again, Mike,' she said eventually.

He grunted, unable to meet her gaze, stroking the stubble on his face.

'It's all fine,' Mum said. 'We're all mates again now. All sorted.'

'Well,' Elle said, 'that's good. Glad to hear it.'

She retreated to her room. A bottle of wine she'd been working on when she'd fallen asleep last night still had a third in it. She swallowed a mouthful from the bottle, took out her phone, and began work on the next questionnaire.

Chapter Two

1

A taxi dropped Elle at the front of Oxford airport on the first Friday in January, just over a month after she'd found out about Mike and Mum's scam. Her guilt about her drunken deception kept company and swapped stories with the low-level imposter syndrome she always felt when entering a new social situation.

Once inside the empty main building, she carried her bulging suitcase to the front while trying not to panic about the quiet. She hoped she hadn't got the wrong date. Hoped it hadn't all been a wicked trick. It was almost 7 p.m. Right on time.

She took a deep breath and rolled her shoulders. No, she'd got the right date. It had been on the paperwork she'd already checked twice in the taxi. And it wasn't a trick. This was just her conscience working hard to ruin things for her, as usual, and she had no time for that gullible old fool anymore. She was

Holiday Elle now, fiery and free, had been the moment she said goodbye to Mum.

Finally, a man peered out from the back office.

'Are you here for the Apollo flight?'

'I don't think I'm going to space.'

The man gave a weak smile and she wished the joke back.

'Apollo Wellbeing?' he said. She nodded. 'They'll come and get you.' He went back to what he'd been doing.

Hearing the name of the company out loud had set her nerves squirming again. It would be fine though, she'd been over it a million times in the last four weeks. The regret. The urges to come clean and do the right thing. Thing was, as the application process had gone on, it became increasingly clear that the questionnaire Elle took initially was far less significant than she'd first assumed. So even if she had lied on every question, from the second questionnaire on she'd been completely truthful. Her medical history. Her life story. Her reasons for wanting to apply for the trial. In fact, she'd practically come clean in her phone interview with a researcher from the company, a serious-sounding American woman called Jess.

'I wasn't sure how to answer some of those things in the questionnaires,' she'd said, 'so I just chose ones sort of...impulsively sometimes. I'm a bit worried they might not...reflect me fully.'

'Well, I think that's okay,' Jess had said. 'There's a lot of factors that come into play when we make our final selection, but impulsive answers are fine. And they might be more accurate than you think.'

Who knew, maybe that was right? Maybe drunk Elle was the real Elle. Or at least who she was becoming now. Because standing here in this small airport, she certainly didn't want be Elle Ronson anymore. What had that ever got her? She'd been played time and time again, and all she had to show for it was her Norman Bates life – only without the nice motel. And what better time, what better situation, to reinvent herself?

Five minutes passed, and she actively suppressed the rising conviction that the punchline she'd been dreading was about to land. Then, from around the corner came quick footsteps, and a slim, clean-shaven black guy in a dark-blue polo shirt bearing the Apollo Wellbeing logo appeared, smiling apologetically. She put him somewhere in his mid-to-late twenties, although he strode with the confidence of someone older.

'Are you Elle?'

'Yes,' she said, her relief erupting unbidden.

'Hi, Elle. Benji.' He shook her hand. 'Sorry, we've had people coming one-by-one and you're our last. I just got a little behind. Have you been here long?'

'No, a few minutes.'

'Oh, great.' He blew out a breath and gestured she should follow. They started walking. 'On behalf of Apollo Wellbeing, thank you so much for agreeing to help us with our trial. I'm going to take you to the jet now and then we'll get straight off. Where have you had to come from, Elle?'

'Well, I got a cab in from the city centre, but I came up on the train this morning from a place called Marlstone.'

They turned a corner and arrived at a single scanning machine operated by two security personnel. Once her bags had been checked, she walked straight through to an empty departures lounge. Oxford Airport didn't handle commercial airlines, and a fair amount of its business was handling the private jets of the rich and famous. Having looked this up beforehand, Elle still hadn't quite expected things to be *this* smooth. This exclusive.

'So Marlstone,' Benji said, picking up their conversation. 'Near Birmingham, yeah? I know it well.'

'Really?'

'Yeah, I did a degree at Birmingham Uni, Sociology. We used to go out in Marlstone. Posh, isn't it?'

'Not the bit I'm from.'

He laughed. 'I feel you there.'

He led her through to a set of double doors and outside onto the brightly lit tarmac apron. They walked along a coned-off path towards one of the jets, the largest of the many parked nearby. It wasn't much smaller than the commercial plane she'd taken to Spain all those years before.

She ascended steps built into the door, and once she was inside a female flight attendant handed her a glass of champagne with a textbook welcome-grin. Benji showed her to a seat at the front of the cabin, the faces and gazes of other passengers, other *participants*, overwhelming her. A long-haired rocker type in an Anthrax T-shirt. A blond He-Man in white jeans. A punky woman in an oversized Hawaiian shirt. Everyone sitting alone. Then she noticed the plane's interior. White and minimalist. Hardwood floors. Chunky leather recliners. And was that a bloody lounge area with sofas?

She sat down, a little tipsy already without having taken a sip of bubbly. This was the real deal, wasn't it? This was money. This was important.

They would *absolutely* find her out.

'We've had a no-show,' Benji said, taking her bag and storing it above her head, 'so there's plenty of room.'

'This is so…swanky.'

Benji raised his eyebrows, as if to say, You've seen nothing yet.

2

After a brief, upbeat welcome speech before take-off, Benji made a final plea for people to declare if they'd snuck a phone or any other GPS-connected device through security with them.

'It's fine to tell us now if you forgot,' Benji said, 'but if it gets to the trial complex then Apollo Wellbeing will be very black and white about contract breaches. They may end up pulling the whole thing, which could mean none of you get paid.'

Elle had read the summary sheet of the forty-page contract so many times she could probably recite it by heart and her phone was safely locked in a drawer back at the flat. She didn't want Mum accessing her messages or using her data.

'Certain information from the outside world, once the trial starts, might bias the results. So if you thought it wasn't a serious thing, or if you've just forgotten to take it out of your pocket... Anyone? No?'

Benji looked pleased with the silence.

'Good stuff. One last thing, your personal screens today have a selection of films and box sets on them, but there's no Wi-Fi on the plane, even though you'll see browser windows and apps.' Someone booed and Benji grinned. 'You'll just have to get to know each other, won't you?'

A small applause ran through the cabin when he was done. Someone near the back, the punky woman maybe, yelled out, 'Yeah, science, woo,' which got a laugh. Benji, meanwhile, vanished into the front part of the plane.

3

Once they were airborne, the pilot made his introductions, warning them of upcoming turbulence, which in the end kept everyone in their seats for the entire flight. Every so often Benji checked in on her like they were old friends, sitting with her at one point and laughing with her about places around Birmingham they both knew: clubs and pubs, the Waterstones, the shopping centre in Marlstone. She liked his generous smile, and the way he made the perfect amount of eye contact when they talked.

'Are you here for the whole trial?' she said. A strong wind shook the plane but Benji's expression showed no sign of alarm.

'The whole month.'

'What's the place we're staying like?'

Benji shrugged. 'This is my first time.' He dropped his voice to a whisper. 'I'm new. Don't tell the others.'

'Oh wow, so you're in the same boat as us.'

'Same boat, same plane. I've seen photos though, it's well nice.'

'Do you get much time off to enjoy it?'

'Yeah, I hope so. I get some downtime when there isn't stuff to do. But I'm kind of the only one of me there, so I'm sort of technically meant to be on it all the time really. To troubleshoot and that. There's not like, hours, or anything.'

'That sounds…stressful.'

'Nah, not at all. Trust me, this looks like the best job I've ever had. Mainly all I have to do is hang out with everyone and make sure you're having fun. Make sure people are respectful and turn up to stuff on time. And keep an eye out for any side-effects to the medication.'

'Have they said anything about side-effects?' Elle only had limited space left for worries, and the trial literature had put her at ease about any possible bad reactions. He'd probably been joking, but hearing Benji mention side-effects underlined their possibility.

'Not really, no. They've told me it's a really small dose of a drug that's pretty well understood, but they just have to be super cautious for legal reasons.' He made a warding-off gesture with his palms. 'But I'm definitely not the guy to speak to about the medical stuff. The trial staff will be around the whole time on site if you've got any questions.'

Elle took a sip from her glass, her anxiety abating once more. In her conversation with Jess, and in the trial paperwork, the study drug was described as one that would affect certain problem-solving and decision-making chemicals in the brain in a way that would only be detectable to very sensitive tests. They weren't able to say too much about which chemicals, because to do so might bias results, although everything would be revealed in a full debrief once the trial was complete. The main thing was that participants should just concentrate on enjoying their holiday.

'This trial is largely about finding a balance of the drug that's most effective,' Jess had told her. 'And we're close to sure about that, too. Even if you're not on the placebo, you won't really notice the effects. It's the equivalent of drinking a thimble of wine.'

By the time they were due to land Elle was a little tipsy from the three drinks she'd knocked back to settle her nerves. She watched out of the window for signs of civilisation and saw only darkness until the runway lights illuminated the ground not far below them. The plane touched down and Elle relaxed her grip on the arm rest.

'Ladies and gentlemen,' the pilot said, 'we hope you enjoyed your flight with us today, despite the unusual conditions. I'm pleased to report that there's no sign of stormy weather here, though. The temperature outside is twenty degrees, which bodes well for you all tomorrow. Rumour has it there's a heatwave, too, so you've come at a good time for sun. On behalf of myself and Laura, and of course, Benji, we hope you enjoy the rest of your stay here in the Canary Islands.'

A cheer went up, and Benji began to issue instructions for

disembarking. Elle missed the start of what he was saying though, because something the pilot said had struck her as curious.

'The Canary Islands.' That's what he'd said.

Not Lanzarote. Not Fuerteventura. *The Canary Islands.*

Just like in the advert, and just like in the paperwork. In fact, now she came to think of it, no one, so far, had told them *which* Canary Island, exactly, they were on.

4

Benji led the group away from the plane's mechanical heat and into the gentle warmth of the night air. A minibus was parked near the corner of a squat building at the far end of the runway. Elle checked her watch. It had just gone 11 p.m. UK and Canary Island time.

Even though it was dark, it was clear that they hadn't landed at a major airport, if indeed 'airport' was even the right term. It was little more than a landing strip, and other than the runway lights, only two tall floodlights illuminated the entire area. All the buildings along the runway's edge looked more like maintenance sheds.

Somehow Elle now lagged behind the rest of the group, which was a real Home Elle sort of thing to do. Holiday Elle wasn't afraid of making a tit of herself with strangers. Holiday Elle got stuck in and made friends right from the off.

She caught up to the next slowest person in the group, a woman in a halterneck crop top with straight, dark hair running down to the small of her back. 'This place isn't quite what I expected.'

The woman looked up, smiled, and said, 'Yeah, it's nice and warm though, isn't it?'

And like that, she'd made a friend. Everything was going to

be brilliant. The woman was Halimah – *everyone calls me Hallie* – from Kent, and when Elle introduced herself as Elle from Birmingham, Hallie threw her arms around her and told her how much she *loved* Birmingham. Taken aback – because no one liked Birmingham that much, surely – Elle laughed and squeezed back.

The confident way Hallie dressed and carried herself gave Elle the impression she might be the sort of person who asked important questions well before packing her bags, so she said to her, 'Bit of a ditzy question, but do you know *which* Canary island this is?'

Hallie made an exaggerated out-of-her depth face. 'No idea, sorry.'

'They haven't told us.' A man wearing Buddy Holly glasses and a long, dark coat slowed his pace to join them. 'Looking at the terrain, I'm thinking this is Lanzarote.' He was pointing at an indistinct point in the blackness beyond the minibus.

'Aren't they all pretty much interchangeable?' Hallie said.

'Not really,' Buddy Holly said. 'Lanzarote's covered in cooled lava. The rock's obsidian. It's an active volcano, too. Fuerteventura, well that has golden, sandy beaches. And Tenerife is lush, and has a great big mountain in the middle. Spain's tallest. We'll see that come morning if we're there.'

Hallie widened her eyes at this sudden eruption of facts.

'And your guess is Lanzarote?' Elle said.

He nodded. 'Unless we're on one of the small ones, and there's a fair few of those.'

'How do you know so much, then?' Hallie said, sounding so impressed she might have been being sarcastic.

'Well, cards on the table, I'm a reservist for the Air Force, so I know a bit about topography and geography. Not to mention reconnaissance.'

'Reconnaissance? Impressive.' Now Hallie was definitely being sarcastic.

'I like to know what I'm standing on at all times.'

'Well, I can see you're going to be quite useful to know,' Elle said, trying to ignore Hallie's eye roll. 'I'm Elle.'

'Charlie.' He held out his hand and shook Elle's firmly. 'And I'll tell you one other thing. There's a reason they haven't told us which island we're on.'

'Really?' Elle said. 'Why's that?'

'Because they don't want us to know.' His flat expression broke with the tiniest smile.

'Why wouldn't they want us to know?' Hallie said.

'Don't know yet. Likely something to do with the trial. Maybe they're deliberately disorienting us.'

Hallie studied Charlie with undiluted scepticism now.

'You think?' Elle said, hoping he hadn't caught the face Hallie had made.

'We'll find out soon enough. But think about it… No phones allowed. No mention of the island's name. Very vague write-up about what this trial's even studying in the information pack. Have you wondered yet why they're even having it on an island rather than in some cheapo digs back home?'

'You don't think they're being straight with us?' Elle said, aware Hallie was starting to pull ahead of them.

'My opinion?' He dropped his voice. 'I'm not convinced this is a drug trial at all.'

5

At the bus, Hallie made a comment about Charlie freaking her out, and that for the sake of her beauty sleep she was making a break for it. When they climbed aboard she sat beside the blond He-Man at the front of the bus, while Elle ended up trapped in the window seat beside Charlie near the back. He seemed harmless enough, even if his pale face and intense stare told the story of a man who spent too much time online. But he was a familiar enough sort, an information sponge in desperate need of a squeeze. Elle had a knack of drawing oddballs, and she had quietly come to accept this dubious gift.

Charlie chose to talk to a man with floppy dark hair and a well-groomed beard in the seat across the aisle anyway, diving straight into how suspicious it was that no one had checked their passports yet, and how unusual it was that a forty-ton plane had only one pilot.

'It's just not the done thing.'

Now that she was cut off from everyone, Elle's hand twitched on instinct, desperate for a mobile phone to occupy it. But given that wasn't an option, she stared out the window at the darkness beyond the reach of the floodlights instead.

Eventually Benji appeared at the front of the bus. He introduced their driver, Paul, one of the security staff, whose silvery hair and moustache brought to mind a terrier. The journey ahead would be a short one, Benji said, and once their luggage had been loaded into the back of the vehicle, they'd be off.

The engine started, and while they drove Elle watched for signs of life – in vain, but for the occasional curious goat raising its head. Alien perfumes and aftershaves intensified in the dark; the chatter of strangers grew oppressive. The further they drove from the lights of the little airport, the more plausible Charlie's conspiratorial words became. Nerves began to roil in her belly.

He'd been right about there being a certain *fuzziness* to the trial literature. Once she'd been selected, the messaging had almost entirely been: it's all good, don't worry about a thing, everything will be explained when you get here – you're about to have the time of your life. It stood in contrast to all that fine print in the giant contract that she, being honest, had barely even skim-read before signing. Perhaps she should have worried more, not relied so much on the summary sheet. What exactly was it she'd consented to?

She tapped Charlie on the shoulder. He finished what he was saying to the posh man first before slowly shifting his position to face her.

'You okay?'

Seeing his comical glasses once more, she almost stopped herself. 'Well…it's just, I wondered…if you think there's something funny going on here, why did you come?'

'You still thinking about what I said?' He nodded, conveying his belief she'd made the right choice. 'Yeah, got to wonder where they're taking us. We're about five miles in now and I've not seen a light out there. And have you noticed the road's paved but there are no markings?'

She hadn't, no. 'Are you worried?'

'Me? No. I've got training, so I can handle myself. And, most importantly, I believe they'll pay us, whatever this trial ends up really being about. That's why I'm here, the money. I've got big plans for it. If I got a sense they weren't going to pay me, though…that would be different. Just stay vigilant, Elle. Things aren't what they seem here, that's for sure. But if you're worried about anything at any point, you come find me.'

6

Eventually a light appeared on the horizon. They drew closer, and it became clear that it emanated from within a high-walled compound ahead of them. The road turned sharply left once they reached the white brickwork, and curved gradually rightward along its edge until the bus slowed, turned back on itself, and stopped.

'Here we are,' Benji said.

Paul climbed out and heaved open a sliding gate before returning to the idling bus and easing it inside. Another goat, piebald and scrawny, watched their arrival just metres from the bus. On its forehead a white patch shaped like a lightning bolt marked the darker fur there. It appeared to stare right at Elle through the window before running off.

'Bye, Harry,' Elle said.

The bus stopped at the crown of an arched driveway and they climbed out. Terracotta steps led up to a curved white building which stood two storeys high and stretched from wall to wall. To Elle's left, beyond a garden filled with spiky, hardy-looking plants, stood a tennis court. On the other side, a five-a-side pitch was illuminated beneath its own set of lights.

As if he already knew the place intimately, Benji led everyone up the stairs and into a white-tiled, cavernous atrium. Much like the plane, the aesthetic inside was clean and modern – more of a conference facility than the hospital-like building Elle had been imagining. The central reception desk, a sleek bracket, like the building in miniature, had been set up with glasses of champagne. Once people had helped themselves to a flute, they assembled in front of the desk where Benji stood with a group of staff members in different coloured versions of the Apollo polo top.

'Okay,' he said, his voice echoing through the building. 'Thanks so much for taking time out of your busy lives to come all the way here to help science.'

'Woo, science,' the punky woman said again.

'I know it's late, and we've got an earlyish start tomorrow, but I just wanted to very quickly introduce you to our small team and run through some basics before you get a well-earned rest. You've already met Paul, and he's one half of the security team here. The other half is Monique—'

A tall woman in a purple polo shirt matching Paul's and Benji's raised her hand from the far end of the reception desk before folding her muscular arms. Paul stood beside her, his arms folded too. The pair made a formidable-looking team.

'—and these two will be your point of contact at the front desk at all hours. Any worries or security concerns, especially if I'm not about, ask them. Next to them is Carl, and he's our on-site cook and a solid table tennis player – so I'm told.'

Carl was about six-foot-five, and looked as if he could mash the security team with one fist. His raised hand appeared larger than Paul's head.

'Rosie and César, who aren't here at the moment, are our cleaning team. Please leave the Do Not Disturb sign on your door if you don't want your room cleaned every day. We'd appreciate you doing this at least occasionally – they're a small team and this is a big building.'

Elle watched on, impressed by Benji's professionalism. It was hard to believe he'd never been here before, had never met most of these people before. He was acting like they were all old friends.

'And last of all—'

A bleat from behind them all cut Benji off. The Harry Potter goat from outside clip-clopped past them all from the direction of the open double doors. Laughter broke out, and increased when Benji turned to the man and woman in white lab coats beside him and said, deadpan, 'Is he on the trial?'

'Someone's left the gate open,' Monique said with an eye roll.

'Little bugger,' Paul said, and sprang to life. The goat cottoned on to his approach, and ran off, deeper into the atrium, much to the group's delight. When it was clear the goat wasn't getting caught any time soon, Benji shrugged and went on:

'So... I'd like to hand you over to Dr George Lineker and Dr Jess Utterson, as they are the reason that we're all here, and I think...they're going to do a little introduction.' Benji looked to the two white coats, and Dr Utterson nodded, stepping forward to take Benji's place in front of the assembly. She looked considerably younger than Dr Lineker, whose whitening goatee and pronounced widow's peak put him in his early fifties at least. Dr Utterson, though, looked around Elle's age.

'Thanks, Benji,' she said, clasping one hand over the other and smiling. 'I—'

The coconut-shell knocks of the goat's hooves grew close again, as did the stomp and curse of Paul's fruitless chase.

Her mouth twitched to one side, and she grabbed the two interlocking rings on her necklace and squeezed. 'I don't want to be boring, as you'll know most of this from the paperwork we sent and the conversations we've had. But we did just want to go over the basics once more so that everyone is on the same page before the trial starts tomorrow. And so you can put names to the people prodding and poking you.'

Dr Utterson sounded a little out of breath, and her hands were trembling slightly. Elle recognised her voice and accent as belonging to the woman she'd spoken to on the phone.

'So, I'm Dr Utterson, but please, there's no need to call me that. Jess is much less formal, thank you. First, these white coats —these are to let you know when we're working and when we're not. Myself and Dr Lineker will be on site at all times, and we are in charge of your health and wellbeing while you're here. I'm a co-investigator here on what we're calling the Capricorn trial, and Dr Lineker is the chief and principal Investigator. Both of us are based at the same research institute in Oxford. I'm a psychologist, and spent my early career working in prisons and hospitals. Dr Lineker began his career as a hospital doctor, before moving into psychiatry, and currently works in research.'

She looked to him for reassurance and he nodded, a little smile peeking out from one side of the hand pressed to his mouth.

'As Capricorn is a very small trial, both of us will be doing a lot of different bits and pieces that a larger trial would have huge teams—'

Another grunt echoed around the atrium, and Carl and Monique both left their positions to go and assist Paul. Dr Lineker tutted.

Jess continued: 'So...a few things might seem a little unorthodox, but don't worry, and if you have any questions, obviously we will answer what we can. You'll have noticed in the paperwork that there are certain things we *can't* tell you about the trial until it's complete, but this is what we can say. If you're familiar with trial phases, think of this one as a sort of phase 0.5 trial, because it's somewhere between what's been called a phase 0 trial, which is when very low doses of drugs are given to patients to test for harms, and a phase 1 trial, which is a first-in-human trial, testing things like dosage amounts, efficacy, and side-effects. Our trial is the best of both worlds for you, as we'll be giving you a very low dose of the drug, so side-effects are highly unlikely, and we're extremely confident that our drug isn't harmful. Yet even at this low level, we are expecting to see very real results, too, so your input is vital to the goals of the trial. Ultimately, once we've attracted enough funding and built the case for this drug with this trial and the others we plan to run, it has the potential to be a complete game-changer for the whole world.'

The tension in Elle's back and shoulders had begun to dissipate now. The more Jess talked, the fewer concerns she had. These were researchers from Oxford University. They knew their stuff. And she'd said this was just one of a number of trials. That meant to some extent she was off the hook for the lies she might have told getting here. The more data they had, the less significant her results were in the scheme of things.

'You have all been selected because you showed a diverse range of thinking styles in our pre-trial screening. We designed some complicated measures behind the scenes to determine that, and no two of you have exactly the same traits. But what you all have in common is, you are all extremely interesting thinkers – especially to us.'

This received a murmur of laughter, and Elle further relaxed into her deceit. If interesting was what they wanted, someone who lied to escape their mum wasn't exactly normal, was it? Elle shook her head. She needed to drop all this worry. She was meant to be owning this now.

Applause broke out, and Carl the cook walked past in the direction of the front doors grinning, his huge arms holding the terrified goat around its torso and neck. Paul and Monique followed, both looking like they'd rather be somewhere else.

'Great,' Jess said. 'Hopefully he won't be butting in anymore.'

Elle laughed, as did a few of the others. Jess shot her a grateful look and soldiered on: 'Okay, so we're studying how the drug impacts decision-making and problem-solving on a range of tests. You shouldn't notice the effect of the drug at this dose, but, and this is a *big* but which all trial investigators must stress, if you do feel unusual, unwell, or experience anything unexpected, please let us know immediately. Whether we're in a white coat or not. Whether we're asleep or eating or walking along the beach. Again, we don't expect this to happen, but we have to anticipate this as part of the trial protocol. It's just good science.'

She checked her watch, looked at Dr Lineker, who nodded, and once more addressed the group.

'I'm nearly done, I promise. Our trial then, is randomised, so some of you will receive the active drug and some of you will receive a placebo, which is just a sugar pill. It's double-blinded, so neither you nor we will know which drug you receive. Tomorrow, you'll receive a quick medical once-over, then be given a series of tests one-on-one. These will form our baseline. You will then take the pill every morning until the end of the trial, and at both the two-week stage, and at the end of the trial, we will repeat the tests conducted on day one to compare against the baseline. Tomorrow morning will be one of our rare early starts I'm afraid. But if everyone stays near their rooms until they are called, you are free to do as you please once the tests have been done. Breakfast will be served from six until nine, but there is milk and cereal in your rooms if you're lucky enough to get a lie-in. And don't spend too much time perfecting your hair before coming down, as we will be covering your head in conductive gel, which I guarantee won't work with whatever look you're trying to achieve. Also, bring a towel.

'Oh, and one more thing. I don't want to end on a downer, but we wanted to just ask you to keep in mind at all times the participant's assurance obligation in your contracts. You will only be paid your fee if you complete the full trial and adhere to the trial rules. Only under the extraordinary circumstances detailed will any portion of the fee be paid if the trial isn't followed to completion.'

7

'Right,' she said, and gave Dr Lineker a final glance. He made a cutting gesture with his hand and shook his head. 'I think that's enough. There will be plenty of time for questions one-to-one, but if anyone has anything pressing now... Yes, I think you're Halimah, is that right?'

'Well remembered,' Hallie said. 'Hallie's fine, though. I just wanted to ask what the, like, internet situation is, exactly. It says there's Wi-Fi but there's a firewall or something? How does it work?'

'Yes, so I know it might seem quite strict, but Dr Lineker and I have both had experiences of trial results being affected by participants going online and looking up various things that have impacted the blinding procedure. It's a hazard of the modern age, but one we've planned for – especially as elements of our trial are searchable online. So each of you has a TV, with all the subscription streaming services on it. There's a PlayStation, too, and you've all been given a tablet which has pre-loaded apps on it. There is a web browser on it, but we've had to be quite strict about what it can open and what it can't, so you might find weird things you search don't get past the firewall. There's no email, I'm afraid, and social media is a no-no too, as this trial is in a commercially sensitive phase. But if you do want to send messages out to relatives or friends, you can do that through us via the company email.' She pointed to the muscly blond man from the bus. 'Harrison, is it?'

'Guilty as charged, yes. I just wanted to know why bring us all this way? And what is this place? It doesn't look like a medical facility.'

She paused and looked up at the ceiling far above her head. Dr Lineker looked as if he was about to speak.

'It's complicated,' she said, beating him to it. 'But essentially it was more practical for a number of reasons. Commercial sensitivity is one, but also getting a trial in place requires time and paperwork, as you can imagine, and this was the place that worked. Also, I'd add, a good recruitment pool was in our minds too, as was creating a positive experience for you all. This place, which yes, was originally designed as an exclusive leisure and business facility, was somewhere that ticked a lot of boxes for us, and also was available to us in our timeframe. Our trial also had fewer demands than other types of trial, so we don't need a full hospital set-up.'

'Where are we…' a voice near Elle said. It was Charlie, his arm coming into the air as an afterthought. '…exactly? Which island?'

For the first time Jess looked genuinely fazed, and she turned to Dr Lineker now, who stepped beside her and lowered the hand from his face.

'Uh, I think I'd like to draw this to a close now, and as Dr Utterson said, we can pick up specific questions in the morning. To answer that final question, though,' he forced a laugh, 'we're on one of the Canary Islands, but embarrassingly, the exact name, which I always get mixed up anyway, escapes me right now.' He looked up and down the row of staff for backup, but none of them helped out. 'It's actually the choice of our sponsors, and I'm afraid we've all been extremely busy the last week or so. But I'll…look it up, and if you're still interested we can talk tomorrow. Sorry.'

Charlie, whose hand was still raised, brought it down slowly and turned to Elle. He gave her a sideways smile, as if to say, *I told you so*, and she had to admit, it was a bit of strange answer.

Chapter Three

1

A knock on Elle's door woke her the next morning. She'd gone to sleep beneath a single sheet, but now the room was chilly, and before opening the door she put on a dressing gown and checked herself in the wall mirror.

Benji stood in the corridor holding out a mug with an apologetic smile. 'Sorry, Elle, you're up.'

She took the mug and sipped. Fresh coffee. 'What time is it?'

'Ten to seven.' He pointed at her drink. 'Is that okay? I can bring you a tea if you'd prefer.'

'No it's perfect. Thank you. How did you know?'

'Lucky guess. Let me give you some space, and I'll come back in twenty minutes and walk you over. Sorry to wake you.'

'Oh no, it's fine. Could have been much earlier.'

'Well, you were one of the sensible ones. A few were up pretty late last night.'

'Really?'

He nodded while giving an exaggerated side-eye. 'Oh yes.'

She closed the door when he'd gone and crossed the room to open the curtains. Given the room temperature, Elle expected to see clouds. Instead, her small balcony was already warming in the early morning sun. She'd not been able to appreciate it last night, but up here on the first floor she had a view of the glistening infinity pool at the back of the complex, and beyond that the sea. They were perched high above a cove of black-and-ochre cliffs, and Elle recalled that the literature had mentioned there being a private beach somewhere.

This would do. This would definitely do.

2

She washed her face and put on some light make-up, just enough to brighten her appearance. The bathroom mirror was unkind, making her red hair look lank and her pale-blue eyes appear milky. A kind ex had once said she reminded him of Emma Stone, but in light like this all she saw was Mum. She snorted. 1,000 miles away and she still couldn't escape her.

Elle hoped she was okay. Hoped she hadn't set the house on fire trying to cook or thrown the telly out the window trying to work the Chromecast. Was she still in bed at home, or had she spent the night out somewhere? What if she was lonely? As much as she didn't want Mum in her head dampening her excitement, changing a lifetime habit wasn't going to be easy. They'd not left on the best terms. Mum had feigned enthusiasm when Elle first told her about the trial. But since then she'd been sullen and moody, barely speaking to Elle unless she had to. She didn't seem to believe Elle when she said the trip and accommodation was all free, perhaps suspecting Elle of having more money hidden away.

'What are they after?' she'd said. 'You don't get anything for free in this life.'

Elle hadn't dared mention they were actually paying *her*.

Benji returned as promised, and she followed him, towel in hand, down the accommodation corridor and out onto a suspended walkway hanging high above the atrium floor. At the bottom of the grand central staircase, Benji led her past the reception desk and towards a room on the corridor beneath their accommodation.

Benji left her with Dr Utterson – no, *Jess* – who sat her down in a mostly empty room at a table set up against the far wall. She began to feel nervous and exposed again. Pleasantries out of the way, Jess said, 'This morning we're going to take some baseline data. I'm going to run tests with an EEG machine first in this room, and after that you'll move on to Dr Lineker. Do you know what an EEG does?'

'It measures the brain, I think?' she said, having read about such instruments in her psychology books. What she didn't know, though, was whether the machine might be able to detect her deception.

'Exactly. It measures the electricity created when the cells in your brain talk to each other. We're going to do a few tests, and a special app will measure how you respond. Is that okay?'

Elle nodded. Jess sounded more confident than she had done last night, and yet in other ways she seemed less imposing. She was extremely slight, bony even, and somehow appeared to be much shorter. Elle complimented her necklace, the one she'd noticed her wearing the night before, and Jess smiled and told her it had been a gift from her late mother. Elle didn't know what to say, so told her again it was lovely. She took Elle's temperature with an ear thermometer, and her blood pressure with a cuff. She did her best to make chit-chat and reassuring faces, but Elle could tell it didn't come naturally.

Jess affixed what looked like a white swimming cap covered in electrodes to Elle's head. Wires were connected to a box strapped at the back of her neck, which in turn connected to a laptop at the table's far end. She took a syringe full of gel and emptied it onto Elle's head through holes in the cap, rotating the tip against the skin of her scalp.

'Let me know if this hurts,' Jess said.

'No, it's fine.'

After twenty minutes of setting up, Jess started the first test. She played a steady, pulsing tone through a set of speakers at the other end of the room. Every so often the machine played a higher tone, or a different sound entirely, like a trumpet blart and what sounded like a goat's bleat. When this happened, Elle had to push a button in her right hand that also connected to the laptop.

After forty minutes the tests were complete, and Jess left Elle in the room alone while she went to see if Dr Lineker was ready. Elle's heartbeat quickened, convinced that Jess was right now telling Dr Lineker that her tests hadn't been normal and that they needed to send her home. Five agonising minutes later, Jess opened the door and gestured for Elle to follow her. Walking across the corridor, she looked back towards the atrium where Benji stood waiting in the doorway, engaged in a conversation with a bald man she didn't think she'd seen before. Benji held up his thumb and made a quizzical face. Elle gave him a thumb back.

Dr Lineker sat at a desk in the middle of a smaller room on the other side of the corridor. He stood up and gave her a sweaty handshake. Up close he appeared blotchy and pale; dark swipes marked the skin below his eyes.

'How are you enjoying everything so far?' he asked, speaking quickly through barely parted lips, gaze firmly on the table.

'Yeah, it's lovely here. Thank you. My room's so nice.'

'Yes, the rooms are nice. Yes.' He drew his thumb and fore-finger down either side of his goatee. 'Now, the tests we're going to do…' He paused. 'The tests we're going to do will assess your decisions in various unusual situations. I'll hand you a tablet, and you'll be asked a series of quite detailed questions, and for the reasoning behind your answer. Don't take too long, we want your answers to be instinctive. All in all, this shouldn't take more than twenty minutes.' He paused again, looked to one side for almost five seconds, before returning his attention to the table. Was something distracting him? 'Twenty minutes, it should take, sorry. But do take as long as you need.'

Elle started the first question, in which she was a juror deciding whether to convict a ship's captain who had ordered members of his crew killed to stop the remaining crew starving. Meanwhile Dr Lineker sat in the corner at a laptop studying graphs. Every so often he looked over at her, and Elle tried not to look back. Was that her EEG data? Did he know something?

She returned to the problems on the tablet, which shifted between moral dilemmas, logic problems and practical puzzles. It all brought back cringe-inducing memories of her failed university interview at Oxford. Would she push an overweight man in front of a tram to stop it from running over a greater number of other people? At which interval in a count of ten would a group of people in a circle know the colour of their own black or white hat, based on what colour hats the others were wearing? How many trips did she need to make across to a remote island to stop the inhabitants from starving?

'Some of these seem like you could have actually done them for real out here?' Elle said.

Dr Lineker looked up and narrowed his eyes. 'What do you mean? No, we couldn't do that. It would be unethical. No. We wouldn't do that.'

'Sorry,' Elle said, taken aback by his reaction. 'I was just… It was a joke. I was doing the island one. Ignore me.'

Lesson learned, no mucking about. She ploughed on. When she'd finished the final question, which had asked her to react to various scenarios involving the fair distribution of £1,000 between her and another person, she put down the tablet.

'I think I'm done.'

Dr Lineker stood up and walked over. 'Thank you, Lynn.'

He walked away, and Elle panicked. Should she correct him? If she didn't, her results might get put against the wrong person.

'Sorry, did I just call you Lynn? Elle. I meant, Elle.'

He returned holding out a glass of water and a red-and-white pill. She took them both and swallowed, shaking her head to indicate she hadn't been offended by his error.

'All done,' she said. She stood up to leave.

'May I see your mouth?'

'Sorry?'

'Inside. May I see inside your mouth, please?'

Without further hesitation she obeyed, and Dr Lineker raised a small torch to her face.

'Lift your tongue?'

Again she did as she was told, glad she'd brushed her teeth thoroughly. She'd not expected a dental exam. His face was inches from hers. Tangles of red capillaries gathered in the corners of his eyes. Sweat beads assembled along his roller coaster hairline.

Apparently content, he thanked her and told her she could leave. She was standing at the door when Dr Lineker said, 'If you feel anything unusual, Elle, let us know straight away if you have concerns. Make a note in the diary in your bedside drawer, either way. All data is good data. It's bound to be unrelated to the pill, though, so please don't worry.'

'I won't,' Elle said and left. She wasn't particularly concerned, but grew increasingly close to being so every time they told her not to worry.

3

The atrium now carried the aroma of cooking food, and her stomach rumbled. She bumped into Benji escorting Ted, the floppy-haired posh man from the bus last night, to his tests. There were traces of grey and white at Ted's temples and in his beard which she hadn't noticed last night, and something about his face was vaguely familiar. She felt a bit ridiculous with her head wrapped in a towel, but neither Ted nor Benji seemed to notice. Ted wore long salmon shorts, open-toed sandals and a light-blue dress shirt, open to reveal a shaved, tanned chest. He was handsome in a strong-jawed, blue-eyed way, though the kempt nature of his hair hinted at an accompanying vanity or insecurity.

'Can I ask you something?' Ted said, and the openness of his smile made her grin back at him. 'The pink shorts. Are they awful? I was pretty confident when I packed them but I'm having second thoughts.'

She laughed. 'They're fine. I mean, I can't talk really, can I? I've got a towel on my head.'

'I think it's working for you,' Ted said, turning to Benji for a second opinion.

'Oh, without doubt,' Benji said.

'Anyway,' Ted said, 'see you out at the pool, Elle?' He phrased this like a question.

'Yeah,' she said, smiling even when they started walking away, 'see you out there.'

The canteen was deserted but for Carl towering above a heated serving counter. She cast her gaze over the trays of baked beans, fried toast and sausages. Another counter contained healthier options: yoghurt, cereals, seeds and fruit.

'Any goat on the menu?' she said.

He didn't get it at first, but when he did he gave a short and powerful laugh before launching into a long story about eating goat while serving in Afghanistan. When he was done, she sat looking out at the distant pool through floor-to-ceiling windows. The dark-blue sea beyond it sparkled. It really was starting to feel like a holiday now, wasn't it, despite the tests.

Despite that invasive mouth exam.

No, no, she didn't want to linger on *that*. Yet it had sort of bothered her, the way she'd just obeyed him when he'd asked. It reminded her of that old Milgram experiment, when participants were told to issue electric shocks to other participants, gradually increasing the voltage until it seemed like they were causing real harm. It was all fake really, and the receiving participants had actually been actors or something, but the real participants didn't know, and they'd kept doing it even when the voltage would have been lethal. Afterwards, when asked, they'd all said it was because they were obeying the rules. Obeying the white coat. And that's exactly what she'd done, obeyed the white coat. It made her wonder, what else would she do if asked?

4

Back in her room she slathered on two layers of factor fifty, stopping by four or five asymmetrical freckles to really do a number on them. She paid extra attention to a puffy circular scar on her upper arm. It was too early to swim, and even though she wanted to sit on her balcony with another cup of coffee and read her book, she ought to be sociable.

Wearing a wide-brimmed sun hat and shades, and carrying the latest Megan Abbott and an old Barbara Vine because she wasn't sure what she fancied reading, Elle made her way down to the ground floor and exited the building by the glass doors at the back. The path to the pool was lined with stubby palms that looked like pineapples and tines of chlorine penetrated the coconut scent of her suncream.

She emerged at the centre of the pool area, rows of luxury sun loungers to her left and right. The bright-blue infinity pool itself, shaped like a cartoon smile, glinted beneath the low sun rising to the east of the cove. The far edge of the pool appeared to float over the ocean, and in harmony with the curve of the building and the bay, it bent towards her.

'Nice, isn't it?' said a voice with a Merseyside accent.

A slight man in red swimming shorts, his skin paler than hers, lay on the lounger behind her. He had a thatch of slicked-back auburn hair which had been shaved at the sides and had a wide mouth in which his teeth still didn't seem to fit.

'It's gorgeous,' she said. 'It's blowing my mind actually.'

'I'm Ricoh.'

'Hi, Ricoh, I'm Elle.'

'Lovely to meet you, Elle,' he said, and stood up and gently shook her hand, bowing his head a little bit. 'Going to do a bit of reading?' He nodded at her book.

'Yeah, hope so. Not much else to do, is there?'

'I know. Bit lost without my phone.'

'I know what you mean.'

'This place is proper grammable though, right?'

'Yeah…it's perfect. Do you want one of these?' She held up the two books. 'I've basically packed my whole bookshelf.'

He shrugged. 'Yeah? If you don't mind.'

'What do you like? I see you more as a thoughtful mystery man than an edgy modern noir guy.' She handed over the Barbara Vine.

'Whatever, really. Cheers, Elle. You're a lifesaver.'

She walked away smiling, continuing her exploration. At the end of the pool she passed the blond He-Man from the plane, his huge arms behind his head like he might be asleep behind his sunglasses.

To the pool's right stood a giant hot tub and two table tennis tables, and past that was an opening in the wall beside the pool. Here she found stairs leading down to another patio beneath the pool, which had an equally incredible view of the beach and the sea. More sun loungers were assembled here at the base of a black-and-orange cliff face. Elle didn't descend all the way, but from the halfway point she could see the start of another staircase at the far end. A sign beside it read, 'Beach Access'.

This was incredible. She'd never been anywhere like it.

On her way back, the muscly blond guy held up his hand.

'I like your hat,' he said.

She stopped, reaching up reflexively. 'This old thing?'

He laughed. 'I'm being genuine, it's a great look.'

'Is it?'

'Well, I like a bit of personal style. Have you been in to see the docs yet this morning?'

'Yes, I was there just now.'

'How did it go?'

'Oh, fine. Thanks. Have you been?'

'I was first in.'

'Poor you.'

He flashed his straight, gleaming teeth. 'It meant I got my pick this morning.' He gestured at all the empty loungers with an open hand. 'You coming to sit? Don't feel you have to keep a big space on my account.' He'd briefly glanced down the row, where Ricoh occupied the farthest lounger before the path, and beyond that a woman she hadn't met yet lay on another lounger at least five or six away from Ricoh.

She had indeed been planning on leaving a good-sized, English gap, but she couldn't well do that now. Taking the one beside him, she slipped off her sandals and folded her legs beneath her to keep all of her in the shade of the umbrella. The man introduced himself as Harrison. He worked in London doing something complicated-sounding with software development that also involved finance in some way. He said he wanted to use the trial money to get his own million-pound software idea off the ground.

'What's the idea?' Elle said.

'Too much pipe needed to explain it properly, and it's dull technical stuff. But I've got a few serious investors circling now. Glynn Rogers, an old friend, a walking pound sign really, he'll come on board once he sees the proof of concept. I'm just at the stage where I need a last bit of rocket fuel, Bezos-style, and then we're off. You'll definitely hear about it when it happens though, that should give you the idea of just how big this is.'

'Sounds…exciting.' She stared out at the sea, not quite knowing how to adequately respond. Was 20K really enough to make a difference for a million-pound project like that? It didn't seem like an amount that would be significant, but then again, what did she know?

After a moment, Harrison said, 'Yeah, well, I've not achieved anything yet, have I?'

She turned back to him. 'No, but…it's great you're so focused on something. I'm surprised, actually, that you're out here doing this. You sound like you really have plans. I thought it would be mostly people like me, that sort of just need the money for, you know, life stuff.'

'People like you?' He laughed. 'You seem okay to me. I wouldn't do yourself down. You heard what they said, didn't you? Everyone here was chosen because they're a bit special.'

Elle waved a hand dismissively. 'They didn't say that at all.'

He grinned again. 'They did, they said we were all interesting thinkers.'

'Yeah, whatever that means.'

'Isn't it obvious?'

Elle studied him to see if he was being serious. It was impossible to tell beneath the glasses. 'Honestly, I'm not sure it means much. I'm sure you could fill in those questionnaires completely at random and seem like an "interesting thinker".'

He sat up and leaned towards her. 'Do you want to know my theory?'

'You have a theory?'

'I do.'

'What about?'

'The trial. What they're studying.'

Elle smiled, starting to enjoy the theorising now. 'Go on.'

'I think everyone here is super smart. Not in an IQ way necessarily, well, maybe that… But also in another way. And this drug we're all testing, it's a sort of cognitive enhancement drug, to make us all even smarter or more attentive or something. The way the test is set up; three brain scans, three performance tests, one a baseline, the rest at intervals after having taken the drug to monitor our improvement…'

'You could be right,' she said. 'How do you feel right now? More attentive than usual?'

He was still leaning towards her, and now he lowered his voice, 'Well, obviously. But that's got a lot to do with the person I'm talking to.'

Elle turned away from him to hide an embarrassed smile. He was flirting with her.

'No, seriously,' Harrison said, laughing, 'I'm sure the drugs don't work this quickly, but I do feel pretty relaxed and focused all of a sudden. But then…' He held out his hands to cup the scenery in front of him.

'Well, there is that. You know, there's another guy here, a participant, and he has a theory that this isn't a drug trial at all. I think he suspects something else is going on, although he's a bit cagey about the specifics.'

'Columbine, you mean?'

'Columbine?'

'Yeah, bloke in the coat?'

'Yes, that's him.'

'Right.' Harrison lay back again, not sounding impressed. 'No offence, but that guy is… Hey, so I was going to ask, what did you mean when you said, *people like me* just now? What's a person like you? What brings you here? What do you do?'

'Me? I just needed a holiday. I've been doing…a lot and just needed some downtime.' He bobbed his head with understanding. She told him about her abandoned teaching career after university, her bounding from temp job to temp job afterwards just to keep up with 'a family member's' debts. And about her time at Parkwood inspiring her to study Forensic Psychology.

'That's interesting, I've bounced around a lot myself. And, oddly, I have this cousin, he borrowed a few thou from me and I never saw it again. It really set me back, so I know how you feel.' He sounded contemplative now. Regretful, maybe.

'Maybe that's why we've been picked,' Elle said. 'Dodgy family.'

'Yeah,' he said, 'maybe. So you're just here to power down?'

'Yeah, you know? Do holiday things. Read books. Have some drinks. Maybe play cards or have a game of Scrabble.'

'Snap. I love playing cards. What's your game?'

'Uh… I don't know. Snap.'

He smiled but didn't laugh. 'Well, maybe one of these days we can play Snap, then.'

'Yeah, maybe that would be fun.'

Approaching footsteps drew her attention, and Benji walked towards them from the direction of the building.

'Hi, guys, sorry to interrupt.' He looked from Elle to Harrison and back to Elle. 'Just checking you're both feeling okay.'

Harrison glanced at Elle. 'Yeah, chap, we're good as gold.'

She wasn't sure, but had there been an edge in the way he'd just called Benji 'chap'? If Benji was bothered by it at all, it didn't show.

'That's what we like to hear.' His gaze scanned Harrison's body, his toned pectoral and abdominal muscles. 'Listen, after everyone's done this afternoon we're going to do a proper tour of the place. Show you all the facilities. But until then, anything I can do, give me a shout.'

'Thanks, Benji,' Elle said.

Benji nodded at her. Harrison said nothing, and after seeming to wait for an acknowledgement, Benji left. Oddly, having already passed by the other two on the way over, he then ignored them on the way out. Perhaps he'd already spoken to them this morning.

'I think he's got his eye on you, Elle,' Harrison said.

He sounded light-hearted enough, but still she whipped her head around to glare at him. 'Pardon?'

'He was coming over here to check up on us, didn't you think? Letting me know he's there.'

'Don't be silly.'

'I'm not. A guy like that, in a job like this, you think he's here for his health?'

She supposed she'd not really thought about that before. 'I think he was just being nice.'

Harrison smiled and lay back, his expression skyward and certain.

5

Soon some of the others began to arrive at the pool. The long-haired rocker from the plane strolled over first, dressed in a black System of a Down T-shirt and long black shorts. He introduced himself as Dale, and was an awkwardly tall writer from Newcastle. He spread out on a lounger, not looking entirely comfortable, and began to write secretively in a hard-back blue notebook.

Ted came next, and took up a lounger nearby and started reading a Patricia Highsmith book. Whether it was the book that triggered the notion or not, it struck Elle now why he'd appeared so familiar to her. He reminded her of Winston from work. Something about the beard and eyes, and the patient, kind way he humoured Harrison when the two of them began debating crypto currencies. Both of them spoke with the same regionless accent which in more animated moments would try to drop anchor somewhere in the Thames. Ted, it transpired, ran his own small software business, and after some pressing from Harrison, said he wanted to use the money from the trial to pay off a few debts.

'It's tough out there,' Harrison said, perhaps just a little bit smug.

'Yeah, but when the going gets tough…' Ted countered.

Harrison nodded. 'Yeah, fair play.'

Hallie soon joined them on their side of the pool wrapped in a gossamer shawl which, after ten minutes in the sun, she made a dramatic show of removing. The men watched her dive into the pool, her two-piece swimsuit showing off as much of her body as was decent, and a fraction more. Elle supposed if you had it, flaunt it.

Next down was Genevieve – or Gee, as she preferred – the punky woman from the plane who would later tell them all she was a project manager in Northampton. She stomped over in long shorts and another Hawaiian shirt, caught sight of Dale in the pool, and ran to divebomb him fully clothed. The assembled participants yelled with a mixture of amusement and annoyance as water went everywhere. Gee and Dale took to splashing each other as if they'd known each other longer than a day, and Hallie, who left the pool at that point, informed Elle that the pair had been the last two standing the night before.

Everyone seemed incredibly charming, though the non-stop chatter never ventured out of the shallow end. It was nearly lunchtime when Harrison suggested heading down to the beach. Ted had already left to lie down in his room, but everyone else wanted to go. In a spirit of inclusivity, Elle quick-stepped over the warm tiles to the other side of the patio and asked the woman who'd accidentally ostracised herself there if she wanted to come with them.

The girl raised a flattened hand to shield her eyes and squinted. 'Oh,' she said, and sat up on her elbows. For a moment she looked dumbfounded. Then, in a high, floaty voice, she said, 'Thank you. I'm fine right now. I might come later.'

Elle guessed she was in her early twenties, though her voice sounded like it was coming from a little girl. Her hair was long and dyed ash blonde, while her face glowed with bronzer.

'Okay, well, I'm Elle. Maybe I'll see you down there…' She left a gap so that she might offer her name.

'Maybe see you down there.'

When nothing else was forthcoming, Holiday Elle took command: 'And what was your name, by the way?'

'Becks.'

'Nice to meet you, Becks.'

'You too, Elle.'

6

The set of steps down from the lower patio to the beach was a seemingly endless run of half-turn steel staircases bolted to the cliff wall. It moaned and creaked during their descent, and Elle feared their combined weight might pull the thing down. The beach itself resembled strewn rubble up to a metre in front of the water, at which point the pebbles and stones brought to mind the blackened remnants of a barbecue. They obviously weren't on Fuerteventura. Given the volcanic appearance of everything around them, Elle was coming around to Charlie's view that they were somewhere in the sticks on Lanzarote.

'It's very private,' Dale said.

'Shame the beach is rubbish,' Hallie said. 'You can't sunbathe on this.'

Elle studied the water, which stretched to the horizon uninterrupted by land. She slipped off her sandals and stepped into the water. The coarse sand scraped her skin and squeezed through her toes pleasantly.

'Is it cold?' Hallie said.

'Not too bad.'

'Fuck it, I'm going in,' Gee said, dashing then diving into the water, swimming towards one of three anchored orange pedalos floating in front of a buoy line stretched across the cove's two pincers.

From his position at the end of the line they'd formed, Dale glanced at Ricoh, Hallie, Harrison and Elle. Then, with a shrug, he kicked off his shoes and charged in after Gee.

'Race you,' Ricoh said, and followed Dale in.

Harrison stood between Elle and Hallie. He offered each of them one of his hands. Hallie took him up on the offer but Elle stepped back and shook her head.

'I've not got my swimming stuff on,' she said, looking down at her dress. 'But you go ahead.'

The other two looked at one another and, without wasting another moment, crashed into the water, laughing and screaming. She watched them swim away, reach the pedalo and climb on board, throwing themselves down the slide with the abandon of unleashed toddlers. Elle appreciated that they hadn't pressured her into going with them.

God, she felt old. Other than perhaps Ted – whose beard and manner made his age difficult to determine – everyone here seemed so young. They all looked pristine and wide-eyed. All that supple skin and those big dreams. Her own plans felt about as exciting as the one-piece bathing suit in her suitcase.

She liked them all though, that couldn't be overlooked. The morning had flown by, and only Becks hadn't been overtly friendly – and that was probably just shyness. Even Harrison, with his gym body and rounded vowels, wasn't as cocky as you'd expect. He'd actually been nice.

Elle found a smooth rock and sat down, the warmth radiating through the fabric of her dress. The day was really starting to cook, and the exposed skin on her neck and face sensed the coming threat of the afternoon sun. She stroked her arms as if she might slough off the heat, reached beneath her sleeve to touch the scar once more. She probably needed to get inside for a bit, cool down and read a book in the shade.

During the summer break between her first and second years at university, she'd gone to stay with Granny Alice in

Spain. Granny Alice had worked her whole life as a personal assistant in the city for the same firm, and dreamed for years of retiring to the sun with a sea view and a boat. They'd been out on that boat, a small yacht, and Elle had been learning how to sail it, when Granny Alice caught her scratching at a bleeding mole just beneath the arm of her life jacket.

Granny Alice asked to see it, concerned, having had a skin cancer removed herself the year before. Her tanned face paled. Elle's misshapen, black-and-red island amidst an archipelago of perfectly round, brown freckles wasn't right.

'How long's it been like this, sweetheart?' she'd said.

Elle didn't know, though. A month. Two. She hadn't wanted to bother anyone.

They went to the doctor that afternoon, and, once back in the UK, the mole had been removed and found malignant.

The terrifying wait to hear if it had spread, to find out if any further operations were needed, had been the worst time of her life. She'd come close to leaving university – she might well have packed it in, had she felt like she had anything better to go back to in Marlstone. And even once she'd been given the all clear, and the flesh around the mole, removed as a precaution, had healed, the cancer's parting gift was to have cut short the last time she'd ever seen Granny Alice alive.

Elle looked up. Over on the pedalo the others were yelling and gesturing for her to come and join them. She cupped her hands around her mouth and yelled, 'I've not got my swimming stuff.'

Dale climbed up to the top of the slide, jumped into space and somersaulted, splashing Gee and Hallie, much to their comedy outrage.

With her complexion she couldn't mess around. But she'd stay just a little bit longer, make the most of the weaker sun. She didn't want to come across as unsociable. It certainly didn't feel like January at all. This was the weather she remembered from summers with Granny Alice. She'd known before coming that the Canaries enjoyed warm winters, but she hadn't quite imag—

A scream drifted into the cove from high above. Elle twisted around and looked up. She turned back to the pedalo and the others had stopped cavorting. They were looking her way.

'You okay?' Harrison shouted.

Elle stood up, pointed to the stairs. 'It came from up there.'

They all looked at one another, deciding what to do. Elle hadn't liked the sound at all, it had been sudden and fearful. She turned, and ran towards the steps.

Chapter Four

1

The low hum of the stairs, reverberating from Elle's dash up, continued long after she reached the patio below the infinity pool. Sprawled at the foot of the curved staircase up to the pool lay Becks, her face buried in the crook of one elbow, her other arm outstretched, hand clutching her ankle.

Elle ran over. 'Are you okay?' She kneeled down and placed her hand on Becks's bare side, still trying to catch her breath.

Becks looked up at Elle, face red and eyes teary. 'I think I've broken my ankle.'

'What happened?'

'I slipped at the top and fell all the way down.' She lifted her hand, revealing broken skin glowing a fierce red.

The rapid slaps of footfalls from above preceded the arrival of Paul and Benji. Elle stepped back to let them attend to Becks. Once they'd established she was lucid and in no imminent danger, Paul and Benji took a leg and an arm each and carried her up the stairs. She cried out every so often, while Elle looked on, helpless.

Behind her the stairs began to clang. Elle waited until Gee arrived, out of breath and still dripping sea water from her clothes. Elle filled her in, and the two climbed up to the pool level to find Becks lying on one of the sun loungers, Benji to one side of her.

'If you need me,' Gee said to Benji, 'I'm first-aid trained.'

He shook his head. 'I think we've got this. Paul's just gone for a stretcher and some ice.'

Becks grabbed for Benji's T-shirt, pulled him towards her while squeezing her eyes shut. 'It really hurts.' She moaned and put both her arms around his neck, pushing her face into his chest.

Benji hugged her, rubbed her back and winced at Gee and Elle.

Gee shrugged. 'I'm around if you need me.'

She strolled away towards the building, still dripping with sea water. Elle watched Benji tend to Becks. It felt a bit morbid, but having found Becks, she felt guilty about just leaving.

'We'll sort it,' Benji said. 'Don't worry.'

Elle nodded, paused, and walked off, catching up with Gee by the doors into the building.

'Are the others coming up?' she said.

'Not sure,' Gee said. 'I thought they were behind me.'

In the atrium the cooled air blanketed Elle's body, alerting her to every chilly sweat droplet clinging to her skin.

Charlie was sitting with another participant, Mai – a pretty East Asian woman with intimidatingly stylish short hair – on one of the three sofas arranged in a U by the glass wall overlooking the rear of the building. He signalled for them to come over.

'Were you with her when she fell?' Charlie asked.

Elle shook her head. 'I feel awful, I invited her to come to the beach. She must've decided to follow us. I ran up after I heard her yell out.'

Charlie turned to Mai, who nodded at him knowingly.

On their journey back up the stairs to their rooms, Elle turned to Gee. 'Poor Becks. I really hope she's going to be okay. Imagine being here for a month and not being able to walk.'

'I think she'll live. If it was broken she'd be in a lot more pain.'

'Do you think?' She'd seemed in sufficient agony to Elle, but Gee was obviously made of tougher stuff.

'They'd better not close access to the beach. How she's managed to fall down those stairs...' Gee shook her head, and before splitting off to go to her own room, she added, 'What an idiot.'

2

Over an extended canteen table, the group ate lunch together and talked over the events of the morning: both what had happened at the pool and how their tests had gone. Becks had now been taken to her room, and Benji made a brief appearance to plate up some food for her which he then took back to her room. It was stupid, but Elle felt an odd and unexpected jolt of jealousy.

Benji was good-looking, she'd give him that. And he radiated a sort of worldly wisdom when he made eye contact with you which Elle found deeply attractive. But she couldn't dismiss Harrison's warning though, nor its central logic: why *does* a young man choose a career that throws him into a situation like this, far from home for a month as a rep on a sort of glorified 18–30 holiday? Maybe the pay was really good.

What she had to ask herself, though, was: would Holiday

Elle care if he *was* a bit of a player? Home Elle would, with all her whimsical, old-fashioned notions of settling down with a nice boy one day in the not-too-distant future to raise a family. But maybe Holiday Elle ate players up for breakfast. Especially hot ones. Probably.

Although she was jumping the gun somewhat, because even if he was single – which was far from established – with all the other women around, why would he be interested in her, a brittle autumn leaf in this vibrant summer meadow?

While they discussed the morning's tests, Charlie delivered a long, slightly confusing monologue about how the whole thing might be like the Stanford Prison Experiment.

'The drug trial's a front,' he said. 'They're actually watching our behaviour.'

'Right,' Mai said, lapping it all up. 'Yeah, the security team do look at us all funny, have you noticed? They could be studying us.'

Pointing his fork for emphasis, he said, 'Tell me, this drug's supposed to test decision-making, okay? Why are we allowed to drink, then?'

'Not following,' Harrison said without looking up from his food.

'Alcohol's a central nervous system depressant. In the RAF you don't touch it within twenty-four hours of flying. But we can put it away like we're on holiday. Wouldn't that skew their results?'

'Yeah, right,' said Mai. 'It totally would.'

'Don't you dare mention that to them,' Gee said, holding up a clenched fist. 'If they cut off the booze, I'm coming for you.'

'Depends what they're testing, though,' Harrison said. 'We don't know that.'

'Right,' Mai said, offering Harrison her nods now.

'But that's *my* point,' Charlie said. 'I don't think they're testing the drugs at all.'

Sensing tension, Elle said, 'I see what you're saying. But this morning the doctor definitely checked my mouth to make sure I swallowed the pill. I thought it was weird, to be honest, but why would he do that if the pill wasn't involved at all?'

'For show,' Charlie said. 'If you go to the trouble of having a fake pill, why wouldn't you go the extra mile?'

'I get that,' Elle said. 'But isn't that…sort of over-show-manship?'

'What's too showy in a company of players?' That was Dale, looking wistfully into middle distance.

'Exactly,' Charlie said.

'I mean, aren't you more worried that Becks's fall might have had something to do with the pills? Like, a side-effect?'

'Nah,' Gee said, 'she's just clumsy.'

Some of the others laughed so Elle didn't persist. No one else had the energy to argue with Charlie further, and apparently realising this, he held up his hands and concluded:

'I'm just putting the idea forward, based on my trained observations. Just keep your eyes and mind open, people. Big events, sudden changes. Because that's when you know the trial's *really* begun.'

3

That afternoon, nine of them gathered at the reception desk for Benji's grand tour. Only two participants were missing: Becks, and the shaven-haired man Elle had seen this morning. She knew Becks was recuperating, but what was going on with the other guy? He hadn't been around all day.

Benji arrived and did a head count, before asking them to wait another moment. He ran up to and across the floating landing, disappeared down the accommodation corridor, and burst through a few minutes later holding open the door.

'Announcing tonight's special guest.' His voice bounced around the atrium.

Using crutches to propel herself, Becks appeared with a coy smile. When she emerged again from the lift on the ground floor, Benji beside her, the group cheered.

'So embarrassing,' Becks said.

'Okay, thanks for all coming. As you've probably worked out already, the building itself is very new. It usually functions as a resort for big groups—'

'Big *rich* groups,' Gee laughed.

'Yes, big rich groups. And it's really kitted out to keep you entertained here on the site. Yes, Ricoh.'

'A couple of us went down the beach earlier. But, like, are we not actually allowed to leave this place?'

A few people groaned. Benji wasn't fazed.

'I'll get to the beach in a bit, but no, it's in the contract that for health and safety reasons we can't let you off the site during the trial. As you might have noticed on the way here, this facility was built to be very exclusive, so there's not much to see outside. Certainly not within walking distance. And before you ask, no, you can't borrow the minibus.'

Ricoh smiled, although he still looked worried.

'But no,' Benji said, 'you can't leave, and, to be honest, you won't want to. Let me show you what we've got.'

After walking them through facilities at the front of the complex – the tennis courts, a squash court, the football pitch and a contemplation garden of cacti and aloe vera – Benji led them through the back doors and out into the blaze of an after-noon sun unimpeded by clouds. He briefly showed them the pool area and beach before taking them to an outbuilding tucked behind the table tennis tables. Inside it smelled of bleach and pine, and contained two changing rooms, a sauna, a steam room, and a sun bed. The entire far end, though, was a dedicated laundry room, with washing machines, drying racks and tumble dryers.

'You can use these rooms twenty-four hours, but we do close them for cleaning. To be used respectfully, which I know you all will.'

On the walk back inside, Elle sidled up beside Benji.

'Are we missing someone?'

Benji nodded. 'Yeah. I did go up and remind him, but I'm getting the idea he's…quite into his gaming. He's pretty quiet.'

Once they were in the atrium again, Benji explained the building had two wings, both with upper and lower sections. The upper-west wing was their accommodation, and the lower-west wing was where all the trial business occurred.

'That's where you'll find my office or the staff room if I'm not wandering about.'

The upper-east wing contained staff accommodation, but it was really the lower-east wing that needed the most unpacking. Down here there was a wooden-floored gymnastics room, a white-walled gym, and a top-of-the-line virtual reality suite, with five headsets resting in a wall-affixed docking station.

'You will be the first to use this,' Benji said. 'We're trialling it for a company in San Francisco, and they've given us five games to test. They'd love your feedback.'

Further along the corridor was an enormous games room containing entertainments both digital and analogue. Harrison made everyone jump by smashing the punching bag on a test-your-strength arcade game while Benji was talking.

'Sorry,' he said, holding up his hands. 'Don't know my own strength.'

After that was the snug, where another giant screen had been surrounded by sofas, recliners and bean bags.

'I might run some movie nights,' Benji said, 'but you can literally get any film on the streaming packages we have, any night of the week.'

The walls here were decorated with stills from famous films. Elle caught sight of Jeff Goldblum in his *Jurassic Park* leathers, Katherine Ross as a Stepford Wife, and the sentient robot from *Ex Machina*, before Benji moved them to their final destination, the showstopper.

'And this is obviously ridiculous,' Benji said, switching on the lights. 'Welcome to The Lightning Bar.'

After the oohs and ahs subsided, Elle said, 'Shagadelic,' making Benji laugh.

'Exactly.'

Le Chat Noir glared down from on high at zebra-striped floors. Swirling, multi-coloured murals lined the walls. Orange-upholstered chairs and bar stools were arranged around a chunky, marble-topped counter with The Lightning Bar lit up behind it in neon pink. They even had white ball chairs hanging from the ceiling and framed photographs of JFK, the Beatles and Che Guevara.

'I'll be serving drinks and cocktails six nights a week from eight until eleven. Paul or Monique will hold the fort on my night off.'

Benji pointed to a tiled area in the corner with a small stage. 'And that just about brings us to the end of the tour. Dinner will be served from 5.30 to 7.30. Anyone got any questions?'

'All of this stuff's just open 24/7 then?' Harrison said. 'Gym and everything?'

'The bar isn't, but the other rooms, yeah. We don't want you getting bored.'

'But we definitely can't leave?' Gee said. 'Not even if we want a walk?'

'Afraid not.'

'Not even if we're escorted?' Ricoh said.

'Sorry, no.'

On the way out, Elle hung back, hoping to talk to Benji again. He flicked off the lights and whispered to her, 'This place is nuts, isn't it?' before locking the door.

He looked like he was about to say something else, but further up the corridor Becks yelped with frustration, stuck at a set of automatically closing fire doors. Benji glanced at Elle, made a disappointed face, and dashed off to help Becks.

4

'You look bloody gorgeous,' Hallie said when Elle entered The Lightning Bar that evening.

Elle looked down at herself. All she'd done was put on a loose-fitting floral-print dress and apply the tiniest amount of eye make-up. In all honesty, she felt a bag of spuds, but the compliment gave her a buzz nonetheless, and she thanked her. Hallie clearly knew how to dress, and had changed into an asset-accentuating off-shoulder top and a location-apt blue miniskirt. She hugged Elle with the arm not occupied by a blood-red cocktail.

Hallie whooped, and yelled Elle's name, and started trying to dance to the Roy Orbison song playing from a jukebox in the corner.

'Benji, can't we get some real music on?' Hallie said.

'Real music?' he said. 'You not a fan of the 60s?'

'I want a proper dance.'

'Well, I can look into it. Elle, drink?'

She'd not been at the pool that afternoon, but had decided instead to stay in her room to read, bracing herself for what she anticipated being a late night. Still, the sun on her balcony had dehydrated her, and what she wanted more than anything was a cool beer. But like Hallie, both Mai and Becks had cocktails, so to be sociable, she ordered a mojito. To her amusement, Gee arrived minutes later and immediately ordered – and necked – a pint of Stella.

Soon ten of the participants were seated around tables in front of the bar in a fashion which allowed conversation to move back and forth between them all, including Benji, whose ability to walk the professional–chummy tightrope impressed Elle. The alcohol did its work slowly, unknitting her self-consciousness, allowing for Holiday Elle to take the pilot seat.

Once again, the shaven-headed man wasn't there. He'd not been at dinner either. Elle wanted to know what his story was. What if he was just shy, and was now upstairs wishing someone would invite him down? How sad would that be?

'Anyone know what's going on with that guy with the shaved head?' Elle said.

A few looked at Elle blankly, others didn't respond at all. Charlie nodded, and when he'd finished his gulp of lager, he said, 'I know who you mean. No idea about him, though. Don't even remember him on the plane.'

'He was definitely on the plane,' Benji said. 'His name's Constantine. Seems like a nice enough guy.'

Becks sighed. 'That's such a beautiful name.'

'Seems wrong to leave him up there,' Hallie said.

'Do you want me to go up and invite him down?' Benji said.

'Not necessary.' Hallie grabbed Elle's hand and stood up. 'Come on, we'll go visit him. He won't be able to resist us.'

Elle tried to pull back her hand, but Hallie yanked harder and shot her a glare that Elle had to obey. She stood too. Hallie pulled Elle across the bar to the door, and Benji said, 'Uh, do you want to maybe wait? I'm not sure—'

'We'll be right back.'

Hallie walked quickly, and Elle broke into a jog to keep up. They crossed the atrium, Hallie bidding Monique a loud 'Hello!', before making their way up towards their accommodation. Their shoes clopped like hooves.

'Do you even know which room he's in?' Elle asked.

'Deduction. You grow up with six siblings, you get to know where everyone else is at all times.'

She stopped at a room in the middle of the corridor and knocked. Elle hoped they weren't disturbing him. This was a daft idea. She should have stayed quiet.

'I'm really good at convincing people to come out,' Hallie said. 'And really, we need all the boys on show if we're going to make an informed choice.' She jabbed Elle with her elbow.

What on earth had Elle got herself into? She tried to put her off. 'He's probably gone to bed.'

'Constantine,' Hallie said, and banged the door twice. She put her fists to her hips. When he didn't answer, she tried again, and again. Then she kicked the door, kicked it again, harder, and yelled, 'Constantine, we want you to come out and play.'

'Steady on,' Elle said.

This wasn't fun anymore, and noticing that Hallie was building up to another kick, the unwanted memory of Terry that day in the hospital reception returning to her, she locked arms with Hallie, and tugged her away in the direction of the atrium.

'Let's go,' she said, 'he's obviously busy.'

'What if the pills have messed him up? He could be dead.'

'Well, I'm sure he's not.'

'You know, I've got a bit of a headache,' Hallie said. 'Started earlier. Is your head okay?'

'I'm okay. How bad is—'

The double doors opened, and Benji stepped through.

'He's not answering.' Hallie shrugged and screwed up her face as if to say, His Loss. 'We're worried the pills have killed him.'

'No we're not,' Elle said, laughing a bit too hard.

'Well,' Benji said, 'I'll check on him to make sure. But I think the man just likes his space.'

Hallie let Elle steer her away, and once they were back in the atrium Hallie leaned in and whispered, 'Benji's tasty, isn't he?' Elle laughed, committing to nothing. 'So's that Harrison. You like him, Elle? He was checking you out a few times today. Seems to get on with you.'

'He's fine. Everyone's nice, but… I'm not really looking for anything. I'm just here to get to know people and have a good time.'

'Get to know people.' Her laughter echoed through the building. 'What a load of bollocks. No one's here for that.'

5

Back at the bar another discussion about the trial had ignited. Charlie – who else? – had made the point that he'd found no online presence for Apollo Wellbeing when he'd checked before leaving. This he found suspicious. Ted and Harrison countered that there were a million reasons why the company didn't have a web presence yet – not least that the company might be new or trying to keep its activities a secret. Despite his intensity, though, watching from the outside, Elle thought Charlie's style appeared more playful, and it was possible he might even be, at least a little bit, on the wind-up.

Elle tried keeping out of it by sitting at the bar with Hallie. It wasn't that she wasn't curious, far from it. It was just that the unease she'd felt on arriving the night before had largely been quelled by the impressive surroundings and the entertaining company. There was a sort of freshers week vibe now – not that she'd got much out of her actual freshers week, having lacked the confidence back in the day.

'You want to know something else, too?' Charlie was saying.

'Not particularly,' Harrison said.

'Everyone here is single.'

'How do you know that?'

'My ears are always open. Forewarned is forearmed. So, am I wrong? Anyone here shacked up?'

A silence followed this, and Elle looked up at Hallie, and asked the question by nodding at her. Hallie confirmed with her own nod, and silently asked the question back of Elle. She nodded too.

Harrison blew air through his lips. 'So what?'

'Relationship status was on the questionnaires. It was part of the selection criteria. So, why?'

'I take it you have a theory,' Ted said.

'Seems to me this whole set-up is designed to divert us from the real nature of the trial. All these rooms and entertainments. Everyone single, young, attractive.' He looked at Mai. 'It's all one massive distraction.'

'We're all fiddling, Rome burns?' Dale said, briefly leaving the world of his notebook.

'Exactly.'

Benji re-entered the bar, and Charlie fell silent. Harrison didn't seem impressed, while Ted got up and wandered out with a head shake only Elle noticed.

Hallie pushed into Elle, and brought her head towards hers. 'Is Charlie mad?'

'I'm not sure he's a hundred per cent serious about it all. I think he likes the attention.'

'Should we ask Benji?'

Elle, still a bit embarrassed about what had happened earlier, wasn't keen to draw attention to herself once again with questions about Charlie's conspiracy theory. But it was too late, Hallie had already called him over.

'Everything okay?'

'We want to ask you something.'

'What's that, Hallie?'

She grinned, revealing ever so slightly snaggled canines. 'Are you single, Benji?'

Elle closed her eyes. How bloody awkward.

Benji gave a sideways smile, and said, 'I'm not in a relationship with anyone, no.'

Elle desperately wanted to change the subject. 'Was Constantine okay in his room, Benji? Sorry if we disturbed him.'

Hallie glanced at her with a mixture of amusement and disappointment.

'He was fine,' Benji said. 'He was watching TV with headphones on.'

'So he was feeling okay?' Hallie said.

'He was fine,' Benji repeated.

'Suppose that's good then, day one and no one has had any significant side-effects yet.'

'I'll drink to that,' Elle said, and clinked her second cocktail with Hallie. Hallie appeared to wince at the sound, and doubt briefly crossed her face.

'You don't need to worry about that,' Benji said.

'Really?' Hallie spun a plastic stirrer in her drink. 'You seem confident.'

'I'm just going on what they've told me.'

'Do you know what the trial's *really* about then?' She dropped her voice to a whisper. 'You can tell us.'

He was already shaking his head. 'I know as much as you.'

Hallie narrowed her eyes and murmured.

'What?' Benji said with a laugh.

'I think he knows,' Hallie said to Elle.

Benji shrugged, and rolled his eyes at Elle. 'Everyone's entitled to their opinion.'

6

As the evening progressed, chatter led to dancing, which soon led to karaoke. Home Elle couldn't sing at all, but Holiday Elle gave Queen's 'Don't Stop Me Now' her very best. Really only Mai had any sort of talent, and her version of Britney's 'Toxic' was even better than the real thing. Her voice had vibrato and was in tune and everything.

People wandered in and out, and everyone drank far too much, which was to be expected. Elle was surprised, because even though the four cocktails she put away were more than anything she'd consumed recently, she didn't feel that drunk at all. After her first drink she'd found her level and stayed there. It felt as if she could drink all night, but she didn't.

In fact, no one seemed too drunk. Harrison got a bit close-talky and touchy, and Ricoh's nervous energy made him witter and pace, and it was hard to tell if Hallie was super-pissed or naturally a bit of a party animal. But no one became aggressive or over-emotional. And when at the same time, everyone seemed to tire, and the gradual drift towards their bedrooms began, Elle was genuinely content. In the right place, at the right time. She hadn't thought about Mum, or lying on the questionnaire, for a good few hours.

7

Hallie linked her arm through Elle's and they walked back to the accommodation corridor. Hallie was the only one with a room overlooking the front of the complex instead of the sea; she said she couldn't sleep with the noise of the waves. Outside their facing doors, Hallie hugged Elle and kissed her cheek.

'Aww,' she said. 'I feel like I've known you forever.'

Elle laughed, but worried it sounded mean, and so she squeezed her back and said, 'I know, it's funny, isn't it? How's your head feeling now?'

'Fucking kills. But I'll live. What doesn't kill you makes you stronger, eh?'

Elle had never been in the popular crowd at school; Hallie, by contrast, most clearly had. It felt nice floating along on the wave of her confidence. She was exactly what Holiday Elle needed.

When she pulled out of the hug, Benji came through the doors, escorting Becks back to her room. After the door closed behind them, Hallie's lip curled.

'Maybe *we* need to throw ourselves down a flight of stairs,' Hallie said.

Elle was still laughing when she closed her own bedroom door and took off her shoes. She'd got as far as brushing her teeth when someone knocked on her door. Benji, maybe? Unlikely, but maybe he wanted to check in on everyone before bed. That wasn't so absurd, and crossing the room, she quickly glanced at her reflection in the mirror.

Elle opened the door to Harrison, his eyes droopy and his smile mischievous. He held up a pack of playing cards, and said, 'Fancy a game?'

She tried not to look disappointed. His shirt appeared to have opened by another button, and now he was blocking her doorway, the imposing size of him became apparent. He took a step inside.

'Just a quick game of Crazy Eights or something.'

'Oh, thank you. But I should probably call it a night.'

'Or Snap, if you'd prefer.'

Elle smiled. Perhaps she should say yes. Holiday Elle said yes to everything, didn't she? Or did she? She wasn't exactly sure. But Home Elle or Holiday Elle, if she hadn't been sure before, she was now: she just didn't find Harrison that attractive. And the urge to get him out of her room – before either Hallie, who clearly did like him, or worse, Benji, saw him there and jumped to the wrong conclusion – was powerful.

'Sorry, I really need to be sober for you to truly feel the force of my Snap game.'

'I've found today pretty…full-on,' he said, leaning forwards. 'I don't know about you. And I just feel like I need to do something to unwind.'

'If you want I've got plenty of books I could lend you. I gave one to Ricoh earlier.'

He huffed out a defeated laugh and held up both his hands. 'I'll get going.'

'Definitely another time. I didn't mean, like…' But she did mean it like that, so why backtrack? Because it felt awful, was why. But she wasn't about to let him in just because it was a bit awkward. That really *would* be a Home Elle move.

'Tomorrow?' she said.

'Sure. I'm definitely down with that.'

He stood still for a moment, watching her with an unsteady gaze. For a second, maybe two, the glow of his charm vanished from his eyes, like a projector flickering in a storm. Yet nothing replaced it either; it was as if he'd fallen asleep with his eyes open. Whatever had gone returned with a violent wince followed by a dopey grin.

'Are you okay?' she asked.

'Yeah. Yeah, good. Just had a…little migraine or some-thing.' He shook his head. 'Night, Elle.'

'Night, Harrison.'

He held his ground a while longer, until finally he stepped backwards into the corridor.

Elle stepped forward to shut the door and Harrison walked away. At that moment Benji appeared, and Elle's stomach muscles clenched. He smiled at Harrison when he passed, and Harrison touched his forehead with his fingers in a salute.

Benji held up his hand to Elle without making eye contact, and followed Harrison out to the landing.

Elle closed the door. Damn it, now Benji would assume something was going on with them. Should she go after him, explain what happened? No, it was only the first day, for good-ness' sake. She didn't want to overdo it.

8

In the small kitchenette area of her room she poured herself a glass of water before lying down on the bed. She stared at the ceiling and assessed her levels of drunkenness. It was hard to tell, but she was probably going to be okay.

She rolled onto her side and retrieved the daily diary Dr Lineker had asked them all to complete from her bedside drawer. The hardback's cream cover gleamed beneath the bedroom spots. The Apollo Wellbeing logo was embossed in the corner, and each page had been labelled with the day of the trial. A message on the inside read:

Please use this diary to record how you have felt during the day, thinking of your physical health, mental health and overall wellbeing. Please complete

at the end of each day or at the start of the following day before taking your next day's medication. DO NOT include data from the day/night of your arrival.

With an Apollo Wellbeing-branded pen, she wrote on the page marked 'Day 1':

I have felt normal today, and am feeling positive in all aspects of my health.

She paused. It didn't really feel like enough. She'd had a good time today. She ought to give them more, even if the trial paperwork had stated just a sentence would be fine.

Still, they were giving her £20,000 for a holiday.

I am having a good time.

Why not? She wouldn't think twice about leaving a message in a visitor book at a hotel.

At the bottom of every page three tick boxes awaited completion.

Which of these apply today?
I AM FEELING MYSELF
I AM MOSTLY FEELING MYSELF
I AM NOT FEELING MYSELF

She smiled a little, chewing the pen. Did Holiday Elle count as not feeling herself? There should have been an 'It's complicated' option. Never mind. She ticked the first box and closed the book. She rolled over to put it back, and stayed her hand halfway between the drawer and the bed. She shuffled closer to the drawer, leaning in. Something at the back caught her interest.

She climbed down to the floor and pulled the drawer out as far as it would go, accidentally detaching it from its rails. She muttered a curse and put the drawer on the bed and examined what she'd seen inside.

At the back, where the white base met the wooden side, someone had written something in Biro. The handwriting was compact and calligraphic, but now the drawer was on the bed, she could read it clearly enough. Five words long, it read:

They are taking our souls

Chapter Five

1

The first few days were largely the same. Variations on a theme, rarely major. Elle, a creature of habit, wasn't complaining. She ploughed through two novels and was halfway through a third. The weather remained glorious, the rare clouds no more substantial than mist, and the day temperature never lower than twenty-two degrees. With the company and entertainment available, there was more than enough novelty to pass the time.

On the way into breakfast each day each participant would have to show their completed diary, take their pill and endure a swallow check before being allowed into the canteen. The whole thing was often a mess, with people drifting all over the place and a sweaty-looking Dr Lineker muttering about how it was like trying to herd cats.

After, people would usually drift down to the pool or, less often, the beach, while some, like Charlie or Ricoh, might stay in, gaming or watching TV. In Dale's case, he often went with the crowd and found a spot nearby to work on his novel, while Elle would usually read on her balcony. In the afternoon, only the hardcore sun worshippers went back to hit the loungers. Hallie. Harrison. Becks, who was still hobbling around on her crutches. Once the sun started to cool at around 4 p.m., games would be paused and siestas broken, and some would enjoy another swim or take to the outdoor sports facilities.

Once dinner was finished – the most sociable of all the meals, as everyone was starving at the same time – some started on the indoor entertainments. This was usually the time of day Ricoh started slamming a basketball around in the atrium with Mai or Ted, or Benji would start a pool or darts tournament in the games room. Hallie and Becks usually vanished to their rooms to prepare for the evening, which always consisted of a mass gathering in the bar that would eventually spill out into some of the other rooms or, as on one balmy night, the rocky beach.

Other than Benji – who played the role of barman so well that Elle wasn't surprised when she learned he'd actually done the job before – the staff members tended to vanish in the evenings, only rarely joining them for a drink. Once Elle saw Jess at the bar talking with Ted, and another night Harrison and Paul shared a whisky in the corner. But that was it really.

After Benji shut the bar, the place wouldn't always fall silent. Sometimes the real gluttons for punishment stayed up late, despite the requirement to turn up at breakfast for their pill before nine. Occasionally they'd stumble back to their rooms in twos or threes, talking loudly, having been in the VR suite or watching films. The only other sound at night was the goats outside, whose human-like screams and yells occasionally drifted over the walls.

On the fourth night one had been so loud it woke her up, screeching for almost half an hour in a particularly distressed fashion. She'd hoped it wasn't Harry. Elle had eventually climbed out of bed, unable to believe that no one had asked Security to go and check the thing hadn't broken its leg or fallen down a well. She was half-dressed when the goat fell silent. Elle returned to bed, expecting it to start up again at any moment. But it never did and, before long, she fell asleep.

2

She awoke early the next morning, before Housekeeping had even arrived on site, and, unable to drift off again, she'd made herself a coffee and gone to stroll around the front garden in the soft morning sun. She only saw the goat from a distance, its head wedged under the gap at the bottom of the fence, tongue out, something odd happening with the fur on its neck. But the lightning bolt marking, flies crawling over it now, was distinctive enough for her to identify the animal as Harry. Her appetite for breakfast shrivelled.

Elle found Paul over by the five-a-side pitch, finishing a cigarette. She told him what she'd found, her voice unexpectedly emotional. He made a sad face and threw his butt down. 'Yeah, sorry you had to see that, love. Only just seen it myself. I'll get it shifted.'

A faintly sour smell drifted over on his breath.

'How did it happen?'

Paul shrugged. 'Tried getting back in the hard way and got stuck.' He shrugged again. 'Must have panicked. Broke his neck struggling, looks like.'

'I think I heard him last night. Didn't you hear the screaming?'

'Screaming? Nah, didn't hear a thing. Shame.'

At breakfast later she mentioned the goat to Charlie, interested to see how he might weave it into his theory.

'Yeah, I saw. I watched Paul loading it into the minibus earlier.'

'Not being funny, but you watched?' Becks said with a pout. 'How horrible. I love animals.' She pushed a sausage into her mouth. 'I suppose at least we'll get some sleep now.'

'I could hear it screeching last night,' Hallie said. 'What happened then?'

When Elle repeated what Paul had said, Charlie laughed and shook his head. 'No offence to Paul, but it didn't do that to itself.'

'What do you mean?' Elle said.

He chewed on a piece of toast and said, 'Goat's head was on backwards.'

3

Elle hadn't wanted to believe Charlie, nor his implication that someone in the building had done such a savage thing to get a few more hours' sleep. Yet she knew what she'd seen, and the more she dwelled on what was admittedly a brief glimpse, the less likely it seemed the goat had broken its own neck. And the way it had fallen so suddenly silent last night, too, only supported that idea.

But who would do that? One candidate was Paul, who had a vendetta against the thing, having chased it around unsuccessfully that first night. Maybe he'd been trying to protect their sleep, doing his job diligently in a sort of considerate but cold-blooded way. Only why, then, hadn't he moved it straight away? Why would he have left it out all night and waited until they were all up to do it in full view?

Elle identified at least one video camera that might have caught what actually happened, and the next time she saw Paul she asked him if he'd checked the footage. He gave her a funny look, like the request was somehow distasteful. Why was she asking about footage of a goat dying? Of course, he wasn't to know her suspicions, and immediately she felt her face reddening and an urge to drop the whole thing.

'Listen,' he said, 'cameras have been playing up since we got here, so we don't want to go into that software again unless we absolutely have to. More than our jobs are worth, being honest.'

It was a suspicious thing to say, but Monique later confirmed the glitching software when Elle made a subtle enquiry after Paul went off duty. And Paul leaving the body still didn't make sense, if it had been him who'd killed the goat. So maybe it had been someone else. Perhaps one of the doctors? Or even Monique?

4

One thing she couldn't bring herself to believe was that it had been one of the other participants. She'd got to know them all pretty well by the end of the first week – bar Constantine, who still actively avoided everyone – and despite her paying close attention, none of them had even a whiff of brutality about them. She had to admit, she was warming to Harrison's theory that everyone on the trial had something a bit different about them. But their quirks weren't scary, and she'd come to like them all in different ways.

Hallie told Elle she was a property lawyer over a game of table tennis by the pool one afternoon. She'd moved to Kent after growing up in Manchester, and she planned to use the trial money to build a property portfolio back at home.

'I'm going to specialise in tiny homes,' Hallie said. 'You should come in on it with me with your trial money. It's going be huge.'

'Tiny homes?'

'Yeah, little bijou doll-house things. But for humans. Eco-friendly and economical and all that. It's like, a dream of mine. I'd have done it before now, but I send a lot of my extra money back to the family in Pakistan.' Through the side of her mouth, she added, 'And I buy shoes like they're crack.'

Mai, who had been lying nearby, found this hilarious and broke into giggles. The laughter encouraged conversation and Mai revealed to them that she was a civil servant, but was trying to get into fashion vlogging and influencing. They couldn't check any social media platforms to establish how far she'd got with this endeavour – in fact, the internet on the whole was useless, as seemingly any innocuous search ran smack bang into the firewall – and Mai was too embarrassed to tell them her handle anyway. But Hallie seemed to think she knew her stuff, given that Mai's plan for her money was to buy targeted adverts to really launch her new career.

Knowing about her love of fashion made Mai's friendship with Charlie, a man rarely out of his long coat and cargo trousers, all the more incongruous. The two of them could often be seen walking around the complex, talking with conspiratorial closeness. One afternoon Elle watched them struggle to move a pedalo beyond the buoy line, before Paul turned up to glare at them and they gave up. Apparently he'd disabled the pedals so they couldn't be taken from the cove.

'I just like that he notices stuff no one else does,' Mai said, when Hallie tried drawing her out on the topic. 'It makes me feel safe.'

There was no way either Mai or Hallie had been involved with what happened to the goat. It just didn't fit. As for Charlie, it wasn't out of the question he might be capable of killing an animal in the right circumstances. But why, then, would he have brought up the idea in the first place? And increasingly

Elle tilted towards believing his bullish manner was mostly a front. She sometimes even felt a little sad for him. Attack as a form of defence was his default mode. Had he been bullied at school, perhaps? Had he suffered an overbearing father?

While they were throwing the ball at the basket in the atrium together – the pair of them both useless at it – Charlie told her that in addition to being in the RAF reserve, he was also a National Park warden, an aviation engineer, and, on occasion, a flight school instructor. His big plan, though, was to spend the trial money on buying up old flight simulators using his RAF contacts.

'Then I'm going to set up a virtual flight school. It's going to be a really big deal.' It was one of the few times she'd seen him animated, and she sensed that a more child-like, honest version of Charlie lurked just beneath the surface. When he threw the ball, it struck the brickwork to one side of the basket, and bounced back to him. He caught it and gave a surprised smile, looking momentarily like a little boy.

Harrison, the only other participant she might have at one point suspected of being capable of killing an animal, had come to apologise to her the morning after he visited her room. He seemed genuinely mortified, and explained that he'd been drunk and very homesick. His whole alpha male thing collapsed around him, much to her surprise. He asked for her forgiveness, and she told him an apology wasn't necessary. They'd played cards a couple of times since, and talked about their families. He routinely volunteered for an arthrogryposis charity, because his young cousin suffered with it. Hardly the actions of a goat killer.

After a few conversations with Ted, Elle decided the most morally dubious part of him was that his business sometimes involved being ruthless with winning contracts. But even then, he was the one pointing out his discomfort with the notion. He actually came across as the most grounded of the group, and tended to hang back on the sidelines when the crowd got too large.

He clearly loved games, and excelled at sports – she'd seen him doing football tricks with Gee on the five-a-side pitch and sinking no-look baskets with Charlie and an annoyed-looking Harrison. He played pool and table tennis, often throwing matches towards the end after taking considerable leads – something his opponents didn't seem to notice. Ricoh celebrated one pool comeback like he'd won a gold medal, punching the bag on the test-of-strength game repeatedly.

'How are you so…good at stuff?' she'd asked Ted at the bar later.

'I'm not that good,' he said. 'I think I'm just a natural risk-taker, so when it pays off in things like sports, it makes me look far better than I am.'

She admired Ted's maturity, but found it unnerving at times, too. Especially when he gave her a look that reminded her of Winston, and her guard would involuntarily drop. He was destroying her at darts one evening in the games room, when he said, 'I hope you don't mind me saying, but you seem a bit different from the others.'

Elle began to sweat and took a deep breath. She forced her attention onto the bullseye to avoid his gaze. 'You think? How so?'

'I can't put my finger on it,' he said. 'You like to watch things. You seem more…cautious. Like you're working me out.'

Feeling embarrassed, she apologised, and he laughed in a way that instantly made her less self-conscious.

'You actually… It's just, you sometimes remind me of a friend. It's a bit weird,' she said.

'Someone nice, I hope.'

'Yeah, Winston's the best. I always go to him if I want to talk and need a level head.'

'Good to know.' He threw a dart. 'Well, if you need a... level head, I'll be your trial Winston.'

She smiled, sensing he wasn't entirely convinced that his familiarity was the reason for her watchfulness. Perhaps to deflect from the fact that she actually *was* different from the others, Elle came clean about her mission to work out if anyone had killed the goat.

'So you're trying to deduce who's most likely to be a killer, then? Am I still a suspect?'

'No, definitely not. But how can you tell these things? It probably just hurt itself, didn't it? I'm being paranoid.'

He nodded, still amused, and said, 'How can you tell, indeed.'

After her conversation with Ted she tried to be less noticeably watchful, not wanting to stand out from the others in any way, given her situation. Trying to throw herself into things a bit more, she accepted Gee and Dale's invitation to try cliff jumping with them. They did it most days; swimming out to a spot near the end of the cove, climbing up twenty or so feet, and hurling themselves off. The two of them were like boisterous puppies when together, and utterly fearless. When Elle actually stood up there, having barely made the climb, she was unable to jump. She stared down at the water smashing the rocks numerous times, but only managed to make her head shake. Holiday Elle had her limits. The other two laughed at her, although she didn't think they were being mean-spirited.

Oddly, both seemed quite contemplative when on their own. Gee had strong political opinions which surfaced like hunting sharks at unexpected moments. She'd specialised in managing environmental building projects, and lived with a degree of fatalism related to the planet's poor mid-to-long-term climate prospects.

'Seize the fucking day, I say, before it sets you on fire,' she'd said over drinks one night late in the first week, which was presumably why she wanted to use her money to climb Everest.

On the goat question she had to be ruled out. Among her many causes were animal rights. She only ate meat because she suffered from bouts of anaemia. Case closed.

And, as a suspect, Dale was a non-starter. It was all he could do to stand up straight; he didn't appear physically capable of breaking an animal's neck. He also looked like he might cry when someone told him the goat had died. He seemed genuinely sweet, if a little naive. He was always complimenting people if they made an interesting remark or a funny joke, often writing it down in his blue notebook. He told Elle he was working on a novel based on the trial.

'I'm not a character, am I?' she asked.

'Maybe,' he said. 'You'd make a good character. You really listen to people.'

His plan with the trial money was to self-publish and become as big as E. L. James, he said, though he emphasised that he didn't write 'sexy stuff'.

'I think if my mam were alive, she'd love to see me write a book. She loved books.'

Then there was Becks, who floated around from group to group like an injured ghost. Elle couldn't quite get the measure of her, and often her attempts felt like the endless descent into a gas planet. Her ankle remained a focal point of any conversation – How's it feeling today? Do you want some painkillers? Do you need help with that? – even though she actually had a relatively interesting job as a producer for television.

'Have you worked on any shows I might have heard of?'

Elle said to her while taking her turn to walk her back to her room and hold open the doors.

In a detached and airy way, Becks said, 'You've probably heard of all of them. I've done all the big reality shows.'

'*Love Island*? My mum would—'

'Not that one.'

'Oh. Well, it must be interesting, though.'

'Sometimes.'

'What do you do?'

'This and that, really. A lot of emailing, like we all do.'

Elle would leave such encounters with a vague sense of having conversed with smoke. It reminded her of Mum in some ways, but also of herself, turning back questions and reflecting body language to move the attention around her. Which was why she found herself wanting even more to pierce her outer surface, and one evening she sat with Becks at the bar the whole night, downing cocktail after cocktail, hoping she would open up. But all she learned was that she'd grown up on a farm, which was why she loved animals so much.

Even if that hadn't been true, where the goat was concerned Becks's ankle ruled her out as a suspect. What had happened to Harry required two planted feet.

5

The animal's lifeless face would glide into her mind often, especially after sunset, vivid, and sometimes from a perspective much closer than she had ever been that morning. If it hadn't been someone inside the compound, was it possible someone was prowling around outside? Or perhaps she was overreacting, because no one else seemed bothered.

She narrowed her suspects down to Monique, Carl and Constantine – mostly because she hadn't been able to interact with them enough to rule them out. Not that she had much of a plan, even if she narrowed it down further – but she couldn't just forget about it. It gnawed away at her, an embodiment of the more general unease she had about elements of the trial. And she'd given the animal a name. That felt somehow significant.

Then there was the curious case of Ricoh. It wasn't that she suspected him. In fact she'd really warmed to him. It's just there was something going on with him that made her suspicious.

He was the youngest member of the group at twenty, still at uni in Manchester, studying History. He'd ditched his lectures to pay off his first-year overdraft, which put his motivations in the same bracket as Elle's, and so she felt something of an affinity towards him. However, by the second week of the trial he seemed to be struggling. He paced a lot, never staying still for more than five minutes. Even when seated or lying down, he remained animated. Often he drifted down corridors and paced by sun loungers, only to pace back in the opposite direction just a short time later.

One morning she heard Monique take him aside in the breakfast queue and ask if he'd managed to get back to sleep. Apparently he often walked around after dark, and she'd found him down by the beach at three in the morning. He did appear noticeably tired, his pale complexion highlighting the darker skin beneath his eyes.

He borrowed three more books from Elle, returning the previous book to her each time with a glowing review stripped of any specific story details. Elle suspected he wasn't reading them at all, but using them as a way to talk to her.

'I don't know, when I signed up I thought this'd be easy,' he said to her one afternoon on the beach, after she'd wandered down for some air and found him marching along the tide line.

The sun had nearly gone and there was a chilly seam in the breeze. 'I saw the amount on that ad and imagined being able to buy drinks for my mates, finally. A big, fat round. But I'm just getting a bit restless now. You know what I mean? A bit…bored.'

'Bored?'

'You know, without my phone…seeing the same things. The routine of it.' His eye contact lay a hair the wrong side of intense; Elle bobbed and weaved to avoid it.

'Seriously? But you liked the Linwood Barclay book. That was good, wasn't it?'

'Ah, yeah. It was, it was. But honest though, there's rocks on this beach I've given names.'

Elle laughed, although the genuine stress she heard brought out a mumsiness in which she didn't mind indulging. She almost wanted to tell him that only boring people got bored, something Granny Alice used to dust off when Elle was a girl. But she didn't want to be patronising, and he was clearly in a bad way. She was mostly coping without her phone and the internet, but there had been a few grumbles in the wider camp about the strength of the firewall. And Hallie and Mai sometimes waxed nostalgic about their phones, like they were dead lovers. Harrison, who had some experience with firewalls in his work, muttered once or twice about hacking the system – although so far he'd refrained.

'I don't know,' Ricoh said, 'Maybe it's not even boredom, maybe it just feels like it. Feels like I'm in my own head a lot more somehow, if that makes sense. I'm lying down to go to sleep and I'm sort of…there. Noticing things I've never noticed before. Thinking about… It's weird. Hard to explain.'

'Are you anxious? Is that what you mean?'

He screwed up his face. 'Nah, not… Maybe. It's more

like…it's like a hangover, but the headache bit is like…me. I'm there in my own head. Hello, me. Do you know what I mean?'

Elle didn't, but she wanted to know more about his headache. It reminded her of what Hallie had been complaining about. 'I think so,' she said to encourage him.

'But, like, the thoughts I'm having are…freaking me out a bit. They don't feel like mine, but they also are, which makes no sense. And the only thing that gets rid of it is, like, walking about or doing something with my hands.'

'Have you had much to drink?' She knew the answer; he'd been at the bar every night with the rest of them.

'Not more than usual. But yeah, it's sometimes felt like a hangover. A headache I can't shake off. But I don't know, I'm not a lightweight.'

'It might be the climate – are you drinking lots of water?'

'No, probably not.'

Elle hadn't really had a hangover since being here, despite drinking more than she usually did when not in crisis mode. If it weren't for Harrison's quite vocal daily hangovers, she could almost come to believe Charlie's new theory that the drinks were being watered down for the sake of the trial – another piece of evidence in his increasingly elaborate conspiracy theory.

'Thanks, anyway, Elle,' Ricoh said. 'I feel better, having had this chat. You seem really nice.'

'Oh, thank you. Well, if you ever want to talk, I'm here.'

He smiled, and took a moment to look away from her. She sensed he was about to say something else.

'Hey, you don't think it could be the drugs, do you? This headache.'

She hadn't mentioned the possibility, not wanting to worry him. 'I wouldn't think so,' she said. 'They've been pretty clear about that. But definitely put it in your diary, and if you're worried, you could mention it to the doctors.'

'I don't know. All that participant's obligation stuff. If they send me packing, I might not get my money.'

'Oh, you would.' She looked out at the sea, at the line of buoys marking the edge of their current world, not entirely sure if she was being truthful anymore. 'They're not evil.'

6

As the second week began, Elle pushed Harry's death to the back of her mind as best she could. She was meant to be on holiday, after all. So she threw herself into socialising. She instigated a bowling competition in the atrium. After one of Benji's film nights she dragged others into a poker game – although Ricoh stormed off after consecutive failed bluffs, punching the door on his way out. She even tried cliff jumping a second time before realising she'd made a terrible error and climbing back down again.

One night in the bar, Ted, seeming to want to take Elle's baton, suggested they play a game.

'Have you ever played live-action Cluedo?' he asked. No one had. 'It's a really fun way to get to know each other.'

'How's it work?' Ricoh said.

'Well, we all write down our names on a bit of paper, okay? And then, on different bits of paper, we also all write down a murder location somewhere on this site, and a murder weapon. Then we put the different bits of paper into three separate pint glasses, and we all draw a person, a location and a weapon from the glasses.'

'What do you mean by a weapon?' Elle asked.

'It can be anything really. Ideally something you can conceal on you. A pen. A comb. A cucumber.'

'A cucumber?' Ricoh said, laughing. 'Then what do you do?'

'Well, then you have to get your victim alone in your selected location, take out your murder weapon and say, Sorry, mate, you're dead.'

Everyone wanted to play, including Benji. Ted went on to explain that a murder victim had to 'pass on' their assigned murder to their murderer by handing them their three pieces of paper. Victims then had to declare their death to the group, but remain quiet about the identity of their killer.

'How's it end?' Mai said.

'Well eventually,' he said, 'only two people will be left. And the winner is the one who outwits the other.'

The game added an exciting bit of tension to every social encounter, and Elle felt nervous when alone with anyone. In the first few days victims dropped like flies. Ted, Becks, Dale and Gee were all killed by mid-week, the participants playing with perhaps a bit too much enthusiasm. Becks recounted how her killer had hidden inside her cupboard. She'd been falling asleep when they'd climbed out to 'murder' her. She relayed the story in a matter-of-fact manner, but Elle wasn't sure she'd have been quite so forgiving. Ted made a remark in the bar later that they ought to remain respectful of each other when playing.

'Are you enjoying the game?' he asked Elle that same evening, finding her alone by the jukebox. He smelled like soap and aftershave.

'Yeah, it's a laugh.'

'I thought it might help you.'

Elle furrowed her brow. 'Help me with what?'

'With your search for the killer.' He shrugged with a side-ways smile. 'No better way to find out who's the most devious.' With that he walked off, looking pleased with himself and reminding her of Winston more than ever. Elle couldn't help but smile back.

Elle had drawn Ricoh and her challenge was to murder him with a lip balm in the snug. She managed to locate him in the atrium on one of his late-night wanders after everyone else had gone to their rooms, and after making small talk she told him she'd lost her lip balm. He came to help her look, and, once the snug door closed behind them, she pretended to find the murder weapon behind the sofa.

'Ah, here it is,' she said, already feeling bad about tricking him into the room. 'Now, Ricoh, I need to tell you something.'

When she rose from behind the sofa to kill him she found him staring at her from the other side. His expression was stony. His fists were clenched tight by his sides.

'You better not be murdering me,' he said, barely moving his lips, sounding like he was fighting back real anger.

She felt the way she did around skittish dogs, like she needed to suppress her fear in case the animal reacted to it aggressively. Remembering how badly he'd reacted during the game of poker, she said, 'No,' and waved her hand like it was the silliest idea in the world. 'Not at all. No.'

He grinned, and immediately the charge in the atmosphere disappeared. Still, she felt unsettled by the encounter and wanted to be back in her room. She'd kill him another time. In daylight.

'Hope your head's feeling better,' she said before leaving him. He didn't respond.

By the time she was out in the corridor the whole thing seemed silly, and it was easy to dismiss what she'd felt as being the result of tiredness. Or perhaps it might even be a mild side-effect of the drugs, who knew? But Ricoh didn't follow her. He remained in the snug, alone with whatever feelings were coursing through him.

7

As much as Elle embraced the distractions of life at the complex, they were really just interludes between her talks with Benji. Each conversation they had, no matter how brief, would leave her fizzing for hours afterwards. Was she imagining that he seemed to seek her out more than the others? Or that when she scanned a room for him, she would catch him looking back?

On one of his rare afternoons off they walked down to the beach, Elle half expecting him to pull out an object from his pocket and declare her murdered. He mentioned that she seemed a bit happier than she had done at the end of the previous week. So she shared with him her worries about what happened to the goat. She'd not done it before for fear of sounding paranoid, but enough trust had built up between them that she felt like he wouldn't judge.

'I don't know why I can't let it drop,' she said. 'Well… maybe I do. Before I came here, there was this incident at my work with a patient. He sort of…came at me—'

'God, were you okay?'

'Yes, yes. Fine. He was unwell, but he mentioned goats when he was having this episode. It's given the goat here this… stupid significance. It's so self-important, like people who meet a person with the same name as their dead gran, and think it's a message from beyond the—'

'No, I totally understand. I'd be the same. In fact, I think I've even done what you said about my gran.' She laughed with him, but hoped he'd not been offended. 'Yeah, it's funny. I remember Monique mentioning it, but she said it broke its neck in a panic. If you want, I can ask to see the video?'

'They'll know it's me asking. And Paul said the video software was being problematic.'

Benji nodded. 'Yeah, he has said that. But isn't that what he'd say if he'd done it? I'll make some sly enquiries.'

He smiled and, God, it did things to her.

8

He was probably just being nice. She was reading too much into his professional attention. It was just a small crush to bounce around in her head during quiet times. Utterly harmless if she just played it cool. It was just good to have someone to rely on here, that was all.

Still, as the other participants began to couple up, it did feel like the road to Benji was opening up for her. Hallie had definitely started sleeping with Harrison. She'd heard them outside her door coming and going from Hallie's room. Gee had been open about sleeping with Dale, although she had also made comments about wanting to fuck Mai, Harrison, and even Elle, which Dale hadn't appeared fussed by. Mai and Charlie might well have been sleeping together, but no one really knew. They moved openly in and out of one another's rooms with the easiness of a couple, while never showing any public displays of affection around the other participants.

Elle's only real obstacle was Becks, who had given the distinct impression of liking Benji (although Harrison received a fair bit of her attention, too), and used every opportunity she could to monopolise his attention – easy enough to do, given her condition and associated props. But Benji acted differently around her. Becks never saw the weariness descend on his face when she turned away from him, and once, while Becks was asking for Benji's help getting up from her seat at the bar, Benji actually caught Elle's gaze and offered her the briefest raise of his eyebrows.

Why then, if he was interested in her, hadn't something

happened yet? Yes, he was working, but not all the time. Did it have something to do with their first night when he'd bumped into Harrison leaving her room?

9

Thursday night of the second week, Elle went alone to the bar. Hallie, who usually joined her, had been complaining about her headache all afternoon and had finally given up to lie down in her room. Monique stood behind the bar. Surly and mechanical, she poured Elle a glass of white wine and stared at her without a word.

The vibe wasn't the same without Benji, and, wanting to enjoy the dipping sun, Elle strolled out to the infinity pool and stood by the back wall, glass in hand, thoughts moving with the pleasant slothfulness of a lava lamp. She admired the ocean, glimmering electric. Presuming they really were in the Canaries – although *that* matter had yet to be resolved – this was the Atlantic. Granny Alice's balcony had overlooked the Mediterranean, yet the view was similar enough that it made her feel close by.

They'd had many conversations on that balcony, dinner done and the day in retreat. About life. About the future. About Mum.

'Elle, my Debs has always been special,' she'd said once, 'and I know it's not a fashionable thing to say, but special isn't always a good thing. Five years old and she was stealing from my purse, thinking I didn't know. Five. Had it out with her when she was a bit older. Nicked forty quid for God-knows-what. She was sitting with a pencil, doodling – next thing I know, it's sticking out of her leg and we're rushing her to the hospital. She done it, Elle, to get out of being in trouble.'

Elle shivered now. A part of her, the one that had come

here to escape, knew that Mum had stolen from her. Had cooked up a ruse to get hold of her own daughter's savings. This part raged and boiled. Yet another part, the one never comfortable with the savings Granny Alice had given her, still worried about Mum. What was she doing right now? Was she eating okay? Did she miss Elle? Maybe all this worry about the goat business was really some sort of sublimated guilt about Mum.

She still loved her. God, how could someone *not* love their mum? And in a way, Mum must love her too. When Elle once found a demand letter from a payday loan company in the bin and offered to pay it off, her mum's eyes had actually welled.

'You are a wonderful, generous person, Elle. You're better than all of us.'

And in that moment she'd felt complete. Like moments of this sort were the point of being alive. Whatever she did next about Mum, whatever happened after the trial, she would never hurt her.

Approaching footsteps made her turn, and Benji approached her from the direction of the building.

'Sorry, didn't mean to disturb you.' He was out of uniform, a dark T-shirt hugging his trim upper body and a beer bottle in his hand.

'Oh, you didn't?' She let out a laugh that she immediately regretted. It didn't belong to Holiday Elle.

'You looked deep in thought.'

'I was just wondering which ocean that was. Has anyone worked out which island we're on yet?'

He laughed. 'Yeah, we're on Lanzarote.'

'Great. Charlie will be pleased.'

'Dr Lineker, he's a bit…wrapped up in his work. But he got there in the end.'

'How come *you* didn't know?'

He shrugged. 'To be honest, I just thought the Canary Islands were, like, one thing. Listen, I really didn't mean to disturb you. I'll leave you to it.'

'You don't have to,' she said. Had that bordered on needy? She wasn't sure. Yet it just felt so unnatural to put up any sort of front. Especially if it might seem rude or make him think she might not like him or—

He'd stopped himself mid-stride. After weighing something up, he took a slug of his beer and said, 'Do you want to see something decent?'

10

Benji led her to the cliffs at the far end of the beach, opposite those she'd climbed with Gee and Dale. She followed him up a natural staircase to a spot halfway which hung above the ocean. Spray from the waves smashing the cliff wall below dappled her face and bare legs.

'Wow, what a view,' she said. On realising how isolated they now were, she added, 'Hey, you're not playing Cluedo, are you? Are you going to murder me with that beer?'

'No, you're safe. For now anyway.'

They clinked their drinks, and Elle downed the last of her wine. A surge of bravery possessed her.

'Can I just say something?' Elle said. 'That night you saw Harrison coming out my room.' He made eye contact, and she hesitated. Was she really going to say this? He probably didn't even care.

'Yeah.'

She couldn't say nothing, now she'd started. 'Well…he just turned up wanting to play cards. I know how it might have looked…but he hadn't been inside for longer than a minute, and he came in without being invited.'

'Was he out of line?' Benji frowned.

'No, not really. He's just a harmless puppy, isn't he? I think he was lonely. But…no, I just… Like I said, I don't know why I wanted to tell you that. But it's been bothering me, because you saw us, and so there it is. I mean, I like playing cards, don't get me wrong. Just…not then. And not with him.'

She didn't wait to see his reaction, instead she forced her attention out to sea, even squinting like something far more important had now caught her eye.

'That's good to know,' Benji said.

She pretended not to hear him. Feeling as exposed as the rock walls beneath them.

'I want to say something, too.'

'Yeah?'

'Yeah.'

'Okay.'

'You know Becks?'

'Uh-huh.' She held her breath.

'I think she's trying hard to make it look like there's maybe something happening between us. I know she puts it on specifically around you.'

'Oh. Do you think?' Her voice was so quiet, he might not have heard it above the waves.

'And I don't know why I'm telling you this either, but nothing's going on between us.' He raised his beer, offered the sea a rueful smile. 'Nothing.'

'Okay.' She reached up and brushed her hair behind her ears, heat rising in her chest and her face. 'Good to know.'

'Good to know.'

Together they watched the ocean in silence. At the same time, they both laughed.

'Weird we both made random confessions,' she said.

'Yeah, weird.' He dragged a hand down his face, and when

it came away he met her gaze with sadness. 'Elle... I'm not allowed to get involved with participants.'

'Oh,' she said. 'Oh, right. No.'

'Even if I really, really wanted to because I thought they were absolutely gorgeous and funny and like no one I've ever met before.'

Elle took a breath now. 'But you can't.'

'No.'

'No, of course not.'

'I'd have to pack my bags and I'd lose my payment. It's a one-off for the whole gig and...they really made a big deal at interview about the rules we had to follow. And listen, my dad got himself into a ton of debt back at home. Serious, serious debt. I lent him money and he broke my trust, so you know I—'

'I totally understand, Benji.' And of course she did. How could she not?

'I could tell you more but it's depressing, and I just want things sorted.'

'I understand. Completely.'

In a way this would be easier. Once the disappointment faded, she had the best of both worlds. She knew for certain that this lovely man liked her, which was a much-needed confidence boost after all the aborted relationships she'd had in the last five years. But now they wouldn't end up getting into the mess of actually being together. The terrifying plateau and the crushing decline. In that way it was perfect, forever an idea. A beautiful, unrealised possibility.

She tried to watch the sunset and the sea, though she wanted to keep looking at the bare brown skin of his legs. His strong-looking hand rested inches from hers. No, this disappointment would take a while to pass.

Down on the beach a figure appeared. Ricoh. He began to

pace back and forth on the sand, oblivious to their position high above him. They watched, Elle sharing with Benji the conversation she'd had with Ricoh, explaining how she worried about him a little bit.

'He doesn't sleep much,' Benji said. 'We've been watching him because he sometimes comes out of his room at night and wanders around the centre. Paul's getting really wound up by it. I think Paul likes to have a nap in the staff room, and can't if he's around.'

'I know, I don't think he's been coping. He told me he felt off. Like, not himself and restless. I told him to lay off the alcohol.'

'Yeah,' Benji said with an amused huff.

'I mean... I did wonder if he was having side-effects, you know? From the drug.'

Below, Ricoh took off his T-shirt and started running.

'I doubt it,' Benji said. 'He's been a bit twitchy since the start.'

Ricoh increased his speed, eventually breaking into a sprint, shuttling between cliff walls in a race with himself. He went at it for nearly five minutes before stopping to face the ocean, hands on his knees, back rising and falling.

'Does he seem agitated to you?' Benji said.

Before she could answer, Ricoh ran at the water and dived into an oncoming wave, emerging from beneath the water in an aggressive front crawl. He reached the first pedalo and didn't stop, slowing only when he approached the buoys. Then he vanished beneath the water.

Benji stood up and scowled. 'What is he doing?'

Ricoh appeared again on the other side of the divide. And he kept swimming.

'Shit,' Benji said.

The two of them clambered back down to the beach.

'I can't see him anymore,' Elle said.

Benji stopped, studied the ocean, and bit his lower lip. 'He's not there, is he?'

'I… I don't know.'

Benji ripped off his T-shirt and kicked off his crocs. 'Can you run back and get Paul?'

Elle nodded. Once down to his boxers, Benji gave the ocean a last scan before diving into the channel ploughed by Ricoh. Elle ran up the steps, looking back at the sea to check on Benji's progress and locate any shape that might be Ricoh. She saw nothing, so kept running.

Paul was behind reception, immersed in a magazine. When she told him, he glanced briefly at the security feed on the computer screen. With a minute shake of his head he got to his feet.

'Go get one of the docs, will you?' he said before striding off, leaving in his wake the faint sour smell she now associated with him.

Elle found Jess in her room and the two raced back outside, now trailing Ted, who had been drawn by the commotion. From the steps they could see Benji swimming behind one of the pedalos, inching it towards the shore while a prone Ricoh lay on top. Paul was already swimming out to help Benji, and Ted went after him.

'What happened?' Jess said, trying to catch her breath while Paul and Ted lifted Ricoh onto the beach.

Benji, down on one knee, said, 'He just swam out and disappeared. I don't know how long he was under but I got him breathing again.'

Ricoh coughed, and with his eyes still closed he whispered, 'Sorry. Sorry. I just lost my bearings.'

Everyone appeared to instantly relax. Benji dropped onto his backside and lay back on the floor.

Ted blew air into his cheeks and gave Elle a relieved bob of his eyebrows. The danger apparently having passed, Paul's expression darkened.

'You could have been killed,' he said. 'The bloody buoys are there for a reason.'

'I just…lost my bearings.' His voice was weak, and Jess, still taking his pulse, glowered at Paul. He shook his head, lips pursed and chin jutting, like he'd smelled something bad. 'I just…got lost.'

Chapter Six

1

O nce Ricoh was sitting up and talking clearly, Jess allowed him to be carried inside. When Elle looked up at the cliff face on their way back she spotted several other participants standing at various points of the ascent like spectators at a sporting event: on the staircase, at the balcony on the first patio, two faces even peering over the edge of the infinity pool.

Word soon spread around the complex that Ricoh was going to be okay, and that they were planning on monitoring him on site, rather than taking him to the nearest hospital – wherever that might be. Based on what they knew of their surroundings, it had to be miles from the complex.

An impromptu gathering took place in the bar, and Elle filled people in on what she'd seen.

'Here we go then,' Charlie said.

'What?' Harrison said.

'You think this is part of it?' Mai said, her eyes bulging with excitement.

Harrison studied the assembled faces, and said to Charlie, 'Mate, now isn't the time for that.'

'Listen,' Charlie held up his hands in a gesture of peace, 'I'm just saying—'

'I'd listen to Harrison,' Ted said. Charlie's upper lip curled in response.

Paul walked in and stood at the bar to address them all. He gave a gruff, concise lecture on safety and boundaries, which he summarised with, 'The buoys, like the rules, are there for a reason.'

'Hear, hear,' Harrison said.

Paul glared, not appreciating the support. He was standing at the door now, on his way out. He stared them all down. 'Want my advice? If you want to get paid, you'd better do what you're told.'

When he'd gone, Mai said, 'What did that mean?'

'Means Ricoh nearly cost me my money.' Harrison looked ready to fight someone. 'Means if they have to can the trial, we all go down with it. No money. Nothing.'

'They wouldn't do that, though,' Elle said. Although, could she really back that up?

The others looked at her, clearly not agreeing.

2

With no Benji around, and with the strange atmosphere in the bar, Elle went back to her room. At around eleven she was starting to fall asleep on the sofa reading, when a soft tapping drew her attention to the patio doors. She held still. It came again. Not a random building-sound, but rather distinctly a knuckle on glass.

Elle tentatively approached the window and peered through a gap she made to one side of the curtains. It was

Benji, out on her balcony. She opened the door and through a half-smile said, 'What are you doing?'

'I…wanted to know if you fancied a game of cards?' He held up a pack, and pulled a face like he'd made a faux pas.

Elle laughed. 'A front door is available, you know.'

'Where's the fun in that?'

Elle stepped outside and looked over the edge of the building. 'How did you even get up?'

'Stood on the balcony railing, and used my massive man-strength to haul myself up.'

'How very…1980s of you.'

'I was going for Romeo and Juliet – so what, 1600s?'

'Near enough.'

'Yeah, I wasn't sure, to be honest. Is it creepy? It felt a little bit creepy at points. Less so after I ditched the balaclava, I won't lie.'

'I'm undecided. Isn't this a bit risky, though? Given what you said.'

'Yeah…but you know.' He shrugged. 'It's been a weird day. Besides, coming up this way avoids the cameras.'

'Oh, reconnaissance. How romantic.'

She let him in and closed the door and curtains, dampening a shrill cry from a distant animal somewhere outside the wall. Excitement stirred in her.

'Seriously though, life's short, isn't it?'

Elle faced him, looked into his earnest eyes, and knew she didn't want to spend the rest of the evening playing cards. Harrison's warning about Benji sounded off one final time from a far corner of her mind. But if he was a player, so what? So was Elle.

She took two steps towards him, turned her face upwards and with a hand behind his head, drew him towards her.

Expecting resistance, she found none, and, flushed with confidence, she pushed her body against him. With her free hand she found his, opened his fingers so the cards fell to the floor, and moved his hands to her backside. Then, both of them smiling through their kiss, they stepped clumsily backwards and fell onto the bed.

3

Lying in his arms much later, Elle felt the ominous spread of post-good-time guilt. The black hole beyond bliss.

'You probably need to go, don't you?' she said.

'Do you want me to?' His disappointment was barely concealed.

'No, it's not that. I just meant…in case you get caught.'

'I doubt anyone would notice until morning. If I got up before Rosie and César…' He looked thoughtful for a moment. 'No, I'll go. You're right.'

'You don't have to.'

'No, you're right.'

He kissed the back of her neck and she pressed herself into him. She wished she hadn't said anything. 'It's reassuring, having an insider with me after a day like this. What was all that about?'

He momentarily went still. He released her and sat up against the headboard. 'Can I tell you something?'

'Of course.' Her chest tightened. Home Elle wanted to preempt him, soften the blow by asking if he was seeing someone else before he could break it to her. Spare herself any embarrassment or pity. But hold on, he'd already said he wasn't. And she believed him. So instead, she listened.

'I want to be open with you. I've already broken the rules

tonight, so what does it matter now anyway? I'm already done if you wanted to turn me in.'

She sat up with him. 'I'm not going to *turn you in*. God, anyone would think this place is a prison or something.'

'Well, I'm just saying I don't want to lie to you. So here it is. When I told you and Hallie I knew as much as you lot about the trial, that night at the bar, well, that wasn't strictly true.'

'No?'

He shook his head. 'I was thinking about Ricoh, and what you said to me about him possibly drinking too much. His headaches and his anxiety. I overheard him talking to Jess and Dr Lineker tonight, and he was saying he was having thoughts that weren't his. Thoughts he didn't recognise. Which is like… what does that even mean? And he said he was running and swimming because he wanted to turn his head off. He said those words – turn his head off. Which doesn't sound much like alcohol.'

'I don't know. He said his thoughts felt…like a hangover, so I suppose it depends how much he's been putting away.'

'And that's what I want to say to you. I know how much he's been putting away. Like, exactly how much.'

'Well you run the bar—'

'One of my briefs, the only one they told me not to talk about, was that I'm in charge of making sure no one gets too drunk.'

She dwelled on this a moment before asking, 'Why aren't you allowed to talk about that?'

'Well, you might not like me when I tell you. But I've been mixing up the drinks. Throwing non-alcoholic beers and mock-tails in with the real stuff. They asked me to keep an eye on what everyone's been having.'

Elle didn't understand. 'What, my drinks?' Although she already knew the answer.

'Yes. I'm sorry.'

She supposed he expected her to be outraged. Instead, she laughed. 'Why?'

'They told me that it's really important everyone has a good time. But, you know, not too much of a good time. That it's important people get through the trial unscathed and are up each morning for the drugs. Tipsy, not smashed. That's the idea.'

Elle wasn't sure how to feel. Confused? Upset? Did she even care at all? 'Well, at least I know why I haven't been getting a hangover.'

'It feels really wrong now I know everyone. Especially you. But then it's in all your contracts apparently, and it's in mine. They are allowed to control food and drink intake in relation to the trial.'

That one hadn't been included on the summary sheet. 'I must have missed that.'

'It's a book. It's no wonder. But I wanted to be honest with you, Elle. I can't bullshit you anymore.'

She smiled. Shook her head. 'I suppose…if it was in the contract… I mean, it's not like any of us are paying for the drinks. So you're not really…robbing us or anything.'

'It's a nice way to frame it. I kept telling myself that's it's not that different from what we do anyway in bar work, when punters start getting a bit rowdy and stuff. Water the drinks down… But…it's not the same really. I'm really sorry.'

'It's…odd. But it's more just funny that I didn't really notice. I mean I did, sort of, but also…the idea of being drunk made me think I was drunk.'

She fell quiet. She'd been talking just to hold back the silence.

'I mean, I only start switching later in the night,' Benji said, 'so some of the drinks are alcoholic. And keeping track of what everyone has is a bloody nightmare. But listen, that's what's weird about this Ricoh thing, right. It's shaken me up, because he asked the doctors if it was the drugs. He insisted it started when he took the pills. And the way they were all acting in there, all these silent glances at each other, the doctors…They were rattled. I started thinking… I don't know, maybe you were right. Maybe he is having side-effects.'

'Oh.'

'You said he told you it started with a headache that he thought was a hangover. Have you felt anything like that?'

No, she hadn't, but Hallie and Harrison had. They'd been complaining more and more the last week, too. Should she tell him?

'You okay?' Benji said. 'You've gone quiet.'

'Just thinking. I suppose I might be on the placebo.'

'I hope so.'

'God, what if they've messed up? What if people get really sick? Wasn't there a trial in the noughties where that happened?'

'I shouldn't have said anything. Sorry… Ricoh was pretty jittery when he got here, wasn't he? It's the isolation and the boredom. I was only mentioning it because I dismissed you earlier when you suggested it. I just meant, it wasn't so out there, as an idea.'

He was good at being reassuring, Benji, but the damage was already done. Did she really have to go down tomorrow and take another pill, knowing it might be harmful? Was she going to want to swim out into the ocean to escape her own thoughts?

No, she'd surely have felt something by now. She must be on the placebo, or the drug wasn't affecting her at all. Like Benji said, Ricoh arrived in a bad way and no one had noticed, that was all. Or the drugs had worsened an underlying condition. What was she going to do, arrive at breakfast and cause a massive fuss? With all this talk in the air about Ricoh blowing the trial and everyone's money, she didn't really want to cause a scene based on little more than a conspiracy theory.

Then again, some conspiracies were real, weren't they? Like the booze being weakened. Charlie had known all along about that, hadn't he? Which raised the obvious question: what else was he right about?

4

When the pills were given out the next day, and there was no mention of what happened to Ricoh, Elle made up her mind. She found Charlie and Mai together in the VR lounge, Charlie barking instructions in forces-ese while the two of them fired plastic computer guns into mid-air. Elle hadn't played much, but knew enough that if she put on the headgear and earphones, grabbed a gun, and entered her name, she would appear in their game.

It wasn't that she expected to get anything useful out of the two of them necessarily. She'd come here on a feeling, that was all.

She joined the game, arriving in a digitally rendered super-market, deserted and intermittently illuminated by emergency lighting. From behind the half-stocked shelves emanated the shuffle and groan of zombies.

'We're around the back, Elle,' Mai said.

Elle found a rear exit and joined them, the hordes closing in almost immediately. She helped them murder countless zombies on their way out of whatever American city this was, and once out in the safety of the countryside, deep into a preg-nantly quiet forest, Elle said, 'Charlie, what did you mean about Ricoh's accident yesterday? In the bar. Before Harrison got involved.'

'Nothing.'

'He was trying to say that he was right,' Mai said. 'That what happened to Ricoh is probably the next level of whatever it is they're going to do to us.'

'So you think what happened with Ricoh is part of…the *real* trial?'

'Yes,' Mai said.

'Not necessarily,' Charlie said. 'It just might be. You were there to see the whole thing, weren't you?'

'Yes.'

'Tad coincidental, don't you think? Guy does something like that out of nowhere just when people happen to be around to see it.'

Elle already sensed she might have come to the wrong people. She'd try and hear them out, though. 'I don't know, Charlie. It wasn't really out of nowhere. He hadn't been feeling right before then – he told me.'

'Funny that,' Mai said. 'Funny that he spoke to you, then did that in front of you.'

'I don't follow. I'm not part of all this, if that's what you think.'

'We're not saying that,' Mai said.

Their whole shtick had a rehearsed quality to it. 'I don't know what you are saying. But don't you think it's more likely Ricoh was having some sort of side-effect or something? That this pill they've been giving us isn't as safe as they've made out?'

'What makes you say that?' Mai said.

She paused. Telling them about the alcohol would drop Benji in it. 'Well, I was thinking about what Charlie said about the drinks the other day. About them being watered down. Because some people are saying they've been having hangovers.

But I haven't, even though I'm a bit of a lightweight and have been putting a lot away.'

'Uh-huh,' Charlie said. 'They're definitely doing that. It's not even a question.'

'But maybe that's just them being cheap,' Mai said.

'Could be,' Charlie said.

'But what's causing the hangovers then?'

'Heat,' Charlie said.

'Yeah, yeah. Dehydration.'

Not quite understanding how they had become the sceptics and she the conspiracy theorist, she tried a different tactic.

'I also found something odd in my bedside drawer.' She told them about the scrawled message.

Charlie and Mai fell silent. They both stopped their virtual walking.

'Okay,' Charlie said, 'everyone out of the game.'

Charlie's avatar vanished. Elle removed her headset and headphones.

'We can't talk about this on mic,' Charlie said. 'Can you show us?'

'Well, yeah. But it's really nothing more than what I said.'

'I think we need to see it ourselves,' Mai said.

'Now?'

Charlie scanned the room. 'Not right now. We'll pick a time when they're convinced nothing's come from this conversation. Just in case they heard all that.' He cupped one hand over his mouth as if to prevent someone reading his lips. 'Mai and I have eyed all the cameras in this building, and we have collated the logical blind spots.'

Elle suppressed a laugh, pleased that everyone's default statuses had been re-established. Really though, what had she expected, coming here?

'What do you think it means then? My message.'

'Someone has tried to communicate with you,' Charlie said. 'Someone wants you to think there were trials here before.'

'Maybe there were,' Mai said. 'Maybe that's why they are so strict about the internet, Charlie. Perhaps someone raised the alarm.'

Charlie mulled on this one, concluding with a sceptical dip of his brow. 'Scrub that. The firewall issue is deeper than that. I've tried a few tricks of the trade to get around it and it's armour plated. Like, big-money strong. Can't browse, can't message. Can't even open a maps application to find out our location.'

'Benji told me we're on Lanzarote,' Elle said. 'Which is what you thought, isn't it?'

'I've changed my mind,' Charlie said. 'Terrain's a match, but doesn't quite fit.'

'Why not?'

'Sun arcs over the cove left to right. We're facing pretty much south on a coast. There's coast around Arrecife that might fit. But it's built up and by an airport. We'd see the jets landing. Which leaves the coast around Playa Blanca, also built up and with loud roads. Might be some quiet spots on the west coast, but we drove five or so miles east from the airport. And why can't we see Fuerteventura from here? It should be visible.'

'Also, Elle, I wouldn't trust what Benji says, anyway,' Mai said.

'Why not?'

'Can't trust anyone associated with the trial.'

'I don't think Benji has any idea what's—'

'Is that what he's told you?' Charlie said. 'You want to believe him, that's your choice. But I'd be mindful what you tell him. Tell us, how did you and him come across Ricoh?'

'We were chatting and…climbed up on the cliffs.'

'Who led the way?' Mai said.

Elle hesitated, and growing a bit irritated with the inquisi-
tion, she said, 'I think I did. Can't really remember.' The other
two exchanged looks, and Charlie made an unsure humming
sound. 'What is it you think is going on? Why would you say
that someone *wants* me to think trials took place here?'

'If you're going to take the red pill with us now,' Charlie
said, 'you really need to keep your mind and eyes open. Stay
awake, okay? You were the one who found Becks, right? You
found the goat, too.'

'Well, I think Paul did actual—'

'You were the one who witnessed Ricoh. And now there's
this message in your room. There's no messages in our rooms.
So don't you see? You could be at the very heart of all their
plans.'

Red pills. *Their* plans. Stay awake. That was conspiracy
theory bingo, and Elle was done. Despite the other two
insisting she at least play the zombie game to a logical point so
as not to make 'them' suspicious, she left, their promise to seek
her out again preceding her exit.

5

Back in her room, she sat on the edge of her bed staring at the
message in the drawer again. Charlie and Mai were certainly
unique thinkers, although more in the mould of those that
easily made the transition from message boards to storming
government buildings. At least talking to them made her feel a
little bit saner.

Still, it was true she'd been present for both accidents. The
site was small enough, but was it *that* small? And Benji *had* led
her up there to what was essentially a viewing platform for
what had happened with Ricoh. Given his admission about the
drinks thing, what was to stop him lying again if it meant

guiding her down whatever pathway was required by the trial? Deceit was built into all their contracts, after all. After Benji's 'moment of honesty' the other night, she'd been feeling guilty about not mentioning that she'd lied her way here, had felt as if she might blurt out the truth to him to balance the books in their burgeoning relationship. But maybe his confession had been a trap to get her to disclose something in return. Could she trust him?

Elle closed the drawer and shook her head. It was too wild even for her newly suspicious mind. The headaches, the accidents, the message: it was probably coincidental. And if there was something unusual going on, the theory that best fitted the evidence was that the drug was having unexpected side-effects. Perhaps, given all his talk of intrusive thoughts, the drugs had even made Ricoh kill Harry the goat. It wasn't an exact fit, but it trounced the alternative, didn't it?

Suppose for a moment she was being led, though. Suppose that she, of all the trial participants, had been *chosen* for this particular role. Why would they do that? What made her special in comparison to the others?

That was easy enough. She wasn't supposed to be here.

Have you ever robbed someone?

Not yet she hadn't, but she was in the process of robbing Apollo Wellbeing, having lied to be here. Did they somehow know? Had her selection been deliberate, the process designed to find someone nasty enough to deceive a clinical tri—

Elle stood up and poured herself a glass of water, downing it in one and immediately pouring a second from the bottle. Dehydration. There. Easy enough thing to happen on an island like this. Alcohol wasn't the only thing that caused headaches. It was affecting her thinking, certainly. Note to self: she needed to spend less time in the company of conspiracy theorists, more time outside in the sun with normal people.

She lay on the bed again and closed her eyes. She'd feel better in time. This was just shock. She'd watched a man nearly drown. Things would settle down soon enough. Then she could get back to enjoying her holiday. The holiday she deserved. The one she'd bloody earned and needed to stop trying to ruin for herself.

Chapter Seven

1

The trial reached the halfway point. Across the Saturday morning and early afternoon, the participants all completed their second round of tests.

'How do you feel?' Jess asked Elle while injecting gel through the holes in the EEG cap. 'Any different from last time?'

Did a medium-wattage paranoia count? 'No. I feel fine.'

'Nothing at all?'

Elle shifted in her seat. 'No. Should I?'

'No. Just being thorough.'

The clinical parts of the trial were identical, the same trumpet blarts and goat bleats. This time, though, the dilemmas posed by Dr Lineker were slightly different. The overweight men and monochrome hats from round one had been replaced with runaway trains and vets organising a conference.

2

Ricoh appeared at the bar that night for the first time since his accident, his shoulders hunched and head down. Gee fetched him a drink, ordering him to neck it, which he resisted. Harrison glared at him, stiff-backed on his stool.

'How are you, pal?' Ted asked.

'Good, yeah, thanks.' He sank half the pint, and from one of the stools Elle glanced to Benji, who busied himself behind the bar with his back to her. Ricoh drinking didn't seem like a good idea, and she hoped his beer had been watered down. 'Just got a bit too overenthusiastic with the exercise. Stupid.'

'Need to take it easy, mate,' Harrison said. 'You're not exactly cut out to break swimming records.'

Ricoh folded his slender arms. 'No? You don't think.'

'I think all of us here would appreciate you keeping the exercise safer, like…the gym, maybe.' He gave Ricoh a subtle once-over. 'You know where that is, don't you?'

Gee snickered at this less-than-sly dig, while Ted's face twitched uneasily.

'That funny, is it, Gee?' Ricoh said. 'You go to the gym a lot then, do you?'

'Take it on the chin, mate,' Harrison said. 'Just a joke.'

Ricoh looked around the room. 'Sorry, am I not in on something? You'd all appreciate me being safer… What's that mean?'

From Elle's position at the bar she watched his leg bounce up and down under the table.

Hallie, sitting beside Harrison, shoved his arm. 'Give it a rest.' Elle hadn't seen much of her in the last few days, and she looked weary.

Harrison turned to her and laughed. 'What? Listen, I'm

not saying anything we're not all thinking. May as well be honest.'

'What's that then?' Ricoh said, meeting Harrison's stare.

'Listen, if you bloody kill yourself, mate, we might all go home with nothing. So just…sort it out.'

'Woah,' Benji called from behind the bar. 'Hold on a second.'

'That's not true, Ricoh,' Elle said, stunned by Harrison's sudden attack.

Hallie leaned away from Harrison, regarding him with disgust.

Ted got to his feet and held up a hand. 'Okay, folks, my headache just got worse, think I might have an early night. Ricoh, pal, glad to see you're feeling better.'

'Thanks,' Ricoh said. 'You don't have to go. Listen, hey, I can hear what you're saying. But none of you have to worry about me. Just… I was just getting a bit…you know, stir crazy?'

'Oh, mate,' Gee said. 'Tell me about it. I chose this trial instead of the three peaks, and now I'm climbing the walls.'

'Climbing the walls, now there's a plan,' Ricoh said, turning now to Harrison. 'Anyway, *mate*. Gym's not really not my crowd, if you get me?'

Harrison tilted his head. 'Not your crowd? What, you mean, people who like being strong?'

Ricoh smiled. 'Nice one. No, I mean you need a quiet mind to do all that pumping iron, don't you? Nice and still up there. No distractions.'

'Sorry, I didn't catch that. Can you say it again?' Harrison's blue eyes burned into Ricoh and he leaned forward.

Ricoh shook his head with a bitter smile. 'Sorry, guys, I can't hack him tonight. He can dish but he can't take.' He stood up.

He turned and walked to the door. Elle called weakly after

him, but he ignored her. Instead, on his way past a table, he kicked it over and walked out the door.

'Yeah, nice job, everyone,' Benji said, shaking his head. He came around the bar and followed Ricoh out.

'Fuck me, Harrison,' Hallie said.

'Well…we were all thinking it,' Gee said.

'No we weren't,' Elle said, and Gee flicked a surprised scowl at her.

Harrison folded his arms. 'No, I'm sorry, everyone. That was uncalled for. Look, I think I got too much sun today. I've got a splitting headache and—'

'Join the club,' Hallie said, 'but you don't see me being a wanker.'

'Yes, Halimah, you've made your own suffering very clear to everyone.'

'You,' she said, getting up and throwing her purse over her shoulder, 'can fuck off.' She looked at Becks. 'He's all yours.'

Becks's eyes widened. Harrison's face did even less, and, when the door closed behind Hallie, he blinked with heavy lids.

Benji soon returned, and he was shaking his head. He took up his position behind the bar and looked at Harrison. 'What was all that about?'

'Sorry, Benji,' he said. 'I'll apologise.'

'Well, I'd let them cool off first.'

'Good idea.' He sighed and rubbed his temples with the thumb and middle finger of his right hand. He went to the bar and asked for a water.

Benji poured him one and handed it over, his gaze flicking to Elle and back. 'How long's this headache been going on for?'

'It's fine. Just need to keep my fluids up. Easy to forget.'

'So more than a day?'

'I'm fine, Benji,' he said, just a little too sharply, and walked away.

3

Elle waited for the atmosphere to sweeten, and when it didn't she went to her room just after ten. She listened in at Hallie's door, but decided against knocking when she heard nothing. She was probably asleep. Elle lay reading on her sofa in the hope that Benji would come again once his shift ended. He'd been to see her three nights in a row now, and she'd be disappointed if he didn't come tonight. She had questions. About Harrison. About Hallie. About Ted.

At twenty to midnight she was falling asleep when the ping of a foot catching on the top of the balcony rail jerked her fully awake. A knock on the glass followed. Elle went over to let Benji inside.

Only it wasn't Benji. It was Charlie, standing on her balcony in his coat, while behind him was Mai, one leg already over the rail.

'What are you doing?' she said, sliding open the door. 'If this is part of Cluedo, then—'

'If I wanted to murder you, I wouldn't knock,' he said. 'We needed to talk to you.' His body language indicated he wanted her to move out the way so he could come inside. 'And we needed to evade the cameras.'

Elle stood still for a moment, ultimately deciding that she had brought this upon herself, and reluctantly stepped aside to let them both in. It would be quicker than arguing.

'What happened in the bar tonight?' Mai said. 'Becks said there'd been an argument.'

She told them what they'd missed, and the two nodded like it all made perfect sense.

Charlie had picked up the paperback she'd left on the TV table and absently bounced its corner against the palm of his hand while he listened.

'Things are ratcheting up,' Charlie said.

'You think Ricoh might be in on all this?' Mai said.

'In on what?' Elle said.

'What's really happening here.'

'Guys,' Elle said, 'I think everyone was just tired. What was it you wanted to talk about?'

'We're taking things to the next level,' Charlie said. 'You in?'

'I don't know what the next level is.'

'We need to know more, Elle,' Charlie said. 'The more I think about it, the more I think there might be danger ahead. Bringing us out to this deserted facility. Pretending it's Lanzarote. Telling us nothing… What's around the corner, Elle?'

'We *need* to know more,' Mai reiterated.

'Dr Lineker's office,' Charlie said, 'that's where they get the drugs from. It's also where they store all the trial documents.'

'We watched them today,' Mai said.

Elle's chest constricted. 'Okay, I think you need to slow down. If you see anything about the trial, and they find out—'

'But they won't find out.' Charlie smiled like this was something he was particularly proud of. 'We've studied the security patrols and camera positions. It'll be a cakewalk.'

'You'll get thrown off the trial. You won't get your money. And, truthfully, there's not enough evidence to justify us doing that.'

'Well, that's why we need to do this,' Mai said, and looked to Charlie.

'We won't get caught,' he said. 'I have considerable experience with discreet operations.'

Elle stared at the two of them, regretting ever having sat next to Charlie on the bus that first night. Had she caused this?

Pushed them deeper into this imaginary world by going to them with her questions in the VR lounge?

'Okay, well I'll be honest,' she said. 'My *only* concern was about side-effects, based on what happened to Ricoh—'

'Right. We can take a closer look at the pills, too,' Charlie said. 'And find out what they're keeping from us.'

'Charlie, if this was…some sort of…social experiment or whatever, we'd know more by now. It's been two weeks. I still don't even know what it is you're imagining might happen.'

Now they stared at her. Eventually, Charlie shook his head with disappointment and put down Elle's book. 'Well, it would have been easier with three.'

'No, don't give up on her,' Mai said.

'I think it's clear where she stands.'

Without another word, the two left through the door of the patio. Did they believe she was in on it now?

'Why don't you just go out the front,' Elle said, standing in the doorway. 'It's safer.'

'No, this way is definitely safer,' Charlie said, one leg already over the railing.

'Just…maybe give it a few days,' she said. 'See if anything else happens, now we've done the second set of tests.'

'Can you do us a favour?' Charlie said. 'Keep to yourself what we've discussed here this evening.'

With that, he crouched down on the other side of the balustrade, grabbed a rail in each hand, and lowered himself down before dropping. A moment later Elle heard his shoes land on the path below.

Mai turned to her now on the balcony and closed the gap between them. 'I understand your position, Elle.' Her serious tone, in a voice close to a whisper, was unintentionally comic.

'I worry about what happens with the trial if you're caught,' Elle said. 'Is it worth the risk?'

She shook her head. 'You have to trust me. There are greater forces at work here. Charlie is right to be concerned.' She went still, apparently listening for something. Then she said, 'Everyone here thinks that I'm this naive civil servant, Elle. But that's just my cover. Okay? Not even Charlie knows this, but I've actually been sent here to find out what's going on with this trial.'

Elle studied her face for any hint of humour. She was deadly serious. 'Sent here? By…?'

'The government, Elle.' She raised her eyebrows and pursed her lips, as if this closed any doubtful case Elle might have opened. It took every ounce of Elle's concentration not to smile. 'So if you change your mind, come and find me. We can talk alone if you want, you really can trust me. I'm here for you.'

Elle had no idea what to say. Why would Mai be blowing her cover this way if she really was a secret agent? Elle held her breath and bit the inside of her lip. Mai nodded, turned, and exited the same way Charlie had – only with far more agility and confidence.

4

'It was odd,' she recalled to Benji later in bed. 'She acts so… wide-eyed, and all of a sudden she was all business-like and together.'

Benji was grinning. 'Do you believe her?'

'Obviously not. But then…it's no more batshit than anything else I've been thinking lately. And why would she lie?'

'Why does anyone lie?' Benji said. 'I've got my doubts about Charlie's whole RAF thing. So maybe they're involved in, I don't know, a fantasy play thing.'

'Maybe. I've wondered about Charlie too. I just assumed he

was just a bit socially awkward and maybe he was trying to impress people with his inside information.'

'Has he impressed you?'

'I don't want to be mean. And it's not like everything he says is mad. You should have heard him talking about why he doesn't think we're on Lanzarote. All this stuff about the arc of the sun.'

The two of them sat in silence before Benji said, 'Do you think they're really going to do something then?'

'I honestly don't know. Can you tell Paul or Monique you overheard something? Maybe if they change up our routines a bit, it might put them off if they do decide to do something stupid.'

'Problem is, if I tell those two, I don't know what'll happen. They take their job *very* seriously. They'll be wanting names, dates, all that. And given it's my job, I have to tell them everything if I want them to take me seriously. And if I do that, those two might drag your name into it.'

'Yeah, I suppose.'

Benji shrugged. 'That room is locked, and they have to somehow get by security and the cameras and all of that. It won't be easy for them to get in.'

'They were really confident about their surveillance.'

'More fantasy?'

'They knew enough about the cameras that they came up the same way as you.'

Benji nodded, sinking back into his own thoughts. 'That's interesting.'

5

Elle took her pill the next morning, experiencing another flicker of concern after she'd swallowed. But overnight,

Charlie and Mai's visit had pushed her back towards the idea that the doctors knew what they were doing. Ricoh even made a brief appearance at breakfast and took his pill, so he couldn't be *too* concerned about side-effects. Neither doctor mentioned any sort of office break-in either, which had been Elle's most pressing concern. Perhaps she'd changed their minds.

Charlie and Mai ignored her and avoided eye contact when their paths crossed later that morning. That was fine by her. By the afternoon her concerns had shifted because she'd encountered a now crutchless Becks lying on Harrison at the pool. On Elle's arrival, Becks planted a lingering kiss on his lips, climbed from the lounger, and bounded off to get drinks. She smiled at Elle on her way past, the cat that got the cream. Her ankle certainly seemed a lot better.

'What?' Harrison said, peering over the top of his sunglasses at her.

'Sorry, nothing. It's none of my business. I just sort of thought you and Hallie were…'

He shrugged. 'Hey, we're all here to have fun, aren't we? She knows that.'

Elle went straight to Hallie's room and it was over a minute before she answered. She wore a diaphanous dressing gown and a blank expression, her face puffy and wan.

'Hi,' Elle said, 'you okay? I…feel like I haven't seen you for ages.'

Hallie shook her head. 'I've not been feeling right. Doctors told me I've got a bug.'

'Oh, sorry to hear that.' Elle made a sympathetic face. Hallie stared through her.

'It's been since I started taking these pills, you know? It's just worse now.'

Elle swallowed. 'Did you tell them that?'

'Yeah, they said it wasn't connected. Gave me paracetamol and told me to rest.'

Hallie's eyes closed and for a second remained there. As if she'd fallen asleep.

'Maybe you should rest,' Elle said. 'I just wanted to see if everything else was…okay? Seemed like maybe you and Harrison…last night at the bar.'

'That boy's damaged,' she said, and shook her head like there was nothing to be done.

'That's crap.'

'Doesn't bother me. He's a creep. I caught him in my drawer trying to steal a pair of knickers.'

'Really?'

'Worse, he tried to charm his way out of it. Said he liked collecting souvenirs.'

'You're joking?'

'Like I should be flattered.' She closed her eyes and shook her head again. 'Small dick, too. Sorry, I need to lie down, mate. My head's killing me. I just…really don't feel myself.'

'Yeah, of course,' Elle said. 'We'll catch up when you're better. It's not the same without you.'

'You're doing okay, though, eh?' Hallie's gaze flicked to and from Elle's bedroom door. 'Who is it? Benji?'

She burned with embarrassment. 'What? No. What? Did you hear something?' She didn't want to admit to it, but given everything that was happening, she equally didn't want her thinking it was Harrison.

'Maybe.'

Elle gave her a playful smile, letting her in on a secret without actually letting her in on it. God, how loud had they been? She was certain they'd been discreet. 'I'm sure you must be mistaken. Benji's not allowed to get involved with the riff-raff. He'd get in serious trouble.'

'My bad,' Hallie said, with a twitch of her old smile.

6

That night, Elle made Benji whisper and tiptoe around. She didn't send him away though. Much later, they agreed they both needed to get some sleep, laughing, because embedded within this decision to part tonight was the explicit acknowledgement that they couldn't trust themselves in the same bed. It was like that between them. Exciting. A little out of control. Holiday Elle had optimistically bought a pack of condoms at the train station back in Oxford, and it was becoming likely that if Benji didn't have any, they would soon run out.

When she awoke the next morning she did so with a regretful sweep of her arm across the bare sheet. She buried her head in his pillow, grinning dopily at the lightest remnants of his woody aftershave. For now, it was just a holiday romance, but she couldn't deny it had also come to symbolise the new start she was making out here. Might he even be part of it?

She queued for her pill at breakfast, still thinking about the night before until Dr Lineker and Jess greeted her. They appeared nervous when they checked her trial diary entry.

Jess handed over the little paper pill pot with a shaky hand. 'Can we ask that you just wait in the canteen? We need to address the group.'

'Yeah, of course.' Elle had an urge to gulp. 'Everything okay?'

Jess didn't answer so Elle moved on. She sat with Gee and Dale. Both stared at their breakfast, glum. They looked hungover, but obviously that couldn't be the case.

'You two okay?' she said.

'Don't know,' Gee said. 'Really starting to get a bit…itchy.'

'Itchy?'

'She's bored,' Dale said. 'She wants to break out and go exploring. I've told her she can't and she's not happy about it.'

'Dale is a fucking pussy.'

Dale nodded agreeably. 'True enough. But just keep the ship steady, captain,' he said. 'Land's in sight.'

Harrison and Becks entered, the former looking tanned and tired, the latter sunburned and sleepy. They slumped down with their trays at the table behind Elle just as Ted came in, followed by Mai and Charlie. Elle watched Jess tell Charlie something after his mouth check, and he nodded. The first thing he did afterwards was find Elle's gaze and nod once.

She looked away. 'What do you think they want to talk to us about?' she said to no one in particular.

Ted, who had joined them, shrugged. 'They really don't seem happy.'

'Health and safety, I reckon,' Gee said. 'They bollocked me yesterday for cliff diving.'

'Oh, here we go,' Dale said, looking up at the entrance.

Both Monique and Paul entered the canteen and stood staring sourly by the windows. Then Benji appeared, his expression solemn, Hallie and Ricoh coming in behind him. Last of all, Constantine entered, and Benji gestured for him to take a seat. If *he* had been asked to come downstairs for this, it had to be serious.

Dr Lineker and Jess marched through the tables to stand before the serving counter, where Carl stood looking surly with his arms folded. Elle tried to catch Benji's gaze, but he wasn't making any attempt to look at her. He appeared determined. Almost angry. What was going on?

Jess stepped forward. 'To start with, we just want to thank you for getting this far into the trial.' She sounded more nervous than she had on the first night, only heightening Elle's own agitation. 'We're all incredibly grateful for your patience and input so far, and very much hope you're having a pleasant stay.'

No one spoke up to affirm or contest this. Not that it looked like Jess wanted an answer.

'Unfortunately, while conducting a routine stocktake of the trial medication, we've become aware that a number of pills have gone missing.'

Dr Lineker, arms crossed tight against his chest, looked as if he might throw up. Elle resisted the alarmingly strong impulse to look for Charlie and Mai, hoping the heat in her face wasn't as noticeable on the outside as it felt.

'These were pills accounted for in a stocktake two days ago. There is no way to get to the drugs without getting through two locks and evading the security cameras on the corridor and in the atrium. It would appear that video footage from the last two nights might have been tampered with manually.'

Over by the windows Monique's gaze dropped to the floor and she pushed her tongue up beneath her top lip.

'We can't be sure, but a big concern is that some of the key trial information may have been compromised, as it was also stored in this room.'

Jess paused to let this sink in. Elle turned to check Benji's reaction, but he was still facing the front, face impassive. When she turned back Jess was looking directly at her before addressing the group again.

'If we don't know who accessed the room, it means any one of you might be aware of something that would bias our results. That bias would essentially render this trial useless. We also have to consider that, given the organised nature of the break-in, this was a deliberate theft of intellectual property, possibly by an outside commercial organisation. This would necessitate the involvement of the police, and possible criminal proceedings.'

Again, she stopped, and surveyed the room.

'We're not answering questions, Harrison,' Dr Lineker said.

Elle turned to see Harrison's hand coming back down. Still, he spoke: 'If the trial's useless, we still get our money, don't we? Sounds like extenuating circumstances to me.'

'No questions, please,' Dr Lineker said. 'Just listen to Dr Utterson for now.'

Harrison's mouth formed a frustrated line and the muscles of his jaw flexed.

'This is all hypothetical, of course,' Jess said, 'We don't *want* the trial compromised. It would be a serious setback. We are very much hoping that this is a…prank or an act of boredom that has just gone a bit too far. We know that some of you have been finding the restrictions here hardgoing, and we are sympathetic. So we want to leave the door open for someone to rectify this. Come forward, return the pills, and assure us that the trial hasn't been compromised. If we're satisfied, we can continue.

'If you want to tell us anything, we are in our offices all day, and in our rooms and the staff room this evening. If you would like more privacy, we will be administering your pill tomorrow morning in our offices on a one-to-one basis. Benji will come to collect you and at that point you will have a chance in private to tell us if you know anything.' She took a breath, and now addressed the floor. 'And there will be a financial reward for any meaningful information.'

'But that's the line drawn,' Dr Lineker said, his face red and his hand over his mouth, as if he didn't trust it uncovered.

Jess took a breath. 'After that we will, sadly, have to treat the trial as compromised.'

'What does that mean?' Becks said, sounding irritated.

'It means we go home. Tomorrow night,' said Jess.

Anger, surprise and disappointment blended into a single

drone, and Jess held up a hand in an attempt to still the commotion.

'The money,' Harrison said again, the anger in his voice cutting through the noise.

'If you read your contract, you will see—'

'No,' Dr Lineker said, cutting Jess short. 'No, you get nothing. The money depends on full completion of the trial.'

With that, head shaking, he walked through the canteen and Jess, somewhat stunned, followed. Elle watched them leave, and when she turned to look at Benji again he was finally looking back, wide-eyed now.

'Whichever one of you bloody did it,' Harrison said, rising to his feet, 'you'd better get this sorted pronto.'

Chapter Eight

1

Trying to find somewhere quiet to speak with Benji was impossible that morning. Elle sat out by the pool under the shade of a parasol, hoping he'd pass by and they would get a moment alone. The other loungers remained empty, no one apparently in the mood to enjoy themselves, even though it might be their last day.

When Charlie and Mai walked by, heading back from the beach, she expected them to at least acknowledge her. Instead, they breezed past in silence.

Before they were out of earshot, she called out to them, 'What did you think about what the doctors said?'

They stopped, looked at one another, and walked over.

'What did *you* think?' Charlie said.

'I think… I might be in a really difficult position.'

'Why?' Mai said.

'You know why.' She tried to keep her voice down. 'Was it you?'

With a slow blink to indicate his disappointment with her, Charlie said, 'Let me put it this way, if we *didn't* do it, what would you conclude?'

'But was it you?'

'I'll tell you what you'd have to conclude – you'd have to conclude *someone else* did something very similar to what we were planning to do. Which is a really big coincidence, wouldn't you say?'

She laughed. They were ridiculous. 'Of course I would.'

'So don't you see? It's just another part of it.'

'Really?' Elle rolled her eyes. 'Charlie, I don't see—'

'It's what he's been saying all along,' Mai said. 'They must have overheard our plan—'

'Wall mics, no doubt—'

'—and they're now using it against us. Making conflict to see how we react.'

'But we're not buying it.'

'No.'

Elle closed her eyes, exhausted, and when she opened them Charlie was kneeling beside her. 'You can believe what you want, Elle. But reality has opinions too.'

2

At lunch Elle sat opposite Ted, who was trying to remain positive about the trial continuing. She could tell he was anxious, though. Still, his presence was comforting, and she wanted to talk to him about Mai and Charlie. To get his opinion. She was debating whether to say something when Ricoh walked behind Ted carrying a steaming mug back from the serving trays. It was unclear what happened, whether he lost his footing or his hold on the mug, but Ricoh jerked like he'd been shot, and the contents of his mug spilled over Ted's shoulder and arm.

Ted cursed and sprang to his feet. Droplets of hot coffee splashed Elle's face. Ricoh began apologising, while Ted quickly took off the shirt he was wearing.

'Sorry, mate,' Ricoh said. 'I lost my grip.'

'It's fine,' Ted said, clutching his burned hand and wincing.

'It's not, mate – your skin's all red. Come on, quick, let's get it under a tap.'

'I'll be fine.'

'No, come on, you don't want to make it worse.'

He let Ricoh lead him behind the serving counter and into the kitchen, while Elle grabbed a cloth and a wad of napkins from Carl to clean up the table. It was ten minutes later when Ricoh emerged alone, looking like he might start laughing. He walked quickly past her without making eye contact and out through the canteen doors.

Shortly after Ted walked out, his lower arm and hand a less angry red now. Still topless, he collected his soaked shirt from Elle, and when she asked if he was okay, he nodded, but his expression betrayed bemusement.

'You look…troubled.'

He met her gaze. 'No, it's just… No. Forget it. I'm just going to change my shirt.'

Before he could walk away, she said, 'Did something happen?'

He studied her briefly, seemed to make a decision, and sat back down. 'He just murdered me.'

'What?'

Ted laughed. 'He just spilled hot coffee on me, took me to the kitchen, and while I had my hand under the tap, he took out a pen and said, 'Mate, while we're here, you're dead.' What do you think of that?'

'Seriously?' A pen had been her suggestion for a murder

weapon. 'Oh my God. You have to tell Dr Lineker. That's so… he's not well.'

'Well…maybe. Ricoh insisted it was an accident, though. And I think old George has enough on his plate at the moment.' He looked into her eyes, shaking his head, and again she was struck by how mature he seemed. How calm and like Winston. 'If it wasn't an accident, though…that's a twisted bit of genius, don't you think?'

'It's twisted.'

'What's going on in a head like that, do you think?'

Elle didn't know what to say, not without sounding mean. So she shrugged. 'Does it hurt?'

He looked down at his hand again, inspected the front and the back. 'Not really. It'll be fine.' He walked off, shaking his head again, and Elle heard him mutter something under his breath. It sounded like, 'Bloody psychopath.'

3

She finally found Benji late that afternoon, on his own at the five-a-side cage looking up at a ball caught in the netting. He shook the fence back and forth, the sound made by the repeating strikes against the metal panels at the base escalating into a loud roar.

'You okay?' he said, not looking away from the ball.

'I thought you'd come and find me. What are we going to do about Mai and Charlie?'

'I don't know, Elle. I'm really hoping they just come clean.'

'They said it wasn't them. They're saying this is all part of the *real* trial.'

'Of course they are. Well, the latest news is apparently Paul and Monique are going to search everyone's rooms tomorrow.'

'Search the rooms. Can they do that?'

'Apparently they can. It's in the contract.'

'That's…' She stopped herself. Because she hadn't read the entire bloody thing, had she? So what right did she have to turn around at this point and express outrage that she'd signed it?

'It's mad, Elle. They've asked me to gather everyone to watch a film while Carl guards the corridor doors when they do it. I've been at a planning meeting all morning, and everyone's in a real panic about it. I really think they might pull the trial.'

'Surely they can't. Not now they're got this far through it.'

'I don't know. They may just want to cut their losses. You heard what Lineker said. They don't have to pay the participant fees if the trial is aborted because participants broke the rules. They were arguing about it, so it's not decided, but that might be their best option financially if they want to start again.'

'That's ridiculous. Would *you* still get paid?'

He nodded. 'Yes, but none of you would.'

'We should just go and tell them what we know about Mai and Charlie. They won't cancel then, will they?'

'We could. But if we do, those two will know you turned them in. They might turn around and say you were in on it, and then the doctors will have questions about why you didn't report it before it happened.'

Elle stared at Benji. That wasn't fair. She *had* reported it. To Benji. 'So…do you think I should stay quiet?'

'I don't know what to do. Maybe things will play out in their own way. Maybe Lineker *is* just bluffing. Maybe Charlie and Mai will confess and hand back the pills.'

'How likely is that, though?'

'If I'm reading the vibe, Lineker's biggest concern is an… inside job. He's worried someone on the trial may have cut a deal with a rival company to get a sample of the drug to them.

There's a chance if they're convinced it's not that, they might cool off.'

Elle had come outside without sun cream, and even though the day was beginning to cool, the lack of shade on the pitch made it feel like each freckle on her bare shoulders and face was frying. 'Isn't that why I should tell them? Charlie's just a conspiracy theorist, he's harmless.'

'But what about Mai? Even if she's bluffing, Lineker might not take the chance.'

Elle fell silent. She reached up to her shoulder and covered her old scar with her hand, the urge to get back into the cool building getting stronger. Was Benji right, or was he trying to cover his own back? 'I need to think about this.'

'Yeah, of course. But can we talk about it again before you decide anything? Just don't do anything you don't need to.'

Elle nodded.

4

Everyone eyed each other warily over breakfast the next morning. Conversations flared but soon died. Charlie and Mai sat in the corner, eating and gazing out the window. Dale, Gee and Ted sat nearby in a group. Ricoh and Becks ate alone, the former looking up at Ted every so often, like he might be expecting reprisals. Harrison, Hallie and Constantine were all absent.

Elle picked at her food, still thinking about Charlie and Mai. She was going to have to say something tonight, there was no escaping it. Even if it cost her a place here, it could be the only way to give the others a fair chance of continuing. In many ways it was karma. She wasn't supposed to be here anyway.

She knew Benji wanted to speak to her again before she

said anything, but she didn't trust herself around him. She liked him a lot, and really believed they could keep things going after the trial. But when talking to him the day before, she'd felt that old impulse to please taking over, and she needed a clear head. She'd asked him not to visit her, too, telling him she needed more sleep. Really, it was because if she spoke with him again, he would change her mind. Too much was at stake for her to just stay quiet. There was no doubt Mai and Charlie had stolen the pills, she just didn't know how.

Her plan was to speak with Dr Lineker once her turn came to go to his office for pills.

Only then Benji strode into the canteen and changed everything. It was immediately obvious from his body language that he was about to address the room.

'Everyone, I've got some good news.' He paused to let people attune their attention. 'The issue that was raised this morning has now been resolved. Which, obviously, means that we'll be staying here to complete the trial.'

A murmur of relief passed through the room, and Benji nodded, clearly relieved himself.

'Who was it?' Charlie said, not sounding particularly surprised or guilty.

'I think it's been put down as a misunderstanding, so I think the idea is, we just move on.'

Benji left without another word, presumably to share the news with those not present. Elle had no idea what had happened, but decided she'd ask Benji later. It was great news really, and after the weight of obligation lifted, her appetite started to return.

She scanned the room to gauge the other reactions, her gaze alighting on Ricoh sitting on his own in the far corner of the room. He was slumped over the table, face pressed into his hands. His back rose and fell quickly, and his arms were shaking.

Elle stood up, ready to go over to him. But before she could move, he got up, leaving behind an entire plate of food, and walked out of the canteen shaking his head. He hadn't seemed happy about the announcement at all.

5

Benji knocked on her window just after midnight, all slow smiles and heavy eyelids. He'd brought a bottle of wine from the bar and two glasses, and proceeded to pour them both a glass.

'What a weird, weird, day,' he said, and sat next to her on the sofa.

'So what happened? Did Charlie and Mai have anything to do with it?'

'No. It was Harrison.'

'What?'

'He handed himself in. They questioned him, and he claimed he was coming out of his tests the other day and saw the door to Dr Lineker's office ajar.'

'The room with two locks was left ajar?'

'Apparently the door has been sticking, Dr Lineker said. He seemed rather embarrassed about it. I checked, too, and the latch *was* heavy, and Paul was fuming they hadn't told him. Harrison said he was curious, looked inside, and took a bottle of pills.'

'Why?'

'As a souvenir, he said.'

'As a souvenir?'

'Yeah, a souvenir.'

It sounded ridiculous, but it struck Elle that it was exactly what he'd said to Hallie when he'd been caught stealing her underwear. 'Did he elaborate?'

'He said he just grabbed it and walked out, and only when he got back to his room did he realise how stupid he'd been. He went to take it back but the door was locked again, so he decided he'd just get rid of it in case he was caught. Apparently he chucked it into the sea from the cliffs.'

Elle shook her head. 'And he just…admitted all this suddenly? He's been the most vocal of anyone about not doing anything to jeopardise the trial. He humiliated Ricoh about it in the bar. So what, on an impulse he nearly sabotaged the whole thing? What did Dr Lineker and Jess make of it?'

'Oh, they bought the whole thing. Jess told me they knew from his personality tests that he was impulsive. That it fitted. They believed everything.'

'Did you?'

'Well, part of me thinks, was he just saying it to make sure the trial didn't get canned? But then, why risk his own money for that? He can't have thought they'd give him the reward for the information. Unless he thought he was going to lose his fee anyway, so did it hoping they'd show mercy on him. If he did that, it worked. They're not going to kick him off.'

'What about all that biasing-the-trial stuff?'

'They took him at his word that he didn't read anything compromising. They reckoned it made sense that he couldn't have been there that long, and said the most sensitive trial materials were all encrypted on the computers. To me, it just felt like they were relieved it wasn't some sort of corporate espionage. That was their main concern, like they're on edge, expecting it.'

'And what about the camera footage being tampered with?'

'They couldn't see any footage of the incident, so it was suspicious. But now Paul seems happy enough that it was part of the ongoing issue with the security cameras. The cameras aren't saving a lot of footage and keep glitching.'

'But isn't *that* weird? The camera system all runs through the computers, doesn't it? And they're saying the information is all encrypted on computers… Doesn't Harrison work in computing? Is it possible he messed with things?'

'They don't seem to think so.'

'So that's it then,' she said. 'Just like that, we just go back to normal?'

He laughed. 'Like I said, a weird day.'

Elle sipped her wine. 'Yeah, weird day.'

6

Elle was drifting off in Benji's arms, but voices out in the corridor anchored her to the waking world. Interminable chatter, pushing her closer to the embarrassing act of getting up and asking them to be quiet. But no, that wasn't her style. Especially not with this group. She'd never live it down.

Then the wailing started. Deep, chesty sobs and moans from much further down the corridor.

'What is going on out there?' Benji said.

Elle stepped out from under the sheet, put on her dressing gown, and went to the door. Behind her she could hear Benji getting dressed. Outside, Gee, Becks and Mai all stood in their doorways. Becks wore a distant smile. Mai looked perplexed.

'Ricoh,' Gee said to Elle, pointing at his door and shaking her head.

'How long's it been going on?'

'Half an hour.' Gee was in the room next to Ricoh's. 'He's been getting louder and louder.'

'He sounds really sad,' Becks said.

'Has anyone checked on him?' Elle said.

Gee's face crumpled in disgust. 'Above my pay grade, boss.'

From behind Becks, Harrison said, 'Just leave him alone. He's an attention-seeker.'

No one moved. The moans continued, shaping themselves into words: 'I need to leave.'

Benji, out of sight behind her, touched Elle's shoulder and she stepped back into her room.

'I'm going to go and wake up Lineker,' he said.

Elle nodded, and Benji left through the balcony doors. Unable to stand there doing nothing, she put on her jeans and a top. Had this really been going on half an hour and they'd done nothing? Told no one. Stood there gossiping about it.

She endured a gauntlet of stares on her way to Ricoh's door. She rapped three times. Ricoh didn't answer. Likely he couldn't even hear her above his crying. She knocked louder. It did nothing to interrupt what was clearly a pattern: soft cries rising into mournful cries, scraping his throat the way the pedalo had against the sea floor, before finally, when the misery found the words, he would say, 'I have to go' or 'I need to leave' or 'I want to go home.'

Soon footsteps echoed through the atrium, preceding the arrival of Dr Lineker, Paul and Benji. Dr Lineker came through first, still looking half asleep and with a Queen T-shirt and shorts on beneath his open white coat. The effect was oddly disquieting, and Elle stepped back from Ricoh's door while they listened in.

'He's not answering,' Elle said.

'It's all under control,' Dr Lineker said. Elle hoped that wasn't panic she saw in his eyes. 'Everyone go back to your rooms.'

No one moved.

'Come on, you lot,' Paul said. 'You're not helping.'

Before he could get to cracking heads, Dr Lineker asked

Paul to open the door. He took out a bunch of keys from his pocket, and let the three of them in.

Ricoh's broken voice escaped: 'You need to let me go. I can't stay here, Dr Lineker. I'm being fucking poisoned. I'm done. I want to—'

Paul shut the door, impressing his last set of verbal instructions on them again with a final glare.

Elle listened, stunned. Ted had joined them in his doorway by then, as had Charlie. The soft murmur of men's voices from inside the room was occasionally punctured by Ricoh's shouts and sobs.

'It's the pills, isn't it?' Becks said.

'It's not the bloody pills,' Harrison said, his hand drifting up to rub his temple. 'He's just weak. But it's obvious how this is going to play out now. They have to be cautious, and that stupid, stupid bastard is going to blow the whole thing.' He hit the door frame with the side of his clenched fist.

'Hey,' Ted said, 'we don't know that, Harrison. I'm sure he's in good hands. Let's not make this worse.'

Elle nodded, amazed at Harrison's balls given what he'd nearly caused.

'If the trial isn't completed, chap, no one gets paid.'

'Well… I know that,' Ted said. 'But that's…no, listen. It's more complicated than that. Let's just see what happens.'

'I can already see what happens,' Harrison said. 'If Ricoh fucks this up for us…' Harrison pushed his hand to his head again, winced now, and retreated back into Becks's room, punching the door again on the way. She gave everyone a look that said, *What can I do?* before following him. Keen to set an example, Elle went back into her room too.

7

She lay on her bed with her television playing ocean sounds from Spotify. It was something she did often when Mum came back late with guests, and it reminded her of Granny Alice, who used to listen to tapes of ocean sounds before she moved to Spain because it made her feel as if she lived by the sea. It didn't quite cover up all the noise in the corridor, but that wasn't a problem really. She was too wound up to sleep. That look she'd seen on Dr Lineker's face, it hadn't belonged to a man in control.

If that had been her only concern, though…

Where had Hallie been tonight? All that noise from Ricoh and not even a peek out to check. Then Harrison, that little touch of his forehead? And stealing those pills – so impulsive and out of character. How aggressive he seemed, too. He'd looked ready to kill Ricoh.

What was happening to them? They weren't the people they'd been at the start of the trial, that was certain, and the only question was, what was causing it? The psychological wear, or the drugs?

They were over halfway through the trial. Less than two weeks left now. Still, she didn't want to take the pills anymore. Not until she knew they were safe. It was good that Becks had blurted out her concerns. That meant the issue was out there. It would be easier to ask the question. Tomorrow, maybe. They could go together. Get reassurance.

She wished Benji were still there. Hoped he would come back.

He didn't, and when Elle finally switched off long enough to fall sleep, dawn light had appeared at the edge of her curtains.

8

Someone was knocking at her door. Elle jolted awake. The bedside clock reported it was almost 10 a.m.

'One moment.'

She found some clothes and opened the door. Benji stood in the corridor wearing his uniform.

'I'm so sorry,' she said. 'I didn't fall asleep until late. Have I missed my pill?'

'It's fine, there's been a change of plan. George has – Dr Lineker has said they're going to bring them to everyone's rooms.' He paused to glance down the corridor. His unease was buried crudely beneath the topsoil of his professionalism. 'At some point.'

'What's happening, Benji?' She'd lowered her voice to entice him out of work mode, but he didn't take the bait.

'We're asking people to remain up here on the corridor this morning. There's been an incident that we're looking into, and at this point we're asking for your cooperation.'

'Benji,' she said, annoyed with his abruptness and formality.

He shook his head. 'It's Ricoh.'

'What?'

He looked around.

'He's disappeared.'

Dear Alex,

Thanks for sending me over your thoughts. As always, your input is invaluable, and I am incredibly grateful for all your support, both intellectual and material, in making these early tests of our drug a success. I appreciate you have concerns based on how patient 3 reacted to this version of SB. She'll feel herself once more when the drug's fully left her system. However, I firmly see this aberration as a positive learning experience – and the girl neither harmed herself nor anyone else at the complex. With some simple tweaks, we can now make sure the drug doesn't overwhelm participants with certain dispositions, slow down the delivery. That's really what I think happened in this young lady's case. Incidentally, we did find three or four messages she left at the complex, and managed to remove them before we packed up.

Also good news, is that patients 1, 2, and 4 never experienced anything negative, and patients 1 and 2 both had quite positive reactions, I would say. Yes, the effect is small, but it is noticeable. I really wish you had been here with us to see for yourself. Perhaps it's something you could consider if you agree that these findings warrant us attempting an initial small trial-like set-up with a more substantial dose. Given the stakes, I should think twenty participants might be enough to bring in the requisite investment. Maybe even as few as ten.

I do think that we ought to press ahead as soon as possible, though, especially given your concerns about potential leaks within your organisation. The last thing we want is to be beaten to the punch. There are no second-place medals where SB is concerned. Winner takes all.

Finally, in answer to your last question, about my personal motivations for all this. You've been very candid with me, so I'll do you the same courtesy.

My father was a large presence in our house when I was growing up. He wasn't a particularly kind man, and when he died the nicest thing anyone said about him at his funeral was that he got things done. One of my strongest memories of him is of being stuck in a traffic jam, just the two of us. My father, angry, frustrated, and late, used the hard shoulder to try and sneak off at the next junction. When the police lights appeared behind us, he turned and hit me in the face. I was too shocked to even cry. And when the police asked what he was doing on the shoulder through his open window, he told them he'd had to get me home because my nose had started bleeding and that I was a haemophiliac. They believed him too, because the blood was gushing by then. So they let him go.

As you can imagine, in such an environment self-belief was hard to come by. But then there was my mother. When I was ten, she bought me a chemistry set because a teacher had told her I'd shown an interest in science. She did this sort of thing often. Quiet attentiveness. Only, when I opened it, my father declared it was a waste of money, and that I didn't have two brain cells to rub together. For a second, doubt overcame my mother's face, and I hated my father so much for poisoning her faith in me that way, and wanted to prove more than anything that she hadn't made a mistake. That it was my father who was in error.

Life is short, Alex, and rarely does a scientist stumble across something as career-defining as SB. Even though my mother passed five years ago, I still believe that the success of this drug will be the validation of my mother's faith in me all those years ago.

I hope you can see now that, like you, I am as determined personally as I am professionally, to make Apollo Wellbeing and SB a success. And suffice to say, I think our teething troubles are over now, and we can honestly begin looking forward to enjoying the fruits of our considerable labour. Let's change the world, Alex.

Warm regards,
George Lineker

Part Two

Adverse Events

Chapter Nine

1

At lunchtime Benji wheeled a dining cart into the participant corridor and handed out trays of food. He had no pills with him, and no information about when their incarceration might end. Elle and seven of the others ate communally on the corridor floor. Hallie took her food into her room, acknowledging no one, while Constantine's door stayed firmly shut until Benji left. When he did appear it was so sudden, it made Elle jump. He wore pressed trousers and a black shirt, open at the neck, with his sleeves rolled up like some try-hard CEO.

'Alright, chap,' Harrison said.

Constantine might have acknowledged this with a nod, although it had been so minuscule, it was impossible for Elle to be sure. He strode towards the double doors at the end of the corridor.

'It's locked,' Harrison said.

Constantine ignored him.

'Mate, they've locked it,' Gee said, grinning with disbelief at Harrison.

He continued, undeterred. At the doors, he raised his leg and pushed against the left door. When that didn't work he used his shoulder on the right. His expression remained blank, although his narrow eyes made him appear constantly sceptical. He gave up, and returned to his room without another word. He collected his tray from the floor, knees bent, back straight, and slammed the door.

'So the undead have risen,' Harrison said, shaking his head. 'This is a bloody joke. Are they going to keep us here all day? If Ricoh's gone, leave him to it. Dock his fee and move on. Why are *we* being imprisoned?'

No one else spoke. For Benji's sake, really – not that *he'd* been particularly forthcoming with her yet – Elle said: 'I'm sure they'll have a handle on things soon. If something…bad has happened, they probably just want to keep us from the worst of it.'

'He'll have walked to the nearest town,' Gee said. 'I'd check the clubs.'

'Or he's collapsed in the desert somewhere,' Mai said.

Dale opened his notebook, began to write something, and said, 'Maybe he went for another epic swim.'

'Listen,' Harrison said, 'he's probably hiding in the building. The bloke's an attention-seeker.' He'd clearly made his mind up on Ricoh, so Elle didn't expend any energy trying to convince him otherwise. In a way, she hoped Harrison was right.

2

When Benji came back for the trays an hour later, Harrison demanded answers.

'I don't have updates yet,' Benji said. 'There's a lot of decisions being made that I'm not part of.'

'Any timeline?'

'I doubt it will be long, but I can only tell you what I've been told, Harrison.' He was firm but not aggressive, sensing the tension bubbling like magma. He sounded as baffled and put out as they were.

Harrison winced like he'd done the night before, this time putting his hand to his forehead and massaging his temple with his thumb.

'You okay?' Benji asked.

'It's nothing. Just a—' He closed his eyes, clearly waiting on another bolt of pain to pass.

'Can you at least tell us if we're locked in here because you're worried about us getting out,' Dale said, 'or are you worried about him getting in?'

'The doctors are doing this for *your* safety. We're trying to manage resources while Ricoh is found. I'm sure you can imagine it's not easy with a small staff.'

'Aye, but what does that mean exactly – our safety. *What* are we being kept safe from?'

Benji collected Constantine and Hallie's plates from outside their doors and pushed the dining cart back up the corridor. Harrison got up and followed him. It seemed for a moment as though he might actually rush Benji. Instead, he stood inches from the door to the atrium and glared at him through the rectangle of glass while Benji locked it from the other side.

Even though she wanted to defend Benji, and Harrison *was* being aggressive, Elle couldn't deny how much it suddenly felt like they were prisoners. And she really didn't like being on the inmate side of the divide.

'You tell them,' Harrison said, pointing, 'Ricoh's problems shouldn't be ours.'

When Harrison sat back down in his doorway, Becks touched his leg and said, 'There's nothing really keeping us here. We could easily climb down from the balcony and get out, couldn't we?'

'Or break down the doors,' Gee said.

Harrison closed his eyes and eventually shook his head. When he spoke, he addressed them all: 'Let's not give them any reasons not to pay us what we're owed. They'd probably love us doing something that violates our contract. Maybe they're even trying to make it happen. Makes their lives a lot easier. But let's give them nothing, okay? I'm getting Glynn fucking Rogers on board when I get home, and there's nothing they can do.'

3

All the uncritical talk of mutiny unsettled Elle. Things felt more normal on the quiet of her balcony, a book on her lap and the sea ahead of her stretching to the freedom beyond the horizon. Easier to pretend this was a lovely sunny holiday rather than Alcatraz.

As the afternoon wore on, the muffled corridor sounds grew more agitated. Laughter increasingly hysterical. Conversations short and voices aggressive. Footsteps rapid. Dale and Gee came out on Gee's balcony at one point, waved over at Elle, and began to speculate loudly about jumping down for a quick swim in the pool. At this rate, full compliance might not last the afternoon.

Just after 4 p.m., Benji returned – and not a moment too soon. Behind him stood Monique and Paul, both now wearing what looked like pepper spray canisters on the belts of their trousers. What was happening?

'Okay, good news,' Benji said to the reassembled participants. 'The decision has been made that it's safe for you to leave your rooms.'

'Finally,' Harrison said.

'What we'd ask,' Benji continued, addressing them with only traces of his earlier assertiveness, 'is that you try to stay inside as much as you can. And if you do go outside, we ask that you go with at least one other person.'

'Why?'

Everyone turned. Constantine stood in his doorway. Elle didn't think any of them had heard him speak before. His voice rumbled, assured and authoritative.

'Guys, I'm just the messenger, okay?' Benji said. 'So to save time, there are still some unknowns about what has happened with Ricoh, and so we are putting in a few additional rules to enable you to remain safe while still enjoying an acceptable level of freedom.'

'Does that mean you can't find him?' Gee said.

'Is he dangerous?' Becks added.

Benji ignored them, and was grateful for Constantine's interruption.

'What about the trial? Has it been abandoned?'

'No, it's still ongoing.'

'But we haven't received a dose today.'

'Can these questions wait?' Harrison said, not bothering to turn and address Constantine directly. 'Are we free to leave, Benji?'

'Absolutely,' Benji said, standing aside. 'Go ahead. And for those of you with questions, the doctors will address everyone later tonight, and they will definitely have more meaningful answers than me.'

Constantine retreated back into his room, and the others pushed through the door while Elle stood waiting in her doorway. When they'd all gone, she knocked on Hallie's door. She waited, knocked again, and when she didn't come, Elle left, assuming she was still asleep.

4

Jess gave a short debriefing in the canteen after dinner, Dr Lineker behind her, sentinel and silent.

'All evidence indicates that Ricoh has voluntarily left the trial,' she said. 'We're obviously working hard to track him down, and as some of you have suggested, he may turn up somewhere else on the island and be trying to get home a different way. I think you were aware Ricoh was struggling being here. We think he was hoping we would be going home after the incident with the pills, but when this was resolved, it upset him. We know he took a bag of belongings with him, and we assume that he left some time in the night, although our state-of-the-art security cameras on site haven't been able to shed much light on specifics.'

Paul and Monique didn't react to this obvious dig.

'He said it was the pills doing it,' Becks said. 'We heard.'

'It wasn't,' Jess said, calm and quick, as if she'd clearly anticipated the question. 'There's no evidence of that at all. We've followed his behaviour quite closely, and Ricoh had been rather unsettled by the situation here.'

'Why the lockdown then? And why no pills yet?' Harrison said.

'I'll leave time for questions at the end, Harrison, but I don't think what you experienced was a lockdown.'

'The doors were locked with us behind them.'

Jess glanced briefly at the ceiling, composing herself. 'Simply, guys, the issue is one of staffing. Okay? To accord with our own standard operating procedures, we needed to put in place a plan to make sure there were enough of us on site to keep you safe, and the only way we could do that and maintain an effective investigation into Ricoh's abscondence was to keep a closer eye on you. Not because we believe you are in any danger, but simply so that we have done things by the book in terms of risk. You wouldn't believe the boxes we need to tick in order to run a trial like this.'

'Is that why you want us in groups now?' Ted said. 'To lower risk?'

She stared at him, perhaps impressed that at least one of them understood the situation. 'Yes. Yes, exactly. If, for example, one of you fell down a flight of stairs, and this wasn't caught by a member of staff because they were dealing with what has happened to Ricoh, we would be in trouble. So yes, this is an extra precaution, which we have to balance against keeping you all in one place.'

Ted nodded and pushed out his lower lip. 'Yeah, makes sense.'

Harrison, sitting across from Elle, shook his head and smirked as if he didn't buy it. She was with Ted though, it sounded plausible. She had a sense of clinical trial bureaucracy from reading around for her degree, but the hoops researchers had to jump through to actually get funding and ethics approval likely dwarfed even her expectations.

Despite feeling somewhat reassured, Elle hadn't expected Dr Lineker to bring out the tray of medication cups from the lower portion of the dining cart.

'So who wants to be first?'

No one answered. The room filled with the susurrations of nervous shifting.

Harrison eventually got up, still shaking his head. He took his pill and without prompting opened his mouth and stuck his tongue out obscenely. He pushed his face so close to Jess's that she had to pull back from him.

'Do you not want to see my diary?' asked Harrison.

'We'll check up tomorrow,' Dr Lineker said. 'Just make sure you fill it in.'

Ted got up next, and Constantine came to the front after him before marching out of the room. Charlie and Mai went together, the peer pressure rising.

Elle didn't want to be last. Still, she remained seated.

Becks stood up now. Her face was hard to read, as always, but she didn't exactly bound towards the doctors. When Jess held out the cup Becks's hand stayed at her side. Jess shook the cup once to encourage her.

Her face screwed up like a child refusing vegetables. 'No. I don't think I want it.'

'Jesus,' Harrison said from the back of the room.

Dr Lineker scowled at him, and stepped towards Becks. 'It's been a long day. I'm sure there's been a lot of speculation, so I understand your hesitation. But the problem is, if you don't take the pill you won't be part of the trial anymore. Which would be a shame, because you've already put in so much work.'

'Just take it,' Harrison said. 'Don't give them an inch.'

'Harrison, that is not helpful,' Dr Lineker said, in an aggressive tone that was equally unhelpful.

'Will you really not pay us, George?' Becks said with a familiarity that felt vulgar to Elle.

'Maybe if there's something you're worried about, we can talk in my office.'

'You're not going to, are you?' Her voice tightened to the point of becoming a sob.

Elle stood up, wanting to reassure her. To tell her to wait if she wanted to. Jess noticed her approach and held out a little paper cup with Elle's name written in Biro on the side. She looked relieved to see Elle, and widened her eyes and nodded, communicating to Elle that if she took the pill now it might encourage Becks.

Elle was pleased Jess aligned herself with her like that. That her perception of Elle was that she was sensible and influential. She took the cup and brought it to her lips.

Jess turned back to Becks.

Elle opened her mouth and stopped. Was she so easy to control still, even after everything she'd been through? One little bit of non-verbal flattery and she was abandoning her instincts. Becks had a right to be concerned, didn't she? They'd said nothing of substance to assure them just now. Taking the pill now didn't make her more sensible than Becks. She'd be obeying just because of the white coat at this point. She was one of those participants in the Milgram experiment.

Jess glanced back at Elle again, and immediately back to Becks. In the corner of her eye Elle noticed Benji watching her from the edge of the room. She tipped the cup and the pill fell onto her tongue.

Becks was still crying and Jess looked as if she was fighting an urge to console her. Elle pushed the pill beneath her tongue and opened her mouth. Jess didn't even look. So Elle turned away, beginning the journey back to her room, expecting to be called back at any moment.

She wasn't, and by the time she shut her room's door her mouth was filled with bitter saliva from the disintegrating pill. She plucked it out, spat into the sink, and put the pill down on the side.

5

Benji lay on Elle's sofa, a hand on his forehead, never raising his voice much above a whisper.

'I feel like I'm letting you all down,' he said, 'but I don't know what to do. You ever get the sense you're on the outside looking in? That's what it feels like with them. Maybe from the start, but definitely since Ricoh ran off. The way they're acting now…'

'What do you mean?'

'The doctors. Paul and Monique. Making secret calls I never hear. Acting shifty when I offer to help. Wearing pepper spray. They know something about Ricoh and they're not telling me, I'm sure of it. And the security cameras. I just get the feeling Paul's lying about them. We don't even know if Ricoh is on site or not because there's no footage, right? And he's like, the system's still acting up. So why haven't they got someone to fix it yet? They can afford to pay everyone twenty thousand pounds, but because there's only one IT guy on the island we just have to put up with a useless system.'

'Yet security is apparently so important, they're willing to lock us down in a corridor for safety reasons at a moment's notice?' She'd chosen her pronoun carefully, even though Benji had very much been a part of that *they*.

'Exactly.' He pushed his palm into his right eye and shook his head. 'When I told Mum about this gig, she said it was too good to be true. She's always right. This all just feels dodgy, man.'

'I've been thinking about what we talked about before,' Elle said, 'about side-effects. Do you still think that might be true?'

He stared at her for a long time. 'They've not said anything specifically, but… I've heard nothing to convince me it isn't the pills. Did you hear him, Elle? Saying he'd been poisoned. He was in such a bad way, like… I've never seen a face like his before. It was like proper distress. The pepper spray went on the belts after that, which doesn't smack to me of being in control.'

'Have they called the police about Ricoh?'

'They said so. But no one's come yet. Again, I kept feeling like I was being fed a load of bullshit. I'll say this, I couldn't believe it when they pulled out the pills earlier. I wonder if they're playing for time a bit, maybe hoping Ricoh will just wander back here or something and they can carry on as normal. But... I mean, what is going on with Hallie? She doesn't seem herself. And Harrison, is it me or does he seem like he's...coked up or something? I mean, who the hell is Glynn Rogers?'

Elle couldn't help but laugh. 'It's an investor he knows. But you know what all three have in common, don't you?'

'What?'

'Headaches. It wasn't just Ricoh. Going right back to the first week.'

'Has anyone else reported headaches since?'

'Not that I've heard about.'

He fell still, staring at his hands. Eventually he began shaking his head. 'Elle, I really like you. I'm sorry you're here and I'm having to trot out all this party-line shit to you in public. You're the best thing that's come out of this job. If I come away from here...if they call it off or whatever, I can live with that. Worse case is I'm back to square one with Dad and his debt. But it'll be fine, because we'll still...uh...' He smiled. 'Keep seeing each other.'

He hadn't asked a question in words or tone, but a gleaming hook awaiting a catch it most definitely was. Despite herself, Elle couldn't help but return the smile. 'Yeah, I'd like to. And if you want to as well.'

'Oh, I want to.'

She stood up from her perch on the edge of the bed and went to sit with him. She felt an overwhelming urge to tell him now about how she shouldn't be there. That she was a fraud. Just something to level them up, now he was giving so much of himself to her. They kissed, and when they stopped his face was fearful again.

'Listen, there's less than two weeks left. I'm going to watch your back the whole time, okay? Try not to worry.'

'I'll be fine,' she said. 'It's you I'm worried about. You're in the belly of the beast.'

'Do you think you'll keep taking the pill?'

'I've had no side-effects. I'm definitely on the placebo.'

He wouldn't break eye contact, and Elle found she had to. 'So you are going to keep taking it?'

The pill was still by the sink in the bathroom. She needed to move it if she was going to lie. But as much as she trusted Benji, and she had fallen for him so quickly despite herself, for her own peace of mind she wanted to hold something back.

'I'll give it some thought,' she said, getting up from the sofa.

When he'd gone she went to the toilet and locked the door. She deposited the pill on a sheet of tissue paper, wrapped it up, and threw it into the toilet. After counting to sixty, she flushed and watched it disappear.

6

At breakfast, Dr Lineker and Jess appeared tired and distracted, barely casting a glance at her diary. They didn't notice Elle leaving her pill in the cup after bringing it up and pretending to swallow. She scooped it out with her fingers while they checked her empty mouth. Later, she was discarding the pill in her toilet when someone banged twice on her door. On the way to and from breakfast she'd knocked on Hallie's door but received no answer. She hoped it would be her.

But it was Harrison, sounding out of breath. 'Hey, your mate might be about to do a Ricoh. You think you could stage an intervention, pronto?'

He was talking about Hallie, apparently outside acting spaced out and strange. A group of them had come across her on their way to the beach.

'Have you told the doctors?'

'Of course I haven't,' he said. 'I'm telling *you*. She's out there on her own, but if they get wind of it we're all going home, aren't we?'

Despite being irritated by his demanding tone, she didn't bite back. Instead she let Harrison lead her out to the pool.

'She's down there,' he said, pointing in the direction of the lower patio. His job done, he walked off, like the whole thing wasn't his problem.

Elle descended the steps and at first didn't see her. When she did, she felt the immediate downward pull of dread. Hallie had climbed over a waist-high fence, crossed the small, rectangular rock garden on the other side, and now sat looking out to sea with her legs dangling over the drop to the beach.

Elle didn't want to move any closer for fear of startling her, and so instead she spoke her name as softly as she could without being inaudible. Hallie ignored her.

'Hallie,' she repeated.

She turned now, gave Elle a dead-eyed smile, and spoke in a low, dry voice. 'Hi, Elle.'

'Is everything okay?'

'I can't get over the view.'

Hallie faced the ocean again, and Elle approached the fence. 'I don't think we're meant to be out on our own. They said we have to come outside in groups. Because of Ricoh.'

'Oh, I know. Poor Ricoh.'

Elle waited for her to say more, but Hallie was done. Far below the sea hissed and crashed.

'Do you want to come back with me?' Elle said. 'We can talk?'

'What about?'

'About anything. I'm worried about you.'

'Want to sit with me? It really is beautiful.'

'Yes. Can we sit on a lounger though?'

'I can't move, Elle. I'm in the middle of my own little trial.' Hallie leaned forward over the drop and Elle gripped the railing of the fence in front of her until she leaned back again. 'Elle, Ricoh was right, you know? They are poisoning us.'

'What makes you say that?'

'They've done something to me. I can't really explain what it is. It was just a headache at first…but now I think that's just how my brain interpreted what was happening. How it interpreted whatever the drug is doing to me. Because it never leaves.'

Already Elle had heard enough to know she was out of her depth. This sort of thing required expertise. Training. One wrong turn and you might have to arm yourself with a fire extinguisher. She had to get back and alert Dr Lineker, but she feared what might happen if she left Hallie alone.

'What does being up here have to do with how you feel?' Elle said. Questions. She had to keep asking questions.

'Well, I need to do something quite extreme. It's a test.'

'Why?'

'It's hard to describe. There are things in my head now that weren't there before, Elle. Thoughts and feelings. And they're awful, Elle. I don't… I don't feel like myself and I want to understand that.'

Elle swallowed.

They are taking our souls.

'It's like I am…synthetic. Like I'm inauthentic. These things inside me aren't mine. So I need to feel something that does belong to me.'

She stood up, put both of her trembling arms to one side,

and turned back to Elle with a smile. She was going to jump, and Elle knew she would forever look back on this moment and wonder if she could have done anything different.

'You're really scaring me, Hallie. Please come and sit with me?'

Hallie lowered her arms. Her shoulders slumped. She appeared disappointed.

'I didn't mean to scare you,' Hallie said, smiling in a way that was some distance from reassuring. She walked over and sat down next to Elle on the safe side of the rock garden, the fence still between them. 'But you need to know, Dr Lineker has put something terrible inside us.'

7

She managed to entice Hallie back over the fence, but she wouldn't return to the building with Elle. So Elle waited with her for almost half an hour, not wanting to leave her alone, hoping someone would see her waving at the two cameras at either end of the lower patio or come down to help her. Harrison would surely have alerted the doctors by now.

But no one came, and soon Hallie began to cry, putting her face in her lap and moaning about how much her head hurt. Elle couldn't just sit beside her. What if she was having an aneurysm? Elle tried once more to convince Hallie to come back, and when she ignored her, Elle told her to wait and went to look for Benji. When she couldn't find him, she went to the doctors. Jess wasn't in her room, so she reluctantly knocked on Dr Lineker's door.

'Come in.'

She peered inside. Dr Lineker was sitting at his desk in the middle of the room, a laptop and a pile of papers in front of him. He turned around as he closed his laptop, and immediately afterwards he turned over the top sheet of paper on his pile so the blank side faced upwards. He smiled, but didn't try to conceal the effort it took. In the unnatural light of this windowless office, his face appeared only a shade or two away from the grey hairs on his head.

'Hi, I'm sorry to interrupt. I tried everyone else first.'

'It's fine, Elle. Can I help?'

'Hallie is acting really strange. I think there's something wrong with her.'

'She's been a little under the weather, yes. Likely a virus.'

'I've just talked her down from the edge of a cliff. And she was saying a lot of stuff that didn't make much sense. About the pills. Can you come and talk to her?'

His tongue popped out of his mouth to touch his top lip. He looked up, as if he was searching for the right protocol from a pile stored in his brain. 'Uh…Where is she now?'

'She's down on the lower patio between the pool and the beach. She won't move.'

He stood up. 'I'll…head down. Thank you.'

The two of them walked together, and when Dr Lineker realised that Elle was coming with him, he shook his head. 'If you could stay here for now.'

'Oh, okay, sure.' She had to ask him before he left, 'Do you think she's right? Is it possible the trial drugs—'

'No. No, no, no. I suspect she's having some very mild post-viral reaction.' He spoke quickly, giving the impression that she was taking up time he didn't really have to spare. 'She's not been feeling herself. We must nip this side-effect talk in the bud.'

'It really didn't seem like a virus.'

'Viruses are bastards. They adapt, mutate, and certainly, yes, they are known to cause psychological effects. Especially in an environment that's a little bit different. And maybe when someone feels a bit homesick.'

'So it's absolutely not a side-effect?'

He raised his voice. 'No.' Apparently realising how close he'd been to shouting, he turned to look at the door. 'That's not what's happening.'

Dr Lineker gave her another fake smile and strode away, while Elle, still worried, went to sit on the sofas by the window, not wanting to stray too far from the scene. Where the hell was Benji? She needed to talk to him. She had only a layman's understanding of viruses, and clinical medicine, and what she knew about mental health was limited to her work and the pre-reading she'd done for her course. But having recently woken up to being the victim of a consummate bullshit artist her whole life, she knew one thing with absolute certainty: Dr Lineker had been lying.

8

Half an hour passed, the atrium silent but for the occasional echoing footfall and the chatter of the others going to lunch. Despite the cooking smells and her whingeing stomach, Elle couldn't eat until she knew what was happening.

The pool area had been deserted when she'd left Hallie earlier. No one had been outside since. So it wasn't like anyone could check in on the situation for her. She paced. Sat down again. Paced a bit more.

'You okay?' Benji said, walking over from the direction of the corridor.

'Think so.' His own expression appeared as troubled as hers must have looked to him. God, it was good to see him. 'You? What's the latest with Ricoh?'

'Nothing still. Jess and Paul have gone out in the minibus

again to search the area before it gets too hot. It's needle-in-haystack stuff, though. Are you waiting for someone here?'

'Lineker,' she said, glancing back through the giant atrium windows. She told him what had happened earlier. About how almost half an hour had gone by since he'd left.

'Do you want to go out and check?'

She wasn't sure. She didn't want to interrupt. But then again, where were they? Something felt off. Jess was the psychologist of the two, wasn't she? Dr Lineker was a psychiatrist. A pharmaceutical man. Was he really the best person to be down there talking to Hallie? Yes, he was better placed than Elle, that was for sure. Still, she couldn't shift the idea that his priority at this point was his precious game-changing drug. That he'd be down there now looking after the welfare of his trial and not Hallie.

'You know,' Elle said, 'I asked him directly about the side-effects.'

'Yeah?'

'I'm certain he's lying.'

'Come on,' Benji said, and she followed him.

Outside the temperature had noticeably risen. A demand for cover shot to her brain from the panicky skin of her exposed shoulders. They approached the stairs in silence, Benji going first and shaking his head when he rounded the bend.

'There's no one here.'

'Maybe they went to walk on the beach.'

The two of them descended the rest of the way and stood at the fence in front of the rock garden.

'She was really standing out there?'

'Yes.'

Benji shook his head before leading the way to the stairs. They began to navigate the switchbacks, but after the first two they had a clear view of most of the beach. No one was down there.

'Could they have gone up to our cliff-top spot?'

Benji peered over the edge, pushing his head down towards his chin and leaning over. He leaned back suddenly, and turned to Elle without looking at her.

'Stay here, okay?' he said.

'What? What is it?'

He jogged down without reply, and the alien drone of the steps bounced between her ears and the cliff wall. With some trepidation she followed, not sure whether to look over the side to see what he'd seen.

'Elle, do not come down here.' He was shouting. 'Go and find Monique. Tell her to call the police and an ambulance.'

'Benji what is it? Is it Hallie?'

'No. Just go up, okay. You don't want to see this.'

She couldn't help it. Elle peered over the side. Three flights below she could see Benji crouched on the beach by the bottom of the last staircase. His body position prevented a full view of what he'd found, but she saw enough to make her turn back. Turn back and run, while trying to delete what she'd just seen from her mind. Unnatural angles. Stillness.

A bloody white coat.

Chapter Ten

1

She found Monique in the canteen, talking with Carl by the counter while Ted, Dale, Gee and Becks ate lunch. Once Elle had explained the situation, Monique stationed Carl at the back doors to prevent anyone going outside, while she went to the office to call Jess and Paul. She returned and jogged out to join Benji.

Not knowing what to do, and unable to shake off what she'd seen, or thought she'd seen, Elle waited in the atrium. Ten minutes later Jess and Paul came running in through the front doors. Elle told them what had happened.

'So where is Hallie now?' Jess asked, her fingers agitatedly playing with the rings on her necklace.

'I don't know,' Elle said. There were really only two options though, since she couldn't have returned to the building without Elle seeing her. So either her body had been on the beach out of sight, an even more dreadful accident having occurred, or she was still out there. And if she was still out there, it wasn't a stretch to assume Hallie knew what had happened. She might even have been involved in some way, hard as that was to imagine.

'Please go back to your room,' Paul said when he'd heard enough. 'And don't say a word to anyone for the time being.'

She did as she was told, thirsty for order. When she reached her door she looked across the corridor. The urge to knock on Hallie's door was overwhelming. Of course she wouldn't answer. Yet Elle found herself standing in front of the door anyway. Listening, fist raised. And from inside came a noise, a soft *clunk*.

'Hallie?' She knocked and waited. Perhaps the noise had been the air conditioning, or maybe the wind moving a blind through an open window.

Elle listened harder. Could she sense someone close now? Waiting just on the other side of the door. Listening back, ear to the wood.

She stepped away, wanting to return to the atrium. Being alone now was a terrible idea after what she'd seen. The corridor felt too narrow, too enclosed. And suppose Hallie *was* inside her room. Did she really want to see her right now, especially if she had been responsible for the accident? Elle had heard Hallie accuse Dr Lineker of trying to poison her right before. Could she have pushed him? Some might view that as a motive, and that meant an unstable Hallie might see Elle as a threat.

Or was she being paranoid? Was her overworked nervous system on edge?

She startled, the doors at the other end of the corridor bursting open. Ted, such a laid-back presence usually, charged towards her. He ran a hand through his hair, pushing hard against his hairline.

'There's a rumour going about that something's happened to Dr Lineker. Do you know anything?'

Feeling trapped, desperate not to have to lie or explain herself, she took a step towards her door and grabbed the handle.

'Wait.' He ran the last few steps towards her, but stopped to leave a respectable distance between them.

'Ted, I'm not feeling great.'

'Join the club, Elle. Just…please. Tell me what you heard. I won't tell the others.' Perhaps aware he'd been raising his voice, he softened his approach. 'All of this is…just so unsettling, isn't it?' His eyes were bloodshot, his face drawn.

She had no energy left to lie. And why the hell should she, really? She wasn't working for the trial.

'I don't know… All I saw was Dr Lineker's white coat covered in blood at the foot of the cliff stairs. I think he must've fallen.'

'Down the stairs?'

'It looked worse than that. I think he fell from the cliff. He'd gone to see Hallie, she'd been up there acting strange.'

'Oh, Jesus. So who's down there now?'

'All of them. Benji, Monique. Paul. Carl's on the atrium door.'

'Yeah, I just spoke with Carl.' He closed his eyes, pushing at his hairline once more. Had that been a wince? 'So they've left us up here alone. Where is Hallie now?'

'I don't know. I checked her room, but…she's not answering. I heard a noise inside, but I don't think it was her. I think she's still down on the beach somewhere.'

Ted went to listen at Hallie's door, and after a moment knocked on it. He called her name and waited. Nothing. He squeezed his eyes with his thumb and forefinger, leaning back to let the wall take his weight.

'We should both go back to the atrium,' he said. 'Safety in numbers and all that. We can get them to check in Hallie's room, just in case.' He gave a weak smile and shook his head. 'This whole thing's coming apart.' He winced again, and this time he pushed both palms into his eyes.

'Are you okay?' Elle said, not wanting him to say what he did, but knowing it was coming before asking.

'It's nothing.' He looked at his hands. 'Just a headache.'

2

Everyone left in the building gathered in the atrium, including Constantine, who stood on the floating landing with his arms folded. Some sat on the sofa by the windows, others slumped against the walls or stretched out on the floor. At one point Gee began to bounce a basketball at the base of the atrium hoop, but soon stopped after Carl shot her a look.

Monique and Jess returned first, their faces expressionless. They stood side by side, and Monique gestured for everyone to gather around.

'Everyone,' Jess said, 'this is very—' She turned away, and stepped to one side. Monique looked about to speak, but Jess turned back again, wiped her eyes and tucked her bottom lip back in.

'This is very difficult to say, but there's been a terrible, terrible accident. Unfortunately, Dr Lineker has died.'

A hush fell over the atrium. Dale's distinct voice, enunciating every syllable, eventually brought it to an end by declaring, 'Fucking hell.'

'What happened?' Gee said.

'It looks like he may have fallen. We don't know. But we'd be grateful if you could just give us the time to process this, and to work out what's next for all of us.'

'What a waste,' Dale said. 'A very intelligent man.'

'What happens now?' Harrison said.

'It's too early to—'

'I don't mean to go on about it, but this…accident isn't our fault. You intend to pay us, don't you?'

Jess glared at him. The rise and fall of her chest quickened.

Monique took over. 'I need all of you to go back to your rooms, please. Just while we get a handle on this.'

'That's what you said last time,' Harrison said. 'And we were locked up all bloody day.'

'Harrison, come on,' Ted said.

He shrugged. 'What? Fuck off, Ted. Who asked you? No one. No one asks you anything, ever.'

Ted gave a dismissive laugh which only increased the forward thrust of Harrison's chest.

'Where's Hallie?' Becks asked Jess.

'We don't know.' She answered like the question had been a non-sequitur, but Elle was pleased someone had asked.

'Well, don't you think you should? I mean, I don't want to call her a crazy bitch, exactly, but she was on that cliff being a crazy bitch before. And not being funny, but now Dr Lineker is dead at the bottom. I don't want to get locked up with her wandering about.'

'The team will establish that the corridor is safe before we all go back inside,' Jess said.

'Do you want me to run down there and get Paul, Monique?' Ted said. 'Would that help in any way?'

'Yes,' Monique said, looking genuinely startled that one of them had said something helpful. 'Yes, it would, thank you.'

'What are you trying to prove?' Harrison said. 'Sucking up won't get us anywhere.'

'I've nothing to prove,' Ted said. 'Do you?'

Harrison sneered, nodding like he'd finally seen Ted's true colours.

3

They waited for Ted's return. Conversation broke out in quiet pockets. Gee and Dale inappropriately amused. Becks and Harrison revolutionaries without a cause. Charlie and Mai deep in conference.

Elle considered talking to Constantine, who paced the atrium alone, arms folded. Then Charlie and Mai approached her, both with an air of smugness.

'So,' Charlie said, 'any thoughts?'

'What do you mean?' She had nothing for them. Not even a pinch of goodwill to keep her civil.

'Two missing people. The principal investigator dead in mysterious circumstances?'

'I saw him, Charlie. I saw his body.'

'It was you that found him,' Mai said, as if Elle hadn't just told her this. 'Again.'

'Uh-huh.' Elle tried to move away but they followed her. 'Guys, no offence, but this isn't a game. Give me some space. Please.'

They backed off, showing no signs of being hurt.

Five minutes passed before Ted and Paul returned without Benji. The assembled participants had reconvened at the foot of the stairs behind the reception desk. Monique and Paul went upstairs to open Hallie's room with a skeleton key while Carl remained at the back door watching over them all. They returned shortly, Paul jogging down and shaking his head.

'She's not up there. So can you all go back to your rooms while we get this sorted. Please.'

'We'll make sure to keep you informed,' Jess said, like it

might somehow ameliorate what was happening. 'With regular updates. I am sorry.'

'Okay, everyone,' Monique said, making a sweeping gesture towards the stairs.

Constantine couldn't wait. He led the way, running up the landing before Becks, Gee, and Dale could start their trudge towards the stairs. Ted followed next, and Elle went to follow him when Jess put her hand on her shoulder and quietly said, 'Could you just stay behind with us?' She gave her a genuine smile. 'We'd like to know what you saw.'

'Harrison,' Paul said, his tone sharp enough to turn Elle's head.

Harrison stood leaning with his back against the edge of the marble reception desk. His arms were folded, and his mouth was a defiant line.

'Do you not think we all need to discuss this?'

Paul took a step down. 'Come on, mate. Let's not make this shit shower any worse.'

Elle didn't like his casual use of profanity. It somehow underscored the slipping of order.

'No, I'm fine here for now. At least until we have assurances that we're getting what we're owed.'

'Give it a rest, Harrison,' Ted said.

Harrison blinked. Then he squinted, gritting his teeth. 'Look, I'm more than happy to keep taking your pills, and giving you brain scans, and answering stupid questions. And I'll take your orders to stay in my room if that's what's required.'

'It is,' Monique said.

'But all of those things have a price. And while you've got two psychos wandering about unaccounted for, and a dead guy out there who probably ended up that way because of one of them—'

'Harrison, we don't know what happened,' Jess said.

'No, *we* don't. But what *you* know is whether or not you intend to pay us our money. If you do, I will willingly go to my room and put my safety in your hands, knowing you are people who keep your word. If you're not, then we don't have to do anything that puts our personal safety at risk.'

Paul had reached Harrison now and stood sideways on to him, his arm extended towards the stairs. 'You done?'

'Bloke thinks he's Jordan Belfort,' Constantine muttered from up in the gods.

'Oh, you got something to say now, Nosferatu?'

'We can give you straight answers, Harrison. Can you just give us some time to get a handle on things?' Jess said. 'Like… five minutes to grieve and process. Please.'

Paul reached out with his free arm to touch Harrison's elbow. Harrison yanked it back.

'Harrison, shall we just go up?' Becks said, her voice flat, her face almost bored-looking.

'No,' Harrison said. 'This lot are out of their depth, and they are trying to shaft us. Are you telling me, that if you knew you weren't getting the money, you'd want to spend any more time locked upstairs? Wouldn't you want to enjoy every last moment we have here in complete freedom? Out where you can see someone if they're coming for you.'

'No one's stiffing anyone here. You'll get what's coming to you,' Paul said.

'Oh, you sure of that, are you, Paul? You can't even run your own security systems, and I'm supposed to trust that you know the ins and outs of our contracts. Unless…sorry, was that an attempt to threaten me? I'll get what's coming to me. Is that what you meant?'

'Come on.' Paul moved in aggressively, putting an arm around him and pulling him towards the stairs. 'Let's have a chat.'

Elle had already rubbed up against the limits of her own crisis-management skills today, and she knew this move wasn't a good idea.

Harrison didn't budge, so Paul pulled harder. 'Let's go, mate, before you say something you regret.'

'That *I'll* regret.' Harrison flung up his arms to break Paul's hold on him, but caught Paul in the face in the process.

Paul wheeled away, swearing, his hands going up to his eyes. 'You little fucker.'

'Oh, come on, I barely touched you. That was an accident.'

Paul swivelled around and held up the pepper spray canister towards Harrison. 'Right, get up the fucking stairs, you little prick. Now.'

'Oh, right. I see. This is how it's going to go, is it? You're going to *make* me. Is that a good idea? Really?'

'You're not giving me much choice, are you? If it means getting you to do the smart thing…'

Harrison shrugged, licked his top teeth from inside a closed mouth, and walked towards the stairs. Elle's tension abated a fraction, and when Harrison passed Paul she saw the security man's face soften with relief.

Then Harrison threw out his left hand at Paul, knocking the pepper spray away from him. He tried to grab it from Paul's hand, and the two of them began to grapple. For a few seconds they were a perfect match in strength, and they pushed and tugged while their feet remained planted, grunting and huffing, everyone else watching on in silent disbelief.

Harrison, the taller of the two, began to gain the upper hand, and managed to spin Paul around so his back was to the reception desk. The pepper spray fired, and it drifted through the air in the direction of the stairs. Some went into Jess's eyes, some into Monique's, and both of them cried out and stumbled away.

With a yell, Harrison pushed Paul away, and having lost his balance, Paul stumbled until the reception desk struck the small of his back. He cried out, and dropped the canister. It clattered on the tiles. He bent over to pick it up, stood back up and spun around to face Harrison. His face was bright red. 'Now listen.'

Harrison had already closed in, and pushed Paul while sticking a leg behind him – a playground bully's trick. Paul tumbled backwards helpless, arms flailing. The base of his skull struck the marble edge of the reception desk and he collapsed to the floor. A dreadful, nasal groan escaped from his lips; both hands rose to cover his head.

'Fuck me, Harrison, chill out,' Gee said, an absurd remark in the context.

Harrison now stood above Paul. He wiped his lips and shook his head, his expression oddly blank. 'You heard me warn him. Man's a belligerent prick.' He bent over and calmly said, 'Glynn Rogers is coming on board.'

Paul rolled onto his stomach, one hand reaching for Harrison's foot. A large amount of blood had pooled on the floor where he'd been lying, and more blood poured from a wound on the back of his head. He tried speaking, managing only more pharyngeal noises.

Elle screamed. She whipped her head around the atrium, looking for help. Carl was making his way over far too slowly, clearly unaware of the gravity of what had happened, due to the stairs impeding his view. Monique and Jess were still crouched over, rubbing their eyes. The others on the stairs watched on with a peculiar detachment that frightened Elle. When she turned back to Harrison, what he'd done seemed to have registered, finally. His eyes were huge, and his hand rose to his mouth like something important might fall out. Paul's outstretched arm had begun to spasm. His whole body shook. His groans intensified.

Harrison shook his head. He stepped back from Paul, stared at the rest of the participants assembled on the stairs, and turned to face what he'd done once more.

'I warned him,' he said. He shook his head as if he had something in his hair that needed freeing. Then, with a grimace, he swung back his right leg like a rugby player about to convert a try, and kicked Paul impossibly hard in the front of the head. Blood flew. Elle screamed again, turning away.

With a look of bafflement on his face, he turned to them all. 'What was I supposed to do? He was suffering.' Once more he shrugged, and that eerie calm settled on his face once again. 'I couldn't just leave him that way. I put him out his misery.'

A moment later, Monique ran at him, dispensing her own pepper spray. Harrison began to shout, dropping to the floor, clutching at his face. She fell on him, striking his stomach and crotch. Her anger intensified, and she began shouting about Paul's family and grandkids. Carl arrived, finally, and helped to subdue a writhing Harrison.

Elle stared at Paul. He lay unmoving, his blood forming a red grid beside him as it funnelled down the joins of the tiled floor. Harrison had put him out his misery. Just like you would an injured animal.

Chapter Eleven

1

Elle locked herself in her bathroom. She only came out when Benji knocked on her door. He stepped inside and held her for not nearly long enough. The rapid beating of his heart beneath his polo shirt was a relief to hear. He was as terrified as her.

'I'm sorry,' he said. 'Are you okay?'

'Yes. What's happening now?'

'I don't know. It's chaos down there.'

'Is Paul…'

He shook his head and bit his lower lip. For a moment, even though his face was right in front of her, it looked far away.

Paul was dead. She had watched Harrison kill him. They all had.

Benji was still needed downstairs. He could see that she didn't want him to leave, and he promised to return soon, which would have to do in the circumstances. Elle sat on her bed and tried to work out what the worst-case scenario would be now, while the view over the ocean taunted her from the other side of windows that might as well have been bars. But this wasn't something which came naturally; her mind would often seize up when it came too close to the truly dreadful. Because…because people were all the same, deep down, weren't they, and fundamentally decent? Despite what you'd seen apparently normal, charming, friendly people do, with your own eyes. If you didn't believe that…well then, how could you ever know who was good? You'd have to just lock yourself away for ever, civil society be damned. People only went awry if they were shunted off course.

Earlier, when they'd been beating Harrison, she'd actually cried out for them to stop, and when they'd dragged him off, she wanted to run down and intervene, in case they did something worse to him out of sight. A ridiculous reaction to have, so soon after what he'd done to Paul.

And yet despite what she'd seen, she didn't believe this was Harrison's fault. Wasn't it obvious to them all now that the pills had to be responsible? This aggression had gradually crept into him. He'd changed before their eyes over the last few weeks. Just like Ricoh. And just like Hallie. They'd all been shunted.

Or was Elle making excuses? Was this like Mum all over again? Denial. Stockholm syndrome. Pathological empathy.

No, she didn't believe that. She'd moved on since coming here. Whatever traces of her previous self might be left, this conclusion was the rational one to draw. Two deaths. Two troubled people. On a single day. If Winston were here, he would agree with her.

The blame lay with the drugs.

2

Benji brought her a tray of dinner at half past five, which she knew she wouldn't eat. He told her Harrison was now hand-cuffed to a pipe in one of the downstairs toilet cubicles.

'In the toilet?'

Benji shrugged. 'Monique didn't want to risk us having to move and escort him when he needed to go.'

She supposed that made sense. 'So the police, are they here? Are they coming?'

In a quiet voice, he said, 'I don't know what's happening, no one is saying anything to me. Monique and Jess have been talking to *someone* on the phone. I thought I heard the name Alex, but who the hell is Alex? They just keep saying, "We're awaiting instructions." From who? Like…what does that mean? Awaiting instructions?'

'Maybe from the police.'

He shook his head. 'Maybe, but they weren't speaking Spanish. And they keep saying, 'It's complicated, it's compli-cated, which is why it's taking so long.' But it's just more bull-shit. Get this, I asked Jess to her face, is it the drugs? And she just clammed up. Went white and panicky, and changed the subject.'

'Oh my God. Benji, we knew it. What the fuck?'

He nodded. 'I know.'

'So at any moment, any one of the others, or even I might…'

'It's going to be okay,' Benji said. 'I'm sure we'd have seen signs before now. I'm sure we'd know. And no one else has said anything about a headache, have they?'

Elle met his gaze and nodded grimly.

3

Sometime after Benji had dropped off their meals, Elle heard voices outside. She opened her door and nodded at Gee, Dale, Becks, Charlie and Mai, who all sat looking up at her from their doorways.

Constantine's door remained closed, but there was nothing unusual about that. Ted wasn't there either. Was he lying on his bed? Eyes squeezed shut, hands on his head. Was that headache really starting to take over now? Was he starting to feel a bit…unlike himself?

She studied the others. They were debating jumping the balcony and swimming in the pool again. Why not enjoy themselves while they were here? Because, let's face it, Harrison had had a point, they were likely going home. Although, then again, maybe there *was* a chance the money was still on offer, and if they just did what they were asked, that side of things might still be covered. Harrison had just lost the plot.

To Elle, it was an outrageous thing to be discussing, given what had happened. Yet what was the right way to deal with watching a man they knew get kicked to death? This was likely shock and denial. Not everyone could just cry on demand.

Becks looked up at her with rheumy eyes. Gee touched her hairline, not unlike how Ted had done earlier. Charlie slumped against the wall, robbed of his usual energy.

On the stairs earlier, when she'd turned around, how funny they'd all looked. Not scared or shocked so much as…what? What had it been?

Perhaps it was just that some of them simply didn't feel like themselves either.

4

Benji updated them in the corridor that evening, although Ted remained in his room. Police specialists from Tenerife were due to fly over, but they couldn't charter a helicopter until the next morning. Once the police had been, a decision would be made about what happened next with the trial – however, none of them could leave until law enforcement said so.

There were head shakes, thrown-up hands, and angry stares. But there was no insurrection, yet.

With time to kill, Elle's mind went into overdrive. Patterns started to form, and memories from the last few weeks leaped out to her. She kept coming back to the game of Cluedo, and something Ted had said about Ricoh after he'd spilled coffee on him. In thrall to a theory, she knocked on Becks's door. When she finally answered she looked annoyed and exhausted.

'Sorry, were you sleeping?' Elle said. 'I just wanted to check you were okay, after everything that happened.'

'I was fine until you woke me up.'

'Oh, sorry. I didn't—' She stopped herself from apologising. She wanted answers. 'I just wanted to know something. Who was it that hid in your cupboard?'

'What, for that game? I thought I wasn't supposed to tell.'

'I think it's safe to say we're not playing anymore.'

Becks shrugged and jerked her head in the direction of Hallie's door. 'Your mate, the nutcase. She was only doing it to try and freak me out. Warning me off Harrison. But I don't scare easily.'

5

Later, Benji came to Elle's room. He used the door this time. He slumped on her sofa again, and Elle made him tea – never having seen a man look so in need of a caffeine hit.

'It's good news about the police,' Elle said.

'It's something.' He took a sip and put it down on the table. 'But I still don't buy it. I'm just their mouthpiece now.'

'You don't?'

'We keep talking about stuff, and they'll start looking at each other. Like they're about to tell me something, like they really want to…but then they'll just carry on. So, like, maybe the police are coming. But, two deaths. People disappearing. And they can't get the police out now? What, Tenerife's got bigger problems than us today?'

'Well…if we're right, and the drug is involved in all this, they're probably in damage-limitation mode, right?'

Benji nodded. 'Yeah. True. I'm wondering if they're holding back because I might not keep doing their bidding if I know the drugs are making people violent. Because some of the participants who are still here *aren't* taking the placebo, right? So who knows what's around the corner?'

'I've been thinking about that a lot.'

'I said to Jess again, "You can tell me, you know. I'm not on the trial. What does that drug you're giving them really do, and how certain are you this stuff happening isn't connected?" And she's like, "That's not something we can discuss. For commercial reasons."' He made speech marks with his fingers. 'Well, I'm done tonight. For commercial reasons. Going to hide up here with you, just in case, you know…'

'One of them's the werewolf?'

He laughed. 'Exactly. How are you dealing with it all now? I can't even imagine…'

Elle's smile was brief. 'I'm okay. I just keep thinking about how he was after he'd done it. Harrison. He was so cold. The way he actually blamed Paul for what he'd done, and then was just...so calm and matter of fact. And then for a moment, it looked as if he understood what he'd done. But then he went and...and said he was putting him out of his misery.'

Benji came and held her. 'God, I don't have the words. I just wish... I could have been there and maybe done something to stop him.'

'It happened so quickly. I'm glad you didn't see it, but also I wish you had, so you'd know what he was like. It was...so eerie. This complete abdication of responsibility. It seemed...psychopathic.'

'Great, just what we need. A bunch of psychotics hiding amongst us.' He stood up and sat back on the sofa.

Elle shook her head. 'Not psychotic. Psychopathic.'

'What's the difference?'

'Someone psychotic has broken with reality. That's not really what's been happening. With psychopathy you're completely *in* reality. You just...don't have a conscience about anything. I don't know, maybe I've had too much time alone to think about this, but do you remember when Ricoh spilled coffee over Ted?'

'Yeah.'

'Well, Ted called him a psychopath. And I didn't think of it until now, but scalding someone to win some stupid game... that's psychopathic. It's calculated, remorseless.'

Benji narrowed his eyes. 'And that's how Harrison seemed.'

'Yes. Psychopaths lack a conscience. Psychotic patients... they're unwell. And they feel regret if they do something bad while having an episode. Psychopaths, though...they lack that little voice in their head telling them not to do something because it's wrong. It doesn't come and go. Most of them don't even think they're unwell at all. From their perspective, that's just who they are. Some of them don't even know they're psychopaths.'

'But they're dangerous to other people.'

'Potentially. Lying, cheating, stealing, they'll do whatever they need to get what they want.'

'Murder?'

'I don't know. People confuse serial killers and psychopaths, but they're not the same. But if the circumstances are right…maybe.'

'Jesus, Elle. So…what, you think the pills could be…' Benji huffed a humourless laugh, '…turning them into psychopaths?'

'I'm definitely not saying that…no. It's just…maybe this is stupid. But I have this friend, Winston, and he works on the high-security wards. He's a librarian, and he used to take books to this one patient who was a criminal psychopath. Winston said he was a totally normal and charming guy to your face, and you could talk about books and films and stuff perfectly nicely with him. If you met him in a pub you'd leave thinking you had a new friend. But then you read his file, and he'd like, brutally attacked people, killed a man, for no real reason, other than a…slight or disagreement over something trivial. And when asked about it, he'd just always say, calm as you like, 'Oh, that bloke had it coming,' or 'He made me do it.' It was so odd. And…I don't know, that story came into my head when I thought about how Harrison seemed.'

Benji nodded. 'Well, he showed no regret when we locked him up downstairs. He just kept talking about the money we owed him, and asking us to be reasonable about it all.'

'He's been getting more and more obsessed with that money. And he showed no remorse about dumping Hallie for Becks. No concern for Ricoh when he was unwell, no concern or sadness for Jess and Dr Lineker just now. Yet at the start of the trial, he was rather full of himself, but he was thoughtful, too. And self-effacing. He even apologised for coming to my room the first night.'

'It's hard though, isn't it?' Benji sighed. 'Maybe he was just on best behaviour at the start.'

'I know. Maybe I'm clutching at straws. But…then I think about Hallie and Ricoh. So what Ricoh did to Ted seemed so out of character, yet he did it to win a game. And, okay, so I asked Becks who hid in her cupboard that night she was murdered, and it was Hallie. Becks reckoned she must have snuck in hours before to do it. It was calculated, and weird, and just doesn't seem like the sort of thing the Hallie I knew would do.'

'Yeah, but devil's advocate, how well do we know anyone here, really?'

'Okay, but also, Ricoh and Hallie both said they had these bad feelings and thoughts they'd not had before, that they felt not themselves, poisoned, inauthentic. Headaches that weren't headaches but more like…being trapped in their head with these alien ideas. Those things happened after the trial started. And do you know what else it reminded me of, what they were saying?'

'What?'

'That message in my drawer, *They are taking our souls.*'

Benji grimaced. 'So…you're thinking that if there were experiments here before, and they experienced the same things…'

'Isn't that how you might describe feeling like you'd lost your conscience? That your soul had been taken. Is that what Ricoh and Hallie were trying to explain? What they've been fighting with.'

'Could be.'

'If the conscience acts like a dam, if it went or weakened,

you would have all these new, frightening thoughts floating in your head that didn't feel like yours, wouldn't you?'

The two of them sat in silence for a moment. Eventually, Benji said, 'I mean…yeah, maybe.'

'And then there's what happened with the goat. Which seemed to have been killed because it was being noisy. Before, I couldn't imagine anyone here doing something so cold-blooded. Now, though…'

She was talking too fast, which she always did when she was trying to convince someone. Like the only way she could change a person's mind was to make her points and show her reasoning, but all within the time-frame of a normal conversation. It never worked though, and she needed to breathe.

'I don't know,' she said, 'maybe I've spent too much time with Charlie—'

'No, I hear what you're—'

'—spinning this mad theory out of nothing, but…is it so far-fetched that a drug we know affects decision-making and problem-solving might unexpectedly muck around with whatever chemicals are involved in conscience? I mean, a lot of those test questions they gave us were ethical dilemmas. And when you're making any choices in real life, your conscience is basically in the car with you the whole time, backseat driving.'

'I suppose. I guess… I've just not read much psychology stuff like you, so… I just don't know what to think.'

'I'm no expert, Benji. I've read a little bit for my degree but… But okay, so I remember reading psychopaths feel certain emotions at a lower wattage. Like, they don't really get worried about stuff. They actually crave danger and excitement. And so there was Hallie, standing on that precipice, leaning over it, without a care in the world. Running her own trial, she said. Like some kid on a slide about to jump off to see if she can fly.'

'Okay.'

'And Ricoh, he told me he was bored. Not just normal boredom, but really suffering with it. It seemed excessive. That is also a psychopathic trait.'

'Maybe that's why he took that daredevil swim.'

'Yeah. Could be. And maybe that's why he ran off.'

'Yeah. Or one of the others did something to him. Someone who had it in for him and had no conscience in their way.'

Neither of them spoke for a moment, both of them well aware who had been angry with him the night before he vanished.

'And Hallie,' Benji said, 'do you think she killed Dr Lineker?'

'I don't know. She seemed so convinced she was being harmed by the trial, but... I don't know.'

'So if psychopaths aren't always killers, how can we predict when they are?'

'When it's in their interests, I suppose.' Elle held up her hands. 'Look, I'm really out my depth. I mean...there's a link between psychopathy and violence, yes. But maybe it's like, only the worst sufferers are dangerous in certain situations. But I can't say.'

'No?'

'All I can say is that when I saw how Harrison was, that term came into my head. Psychopathic. Because...the thing is, he didn't see red. He didn't really...lose it. Everything that happened seemed...rational. Cold. And then Hallie, when I talked to her, she was trying to articulate something but couldn't. And that was scary because she talked a mile a minute before, but...she was composed. Logical. And Ricoh was too. None of them were...'

'Broken from reality?'

'Exactly. Except...they were distressed by the changes they

were feeling. And could that make them more dangerous? I don't know.'

Benji closed his eyes and yawned behind a closed mouth. 'I am so tired.'

'Me too. But my mind won't stop now.'

He got up and put his hands on her shoulders. 'Okay, I think we need to…stop theorising.'

Elle gave a feeble smile, and they shifted to lie beside one another.

'Let's focus, right. Our real worry is who else might become a problem? And how do we avoid them until we get flown the fuck out of here?'

'Can we just lock ourselves in here? Hide under the blankets together?'

'I like that idea.' He kissed her. 'Have you felt anything today, headaches or anything weird?'

'I'm fine. I…flushed my last two pills.'

She waited for his reaction, which was, mercifully, laughter. 'I thought you might.'

'I just didn't tell you before because—' She stopped herself. She ought to tell him everything now. Tell him how she ended up here, and how paranoid she'd felt about being caught. But how would he react now, after all this time?

'It's fine,' Benji said. 'So what about Ted, then?'

'He seemed worse today,' Elle said. 'But I've not seen him much.'

Benji grew tense beside her. 'He was odd down at the beach. I mean, he had just seen Dr Lineker down there, but he seemed…spaced out. Like he was miles away.'

'Maybe we should check on him?'

Benji shut his eyes. 'Maybe.' He let out a sigh, and after a moment Elle twisted her head around to look at him. 'If only there was a way we could…sort of prove who was one or not,' he said.

'I read about this test once,' she said. 'But it's bullshit, apparently.'

'What is it?'

'So…a girl's at her mum's funeral, and this mysterious guy shows up who she's never seen before. It's love at first sight, and she knows he's the one for her. Then the next day she kills her own sister. Why?'

'Are you serious?' Benji said.

'That's the test. But, like I say, I read it was rubbish.'

'What's the answer?'

'It's because she hopes the guy comes to her sister's funeral. Supposedly only psychopaths get the answer right.'

'Well, if we get desperate, we can keep it in the back pocket.'

'Yeah. Maybe we just keep an eye out for any symptoms, like being restless or bored. Especially if they've got also a headache.'

6

Elle hadn't felt tired enough to sleep. Her mind churned with the violent images of the day and snippets of the conversation she'd had with Benji before he'd fallen asleep. He didn't stir when she got up, nor when she returned to the bed to cover him with the blanket and climb in beside him.

She put a palm to his warm back, sliding it around to his stomach. Such trust in her, despite everything else going on. Despite her having been taking the pills until very recently. How could she not have trusted him? She would be honest with him. When the moment was right. He deserved that much, given everything else. If he chose to dislike her for it, then so be it. That was on her.

Sometime after 2 a.m., she did start to sink into sleep. The distant hum of what sounded like an engine briefly roused her once more, but she knew it must have been some trick of her pre-dream brain, so she ignored it, and allowed herself to be immersed by darkness.

7

Elle watched Benji get dressed in a hurry. The bedside clock said it was six, and for a few blissful seconds it was as though the day before hadn't happened. Then, for an even briefer time, it might just have been a bad dream. Then reality jolted her like black coffee, and she was wide awake.

'I'm sorry,' he said, 'I didn't mean to fall asleep. Shit, I need to go.'

'Will you keep me updated?'

'Of course.' He kissed her and turned to leave. 'This is all going to be fine. We'll probably be on a plane by the end of the day.'

It sounded good to her. Better than the bottomless well of despair they'd stumbled into last night.

She lay in bed collecting her thoughts before getting up to make a hot drink. She had only just received her first hit of caffeine when someone knocked at the door. It was Benji, back already and brimming with anxious energy. He walked in and closed the door.

'They've gone.' He brought up both hands to his mouth. 'All of them.'

'What do you mean? Who's gone?'

'Jess, Carl, Monique.'

'What? How do you know?'

He pulled a piece of paper from his pocket, torn from one of the participant diaries.

Benji,

   We've gone to seek help. We couldn't find you to explain but wanted to leave without confrontation. Please hold the fort as best you can and sit tight. We'll come back for you soon.

'It was on the bed in my room with a box of pepper spray canisters. They must have come while we were asleep, and when they couldn't find me they just left. Bastards.'

'Why?'

'Why do you think? They know what we know. There's one dangerous person locked in the downstairs toilet, there's Ricoh and Hallie possibly still hiding somewhere, or might come back any second… If anyone else becomes a danger they won't be able to control it. They already can't control it.'

'So they've just gone and left us?'

'Looks like it. The minibus has gone.'

Elle stared out at the sea, the sun only just above the horizon and the sky a deep blue. 'So…what now?'

He stared beyond her, shaking his head. 'I don't know.'

Chapter Twelve

1

There were only three fewer people in the building now, yet the reverberation of their footsteps in the atrium conjured absence. Elle recalled the sad echoes of her university room when she'd packed up all her belongings to move back in with Mum. The ceiling lights were off and the air conditioner had ceased humming. A heavier coolness permeated the space now.

'Do we still have electricity?' Elle said.

'Things were on in my room, yeah. Just looks like house-keeping haven't turned things on yet. Which I'm guessing means they haven't come.' He put his hands on his hips and surveyed the building.

'What does that mean?'

'Well, like you said, it's damage limitation. Someone's *told* them not to come.'

'How much danger are we in?' Elle said.

She knew he couldn't possibly know, but he said, 'We'll be okay.'

'You really think they're coming back? Because, at the moment, I feel a bit like…a sacrifice.'

'I think they'll come back, I do. If I had to guess, some higher up's run an algorithm and just pulled out the staff in a panic. Which makes me think they'll be back once they can guarantee safety…insurance-wise, or whatever.'

'Which will be when? I mean…how are they not liable for *our* safety, Benji? Insurance-wise.'

'Exactly, they don't want any more problems than necessary. So hopefully it will be quick. Hours. Maybe a day or so.'

'A day or so? No.'

'This trial has been super top secret, right? And this situation is about as bad as it gets on a trial, short of all your volunteers…you know, exploding from the medication or something. So they'll be assembling teams of lawyers way before they call some island police department.'

'You don't think they really called them, then?'

'No. They'll want to have all the i's dotted and t's crossed long before they get anyone in. You ask me, that's who we're going to see here next. Some team of suits and a private security firm, giving everything the once-over before the law gets involved. But, I do think they'll come back. I believe them about that.'

'We can't just sit here for days, Benji. Not with what's happening. Let's leave. Find the police ourselves and report what's happened.'

'Yeah, we could and maybe should. But they asked me to sit tight, which, I don't know, maybe legally means I'm responsible here or something. It was a pretty big set of papers I signed. I think I probably have to wait here with everyone in case anyone gets hurt.'

She instinctively went to argue, but closed her mouth because she was probably being selfish. 'Okay, someone else could go. I could go.'

'Yeah, okay. But we have no idea where we are, or which direction you'd need to walk in. We could be miles from anywhere populated, so we'd have to plan it. Especially if I'm liable now. Because Ricoh and Hallie could be out there, in God knows what state, and any one of the others here might be dangerous if you went in a group. I wouldn't be happy with any of those situations.'

'All of us could go together. Safety in numbers.'

'Is that safe? Besides, there's another problem still tying us to this place.'

'What's that?'

'Harrison.'

2

Benji wanted Elle to wait in the atrium, but there was no way she was going to stay alone in the building. Besides, she wanted to see Harrison. She wanted to understand *everything* about the situation they now found themselves in, know every contour and crevice, just in case she should be tempted into indecision or weakness.

'I'll go in first and check,' Benji said in the corridor outside the men's toilets. 'Just in case.'

'No. It'll be safer together.'

He paused, but didn't argue. He gave Elle a demonstration of how to use the pepper spray canister before they stepped inside. It was rather considerate of the other three to completely abandon Benji, but leave him so well armed. Elle walked into the bathroom, finger on the nozzle, feeling like someone trying to steal a dragon's egg armed with hairspray.

They crept across the wall towards the oversized disabled cubicle. The closed door concealed him, and it squealed when Benji pushed it. Elle gritted her teeth.

Harrison sat with both arms slumped over the closed toilet bowl. One had been handcuffed to the hand rail on the wall. He still wore the same white shirt and dark-blue chino shorts that he'd been wearing the night before, although both were now patterned with red streaks. A duvet, presumably from his room, lay scrunched up around his feet. The formerly white canvas plimsolls he'd been wearing when he killed Paul were set neatly to one side beside a half-empty bottle of water.

'He's still breathing,' Benji said.

'Yes, I am,' Harrison said, opening the eye not swollen shut. 'Were you hoping I wouldn't be?'

'Are you in pain?'

'My balls hurt. And I think my rib's broken.'

'Did they give you any painkillers?' Benji said.

'My turn now. Why are you two down here, not Fred and Rosemary?'

'Do you need anything?' Elle said, staying on message, like they'd agreed.

Harrison looked at her, but only after a moment did his face resemble the person she'd first met. She wanted to step back towards the door. Because at first Elle had seen in his gaze the facial embodiment of the echoing atrium, and something else Winston had said about the prisoner he'd known came back to her. He'd said that every so often, you'd be talking with him, and you'd look up, and it would be like addressing the face on a hollowed-out pumpkin. And when you looked, really searched for that little glimmer in a person's eye that told you they felt things the same way you did, you came back empty.

Just now, that vast blankness in Harrison had almost swallowed her.

Harrison jiggled his handcuffs. 'I'm not a threat to you. You saw it, Elle. Paul attacked me. I acted in self-defence and the clumsy geezer fell. This is all just…ridiculous.'

'We'll come back with breakfast,' Benji said, and turned away from him and gestured for Elle to follow.

Harrison slumped again, defeated, and Elle was surprised by an impulse to make things better for him in some way. To make this undoubtedly necessary imprisonment accord with some set of principles, rather than it resembling Guantanamo Bay.

'Are you sure you don't need anything?' she said again.

'You know Paul wasn't even who he said he was.'

Elle stopped. 'What do you mean?'

Benji's hand touched her arm. When she looked at him he shook his head.

'Do you have an open mind?' Harrison said.

She turned. Her mind was always open. But that felt like a weakness now. As Granny Alice used to say, you didn't want a mind so open, your brain fell out.

3

In the kitchen they retrieved all the cereals they could find and brought them out to the serving counter at the deserted canteen. Like a vampire dragged into sunlight, everything compelling Harrison had said in the toilet turned into the insubstantial dust of mind games now. They had more important things to think about.

'If we're staying, then,' Elle said, 'what do you want to do about everyone else?'

'Are there options?'

'I mean, we could act like nothing happened.' She couldn't believe she'd said such a thing out loud. If the roles had been reversed, how would she have felt, being locked up by Benji and his potentially dangerous lover? Yet she continued: 'If we keep everyone locked in the corridor, the company's team, or whoever, might be back before anyone realises there was a problem.'

'True, I considered that. But you'd have to stay in there, locked up with them, to sell it.'

'I'd be fine. I could lock my door.'

'And suppose it's more like a few days before anyone comes for us, and the others got wind of there just being me left, and that I'd been lying to them… Nah. I don't want to be creating situations that *raise* the tension and conflict. You saw how it played last time. And like you said, psychopaths aren't necessarily violent, are they? It's about the circumstances, yeah?'

'Yes.'

'Right. So if we just try and keep things…you know, as chill as possible. Give anyone whose little voice has gone quiet no trouble at all.'

'Chill as possible.'

'Besides, with Ricoh, Hallie and Harrison, we've had some warning. Okay, so no one will be just…*pop!* Like – *boom!* – psychopath.'

'Unless they're hiding it.'

'Unless they're…yes, there is that. But look – God, Elle, I know this is mad, but I'm already watching the, like, inquest into this in my mind. Someone will ask me, why did you just keep everyone locked up when you knew some of them might be dangerous, Mr Iwobi? You sealed their deaths with your actions. Nah, not for me.'

'I'm sure they, whoever they are, would understand our position. And once they're out, some of them will want to leave the complex.'

'Maybe, maybe not. But right, I think the lowest-risk thing

for me and you to do is to try and get everyone on side. Work together, try and establish who is on the placebo, and hope no one else…falls sick. And if they do, we haven't turned the others against us and can deal with it, with their help.'

Elle couldn't fault his reasoning, even if it felt like they were following the path of least resistance. But to her, at this point, the threat of what the drugs might hypothetically do to the others was less than the very real threat of Harrison. And what might happen if Hallie or Ricoh showed up in a worse way than when they left.

Safety in numbers: instinctively that felt like the best approach.

'Also,' Benji said, 'I don't know anything about this medication at all, but you have to assume that the reason you were all taking it daily was, you needed a certain amount in your body to keep it working.'

'That's a good point. So what, you think the negative effects might just…fade?'

'We can hope so.'

Elle smiled, even though, for all they knew, the drug worked cumulatively. It could take weeks to wear off, and that was presuming the side-effects they were seeing weren't being brought on by some sort of irreversible brain trauma.

But seeing the first beams of optimism shining from Benji's face, she kept her doubts to herself, and said, 'I'll go and find the milk.'

4

Just before 9 a.m., Elle returned to her room until Benji called out to the corridor that breakfast was ready. She opened the door at the same time Becks opened hers. Gee emerged next, Dale standing just behind her. Mai and Charlie followed, again appearing from the same room. Last was Constantine, yanking his door open sharply and whipping his gaze from left to right to take in those already assembled.

Ted didn't emerge, and Elle resisted the impulse to look at Benji.

'Anyone seen Ted?' Benji asked.

'Nah, not since yesterday,' Gee said.

Benji knocked on Ted's door. 'Ted. Ted, can you come out please?' He didn't answer. Benji gave up and returned to the double doors. 'Okay, listen everyone. The remaining members of staff have left the premises to seek assistance.'

'You what?' Gee sounded half amused and half appalled.

'They've gone to get help, so for the time being I'm in charge.'

'To help with what?' Constantine said. 'Why aren't the police here?'

'They've done a runner on you,' Dale said.

Gee laughed. 'Un-fucking-believable.' She turned to Dale. 'Be decent for your book, all this.' He gave her a thumbs up.

'There appear to have been some communication issues,' Benji said, struggling uphill to maintain the breezy, matey authority he'd managed to command over the last few weeks. 'But they've gone to get help now, so it's all in hand.'

'Help for what?' Constantine sounded appalled, like the service in this particular restaurant had not been up to scratch. 'What, in this situation, do we need help with, other than a clear answer about whether the trial is continuing or not?'

'Well, all that's in hand. As is our safety and security, with two members of our party missing. So for now, my view is, I don't see the need to keep you penned up in here while we wait.'

'Wa-hey,' Gee said, not entirely without sarcasm.

'We've put out breakfast—'

'Who's we?' Constantine asked.

'The company. I. I've put out breakfast in the canteen—'

'Carl's gone, too?' Becks said, like this was the worst news of all.

'Yes, they've all gone.'

'When did they go?' Constantine said. 'I saw Monique through the doors yesterday. Did they leave in the night?'

'Yes. That's right.'

'Why would they do that?'

'I can't tell you.'

'Can't meaning won't?'

'Can't meaning I don't know.'

'But did you know they were leaving? In advance.'

Benji said nothing for a moment before choosing to move on. 'I've put out cereals in the canteen. If everyone wants to move from here to there, we can talk more about our situation. Does that sound reasonable?'

'Where's Harrison?' Becks said.

'He's still being…contained.'

'In the toilet?' Becks looked to Gee, and on realising no sympathy lay that way, she looked to Elle. 'Is he still locked in the toilet?'

'Yes,' Benji said. 'He's still in the toilet.'

It was odd, even though Becks had always had a very disconnected way of speaking, Elle couldn't help but notice it now. Had it worsened? Was this the pills flattening out her emotions like a roller? Or was it just more noticeable because now, in her words at least, she sounded as if she really cared?

'Is anyone with him? Could I sit with him?'

'Becks,' Benji said, 'I don't think that's a good idea. But shall we discuss it over breakfast?'

Becks looked at Benji, either with hate or an unfortunately

cast resting face. But he was right to want to keep those two apart, Elle had no doubt.

'Any word on the other two going AWOL?' Charlie said.

Benji shook his head.

'It's the drugs, isn't it?' Becks said. 'You can tell us now. Is that what made Harrison do what he did?'

'Is that why the others cleared off?' Dale added. 'Has it all got a bit John Campbell for them?'

'Guys, I don't get that reference, and I don't have an opinion, but if you're worried about the drugs, I'm not going to make you guys take any more. As far as I'm concerned, the trial is over.'

'How's stopping now going to help us after nearly three weeks of consuming it?' Gee said. 'I get what you're saying, Benji, but any one of this lot could be ready to kick in heads at the drop of a hat. I don't trust anyone.'

'You can all keep asking me about the drugs, but I know as much as you about what they were doing and what they might have done. If you're worried, Gee, you can lock yourself in your room and we'll bring you food.'

She didn't respond. Instead, she looked at each of the other participants, her face set like a bulldog's.

'What's happened to Paul?' Constantine said. 'And Dr Lineker?'

'Well…they're where we left them.' Benji widened his eyes, as if to say, *What else could we have done?* 'We put Paul in the room set aside for medical emergencies.'

'So Dr Lineker is still out on the beach?' Constantine said.

'Oh, poor him,' Becks said.

Benji frowned at Constantine. He looked as if he wanted to ask him why it mattered. But then, if any of them wanted to go to the beach, it certainly did matter. 'I don't know, Constantine. We hadn't moved him yesterday evening because we were leaving him untouched for the police and Forensics. And obviously other things sort of took precedence after that. Did you want to go swimming or something?'

'Not particularly.'

Benji took a deep breath in and held it. Elle knew he was fighting to keep things calm. 'I will definitely check the beach first to make sure the others didn't move him.'

'I think you ought to check on Ted, too,' Mai said. 'Why isn't he answering his door?'

'Damn right,' Gee said.

'Yep. Great idea,' Benji said. 'So if everyone wants to head to the canteen, we'll get started on a plan.'

He stood to one side, holding open the door for the others, who gradually filed past. He gave Elle a pained look when she approached, and she tried to smile.

Something from their conversation earlier had stuck with her, poking now as she watched them all leave. The people running the trial had pulled the emergency cord so quickly. They must have been pretty confident about there being a risk. For it to have happened so decisively, it was almost as if they knew something about what was to come. Like they might have experienced it before.

They are taking our souls.

Constantine was the last out, and Elle followed. Benji tried to arrange his features into something reassuring while holding open the door, and Elle tried to match it with something resembling appreciation.

She hoped they'd made the right call. Because there was no going back now.

5

They were less than halfway across the atrium when Gee stopped before the doors. The rest of the group stopped too.

'What are we doing?' Gee said, staring at the front doors and the gates beyond. 'Fuck all this, let's just get out of here and have a fry-up in a cafe on a beach somewhere. We're meant to be on holiday, aren't we?'

No one spoke, but Elle knew a mutiny when she saw one. She looked to Benji. He wasn't looking back, and appeared not to be panicking yet.

'I'm up for that,' Dale said. 'If we're not taking the pills anymore.'

'Can we stick with the plan and talk it through first?' Benji said. 'I'm not going to stop you doing anything, but at least give me a chance, as the person left in charge here, to convince you why it's not a good idea.'

'Nah,' Gee said, 'I think we've done our time here. Why would we stay here any longer than we have to? Dead bodies lying all over the shop. People going crazy. Someone tied up in a fucking toilet.'

'Right, fine,' Benji said, striding towards the front doors, 'let's all go and have a really good look, shall we?' He'd been doing so well until now, but Elle could sense his irritation was fast rising.

Elle followed, and when she looked back the others were coming too. Outside the air was already warm despite the sun having only been up a few hours. Benji ran down the terracotta steps and jogged across the driveway to the front gate, his elongated shadow ahead of him. He waited for everyone to catch up before yanking back the steel arm holding the gate closed. A padlock lay open on the floor, left behind by the others. Everyone really was now free to leave if they wanted.

The gate roared along a set of tracks embedded in the tarmac, revealing a view of the island interior in daylight for the very first time. The others stood in a line looking out, but Benji gestured for them to follow him. He marched down a stump of road to the point at which it split left and right before circling back around the wall to the coast road. He held out both arms, as if to catch the scenery, the wind flapping the base of his polo shirt. He said nothing; what lay before them said enough.

A desert of ochre rock stretched out to the horizon everywhere Elle looked, only occasionally interrupted by greys, occasional blacks, and patches of green scrub. The ground lay almost entirely flat up to the horizon, but for the slope of a volcanic-looking mountain visible to the east. Without the protection of the walls, the wind out here felt spiteful, mussing hair and throwing dirt in their eyes. It created an illusion of cool, although Elle could already feel the fabric of her thin cardigan baking against her freckled skin.

'Looks like Mars,' Mai said. No one disagreed.

Gee held up a hand over her eyes, despite the sun being behind them. 'How far can we see?'

'Three miles, maybe?' Mai said.

'Depends on elevation,' Charlie said. 'But between three and five here. Probably about six miles west is the airport. Good luck with that cafe, Gee.'

Benji folded his arms and continued to stare out at the barren landscape. Eventually, he turned around and headed back inside, leaving the gate open. Defeated, Elle followed him. She had no doubt the others would do the same.

6

The coffee machine was too confusing to work, and so while the others ate in a humbled silence, Elle made hot drinks using a percolator. She liked being useful. It made her feel safe. As if kindness might work like a suit of armour.

When everyone appeared settled, Benji addressed the group.

'We are miles from anywhere here. And my gut – not on any special knowledge I've been given, I want to add – but my gut says that the vastness out there goes far beyond what we can see. So for any plans you, or we, want to make about leaving here, we need to factor in walking at least five or six miles one way, and another five or six back to here, where we know there is shade, running water, and food. Now, I didn't see much in the way of shelter out there. No rivers or streams or lakes.' He looked at Gee. 'I definitely didn't see any greasy spoons. Everyone, have a think about a possible twelve-mile hike in thirty-degree heat, carrying food and litres of water with you. Or, we could sit tight and wait for the promised help.'

Gee and Dale didn't look impressed. But neither of them said anything to contradict him.

'You guys eat, and we can talk when we've all had a chance to absorb this. But I want to check on Ted.'

For a moment Elle thought he was going to leave her behind with them all. But he asked her and Charlie to join him in trying to locate a skeleton key for the bedrooms. Both the cleaners and the security team had one, so there was a chance one might still be in the building.

'I'll be with you in a minute,' Charlie said, not looking up.

The two of them waited for him in the atrium while he finished his breakfast.

'Why him?' Elle said, a little surprised until she realised choosing any of the others would have been just as odd.

Benji smiled. 'He's the one who scares me least. And, I shouldn't admit this, but sometimes he sort of sounds like he knows what he's talking about. We might need allies. And he's not had a headache that we know of.'

'No, not yet. But really? Charlie?'

'Well, we've got pepper spray, just in case.'

Elle patted her side where the canister was hidden beneath a loose top.

Charlie was still chewing when he appeared. 'What's the plan?'

The three of them made their way towards the stairs. 'I wanted some extra muscle and expertise,' Benji said. 'Ted might still be in there, and I really don't want another Harrison situation on our hands.'

Charlie nodded.

Some rooms, including the staff bedrooms and medical offices, remained inaccessible. But they searched the staff room, the cupboards Benji's keys could open, and behind the reception desk, but found no keys. This left them with the grim task of checking Paul's body, which Charlie volunteered to do without blinking an eye, asserting his constitution was better cut out for it due to his military experiences. He was in and out of the medical room where Paul's body lay in less than a minute.

'Negative,' he said, shaking his head. He touched the handle and let go of it again, blinking as he did so. Had it been for just a little bit longer than a normal blink, wince-like even, or was Elle imagining things now?

'We could climb up to the balcony,' Elle said. 'Maybe his patio doors are open.'

'Worth a try,' Benji said, and to cover his tracks, he added, 'Is it possible, though? To get up that way?'

'It…uh…might be, you know,' Charlie said, also eager to hide his own clambering antics from Benji, although he sounded distant. He definitely looked just a fraction paler than he usually did, too.

'Are you okay?' Elle asked Charlie.

He turned to her sharply. 'I'm top of the line, Elle. I'm just reassessing things based on the new information we have. I didn't expect,' his eyes flicked to the medical room door and back, 'things to happen quite like this.'

'You mean… Are you talking about your whole trial conspiracy again?' Elle said.

'Conspiracy? No. I have a healthy scepticism. As always, Elle. Nothing more, nothing less.'

'But what, you watched what happened to Paul and still thought it wasn't…real or something?'

'It wasn't out the question, but…I don't…'

'Is he serious?' Benji said, eyes bulging.

'I don't know what to think, alright?' His shout echoed in the confines of the corridor. Benji and Elle stared at him.

Finally, Benji said, 'Come on, let's try the balcony.'

7

Elle waited with Charlie while Benji used the rails on the lower balcony to climb up to the one above. He made no real effort to conceal that he was quite practised at the routine, but Charlie had long since vanished into his own world. Again he winced, or perhaps he was just squinting from the sun. She didn't like being out here alone with him. She reached to touch the pepper spray.

'You *sure* you feel okay?' she asked Charlie, stepping into the shade of a tall palm. Up above came the hollow conks of Benji rapping on the glass.

'Stop asking me that, Elle.'

Benji shouted down. 'I can't see him. I'm going to try the door. Yeah, it's open. Ted, are you in? He's not here. Do you two want to come around to the front?'

Elle began to walk to the back door, but Charlie decided anything Benji could do, he could do better. He sprung up onto the lower balcony rail and grabbed the bars above. He was pulling himself up when his hand lost its grip. He fell, the back of his legs striking the top of the rail he'd been standing on. Somehow he managed to grip the rail with his hands, and the rest of his fall was clumsy and slow.

'Jesus,' Elle said, running over.

'I'm okay,' he yelled, getting to his feet immediately. He shook his head, cursing under his breath.

'Do you want to just—'

But he was already making his way up again, this time pulling himself up without an issue. By the time Elle arrived using the stairs, the door had been opened for her. She pretended not to notice that Charlie was limping around Ted's immaculate room, pulling open drawers and looking under the bed like nothing had happened.

'He's gone,' Benji said.

'Is there any sign of trouble or anything?'

'It's spotless,' Benji said. 'Either he went voluntarily or someone's done a great job of cleaning up.'

'This is weird, Benji.' Elle spoke so Charlie couldn't hear. 'Where is he? Where are they all going?'

'I don't know. Maybe they found civilisation.'

'You know,' Elle said, watching Charlie continue his rampage around Ted's room, 'that really doesn't sound like a bad plan at this point.'

'No, it doesn't,' Benji said.

'You still thinking about that inquest?' He nodded. 'Some

of them will walk at some point, Benji. If not today, tomorrow. If we want to keep things chill and keep your conscience clean, maybe we should make a safe plan to search the surrounding terrain.'

He didn't look happy, but he'd clearly run out of counter-arguments.

'His trial diary's not here,' Charlie said, mainly to himself. 'Where's his diary gone? Why would he take it?'

8

Back in the canteen, they shared their findings with the others. Charlie sat next to Mai and began whispering in her ear while she nodded along, staring at Elle. The rest of them looked pensive and muttered about how Ted hadn't been acting like himself in the last few days.

Eventually, Benji addressed them all again. 'All of you are free to do what you want now. I've shown you the terrain, and I've shared with you what I know, so I'm not going to stop anyone if you want to do your own thing at this point. But I think we should stick together and give the others time to get back. For the time being, we can search this place for phones or other ways we can contact the outside world, without having to trek into the wilderness.'

'Internet is down,' Constantine said. 'It was working yesterday.'

Elle put her head in her hands, and the comment caught Benji off guard, making him pause. Given there were already strong restrictions on the internet, why would one of the trial staff have gone to the additional trouble of turning it off entirely on leaving? Unless they were worried that one of those left might be capable of bypassing the firewall. Someone with IT skills. Someone like Harrison.

'There might be a 4G signal or an old landline,' Benji eventually said. 'I think we should try to find a phone first, because for all we know, we could be ten miles from civilisation. Twenty. Thirty. Besides, imagine you get to the horizon, and you get lucky and find a town.' He was looking at Gee. 'Then the cavalry turn up here and you've gone.'

'The police, you mean?' Gee said. 'I've got nothing to say to that lot. I didn't kick anyone's head in.'

'Yeah, that's not our problem,' Dale said.

'Okay, but say you're out having fun, eating your fry-ups somewhere, and we can't find you. How are you going to get home if Apollo Wellbeing want to fly us back tonight?'

No one spoke, and Elle sensed he might finally be getting through. If the drug was having any effect on them in the way she'd theorised, he was right to focus on what they stood to gain from all this.

'Could we just give it until tomorrow, at least?' Elle said. 'Then if they're not here by the end of the day, we can get an early night, go out first thing and see if we have any luck out there. If we find nothing, we can get back before the worst of the sun.'

'What about Harrison?' Everyone turned to Becks. 'We can't leave him here alone. You have to let him come with us.'

'Fuck that and dip it in brown sauce,' Gee said.

'We can't do that, Becks,' Benji said. 'You saw what he did. But we wouldn't leave him alone either.'

'I'll stay with him, then. I don't want to risk my ankle again, anyway.'

Gee blurted out a laugh that resembled a bark. 'Nice try, you waste.'

'What?' Becks's complaint sounded like a child's. 'I wouldn't uncuff him or anything.'

'I'm happy to watch the prick,' Constantine said. Shocked

by the vehemence, Elle looked at him and caught a smile receding into his face.

'Hey,' Becks said, 'you shouldn't call him that.'

Constantine shrugged as if he didn't understand what he'd done wrong. 'I've got no interest in going outside. Someone will come for us eventually. We've got food and water, haven't we?'

Benji nodded. 'There's enough canned goods and frozen stuff to see out a solid apocalypse in there. Provided we have electricity, which, judging by the solar panels on the roof, I think is likely.'

'Good. Then let's do that.' Constantine turned and departed.

'Does anyone else have any major objections to sticking it out just until tomorrow, then?' Benji said. 'Gee, obviously you're free to go, as I said before. I can't make you stay. And you, Dale, if that's what you want to do.'

'I can wait,' Becks said. 'I'm really tired anyway. I think I need a lie down.'

'You okay?' Elle said, noticing the skin around her eyes appeared swollen.

'I was up late.'

'I'm not surprised.'

She shrugged. 'I always find it hard to sleep in the heat.'

'What about you two?' Benji said to Charlie and Mai. 'You're both pretty quiet.'

'I don't like any of it,' Charlie said. 'And I think the sooner we get away from here, the better. But you're right about the logistics. Makes sense to do a reccy tomorrow morning. And in this terrain, we don't want to be out after dark. Liable to break an ankle.'

'Or worse,' Mai said.

'Maybe I *should* stay here then,' Becks said.

'No one trusts you staying here,' Charlie said, 'and we'd

have a lot more sympathy for you if you hadn't been dancing around this place like a ballerina the last week.'

'Fuck you, Columbine.' Becks got up, flicked two fingers at him and walked off.

'Well whatever,' Gee said, 'I'm still going to go for a bit of a walk out the front now. I've got water. I've got a hat. I need to see something different. I could have been doing the three peaks instead of this shit.'

'That's fine,' Benji said. 'But just, you know, don't wander too far. If you did fall and hurt yourself or something...'

'You don't need to worry about her,' Dale said. 'She's the toughest person here. She's hiked Kilimanjaro. She's camped with Kodiak bears in Alaska.'

Charlie sniffed at this, but he said nothing. Benji made a perfectly passable *Is that so?* face and said, 'Well, good to know. Sounds like those skills might be quite useful.'

When they had left, Benji turned to Charlie and Mai.

'Do you want to help us search the building? There's at least one phone on the premises for emergencies. There's back-ups for everything in the kitchen and the store cupboard, so maybe there's another phone. Did you find anything else on Paul, Charlie?'

'Yes, I found a phone and didn't tell you.'

Benji didn't rise to Charlie's sarcasm.

'We'll help,' Mai said, and patted Charlie's hand.

'I need to check on Dr Lineker, too. If possible, maybe erect some sort of...cover. From the weather and stuff.'

'Can't we just bring him up here?' Mai said.

'Well,' Benji said, 'even if I had it in me, which I don't think I do, I think he needs to be left for the police to look at. Doesn't he?'

'You really think they're coming?' Charlie said.

'I hope so.'

'You believe an island like this has a police force?'

'What do you mean?'

'We're not on Lanzarote, Benji.' Charlie smiled at him, as if he was dealing with a child who still believed in Santa. 'I can help with him, though. If we do your building search first, we might find something useful. If not, there are some heavy-duty bags holding the balls in the cupboards. We could repurpose those. Make an evidence tent. I have experience.'

9

The four of them searched the parts of the building they could access. They found nothing except a black sheet of paint-stained tarpaulin stuffed at the back of a cleaning cupboard. Most of the doors remained locked, and without a key there wasn't much hope of getting inside.

'These are serious,' Charlie said, examining one of the doors. 'Four-centimetre timber. Hour-long fire rated. We'd need tools to get through.' He gave the one to Dr Lineker's office a kick anyway before shaking his head.

They were on their way outside when they ran into Gee and Dale coming in through the front door. Both looked out of breath.

'How was your walk?' Elle said.

'Good,' Gee said, eyeing the tarpaulin but saying nothing about it. 'Saw a goat.'

They walked off in the direction of the entertainment corridor, while the other four left through the back door. As a group they descended to the beach, the hollow sound of the staircase a comforting distraction from their isolation. Hallie might still be down here. Might still be dangerous.

Elle didn't want to see Dr Lineker again, and Benji had tried to dissuade her from coming. But she didn't want to be alone and wanted to be useful. Even though she nearly gave up when Mai made a comment about there being so many flies, she helped cover the body and pin down the tarpaulin with rocks.

Mai turned the conversation to lunch once they were back in the main compound, and, despite having no appetite, Elle offered to cook. Benji helped her, and they served up toast and eggs in trays on the front counter and invited the others to come and help themselves. One-by-one the central canteen table filled up with the remaining participants.

Elle forced herself to eat something before she and Benji took eggs and toast to Harrison – providing a spoon rather than a knife and fork, and serving it in a plastic bowl so he couldn't smash a plate to make a weapon. He still sat where he'd been before, and once again Elle couldn't help but feel pity and regret. That only worsened when Benji slid the bowl across the tiles to him, and it tipped over, spilling toast on the floor in the process.

'No butter?' Harrison said.

'I could go back and—'

Benji cut Elle off. 'No. We'll come back for the bowl in a bit.'

Harrison smiled as if he understood, and picked up the toast from the floor and put it in his mouth.

Elle was already out in the corridor when Harrison said, 'Can I have my pill please?'

Benji stopped and turned to face him. 'Harrison, you're not on the trial anymore.'

He wasn't impressed with that. 'Do I get a say?'

'It's not a democracy. And even if it was, I don't think you're eligible to vote.'

'What difference does it make to you if I take them or not?'

'No,' Benji said and walked through the door.

'Have you told her you've got a girlfriend yet?'

Benji stopped just before the door shut, and Elle wanted to shrink. She caught something on his face; perhaps it was guilt, or perhaps it was merely a reaction to whatever was happening on her face. He re-entered the toilet.

'What are you talking about?' Benji said.

'Look, I don't know what your problem is with me. Maybe it's a class thing. Maybe it's a race thing. Or maybe you didn't like me muscling in on Elle when we got here. But you should be honest with her. Tell her about your girlfriend.'

'I literally have no idea what you're talking about, but any feelings I had about you were pretty neutral until you did what you did upstairs.'

'Then why won't you let me have a pill?'

'Why does it even matter?'

'You know.'

'Honestly, I do not.'

'Benji,' Elle said, 'let's go.' He didn't appear to hear her. It was strange to watch, because she knew he was messing with them both. Trying to exploit a situation based solely on an intuition he had about the two of them. His only power was psychological. And despite that, she knew she had to ask Benji later. Worse, she knew that even if he said he didn't have a girlfriend, Harrison's idea was in her head permanently now. At least until she had proof.

'You don't like me,' Harrison said, 'so you don't want me to get my money. That's why you won't let me have the pill.'

'Are you serious?'

'Our contracts are clear, we have to take the pills until the last day of the trial. If I see it through, they have to pay me my money.'

'We are so far beyond that now.'

'If I keep up my end of the bargain, minus the time you've

had me down here, legally they won't have a leg to stand on.'

'Legally? Mate, what do you think they're going to make of what you did? Legally.'

'I have proof it was an accident. Don't worry about that. So can I have my pill, please?'

'No. I'll be back for the bowl.'

'Elle, you heard that. He denied me the pill. I wanted it but he declined. Now, ask him about his girlfriend.'

The door closed. The entire time during the conversation Harrison had remained calm. Reasonable sounding. Had she not seen it for herself, she wouldn't have believed him capable of beating a man to death.

'Think it's safe to say the pills are still in his system,' Elle said, hoping Benji might smile.

To her relief, he did. 'Don't believe anything he said. It's utter bullshit. Last girlfriend I had was a year ago, and we broke up. Couldn't make it work with all my travelling. You know he was trying to mess with us.'

She looked into his eyes. And surprisingly, she did believe him. Completely. 'I know. But he knows how to get in your head.'

10

The canteen had been vacated. Used plates, glasses and cutlery lay discarded on the tables.

'Those utter dicks,' Benji said. 'I should drag them back here.'

'Don't bother,' Elle said, picking up the nearest sauce-stained plate and salving her own irritation by planning what they might cook tonight if they were still there.

That outcome crept closer as the afternoon wore on and the last of the daylight ebbed away. The others appeared restless, the atrium busy with their back and forth. A few took the fibreglass chairs from the canteen and set them up on the road outside the gate to keep a lookout.

At one point Elle found Mai looking lost, and when she asked what she was doing, Mai replied that she was on the hunt for Charlie's suitcase. Apparently someone had gone into his unlocked room, packed up all his clothes, and hidden it somewhere.

'Someone's played a prank?' Elle said, incredulous.

'Yeah. Charlie's not happy.'

She couldn't even begin to unpick the mind of someone who could do that in these circumstances. But then again, this trial did funny things to you, didn't it? Which she knew all too well, because the question she was about to ask Mai, now that she had her alone, spoke volumes about how low things had sunk.

'Mai, what you said to me that day we were on the balcony,' she lowered her voice, 'about your real job. Was it true?'

Mai made a spy-like show of surveying her surroundings before leaning in and saying, 'I can't talk about it here. Let's go outside.'

Elle followed Mai to the pool, which was deserted. Mai kept walking though, and despite the anxiety it provoked in her, Elle followed her down the steps to the lower patio. She was about to ask Mai if they could go back up, when Mai said:

'Yes, it's true about my real job.'

'So is there anything you can do, maybe? To get a message out.'

'Oh,' Mai said, her expression becoming deadly serious. 'My colleagues will step in if necessary.'

She nodded to Elle, and made a face as if she expected a response. Elle nodded back, wishing she'd never asked, cringing inwardly at having been reduced to this. Mai was wearing a small leather bag around her neck, and she reached to open it. From inside she retrieved a spiky green leaf of what looked like aloe. Mai stepped forward and pulled Elle into an awkward hug. She put her mouth to Elle's ear, and like they had been dear old friends for many, many years, she whispered slowly, 'We'll all be fine.'

Then she stepped back and grinned. No pleasure shone from her eyes. She raised the aloe and pretended to cut Elle's throat while making a playful slicing sound. 'You're dead, Elle.'

For a second she had no idea what Mai was talking about. Then it struck her, a cold and clear comprehension. She was still playing Cluedo.

Mai stepped back and clapped her hands, delighted. 'Who was yours? Who was it? It was Ricoh, wasn't it? It has to be.'

Elle hadn't thought about the game in a long time. It took her a moment to answer. 'Yes.'

'Then I win.' She spun around, ran at Elle and kissed her cheek, despite Elle's attempt to step away. 'Fantastic.'

The two of them looked at one another, Mai still grinning, Elle open-mouthed. What was *wrong* with her? Who could still be playing the game after everything that—

'Mai,' Elle said. 'Can I ask you something?'

'About my job?'

'No. No, it's…like one of Dr Lineker's questions.'

Mai grimaced. 'Really?'

She told Mai about the handsome man at the girl's mum's funeral. And at the end of the story, she asked, 'So why did she kill her sister?'

Mai made a disgusted face. 'I'm sorry, but I didn't really follow that. Why was her mum dead? And to be honest with you, I'm sort of bored, now the game's over. Let's go back so I can tell Charlie I won.'

Elle nodded, and as she was leaving, Mai said, 'Don't look like that. Everything will be fine.'

And for the first time, Elle wasn't truly sure it would be.

11

For a brief moment before dinner it appeared the prank on Charlie might escalate. Gee and Dale had been the prime suspects, and Charlie and Dale almost came to blows after an argument on the front drive. Eventually Benji convinced Charlie to cool off in his room, and offered the others a crate of beers if they returned his things.

'But the guy is such an arse,' Gee had said in a sulk.

Within an hour, the suitcase reappeared, and to Elle's relief no one demanded Benji open up the whole bar to them. There would be little he could do to stop them if they did.

When they had returned to the safety of the canteen, Benji's hands were shaking.

'You okay?' she asked.

'Holding it together,' he said with a series of small head shakes.

Elle made a giant pasta bake for everyone with Benji's assistance, and by the time they were done eating it was past 8 p.m., at which point no one believed anyone would be coming for them today.

'Let's get an early night,' Benji said. 'I suggest we get going at sunrise. If we can get in here to eat by six thirty, we'll get a good few hours before the heat becomes too intense. Does that sound good?'

'Roger,' Charlie said, as if he alone had been asked. 'I think we should head for the landing strip. There might be communications equipment of use there. Or even vehicles.'

'What if there's a plane?' Mai said, sounding excited. 'Could you fly us off the island?'

'Yes. I could.'

'Oh for fuck's sake,' Gee said, as Dale laughed.

'I *think*,' Benji said, 'the main thing we need to establish is, just where we are and how we might alert people to our situation. And what I'd suggest is that we follow the roads as a starting point. We should also have an agreed time limit on how far we go and when we turn around. That way, we all stay safe and don't end up dehydrated and in a worse state than we are already. I think we stand a better chance if we split up.'

'Benji,' Charlie said, 'all due respect, but the likelihood of communications equipment at the landing strip is high. We can use a radio and get people to come and get us.'

'I'm not disagreeing with you,' he said, 'but there might be a town three miles east. And we should cover as much ground as we can, just in case we don't find anything.'

'What's the big deal about the sun?' Gee said. 'If we want to keep walking and searching, why can't we? It's not like we're in Iraq or something.'

Gee's face had been an uncomfortable shade of red since the first few days of the trial. If it bothered her, she never let on. If Elle had suffered that type of sunburn she would have been bathing in aftersun lotion for days.

'Gee, I can't make you do anything,' Benji said, 'but my suggestion is, stay cautious. Don't go so far that you can't turn back. Don't run out of water. If you get into trouble, we don't have the resources to mount any sort of rescue. So until we know more, let's just…keep safe.'

'This is a fact-finding mission, people,' Charlie said, clapping his hands. 'This isn't our exit.'

'Oh, give it a rest,' Gee said.

Chapter Thirteen

1

Benji woke the group at 6:30 a.m. with coffees. By the time they had all assembled in the front garden it was gone seven, and soft sunlight had begun to beat back the darkness. Gee turned up in shorts and one of her short-sleeved Hawaiian shirts, and was packed full of barely contained excitement. She didn't bring a hat, and between her and Dale they only had one bottle of water in a shared bag. When Becks arrived, the last one out and half asleep, Benji pushed the cause of sun-appropriate clothing before it became apparent no one was going change their mind. They said farewell to Constantine, who had agreed to stay behind and feed Harrison in their absence, and set off.

Just beyond the front gate they stopped. The air was still but cold, and Elle could feel goose bumps beneath the fabric of her hoodie. She wore her backpack, containing factor fifty, three bottles of water, and crisps and nutrition bars from one of the vending machines. She'd soon warm up once the hiking began.

'Charlie is going to follow the road back to the airport and beyond, west of here,' Benji said, 'and I'm going to head right and check out the east coast. So it's really up to you who you'd like to go with at this point.'

Mai, of course, stepped towards Charlie. But Elle was surprised when Gee and Dale did. Benji's expression hardened at this.

'I remember another road going away from the airport,' Gee said. 'Why would it be there if it didn't go somewhere?'

'Sounds good,' Benji said.

Elle shrugged and went to stand beside Benji. Which left Becks, who made a show of being agonised, throwing her weight from one of her skinny legs to the other, before pointing at Charlie.

'Sorry, Benji, babe. I just like the sound of the airport.'

'You don't have to apologise.' He looked at Elle, and she could tell he suspected they were missing something. Were they all deliberately separating from Benji, the last remaining authority figure?

'Everyone just keep an eye on the time, then. Back here no later than 1 p.m., the earlier, the better. It looks like it's going to be a clear day again.' He looked up at the cloudless sky. 'And if someone isn't back by 3 p.m., we assume the worst. Everyone agreed on that?'

Everyone murmured their assent, and the two teams split apart across the rocky ground, to meet where their road curved around the wall of the building. Once they were following the slope of the road towards the ocean, the other team now out of sight, Benji smiled at her.

'Worked out okay.'

'You think? I feel like they're up to something.'

Benji shrugged. 'We can't fight them. And if we stay locked in there any longer…'

He reached down and squeezed her hand. The road straightened to track the coast, and an egg-yolk sun burned just above the horizon. Under different circumstances it might have been romantic.

2

The road ran along the coast high above the sea for over a mile. They passed a field of solar panels but little else before the paved section abruptly ended. They stopped, and Benji walked up and down the line where the tarmac gave way to rocks and dirt.

'Damn it,' he said.

'Well, at least we know now.'

Pointing to faint tyre tracks in the soil, Benji said, 'Looks like someone kept driving this way and came back again. Do you want to keep going, or should we turn back?'

Convinced this couldn't be all there was, she said, 'I'm fine pressing on. There still might be something here.'

They followed a vague dirt road, the ground crunching beneath them. After another half a mile the sea appeared to be getting further from them, and the land started to tilt downwards. The tyre tracks had gone now, and to call what they were on anything but desert would have been a stretch.

Elle had dressed sensibly in jeans and trainers, while the hat Harrison had liked covered her head. She wore her hair over her ears and neck, while her face was greasy with sun cream. Still, she felt the sun warming up the backs of her hands and the front of her neck.

It hadn't occurred to her until she'd got out here just how trapped she'd felt before. That she'd been functioning with a low-level aggravation at being confined with the others. That didn't mean she was comfortable out here either, though. The relative freedom of the island brought its own emotions. Out here, they were sitting ducks. Her eyes played tricks on her. Rocks and foliage and shadows took on aspects of people in the otherwise homogenous landscape. Like her over-stimulated twenty-first-century brain couldn't cope with the sheer perceptual monotony and so created entertainment for her.

At one point, and she kept this to herself, she thought she saw Hallie sitting by a distant rock, watching them. She'd had to squint and stare for a long time before she realised what she was looking at was another goat, fur the same browny-orange as the rock it stood next to. In her chest her heart drummed the beat of panic, and the adrenaline remained coursing through her body for almost an hour after. It was all too easy to imagine someone sneaking up on them, even though they were surrounded by emptiness and in full daylight.

They'd been walking for two hours, covering somewhere between four and six miles, when up ahead the land dipped again to reveal the sea directly ahead of them, as well as to their right. Some way off still was the corner of whatever landmass this was.

'There's nothing, is there?' Benji said.

'And so now we know that. Which is important.'

Benji walked ahead a little bit, hands pressing into his eyes. He walked in a circle, kicked the ground, and returned to her, looking defeated.

'Just where the hell are we?' Benji said. 'There's no ships in the sea, we never hear any low planes, there's no buildings. I feel like such an idiot for not asking more questions when I got the job.'

'I'm sure we all feel a bit like that.'

He was wavering, desperation at the edge of his voice. Elle

knew then, for certain, that Benji wasn't part of whatever was happening now. Her doubts had never been big, but they had lingered enough for her to hold something of herself back. Even now. But she saw how foolish that was, because the man in front of her was genuine. Genuinely lost. Genuinely scared. Genuinely in need of her.

'Benji,' she said, 'can I tell you something?'

'You've not got a headache, have you?'

'No. Not that. No. It's a confession.' She inhaled deeply. Honesty was the best policy, that's what Granny Alice always said. 'I'm sorry I didn't tell you before, but I shouldn't be here on this trial. I'm a fraud.'

He straightened his back, and appraised her warily. 'What do you mean?'

She took another breath, and told him everything. About her mum scamming her, about getting drunk, about taking the questionnaire and having possibly made up the answers.

'I just kept…kept thinking they'd find me out eventually. That if there was that much money on the line, there was no way I'd slip through.'

He didn't react at first, and when he did finally, he laughed. She didn't know how to take it, but smiled in the hope this was a good thing. Although, even as she was telling him, she burned with shame.

'So you don't actually know whether you lied on the test,' he said, 'you just think you did?'

'No, I'm… I don't know. I don't actually remember it. But on some level I remember… I was so angry with my mum about what she'd done. And I came across this quiz on her Facebook page. I think I was answering…sort of, pretending to be her. Putting in answers…' She gritted her teeth in a grimace. '…I thought she might choose. But, you know – in, like, a mean way.'

'And it worked.'

'And it worked.'

'Wow.' He laughed again.

'Don't laugh.' She was starting to feel ridiculous.

'Sorry, I don't mean to.'

'No, I'm apologising to *you*. Be angry or something. You must think I'm horrible.'

'I don't care. If this lot couldn't even get their selection right, it serves them right. If anything, it's funny, because you're such a nice person. Like, completely genuine and thoughtful and considerate.' Elle's breath caught. 'But you've got a dark side, too. I approve.'

'I feel better for telling you,' she said.

'Thanks for doing it. But it doesn't…change anything. All it does is make me realise this trial is even more of a shit show than I thought it was.'

3

They pushed on for another ten minutes, hoping to catch a glimpse further down the new stretch of the visible east coast. Nothing they saw changed their minds about the likelihood of finding civilisation, and, wanting to be back for the deadline, they retreated with the sun on their backs.

The tarmac eventually came back into view in the distance, appearing like a strip of liquorice on a bed of orange sherbet. It wasn't long after this that the tyre tracks they'd initially followed returned. The pattern of the tread appeared fuzzy, but not indistinct, like it had been driven over in both directions.

'Did you notice when these came back?' Elle said.

'Nope.'

'So they must have stopped somewhere. Why would

someone come all this way out here in a vehicle if there isn't anything here?'

They retraced the tyre tracks to a point at which they veered away from what Elle and Benji had treated like a dirt road. The tracks faded here, the flattening of a small incline running along their route exposing them to the coastal winds, but leaving the road and walking towards the sea, they picked up the tracks again. Possibly some sort of port or lighthouse or desalination facility might sit out of sight further down the coast. Perhaps with communication equipment. Although surely there would be more tyre tracks if that were true.

The ocean loomed ahead of them, the land tilting skyward as the edge approached. Here the tyre tracks turned around and lined up with themselves once more.

'There's nothing here,' Elle said.

'Maybe someone came here for the view. Someone from the facility who wanted a break.'

'Maybe.'

Elle walked towards the cliff edge, driven by intuition and curiosity.

'Careful,' Benji said, the sound of his voice indicating that he was coming up behind her. The wind blew more forcefully here, and it was easy to imagine a sideways gust surprising her and throwing her off balance.

The land ended with a rounded ledge of rock, its texture scab-like. Elle leaned forward slowly and it was immediately clear they were at least a hundred metres above where the ocean slapped the sides of the island. She peered further over, able to see a small shelf of rock two thirds of the way down, which staircased sharply into the water below.

Lying face-up, just short of the ocean, was a body, its middle rounded in an unnatural way, a dark, discoloured ring haloing out from the head.

'Oh, Jesus, Benji.'

She turned abruptly.

'What is it?' he said.

'I think it's Ricoh.'

4

They walked back in silence. Elle couldn't shake what she'd seen, and flitted between tears and nausea when the image of Ricoh's body returned.

Eventually they talked. About what they'd seen and what might have happened. It was possible that Ricoh walked out of the facility and followed the road, and even the tracks, out to that point and jumped off. Yet that didn't seem likely somehow. Ricoh had left at night, and once the tarmac ended the tracks would have been difficult to see. Which meant someone had driven Ricoh out to that point and either made him jump, pushed him, or threw his already dead body over. The tyre tracks looked the right width apart to match the minibus, and the way it turned suggested someone had unloaded something from the back.

Before they'd gone they had scoured the area and found faded shoeprints around the vehicle tyre tracks. Most were patchy or too faded to be useful. None were visible on the rockier section leading up to the cliff.

But two prints at different locations had left faint heel imprints, and at the centre was a four-pointed star.

It wasn't much to go on, and asking to check everyone's shoes would create exactly the sort of confrontation they wanted to avoid. But if there was a way to match them, they would at least know whom they needed to keep at a distance. Or perhaps even contain, if they weren't contained already.

'We should check Harrison's things,' Benji said, the

warming wind beginning to build now. 'He was so angry with Ricoh the night before. He thought that he was going to get everyone sent home. If the pills were affecting his decisions, his conscience, he might have done it to make sure the trial kept going and he got his money. He probably reasoned we'd all think Ricoh had gone off on his own, given that he wanted to leave anyway.'

'Well, yeah, it's exactly what we did.'

Once the wall around the complex came into view, embedded in the rock like some alien sculpture, they never seemed to get closer. Elle increased her pace, and when they finally reached the point where the road curved around to the front of the building, she was out of breath and sweaty.

They climbed the steps and entered the building, and plunging into the wall of cool air in the atrium gave Elle a blissful chill. But pleasant feelings were short-lived, pushed aside by a merciless slug of fear.

Sitting behind the reception desk, smiling at them, was Harrison.

'Hello, hello,' he said, 'welcome back. Where's everyone else?'

The two of them stood staring until Benji stepped forward. 'Coming. Where's Constantine?'

'Somewhere.' Harrison shrugged. In addition to the healing cuts and bruises on his face, a necklace of dark bruising marked his neck. It hadn't been there the last time they had seen him. 'Look, I don't want things to be awkward, okay? So what do you say, shall the three of us have a talk? Clear the air. I promise I'm not after revenge or anything.'

'That's fine, Harrison,' Benji said, holding up his hands. 'Do you want to talk with me first, leave Elle out of it?'

'No, of course not. Boring. No, come on, you don't need to worry about me or anything. Like I told you, what happened with Paul…it was complicated. If you let me explain. But you don't have to worry. No.'

He stepped out from behind the desk and made his way towards them. Just as Dr Lineker and Jess had done on the first night. This was *his* trial now. In his left hand he held a short bat, the sort used to play rounders at school. Dark streaks stained its tip. A pepper spray can was clipped to his belt.

'Where do you want to talk?' Benji said.

He mulled on this. 'The bar. I was hoping you could open up, maybe pour me a whisky.'

5

Having no choice, Benji and Elle followed Harrison to the bar. At the door Benji asked him to leave the bat outside.

'Is it unsettling you? Sorry.' He put it down on the floor. 'I wasn't sure what was happening exactly, so I didn't know what might be waiting for me upstairs. It was very quiet. You have to trust me that I'm not interested in harming you. I actually think we need to stick together.'

Benji used his key to open the door. He ushered Elle in first, putting himself between her and Harrison.

'Elle, would you mind getting Harrison's whisky?' Benji said.

It took her a moment to understand why he'd asked, but it was clear he wanted to keep her far away from him. She nodded and went to pour his drink, a whisky bottle and tumbler falling into her eyeline at first scan. Was it the real thing, or one of the watered-down drinks? She had no idea, and nothing on the bottle helped her decide. At Harrison's request, she added ice from the machine.

Once again she found herself believing Harrison when he said he didn't want to hurt them. Which was madness, given what they knew about him. Yet whatever rage had possessed him to kill Paul wasn't here today. That didn't mean he might not turn at any minute, but it did dampen her fear. He sounded different too, more lucid, more…genuine. Could it mean the drugs might be wearing off? He still didn't sound particularly remorseful.

She pocketed a small corkscrew. Both she and Benji still carried cans of pepper spray, as they'd done since things had nosedived. She had no idea if she had it in her to use either of these weapons, given her track record in conflict situations. But if she could hold on to that mental image of Ricoh's body without being overwhelmed, she might be able to do it. She certainly felt better holding them.

She took the whisky to Harrison, who now sat with Benji at a small table at the back of the bar. She sat down too, glancing down at his bloody shoes. He had them firmly planted on the floor, so she couldn't see the soles. He took a sip, smiled at the ceiling, and after a sniff, gulped down the rest. He asked again about where they'd been, and they told him about their search.

'Why would you do that?' Harrison said.

'Because the staff left to get help. A few of the others didn't want to wait for them, so we compromised and agreed to search for some way of communicating our situation.'

'What's our situation then?'

Benji paused. 'I think we'll have a better idea when the others get back, which should be soon. Where is Constantine?'

'Ah,' he said, and shook his head. 'I've got a lot to tell you, actually. I've been busy. I think you really need to know about Paul, because I think you'll trust me more once you understand.'

'For now, I'm the only staff member on site, so I need to establish the wellbeing and safety of everyone. Where is he, and we can talk afterwards?'

It didn't seem likely that they would ever trust him, but Elle wanted to know what it was he supposedly knew about Paul. It frustrated her that Benji kept shutting him down. Looking back on it, hadn't there been something odd about the argument Paul and Harrison had had that day? Some tension hidden beneath the words just before everything exploded. It lent Harrison's claim credibility.

Harrison dwelled on this and eventually shook his head. 'That won't work. Come on, it won't take that long for me to show you.'

6

They followed Harrison back to the hall. Benji walked unnaturally, shoulders held back as if he was trying to make himself as tall as possible. The friendly atmosphere between them was fragile.

'You two go around the front of the desk. I'll spin the screen around.'

Harrison took his position in the office seat, and brought up the screen which displayed all the security camera footage.

'How did you know the password?' Elle said.

'Paul was an idiot. I watched him putting in his extremely unsecure password more than once. Not exactly ideal behaviour for a security professional. But that's just the tip of the iceberg.'

He opened a folder, and several video icons appeared. He clicked on one, which showed one of the corridors from above the doorway to the atrium.

'You can see the date on it,' Harrison said. 'And the time. This is just after the drugs went missing.'

Crystal-clear footage showed Paul walking up to the door to Dr Lineker's room, looking around, and going inside. The door was swinging shut when Harrison appeared running down the corridor, stopping the door from closing, stepping inside.

'It was Paul who took the pills,' Harrison said. 'I caught him in the act, trying to put them back the night after they found out. Waited up all bloody night to do it and watched him from the landing. Paul wasn't a very happy employee, and if you got him drunk enough he'd tell you how he'd worked for Apollo's parent company for twenty years but they didn't treat him right. No pay rise in a decade. Messed with his pension. Bad hours. No respect. He'd also tell you about his problem with gambling apps and booze, if you knew what to ask.

'What made me suspicious, though, was that I offered to take a look at the broken security system. IT is my background and the worst that could happen was that it would stay broken. But he was very adamant I didn't look at it. Very insistent that he had it all under control. But I knew Monique didn't believe him because she kept raising her eyebrows. Which made me think, why would he be lying about the security cameras inter-mittently blanking out and failing?'

'You're saying he sabotaged it deliberately?' Elle said.

'I'll get to that.'

'Okay, but why did you confess to taking them?'

'Well, Paul offered me a deal once I'd made it clear I was on to him. Paul thought I was a man who appreciated the value of money, and after getting a bit blubbery, he offered to pay me my trial fee if I kept quiet, given the trial looked like it might be over now he'd been caught. It was a good deal, and he would get to keep his job, but I offered him one better. I suspected that had he just returned the pills anonymously, the trial would still have been mothballed because of their worries about data breaches and trial bias. However, if I came forward, and gave them a convincing enough story about why I took them, they might keep me on *and* keep the trial going. That way, I was playing for double my fee if I sold the lie, and I told Paul he'd get to steal his pills. Worst case, I got 20K, which is definitely Glynn Rogers money. But best case – 40K – and Glynn Rogers is sucking my dick.'

'And you trusted Paul, then?'

'Why wouldn't I? He'd clearly stolen the pills, and was in a panic that they'd deduce it was him, for some reason. That's why he was trying to put them back, hoping they'd recount and just assume that they'd made an error.'

'Why was he stealing the drugs?'

'I didn't ask, because I didn't care. I got the impression another company had a tip-off about this pill they're making and paid him off to get some. He told me he was worried because he'd sold info on before, and got a few other people fired when the leaks were discovered. If they put things together, having uncovered his latest theft, which he just hadn't banked on, suspicion might fall on his previous cover-ups as well. I got the impression that this was supposed to be his last big job, but he got cocky.'

'This is all guesswork though, right?' Benji said.

'Not all. Why else would he be taking pills from a trial this secretive?' Harrison's voice remained level and vaguely bored.

'I don't understand,' Benji said. 'If you stood to gain 20K from him, why did you…fight with him?'

'Well, you weren't there, but Elle was. I was doing my best to make sure we all got our money from these bastards, and he saw a chance to get rid of me. He was going to try and do me to get out of it. Stitch me up, or possibly worse. I mean, you heard him. Didn't you?'

Elle didn't know what he meant. 'It all happened so fast, I—'

'He saw me making my stand and clearly decided to use it to get rid of me. I could see it on his face. He was going to get into a fight and kill me. He was smart. I'd have done the same in his shoes. He made it look like I came at him, but really he came at me, didn't he, Elle?'

'Yeah, maybe.'

Elle wasn't sure she had seen or heard any such thing, although she had done her best to forget as much as she could about that day. She didn't want to contradict him, and so instead changed the subject. 'Can you get any other footage up? Can you find out where Hallie went?'

'You and I…great minds. Yes, there's a lot of footage. All of it, in fact, really, if you know where to look.'

'What about the glitch?' Benji said.

'He was bullshitting. Monique didn't look into it closely, but Paul was going into the system and manually deleting footage while pretending to everyone that the cameras were playing up. I found this clip that he hadn't managed to delete – watch this.'

He played a video of Paul accessing one of the trial corridors, recorded by a camera high up in the atrium. The timestamp on the video showed just after two in the morning. Once he'd moved off screen, the footage remained on the empty atrium. Benji looked as if he was about to say something, when Harrison held up his hand.

'Watch, this is interesting.'

Almost a minute had passed when a figure entered the screen, following Paul's route. With the gait of a curious gazelle, Ricoh approached the door and peered through. He watched through the window for a further minute, before suddenly turning to run off in the direction of the stairs, out of sight of the camera.

'I don't understand,' Elle said.

'Well, he liked to walk around at night, didn't he?' Harrison said. 'Clearly he saw something he wasn't supposed to.'

Harrison brought up another video. This showed the

accommodation corridor again, and Paul approaching another door – Ricoh's. He already had a key in his hand and, without looking up, let himself inside, taking out his can of pepper spray after pushing the door open. The time now was three in the morning.

'This is the night Ricoh went missing,' Harrison said. 'So, based on these two videos, what I'm guessing is that Paul either saw that footage of Ricoh watching him. Or, more likely, given how sloppy Paul was, I think Ricoh threatened to out him and Paul killed him for it.'

If they hadn't seen Ricoh's body earlier, their objections might have been stronger. Instead, Elle said weakly, 'But why wouldn't he offer him money, like he did with you? Why kill him?'

'Well, clearly, he never planned to give me the money anyway. But maybe Ricoh gave him a now-or-never ultimatum? I mean, he left it a while before using it against Paul. He clearly knew before they discovered the pills were missing. So maybe he never planned to use it, and was looking forward to getting off the island when Jess and Lineker made their threats about pulling the trial. Only then they found the pills, but Ricoh still wanted off the island. He must have worked out something was up between me and Paul because he'd seen Paul take the pills, so maybe he decided to try and use what he'd seen to cut his own deal.

'You remember how much he was sobbing that night about wanting to go back? Paul was with him, trying to settle him down with the docs. Maybe in a quiet moment, Ricoh told him he saw what he'd done, and that if he didn't help get him off the island, he'd blow the whistle. Maybe he even tried bribing him. Maybe he tried rescuing his fee, too.'

Remembering her conversation with Ricoh, how sweet his motivations had seemed, it didn't quite fit. Although, how well had Elle really known him? And who knew what the medica-tion was doing to him that night? How could she forget how he'd murdered Ted in Cluedo?

'This is all speculation,' Benji said.

'Yeah, perhaps. But this isn't.' Harrison pressed play on a new video.

The footage showed Paul leaving the room forty minutes later, carrying something the size of a body wrapped in one of the blue wool blankets provided in each room.

'Oh, shit,' Benji said.

'So there you go. There's more footage of him bundling the body into the minibus. I assume he must've driven him some-where and buried him. Then came back to cover his tracks. Delete. Delete. Delete.'

'We found Ricoh's body,' Elle said. 'Over the edge of a cliff about two miles from here.'

'Right,' Harrison said, frowning. 'Make it look like he jumped. Makes sense.'

'How did you get all this footage, Harrison?' Benji asked, no longer looking at the screen.

'It was easy enough for me to find. Like I said, Paul made a bit of effort to cover his tracks but the man was sloppy. He didn't delete it very well.

'Anyway, what I'm trying to say to you, is that Paul had it coming really, didn't he? I could just tell he was ready to take me out, so I did what I had to in self-defence. And seeing what he's done to Ricoh now, well, I feel relieved I did what I did, actually. It could've been me over that cliff.'

'Sure, Harrison,' Benji said. 'Makes a lot more sense now. Seeing this.'

He looked at Elle, clearly inviting her on the journey he'd decided was safest for them. 'Yeah, I guess it makes sense.'

'Good,' Harrison said. 'So do you want to know what happened to Dr Lineker, then?'

7

Two cameras overlooked the lower patio area from positions high on the cliff walls: one above the stairs down to the beach, and one above the stairs leading down from the pool. It was the latter camera that caught the incident between Hallie and Dr Lineker, although the rock garden behind the rails was right at the edge of the frame.

Elle and Benji watched as, on screen, Dr Lineker appears, and converses with Hallie from over the rails. She's moved from the lounger where Elle left her and now stands peering over the cliff again. Dr Lineker is agitated, waving his hands and making movements as if he might climb over the rail. Eventually he does, and once over, he appears tentative, scared, and steps carefully over to presumably stand beside her – although now he disappears from the frame. Hallie isn't alarmed by his presence, and after a while the two of them sit beside one another, half of Dr Lineker now back in the frame. And for ten minutes, this is how they stay, seeming to talk to one another without incident.

Then it happens. Dr Lineker leans over, his head touching Hallie's shoulder. She turns, and he seems to push into her. They're far away from the camera, and a little out of focus, so it's hard to make out the precise details. But she appears to push him, hard. And for a second he rocks back the way he came. Then rapidly he tilts forward, and is gone, leaving Hallie staring down at the beach.

Elle took a breath now and found her hand over her mouth. She hadn't known whether to watch, but before pressing Play Harrison had assured her there wasn't much to see. Even so, the moment Dr Lineker went over, she had to stop herself from crying out.

'She pushed him,' Harrison said.

It was impossible to deny, but what had instigated it? Hallie wouldn't have just done something like that unprovoked. It had to be something to do with what he'd done in the moment before. Had he tried grabbing her, perhaps? Had he startled her?

Except it wasn't true to say she hadn't been provoked, was it? Hallie had believed Dr Lineker had been poisoning her. That his trial and his drug were responsible for how she felt. And if he had sat there trying to tell her it was a virus, might she have taken an opportunity to punish him for what he'd done? Especially if the side-effects had muted her conscience and heightened her impulsivity. Was it possible she'd even talked him into coming out there? Lured him, even.

'Was this video deleted?' Elle asked.

'No.'

'So there's a chance Monique and the others saw this footage. Maybe it's why they felt the need to…get more help when they did.'

Elle regretted speaking, because Harrison looked at Benji and said, 'Surely, if that were true, they would have told Benji here, too? Why would they be keeping things from him?'

Not wanting to tell him that the reason Benji had been left behind was because he had spent the night in her room, she turned her attention back to the screen, avoiding eye contact with both men.

On screen Hallie had been sitting down, but now she gets up, climbs over the fence, and walks up to the pool. She hasn't gone down to check on Dr Lineker. And her expression climbing the stairs is flat and focused. She walks slowly, in no rush to call for help. Then she vanishes somewhere before the loungers.

'It took me a moment to work out what she'd done,' Harrison said, 'because there are no cameras around the side of the complex behind the sauna. But look.'

Hallie appears at the front of the building on a camera mounted high up. She walks around to her balcony and climbs up via the lower one – the way everyone on the trial but Elle appeared to be able to do. She emerges later with a bag before exiting through the front gate.

'Where is she going?' Elle asked.

'Who knows?' Harrison said, leaning back from the computer, having manually fast-forwarded the video through the quiet sections. 'Maybe she went looking for Ricoh. Maybe she couldn't live with what she'd done. But now you understand why I wanted to distance myself from her.' Harrison held up his hands and blew air into his cheeks. 'She was a crazy bitch. Anyway, I've only been checking the footage for a few hours, but I've found some other good stuff, speaking of crazy bitches.'

Elle didn't want to be in the same building as Harrison, let alone standing this close. But while his attention was on the screen it wasn't on them. The clock on the wall told her it was nearly 2 p.m., and the others would be back soon. Then the numbers would be in their favour. If she could play for time… maybe ask him about Ted's whereabouts? No, not that, because Harrison wasn't necessarily aware he'd left yet. And the less he knew, the better.

'What else have you seen?' Elle said, and when Benji glanced at her she made a show of looking up at the clock.

Harrison showed them a greatest hits package, occasionally smiling, commentating like a television host. One piece of footage, filmed from above the atrium door, showed Dale and

Gee going out on the upper landing at one in the morning. Dale bends over the handrail with his legs apart, and Gee pulls down his trousers and pants. She pushes a clenched fist in front of his face, before moving it behind him and performing an act which makes him grit his teeth and drop his head. His long hair falls over his face. She then reaches around with her other hand to stroke his enormous cock, visible even across the room.

'There's loads of this,' Harrison said. 'They do it every night, in places where they might get caught. Kitchen, VR room, front steps. Him doing her, her doing him. Disgusting, when you think of it.'

Benji and Elle exchanged a glance, but neither asked him to stop. Thankfully, he only showed one other clip to prove his point, the two of them on Dale's balcony. But what he showed next was worse.

'This is my personal favourite.'

He opened a video, which showed the lower patio once more, this time from the camera above the beach stairs.

Becks appears at the top of the pool stairs, leaning forwards to check she is alone. She takes two steps down, and surveys the area. She pauses, looks up at the second camera above her, and descends to the patio, looking around for any other cameras. Apparently not seeing the one filming the footage they are watching, she climbs back up towards the pool and stops at the top. She then begins to slam her foot and ankle into the corner of the pool wall at the point at which the stairs are attached. She looks in pain, her teeth bared. She stops to check her ankle, her face momentarily composed, and begins bashing it again. After another careful look, she appears satisfied. She takes two steps down, and Elle knows what is coming next. Still, to see a woman deliberately throw herself down a staircase – arms and legs flailing, no measures taken to reduce the impact of each stair striking her head, back or side – is shocking even when expected.

Harrison stopped the video, rewound it, and played it again. Elle was stunned. Had Becks deliberately hurt herself for…attention? What other explanation was there, given how she'd made her injury such a central part of her interactions in those early days? And there was only one word for behaviour like that: psychopathic. That meant the side-effects had started almost immediately.

With a small laugh, Harrison said dryly, 'I know how to pick them, don't I?' He looked Elle straight in the eye. 'Interesting thinkers.' He let that sink in before turning back to the screen and adding, 'But which is the most interesting? You'd have to say, Hallie.'

He opened another video. This camera was positioned over the terracotta steps at the front of the building.

Hallie approaches the front gate from the direction of her balcony. She walks to the right-hand corner of the screen, where she kneels down by the head of a goat stuck beneath the gate. It's Harry, struggling to get free. Hallie takes Harry's head in her hands and appears to whisper into his ear. Then after a glance over her shoulder, she takes the goat's head beneath her armpit and, back to the gate, gets up on her haunches. In one movement, she yanks the head forward, so the goat's body wedges against the other side of the door, and twists the head all the way around. After another quick tug and twist, for good measure maybe, she drops the still head to the floor and walks back to the building. Her expression is the same one she wore in the footage of her leaving the lower patio.

'Christ,' Benji said. Elle had no words left.

'I know,' Harrison said, turning to them with a lazy smile. 'What a collection.'

8

'So tell me something,' Harrison said. 'What was it like outside the complex? How stranded are we?'

'Harrison,' Benji said, 'I'm tired, and I'm hungry and thirsty.'

His expression softened. 'Of course, you two do what you need to. I've made my point. It's entirely up to you who you trust now.'

Benji and Elle remained silent, not moving, waiting for the punchline.

'Well?'

'Can I ask you,' Benji said, 'what do *you* want to do now? Given what you've just shown us.'

'If you've found no signs of life out there, I think we wait for someone to find us here. We have everything we need, don't we? We should just carry on as before, keep taking our pills, and that way, when it all comes out, they have nothing to hold against us. Our case is strong.'

Again the two of them had no response to this. They simply nodded.

He addressed Elle. 'Are you still taking yours?'

She glanced at Benji, who tried changing the subject: 'Shall we pick this up after food?'

He didn't look away from Elle, and that sense of looking into the black opening of a well filled her.

'I don't think… I'm not taking them, no. We've all stopped.'

'Well, you should take them. Can you get mine now, Benji?'

'Yeah, but Harrison…everyone thinks that, you know, the side-effects aren't exactly…helping the situation here. That stuff on the video has shown something is really wrong here. Do you not feel that the pills are affecting you in some way?'

'I feel right as rain,' he said. 'I think all this stuff about the pills is horseshit. People are just making excuses, trying to provide an explanation for bad behaviour. I mean, everything that I've done here has been in response to provocation. Paul. Constantine. *That* bastard tried choking me.' He pointed to his neck. 'That's not any pill. That's just self-preservation.'

9

Before leaving them to it, Harrison marched them to Dr Lineker's office where the pills were stored. He'd already smashed the locks somehow, and the door was ajar. The white plastic tubs sat in a cupboard, neatly lined up in rows on the three shelves. Each bottle had a barcode on, but nothing else to indicate which was the active drug and which was the placebo.

'They must have been scanning the barcodes,' Elle said. 'They probably had some sort of computer software assigning the right pots to each person. They said it was double-blinded, so they wouldn't have known who was getting what until after the trial.'

Harrison looked angry. 'Or the answers are buried in all these notes.' He flicked his hand at the stacked-up paperwork on the desk where Lineker had given his interviews. He removed one of the jars from the cupboard, screwed off the lid, and put the pill in his mouth. He took out another and gave it to Elle. She folded her arms. 'Come on, what is it, 50/50?' he said. 'The contract just says we have to take the pills, it doesn't state which ones. We can't give them anything to hold against us. They're not going to beat me.'

'Hold on,' Benji said. 'If you've both been on the placebo, and now you take the real pill, it will make the results useless.'

'At least we can say we tried.'

'Do you think trying is going to count in a court?' Benji said. Harrison's eyebrows moved towards each other before

Benji added, 'Why don't you let me look through all this and I'll see if I can find out which pill you should be on.'

Harrison made a face like he'd smelled something bad.

'If you want to convince the company we did our best here,' Elle said, 'this would look better than randomly taking whatever was lying around.'

'Getting me to do it works, too,' Benji said, 'as I'm not a researcher. It won't hurt for me to know who is on the placebo and who isn't.'

Harrison took the pill from his mouth and shook his head. 'Fine, but if we don't have an answer by tonight, we just take the things. I don't want us to miss any more days. And when the others get back, we need to convince them to take theirs, Benji. Okay?'

'We can try.'

'We can do better than that.'

10

Once Harrison had left them, Benji and Elle went straight to the men's bathroom.

Constantine's body lay face down in a bloody lake on the toilet floor. Elle glimpsed it in the seconds it took the door to swing open and close again, following a push from Benji.

'We need to get far away from here,' Benji said.

Elle barely heard him. The corridor appeared to stretch around them while she stared at a spot on the wall.

'We might be able to convince the others to…help us over-power him,' Elle said, leaning against the corridor wall. 'They won't all just start taking the pills again, surely?'

'Unless he convinces them into it somehow, which I wouldn't put past him. Or gets enough of them on side to threaten the rest. And then God knows what happens. We can't count on Becks. Twenty thousand quid says she's the one who gave him the keys and the bat before she left. We should have asked to see that video.'

'Maybe.'

'He had the cuff key on the desk just now. Constantine's body was in the toilet, suggesting he got jumped down here. We left the key with Constantine, and Becks was last outside this morning.'

'So where do we go, then?'

'Well, hopefully the others aren't back yet because they found something. But even if they're not, Monique, Jess and Carl *must* have gone somewhere. The housekeepers *must* have come and gone from somewhere every day. Someone must come in to empty the septic tank every so often. This can't just be some rock in the middle of the ocean with a single building on it.'

'Can't it? What if they were coming and going by boat?'

Benji fell silent, but only for moment. 'Then there has to be a harbour. Maybe it has a boat we can take.'

Elle fell silent. It all sounded so weak.

'Elle,' he said, 'I get the sense you and I both need fresh starts when we get back. And maybe you and me, together, we could kill two birds with one stone.'

'I agree.'

He smiled. 'Good. Then let's focus on that. Because we're getting out of here, whatever happens. Boats or no boats. Together.'

They started to kiss, but stopped abruptly. From out in the atrium, a voice cannoned from the walls: 'Benji! Elle!'

It was Charlie. The others were back.

Chapter Fourteen

1

Charlie and Mai stood in front of the reception desk looking dirty and cooked. Charlie wasn't wearing his glasses, which made him look much younger and vulnerable. Harrison was nowhere to be seen. Elle and Benji ran to them, gesturing for them to be quiet.

'What's happening?' Charlie said. His coat had come off for what must have been the first time Elle had seen this holiday. It was tucked under an arm covered in cuts and grazes.

'Someone let Harrison free,' Elle said. 'Constantine's dead, Harrison said he'd attacked him.'

He nodded once. 'Where is he?'

'Around the building somewhere,' Benji said. 'We don't know.'

'What did your recce turn up?' Charlie asked.

'The island's deserted that way,' Elle said, keeping her voice down. 'But we found Ricoh's body. Harrison hacked the secu-

273

rity footage while we were gone, and it looks like Paul killed Ricoh and disposed of his body.'

'How awful,' Mai said.

'What happened with you?' Benji looked Charlie over. 'Where are the others?'

'Becks was right behind us,' Mai said. 'She's *so* slow. But Gee and Dale wanted to keep walking. They tried taking our food and water, but we dealt with them.'

Elle looked at Benji. '*How* did you deal with them?'

'Hit them,' Mai said, like it had been the stupidest question in the world.

'We walked out to the airstrip,' Charlie said. 'No signs of life, as expected, on the way out. The airstrip sheds are tougher than they look and we couldn't penetrate them. But a road ran away from the airstrip along the west coast. We followed it for five miles or so but found nothing.'

'The road kept going, though?' Elle said.

'There was nothing there,' Mai said. 'We could see really far. They've dumped us on a rock. And we were getting hungry, so we wanted to come back, because we had a better plan. But Gee and Dale wanted to just keep going. They said they'd had enough, and told us to give them our backpacks. They had knives with them.'

'Oh, Jesus,' Benji said. 'What then?'

'We had an argument,' Charlie said. 'They wouldn't listen to reason. My glasses got smashed, Dale cut himself.'

'They're such idiots,' Mai said.

'But they were both alive?' Elle said.

Charlie looked annoyed. 'Yes, of course they were. They got the message.' He stopped, shut both eyes tightly and rubbed them.

'Do you have a headache?' Elle asked him.

'No, just...sand in my eye. Wind's picked up now. Dale

needed first aid, ideally, but they'd made their minds up. So we went back to the airstrip, picking Becks up on the way, who decided to come with us. We boarded the plane. There's a radio and enough fuel to get us at least a few hundred miles.'

'The plane's still on this island?' Elle said. 'How did you get inside?'

'It wasn't locked. You don't need a key or anything.'

'Did you call for help?' Benji asked.

'No,' Mai said, 'we didn't know who might be listening in. We wanted to get our things first.'

'Your things?'

'Yes. We're going to take the plane. Charlie's going to fly us out of here.'

'Is that right?' Benji looked at Charlie.

'Yes. I'm able to do that. If that's what we all decide to do. I think the trial is officially FUBAR now, don't you think?'

'He'll fly us all out,' Mai repeated.

'Where was the plane?' Elle said.

'Sitting in an open hangar,' Charlie said.

Elle turned to Benji, a dangerous hope blooming in her chest. 'If the plane's still on the island, does that mean it never left?'

'It means, at the very least, the pilots must have gone somewhere else on this island.'

'Unless, like you said, they got a boat to another, nearby island.'

'Then how did they get there from the airstrip? Did either of you see any sort of vehicle, or a place where a boat could pick someone up, along the road north?' They both shook their heads. 'There just has to be something else that way. Why would they build that road, if not?'

'Unless it just ends, like our road did?' Elle said.

'After five miles?'

Elle took his point, but they couldn't be certain. 'If there's a boat, then Gee and Dale will get there first,' Elle said.

'My guess it that they'll turn around,' Charlie said. 'Dale was bleeding badly. He had to sit down. And they had no water between them. They drank their only bottle in the first few miles.'

'They only took one bottle?' Benji said, looking appalled. 'I thought Gee was some sort of masterful adventurer.'

'I think that was a front,' Charlie said, looking to Mai knowingly. 'She was using it to try and impress people. To control people, like Dale.'

Mai raised her eyebrows, apparently appalled by the idea. 'None of this matters, though,' she said. Because we're flying out of here. We don't need a boat.'

'Charlie,' Benji said, 'be honest with me now. Could you drive that plane?'

He smirked at Mai, and shook his head. 'Pilot. You pilot a plane, Benji.'

'Ladies and gentlemen,' a familiar voice said from above them, 'before we depart, how about everyone just holding on for a minute.'

2

Harrison began descending the stairs. Elle wasn't sure how much he'd heard. Had he been up on the landing the whole time, crouched down behind the mottled-glass balustrade, just as he must have done the night he caught Paul in the act?

'Where is the rest of the group?' Harrison said.

Charlie gave a dismissive frown and addressed Benji. 'Yes, I can pilot that plane. But I do think we ought to wait until the right moment.'

'Oi.' Harrison stood now just metres from them, no bat in

his hand but the pepper spray still at his hip. 'I asked where the others were.'

'Coming,' Benji said.

'All due respect, Harrison,' Charlie said, 'but I'm not sure your input is required here, unless you can offer something practical or constructive.'

Elle's eyes widened, while Benji's closed – both doing so in utter disbelief. Charlie had no intention of placating Harrison.

'You're going to fly the plane, then?' Harrison said, not so much in search of an answer but more to feel the idea out for himself. His face was blank, and Elle was reminded of the first computer she ever used at school, the cursor of which would turn into a rotating sand timer when it processed a task.

'And you all trust him, do you?' Harrison flicked his index finger back and forth in the air to indicate whom he meant. 'To fly a plane.'

'He's an RAF reservist.' Mai folded her arms. 'He's flown more planes than you've had chest shaves.'

'Have you, Charlie?' he said, staring at him.

Charlie met his gaze, and the connection between them felt tangible and dangerous, like an exposed wire. 'Yes. Of course.'

Harrison took a step towards him. 'How many planes have you flown?'

'Well… I'd say in the hundreds.'

'What does RAF stand for, Charlie?'

'Are you being serious?'

'I'm serious. What does RAF stand for?'

He looked baffled. 'Royal Air Force, of course.'

'And what about SAS? What does that stand for?'

Charlie looked disgusted, and shared this look with Mai. 'I don't have time to teach you—'

'Do you not know?'

'Secret Air Service.'

'Secret? I thought it was Special Air Service.'

'No. No, wait. Yes it is, sorry. I thought you meant something else.'

'BVR, Charlie. What does that mean?'

'That's not anything. You're making things—'

'Beyond visual range. It's standard RAF vocabulary.'

'You don't know what you're talking about.'

'PTVR, Charlie. What's that stand for?'

He wiped his hand over his mouth. 'Possible…target vehicle within range.'

'Really? I thought it was Part Time Voluntary Reservist.'

'No one would…it applies to both.'

'Charlie, it almost sounds like you don't know some of these. It almost sounds like you're full of shit and are trying to make yourself seem more important than you are.'

Charlie stuck out his chin and pushed back his shoulders. 'You don't have to fly with us, Harrison. You can wave cheerio to us as we leave.'

'Last one, then. The decider.' He enunciated every letter: 'L. F. A. C. LFAC. What's that?'

'Low-flying aircraft.'

'One out of four, well done.'

Charlie looked pleased and shook his head ruefully. 'You only learn acronyms that are important to you in reserves, Harrison.'

'So LFAC is an important one, is it?'

He paused now, smile gone. 'Yes.'

'So if I told you I made it up, how would you feel? How do you think it would make these three feel? That you're lying to get their trust so they'll get into a bloody plane with—'

Charlie went for him. Benji stepped between them, holding Charlie back. 'I could kill him. It'll be safer for all of us.'

Harrison was leaning away from the conflict, smiling,

looking satisfied. 'You are full of it, mate. Absolutely full of it. Do you still live with your parents, do you? Do you even have a job, or do you sponge off them? Or is it benefits? There's no shame in that. But just pack all the bullshit in before you put someone in real danger.'

Charlie went for him again, and once more Benji was forced into pushing him backwards. This time Elle joined him. Meanwhile Mai stood to one side, just watching, face impassive.

'Please, Harrison,' Elle said. 'Just…enough.'

Charlie pushed Benji away and stomped off, Mai following him up the stairs and towards the bedrooms.

For a moment Harrison appeared lost in some reverie. When he returned to himself and saw them both staring at him, his expression turned regretful. 'I thought it was best you know.'

Behind them the front doors opened. Becks shambled in, face red and hair windswept.

'Harrison,' she said, delight animating her voice but not her face.

'You look abandoned, babe,' Harrison said.

'I was, babe. I was.' She went to him and they shared a small hug before Becks realised she had an audience. 'Oh, how…how did you get up here? Did they let you out?'

If Elle had any doubt left that Becks had been involved in freeing Harrison, she didn't now.

'It's all been sorted, babe. Hasn't it?' He looked at Benji and Elle.

Now the upstairs doors burst open. Mai and Charlie appeared, Mai dragging her suitcase and Charlie hauling his oversized backpack. They walked down the stairs brandishing short, sharp-looking kitchen knives.

Harrison stepped behind the desk and picked up his bat.

'You can't leave,' he said. 'That's just so stupid. You'll have done all this for nothing. We need to keep the trial going as best we can. It's in your contract.'

'I'm taking the plane,' Charlie said. 'I suspect, given the nature of our location – the terrain, the climate, the time it took to get here – there must be populated land within one hundred nautical miles. I'm offering the four of you the chance to come with us.'

'Charlie, you can't fly a plane.'

'We'll see, Harrison.' He sounded certain and confident. Like the entire demonstration before hadn't happened.

'Benji, will you come?' Charlie asked.

Benji's mouth fell open, and he looked down at the floor. 'Charlie, I do believe that you can fly a plane. But I'm just not—'

'Elle, will you come?' He was pointing the knife at her.

And so it had come to this. Scylla and Charybdis. If she stayed here with Harrison, he might well kill them, too. But at least they would have a fighting chance. The Elle she'd left at home might have been inclined to spare Charlie's feelings. Might even have ended up in that plane out of awkwardness. This Elle, though, wasn't even going to dress it up with some false statement of amelioration, the way Benji had done. There was absolutely no chance that Charlie could fly them out of here. And reading between the lines, he might be just as dangerous as Harrison. God knew what had happened to Dale?

'No,' she said, looking him in his eyes and seeing none of the hurt that she feared might make her backtrack.

He moved on. 'Becks, will you come?'

'Not me. I'm tired.'

'I can't let you go,' Harrison said. 'If you go, the trial results won't mean anything. When the dust settles, I want to be able to say I tried my best to make this thing work.'

Harrison started to move towards them, his gait still unbalanced from his beating. Elle turned to Benji in panic. She could see his face working up to step in, and now Mai and Benji were adjusting their stances for the face-off.

'Harrison,' Elle said, 'we can vouch for you. We can tell Apollo Wellbeing that you did your best to keep it going. We can tell them Charlie and Mai had knives.'

He stopped, weighing up his options now. He shifted on the spot, wincing as he did so.

'Go on then,' Harrison said. 'Walk another six miles across the desert after you've already walked God knows how many already. Go for it. And, Mai, when the penny drops on that landing strip and you realise you've backed the wrong horse, you'll be welcome here.'

They began to back up towards the door. Charlie raised his knife and pointed it at Harrison. 'Before we leave, I am going to fly that plane over here, Harrison. I am going to come down really low, so you'll hear me coming, and I want you to come out here and look. Because you'll be able to see us in the cockpit. And we'll be flicking you the Vs and laughing, you moron.'

'I'll look forward to hearing from Mai about how you crashed and burned, trying to work a machine you've never used before.'

It was with both relief and a pang of fear that Elle reacted to the sound of the gate closing behind Mai and Charlie. Harrison didn't appear to react at all.

'I'm hungry,' he said. 'You must be starving, babe.' He put his arm around Becks.

'I'm okay. I could eat, I suppose.'

'Elle, you couldn't cook us up something, could you? Your cooking is really something else. I don't want to overstep the mark here.' He was holding up his hands as if he was at her mercy now, which was a hard trick to pull off while holding up a bloodied rounders bat.

Becks let out a whine. 'My ankle hurts again. They walked so fast and they didn't care.'

'I bet it does, babe.' Harrison smiled at Benji and Elle. 'I bet it does.'

3

Elle made curry in the biggest pan she could find. Not just to keep the peace, but because they needed to eat something for dinner later, and once more keeping busy felt like an invisibility cloak. She was useful, therefore she was protected.

Harrison had explained that while they waited they would all have different jobs and responsibilities. Elle's would be cooking, while Harrison's role would be to keep the place secure in case Hallie came back.

It was at this point he asked about Ted, and they had to admit to him that he had gone missing before they'd sent out their search party.

'I suspect he ran,' Harrison said. 'He seemed the fearful type.'

So she chopped onions, and sliced peppers, just grateful to be in a different room to Harrison. They made her cry, and when the tears wouldn't stop, she was struck by a pure and hateful anger which made her stab the knife down into the chopping block. It stuck in place. How could Jess and Carl have just left her and Benji here this way? Were they sleeping at night? It was so cowardly. Reprehensible.

But who could she really blame but herself? She wasn't even meant to be here, that was the ridiculous thing.

Once she'd brought out the dinner, she excused herself. On

her way out she heard Becks say, 'Benji's job can be to wash up.'

Harrison replied, 'That's a good idea. But he's got something else he's promised to do first.'

Elle went to her room and tried not to collapse on the bed in defeat. They simply couldn't stay here with those two. The hypothetical rescue party might not show up for another few days or so. God knew what would happen in that time, especially when Harrison started taking his pills again.

And what about Becks? She couldn't unsee that video footage, those effortless flips between violence and composure. Elle bet she'd been having headaches too, but was so uncommunicative, she'd not even mentioned it.

Elle's calves ached from their walk on the coast, and her body felt clothed in sweat and grime. She showered, hoping it would re-energise her for their departure. If anything, her exhaustion bedded in, her whole body now heavy with the burden of her endeavours. Undeterred, she put on clothes suitable for another walk, and packed her backpack. Then she waited.

After an hour or so, Elle was starting to worry about Benji. Then he knocked at her door. She let him inside and noticed he was carrying a black notebook.

'Where have you been?' she said.

'I'm sorry, Harrison made me go back to the office to look through Dr Lineker's paperwork. I was waiting for him and Becks to leave the reception before I found you. He was showing her all his favourite videos again.'

'Where are they now?'

'I heard them fucking in Hallie's room.'

'Hallie's?'

'Yeah, they're classy. But I think he's made sure to have a view of the front, in case we make a break for it.'

'Should we just go? While they're busy. How long have they been in there?'

'Not sure. Ten minutes. Twenty. Elle, I need to tell you some things first. Then yes, let's work out the best thing to do.'

'Okay.' She didn't like the tone of his voice. Didn't like the prospect of more surprises. 'What is it?'

'So before I went to Dr Lineker's office, I stopped by Paul first, to check his boot print. Just in case Harrison was up to something. But no, it's unmistakeable. Paul's shoeprint matches the one we found.'

Elle shook her head. 'Do you believe Harrison, then?'

'I think so. I never liked Paul, to be honest, but I just thought he was a grump, not someone who would...kill someone for money. But it did get me thinking. Someone somewhere is going to be majorly disappointed when they don't get their pills.'

'That's a point. Might he have had some sort of getaway planned? Maybe he had a boat somewhere else on the island?'

'Possibly. But there's more. I started going through Lineker's notes, looking for something I could use to stave off Harrison. There were lots of long technical documents. Protocols, tiny print, a ton of jargon and acronyms. I didn't find anything directly related to the pills in the cupboard, but I found this book up there, filled with handwritten notes, just with observations he'd been making. Like his version of our trial diaries. And look at this.'

He put the book down on the desk beneath her television, and opened it to a page with the corner folded down. He pointed at a sentence three lines down, the writing small and hard to decipher on first glance.

Only four of the ten showing first signs of SB-14 effectiveness.

'It's dated the third day we were here,' Benji said.

'I don't—'

And then she did get it.

'Only four of the ten. Of the *ten*?'

'Yeah,' Benji said.

'That makes it sound like…there aren't any placebos?'

'That's how I read it.'

'And wait, aren't there eleven of us?'

'I wondered that, although I think now it might just have been a mistake.'

She stared at Benji before turning back to the page. Other fragments jumped out at her. Words and phrases. 'Ethical dilemmas.' 'Amygdala hypoactivation.' 'Likely covetous, uses hand movements to distract.'

'What else is in here?' Elle said.

'It's too dense to really… I think he's written notes based on the interviews, too. At the back. There's things he's written about people but he's not named anyone. To be honest, I haven't read much of it. I wanted to come and tell you what I'd seen, but a lot of it's quite…vague. Shorthand sort of thing. But there is one other thing. I know what the 'SB' in SB-14 stands for.'

'What?'

'Silver Bullet.'

She muttered the words. What did they mean? Did it mean the drug itself was some sort of silver bullet? A cure of some sort. Or was that too obvious? Did 'silver bullet' refer to what the drug was creating? Were *they* the silver bullets? If so, at what or whom were they to be fired?

'Look at this, too. I found this tucked into the back page of the notebook.'

He held out an envelope, on the front of which was the word *Jess*, written in a much neater version of the handwriting from the notebook.

'You opened it?'

'It wasn't sealed.'

She looked inside: a single sheet of A4 paper.

4

Dear Jess,

I very much hope you're spared from reading this, and that the symptoms that I've been experiencing since arriving here on the island have been unrelated to what I deeply fear is their cause, but that has felt increasingly unlikely in the past few days. Please let me start by apologising if some of what you read here feels rather stuffy or suffers from a 'rehearsed' quality. This is not the first iteration, I'll confess.

I've no doubt that the symptoms I've been feeling have been exacerbated by the multiple levels of deceit on which I have had to operate since we arrived here on the island. I have suffered this stress every moment since we arrived, and it is why I have largely confined myself to my room or office. But I tell you this not for any sympathy, but because I want you to know that I did not deceive you lightly or without regret. I did so out of necessity, and because I wanted to keep your role in what I've decided to do on our behalf to a minimum, just in case the risks I have taken come back to haunt you, Alex and the company.

I have deceived you. I've done so selfishly, for the sole reason that I wanted to get there first. I wanted my name and Silver Bullet to be synonymous. I can tell myself that I did this because only my expertise could have brought Silver Bullet into being, and that without me the project would have died, denying the world what I think we all agree will be a true gift to humanity. However, for a long while you have been more than capable of taking the project forward, likely longer than even I would acknowledge. Yet, I have persisted.

Just over a year ago now, some time after I'd developed the first incarnation of SB, I began to suffer from headaches, which at first I put down to extreme concentration and lack of sleep. Scans revealed that I was suffering from a large intracranial aneurysm. They offered to intervene, but being familiar with the odds of success, given the size, I opted to postpone in order to finish my work. I kept an image of the scan in my phone, and I've looked at it every day. That terrifying ballooned artery, ready to burst — far from slowing me down, it pushed me. Made me work twice as hard, just in case.

They couldn't provide me with a time period, but a time would come, and soon, when the bomb would go off. A subarachnoid haemorrhage. Not a death sentence in all cases, but in mine sadly, a likelihood.

I've been very lucky staving it off this long, particularly given the strain I've put myself under against advice. But that time, I suspect, has come now. I've been experiencing much stronger headaches since being on the island. My vision and concentration have been affected. And my ability to think clearly for extended periods of time has been greatly reduced. There are times I wonder if that clarity went before we even made agreements with Alex to come out here. My symptoms come and go, with a steady worsening over time. But this is something different, and I do fear you may find me cold in my bed one of these mornings, our work incomplete.

But I write this to tell you that you must continue our work, Jess. Despite what I have said, and what I am about to disclose. I do think that once the initial shock has passed you will understand my reasoning and see that, given the time I had left, I had no choice but to cut certain corners. What we have discovered is too important. Everything is there for you now to take this forward without having to resort to skulduggery, as I have. It would make sense for Alex to raise your profile in a more formal capacity at Apollo, and you are more than capable of delivering our findings and winning over investors.

What you must know though, is this: I did not submit Capricorn to an independent review board. I did not seek ethical approval of any sort. I am aware that I gave you this impression, even if I did not state this explicitly. And I know that you were surprised by the timeline, and that I broke your trust in not addressing your concerns. The reality was, I believed I might not even live long enough to see approval on what was already a tricky prospect, given what we were trying to show.

I strongly believed that once we had our results, and they had inspired enough funding, my decisions would be retrospectively vindicated. The regulators are tough, but not stupid. They know results when they see them. This is not something I have ever done before, nor have I done it lightly, but I think in this case, given what I truly believe will come from this, the ends justify the means.

I can't be sorry about this, because it was not without great contemplation that I undertook this decision, knowing that even in the worst-case scenario, as the principal investigator, the buck stopped with me. That it would be my reputation ultimately that would be harmed by my decision. Given that I expected not to be here when my deceit was discovered, I was prepared to take that, in the belief that what we would achieve would overwrite any negative graffiti on my epitaph. And I believe this letter will be more than sufficient to prove that you played no part in this. That I alone was responsible.

But for lying to you, I am so sorry. I would never have made the progress alone that we have achieved together. I fear that we would have needed far more attempts at refining SB if not for your keen insight and observations.

You made a student of me again.

Warmest regards,

George

5

Elle put down the letter, her hand shaking. If the trial hadn't had any ethical approval at all, no one had overseen it. Any questions about the drug, its side-effects, the manufacturing process, recruitment, would only ever have been raised internally, at best. Which on a trial like this, where not even Benji had been allowed to know the full details, meant it was possible that no one had ever raised such questions. Jess might have been the only person to have been in that position scientifically, and the letter made out that Dr Lineker had lied to her, so what *had* she been told?

'What the hell have we been putting in our bodies?' Elle said.

'You were right about it not being the first trial.'

Elle nodded. 'Do you think that's what happened out on the cliff with him and Hallie? Something to do with his aneurysm?'

'Maybe. It did look like he collapsed, didn't it?'

'I assumed she ran off because of what she'd done. That she'd pushed him, but…maybe he fell on her and she just reacted. And then she ran out of here and got…lost out in the desert or something.'

'Or, maybe she's found civilisation. But that doesn't mean she isn't still a danger. And if none of you were taking placebos, that means that any one of them could be as dangerous as Harrison. If we leave here, and we come across them… Gee and Dale too.'

'They called it Silver Bullet,' Elle said. 'What if the additional symptoms aren't side-effects at all? That the drug was actually made to…remove our conscience? Or…or…suppress it. That it's some sort of…military thing.'

Benji raised his eyebrows. 'I don't see how we could find out. But the idea of a drug which turned your conscience on and off at will could have useful applications. In the right hands.'

'It would explain all the secrecy. The location, the security. It would explain why the staff disappeared when things got out of control. If they feared being overwhelmed by us. And… there's something else that bothered me too. We know Paul was deleting the footage of what he was up to, but if he was lying about the system glitching, wouldn't he have gone back and looked at the footage of Hallie killing that goat? Wouldn't that surely have had some repercussions for her? Or what Becks did – wouldn't they have been curious to see what happened? Make sure they weren't liable. So if they did, and then just didn't say anything… It's almost like…'

'They were expecting it.'

'Exactly.'

'And when Harrison stole the drugs. They seemed so happy to accept his explanation about being impulsive. As if they were expecting that too.'

'Well… I don't think there's any point speculating now.' Benji shook his head. 'You still feel fine, don't you?'

She went to confirm this, but she couldn't be sure. Hadn't the whole point of this holiday been to be more selfish? Less anchored by empathy and two-side-ism. Wasn't Holiday Elle created to embrace her inner psychopath, like Winston had suggested? And hadn't she slipped into that role just a bit too easily?

We'll be giving you a very low dose of the drug.

You won't really notice the effects. It's the equivalent of drinking a thimble of wine.

No, Holiday Elle was a choice. She was in control of her. 'I'm fine.'

'That's good. Maybe the drug isn't as effective as they want it to be.'

'Why did they lie about the randomisation? Why say some of us are on placebos?'

'To rule out any effect of expectation. Lineker was in a rush to get results. And he was happy to lie as much as he needed to, if it made the data more reliable. So why not rule out as much bias as possible by just taking away that expectation effect?' Benji glanced down at her bags. 'Are you ready to go?'

'Yes.'

'Okay, then this is what we do. I'll head out and make sure

they're still busy. If they are, I'll get my stuff and come back. Then we go.'

'You're sure? I know it's been almost two days, but what if we miss the rescue party?'

'If help's coming, they're either coming by air or by road, and if it's by road they'll only be coming one way, which is where we'll be walking. So yes. I am. Are you sure?'

'I think so. I just keep thinking there's no way to know what the right thing to do is. I can't believe they'd just leave us here to…what, die? And what if we run into some of the others?'

'I'll go pack what we need.' He glanced at his watch. 'We'll need a torch.'

'And what about what Charlie and Mai said? That they couldn't see anything on that stretch of coast.'

'That obviously didn't convince Gee and Dale. And shit, it feels mad trusting our lives to Gee and Dale, but it's not like we have much of a choice, is it? That road has to go somewhere. There has to be something else on this island.'

'And if there's not?'

'I don't want to think about that. My gut tells me it won't be an issue. I don't see what else we can go on.'

Benji left, and Elle could hear Becks's grunting now from across the hall. Benji turned, took her hands, and whispered, 'I think you're amazing, Elle. I'm going to get us out of here.'

She smiled. 'No, I'm getting us out of here actually. But thank you.'

With that he smiled and left.

6

Elle gave her room a final glance. Often when she left a place in which she'd lived she would feel a soft sense of loss. She felt nothing now, looking back. Not even when her gaze wandered over the pile of books she'd brought with her on the desk, remnants of a more optimistic time.

This was where she and Benji had fallen for each other, hard, and she believed now that she and Benji had a connection strong enough to survive this experience. Might she one day be able to rose-tint this place?

Never. She left, slamming the door behind her.

It was approaching five now. She wasn't really hungry, but not wanting to load up on curry, she forced down some scrambled eggs and toast before filling up her backpack with food and water. Benji soon joined her, ate the remaining eggs, and the two of them walked out of the building in silence, closing the double doors behind them like two teenagers sneaking out in the dead of night. They had reached the bottom of the stairs when a distant rumble and whine floated over the walls and filled the sky above them.

They stopped and looked at each other.

'That sounds like…a plane taking off,' Elle said.

Had Charlie done it? Had he actually managed to get the plane in the air? They started walking again, hoping to catch sight of the plane from outside the wall.

Harrison's voice halted their progress. 'Did you hear that?'

Elle and Benji turned around. Harrison stood on Hallie's balcony, hands on the rail, looking at the sky to their right – the direction of the airstrip.

'Crazy bastard,' he said.

The rumble began to fade. Standing there now with their backpacks on, Harrison hovering like some avian predator, it struck Elle that they'd made a dreadful mistake. Their chance to go had passed.

'Where are they off to?' Becks said, limping to stand beside Harrison.

'We're leaving,' Elle said.

'You can't,' Harrison said. 'No. That's not—' A mild pain appeared to interrupt his thoughts and he shifted his head as if to shake it out. 'What about the trial?'

'Harrison, we're going to look beyond the point Charlie and Mai did. We don't know what happened out there with them but there's every chance there might be help that way.'

'We've all agreed roles here, and now you want to go back on that?'

'You agreed these things with yourself,' Benji said.

Harrison nodded. 'You're a big man at a distance. But how long do you think it will take me to get to you while you're carrying those backpacks? It's not like you can drop them, is it? Bet you've got all your water in there. Which you'll need if you manage to get away from me chasing you down, because you can't come back here.'

'Harrison, why does it matter what we do?' Elle said. 'Just let us look for help.'

'We've agreed on the roles.' He sounded whiny, and perhaps realising this, he changed his tone. 'And…look, my head is getting really bad, okay, and I don't want to be a burden to anyone, so I've stayed quiet about this, but what if I can't look after myself? Becks is not feeling right either, and hardly in the best physical shape after that giant trek today. So we need you. We need to be a team now.'

The way Harrison worked was so transparent now, appealing to sympathy, having already threatened them.

'We'll come back either way,' Benji said, touching Elle's elbow and gently tugging her in the direction of the gate. 'If we find nothing, we'll be back. If we find something, then of course someone will be back.'

'Just stay,' Becks said, like no one had considered the option before. 'Come on, don't make him upset. Jesus.'

They started moving again towards the gates, walking backwards to keep him in their sight.

'You're not giving me a choice,' Harrison said. 'I... I'll have to handcuff you now. Keep walking and it will be worse.'

Elle gave Benji one last look, just to check that they had it in them to do this. The gate was a metre ahead. If he came for them alone, perhaps they could get one over on him. It seemed unlikely they'd get away uninjured. But if they used the pepper spray, and he wasn't expecting it, they'd have a chance.

Both of them turned their backs to him, committing now. And just as she looked away she saw him move, saw him turn. And they were at the gate now, and Benji was pulling the lock aside, and pushing back the door.

That was when she heard it. Another distant roar, and at first it might have been the reverberation of the gate. But then she looked up to the right of the complex, and she saw it flying towards them across the desert, in line with the coast and the road. A speck with three lights at first, but just seconds later clearly a jet, flying at a height her brain could actually understand. A tall tower block, or perhaps The Big One roller coaster in Blackpool, which she'd visited with Granny Alice.

Soon she could hear not just the grumble of its engines, but the high whine too, a sound that seemed to occupy all the available frequencies and made her heart feel like it was swelling and the hairs stand up on the back of her neck. Her lizard brain telling her to panic and flee. That this was something incredibly powerful coming, hungry and fast.

She was able to push past that fear, into a more rational place where she was only scared. The plane was even lower now. Growing larger in her visual field, more defined. Spinning engines and lowered landing gear and—

Should that not have been up by now?

In a matter of seconds the plane's windows were visible,

and it appeared to be coming far too fast, while descending further. The wings tilted leftwards, and could it be possible they were as close to the ground as they seemed?

'Something's wrong,' Benji said, yanking her arm. She allowed herself to be moved further from the building.

On instinct Elle looked back but Harrison was of no concern. He was up on the balcony again looking towards the plane, but surely unable to see it above the wall? But likely he could hear it, because the whole world was the sound of those engines now. And the plane was going to do just what Charlie had said, and fly over the complex to stick it to Harrison.

Only the angle was wrong, and the engines began to sound like they were getting quieter, or slowing down, which ran in defiance of what the plane itself was doing, which was getting closer and closer, to both the building and the ground. A matter of two hundred metres now, maybe, and it was much, much, too low.

'Elle, run.'

Benji grabbed her arm and pulled her, and she did run, and when her lungs began to tighten, she turned back. The plane's nose, now impossibly close to the ground, began to lift up, presumably to bring the rest of the plane with it. But the plane's tail continued downwards in a way that appeared to defy physics. And indeed, physics took exception to this recalcitrance, because there simply wasn't time or room for this manoeuvre, and the black-and-red rock began to consume the metal. Still the plane tried to rise. Inevitably, it failed and fell.

The cockpit snapped off. The middle section broke free and ploughed ahead. It struck the wall, and, with great crashes and squeals, tore into the building itself.

Elle threw her pack down and ran as fast as she could, pursued by an immense wall of heat. Stones and other missiles flew past her. A small object whined insect-like by her ear before something much larger hit her squarely in the back and she crumpled to the ground.

She dragged herself onto her front, back in agony, and called for Benji.

He was nowhere to be seen. All the rest was fire, smoke and dust.

Stillness followed violence, inevitably. The island itself now lay inert in the aftermath of a great upheaval, and the devastation from its volcanic birth was evident in every step of Elle's journey over the barren rockscape in the direction of the west coast.

Her back throbbed. The insides of her nose and throat felt like they had been scoured with jet fuel, and blood seeped down her left cheek from a gash at her temple. Still, she moved quickly, desperate for it all to be over.

It had been a slow start. When she left the complex that morning, the sun still a glowing promise on the horizon, her passage was dim – made all the worse by the smoke erupting from the still-burning wreckage. She'd moved cautiously, a sprained or broken ankle likely a death sentence.

Elle hadn't wanted to waste time walking down the road to the airstrip and back up the west coast, especially given the plane's fate. Instead, despite the risks, she chose to traverse the unpaved hypotenuse in the hope of joining up with the coast road further along.

Some of her way had been smooth, the reddish sand only lightly sprinkled with stones. At other points she would walk around blackened boulders that looked like fallen meteorites. Many hours after setting off she passed the foot of an ancient caldera, the monochromatic surface here like the contents of an ash tray.

Now, sunlight pressed against her neck, and though it was pleasant, bringing much-needed heat to extremities still cold from a night spent on the beach, she knew already that today she would burn. When the plane crashed, she had been dressed for the low evening sun, and wore only a short-sleeved top. The wall near where she'd thrown down her backpack had collapsed, burying her bag and all it contained. She tried to search through the rubble for anything of use, but her distress and disorientation had panicked her.

She didn't have any water now. This was why speed was important. She had to find civilisation before she dropped dead from dehydration. Her last real drink had been with dinner the night before. Already her parched mouth fired panicked warnings to her brain. Yet she welcomed the focus, her concentration centred by thirst, two days' worth of unwanted reflections banished to the darkness of her subconscious. At least for now.

Beyond the caldera she lost sight of the ocean to the south of the island, all around her now sky and rock. If it hadn't been for the smoke cloud far behind her, she might well have lost her bearings and any hope of finding the road. But soon, the land rose, and when it dipped again later the western sea glimmered ahead.

Her watch had been smashed, and although she was able to see the hands, she wasn't convinced it was telling the time accurately anymore. When the road shimmered into view it reported half an hour had passed since she'd first seen the ocean — although it felt more like an hour because nothing out here ever seemed to get closer or further away.

The slope made the journey easier. She resisted running — not that she could have managed it — but she made good time, and when she took her last step on the desert her watch told her it was ten past ten. She'd already done the calculations, and if she'd not wandered too far off course, and Charlie's guesswork about the distance from the airstrip had been correct, she'd be about four or five miles down the coast road here. Soon she would be at the point Charlie and Mai had turned around, while Gee and Dale pressed on.

Had Hallie come this way? Ted too. Were they all waiting for her just a little bit further down the road together in the air-conditioned Shangri-La she and Benji had imagined?

She clung to that hope for the next hour. To do so, she had to forcibly push away thoughts about all the people who didn't emerge from the crash. And though it was painful, she had to fight off thoughts of Benji. If she let him into her head even briefly, she might break down. And the truth was, at this point she couldn't spare the liquid.

She moved more quickly on the smooth, unmarked tarmac strip, not even wide enough for two cars to pass one another. This road had been laid once by a team of workers with vehicles and machinery. They had come from somewhere, brought here with the intention of connecting that airstrip to another place. The sense of connection nourished her.

Pushing on was incrementally difficult; when her neck became too hot she clasped her hands behind her head, palms out, for protection, although holding this position was hard because of the injury she'd sustained to her back from the crash. The road gradually dropped down to the level of the sea, and the blue of the ocean and the salty air made her long to jump in, open her mouth and gulp. When she looked ahead, she tried to ignore the endless land that she still had to put behind her.

People just didn't build roads to nowhere.

Unless they…unless they ran out of money. Or had so much money they could afford to change their mind. Perhaps, on a whim, they decided to locate their fancy complex at the southern tip of the island instead of the north.

She chided her nagging brain for such intrusions. They were ultimately useless. Despite these recurring doubts, urging her to turn back, she had to remember there was no back *to return to. Everything had been doused in jet fuel and returned to the preferred state of matter on this island.*

So she pressed on as fast as she could manage, until up ahead of her something lay in the road. She slowed her approach but didn't stop, and soon she saw movement, skittish birds, crows, flapping and pecking.

It was a body. She stopped, sat down in the road, and allowed her face to succumb to the gravity of grief. Her chest began to heave. She couldn't stand to see another, not today, not ever again. Hadn't today been enough?

Part Three

All-Cause Mortality

Chapter Fifteen

1

After the crash, at least one of the plane's engines had continued to screech. Elle had heard it from where she lay after being floored by what turned out to be half a breeze block. She stood with great effort, crying out with the pain in her back and shoulders. She looked around. Wheels, windows and fragments of fuselage lay scattered across the landscape on either side of where walls had once stood intact. The majority of the plane had punched all the way through both walls, and now lay half on the coast road, crushed and on its side, one torn wing beneath it, the other pointing skyward.

When she turned she saw Benji five metres away, lying on his back. He wasn't moving.

As quickly as the pain allowed, she went to him.

'Benji.' The composure in her voice didn't match her terror. Nothing. She had to blink away tears.

Only then, Benji groaned. He tried to move too. She

crouched by him, let him squeeze her hand until it hurt, and then some more. Blood pooled on the ground under his legs, and she realised his thigh was bleeding heavily.

She tried to remove his trousers, but he yelled, so she tore away the already ripped material around the deep and long wound. She used the clothes in Benji's pack to create a tourniquet above the wound, something Elle had seen on television. How tight did you make it, though? Wouldn't it be worse if you stopped the blood entirely?

She washed the wound with some of the water from the bottle Benji had packed, and used more clothes to press against the wound. It hurt the injury on Elle's back to push too hard, but she made herself do it anyway. Eventually, when most of the few items of clothing Benji had packed were too soaked to be useful, and the bleeding slowed, Elle searched the ruins for anything they could use.

From the look of the flattened cockpit, now just inside the wall on a pile of rubble that was likely the sauna building, the impact had been too powerful for Charlie to survive. And even if, by some miracle, Mai and he had been alive in another part of the plane when it hit the ground, the fire consuming it now would already have claimed them. So Elle knew that she might see things that would disturb her. But she had to save Benji – there couldn't be any more deaths on this island.

She explored to the right of the complex first, and came across the first signs of death on the road not far from the great gouge in the earth where the plane had first struck. An arm poked out from an otherwise empty white shirt, an epaulette on the shoulder with four yellow stripes. The hair on the arm made it seem so *realistic*. That was the word she settled on, and she wouldn't spend any more time looking at it while thinking of another one.

Elle moved on in a state of woozy acceptance. That was until part of the wall beside her fell down in a crash, and she yelled out and stepped back, tripping over her feet and landing on the ground beside the road. A body in a red dress lay on its front, draped over a stump of wall, still stuck in the ground like the root of a stubborn tooth. The person's hands were tied behind their back.

A clothes-shop mannequin – that was all.

Yet the size and shape of it, the colour and style of the hair, made a good facsimile for Jess.

It *had* to be Jess, because her necklace, the one given to her by her late mother with two interlocked rings, lay on the tarmac just metres from where Elle had fallen.

She could take no more. She turned back. As if to fire one more warning, a crash as loud as the initial plane impact preceded a cloud of dust rising from behind a section of the remaining wall. Another part of the building had collapsed.

When she returned to Benji, she found he had fallen unconscious, and had let go of the T-shirt he had been holding to compress the wound. Blood was seeping out onto the ground again. Elle retied the material, whispering his name until his eyes opened. For an instant he appeared not to recognise her. Then he smiled.

She talked to him, and he tried to talk back. She made him drink the water because he'd lost a lot of blood. There was only half a bottle left now, so she took the briefest sip herself and left the rest for him. She told him about what she'd seen, and how both Jess and the captain had been on the plane too. Jess's bound wrists suggested Mai and Charlie had taken them hostage. Perhaps those who had fled the complex had all been hiding at the airstrip, and Charlie and Mai came across them on their second visit. But if they'd been there all along, why hadn't they left already? What had they been waiting for? Had there been an attempt to stop Charlie stealing the plane, or had something else gone on?

Benji wasn't in any state to theorise, but what happened out there made a difference to what they did next. She didn't know who else had been on that plane, and she didn't want to trawl through the wreckage to find out, but there might be others still at the airstrip. Even better, the minibus might be there. If she could access it, even if there were no others at the airstrip, she could use it to search the rest of the island for help.

Except maybe none of those things was true. The airstrip could be deserted. They might have all been staying at another facility further north on the island. Perhaps they'd been dropped off there by someone in the minibus, and that person had left again. If she walked five or so miles that way, she'd end up having to walk that much further north if the airstrip *was* deserted. And that was an hour or two extra while Benji was bleeding to death and their limited supplies were running out.

Even if there was anyone still at the airstrip, holed up with food and water, waiting, they weren't going to be happy to see Elle. Carl and Monique had fled this place in fear of what the drugs might do to the rest of the participants. They weren't about to welcome her. And that assumed they weren't buried in the wreckage. And did she really want to run into Hallie, or Ted?

No, her gut told her their best hope of finding help lay at the end of the west coast road. And the quickest, least energy-consuming way there was to cut across the desert and join the road further north.

But Benji. She couldn't leave him like this. The sun was almost down, and a cool evening wind was picking up. Night was coming, and they needed to find shelter. But the complex was too dangerous to return to, and when she walked around the other side of the building she could see the flames and smoke from inside. The wind blew from the north-east, so if Elle could get Benji down to the level of the sea, he might be spared the brunt of it.

The cove would have been ideal, but it was out of the question because of the descent. He'd tried to stand but his leg hurt too much to bear weight. He suspected something was fractured or broken. And as soon as he put his foot down, the bleeding started to worsen again, any healing undone in an instant. Elle circled the burning fuselage to the building's right, unsure if something might still explode and hoping not to find any more bodies. To the left of the cove, behind the rock pincer jutting out into the sea, the descent to the ocean was kinder. The land sloped gradually to a small pebbly beach.

It took them well over an hour to get from the front of the complex to halfway down, Benji sliding on his backside with Elle braced to break his fall in front. They found a spot where two jutting rocks created a pocket with the slope. Benji would be sheltered from all but the rain here. He was still within shouting distance of the road, too, and would hear any approaching vehicles.

'If I find a car,' Elle said, 'I'll drive back. If I find a boat, I'll sail back.'

'You did say you'd get me out of here.'

She didn't want to leave him, and he didn't want her to leave. But both of them knew that time was running out. She had to at least try to find help. But night was nearly here, and though they agreed it would be hard for her to navigate in the dark, she had a sense that she might be able to do it at a push. But it was a risk. And what if Benji passed out and started bleeding again? He might not survive the night.

So they held each other for the rest of the evening, and when he began to shiver, she squeezed him and rubbed his arms. The wind blasted above them, sending down unwelcome wafts of jet fuel stink, but for the most part they were sheltered.

Elle drifted in and out of sleep, and at one point, when she actually stopped shivering, she feared she'd succumbed to hypothermia. As dawn arrived, Elle got to her feet, had another small sip of water from the bottle at Benji's shivering insistence, and climbed back up the incline. It was hard work, and the rocks and pebbles frequently gave way, causing her to lose her footing. Benji would be fucked if he tried to get back up. If she didn't make it back for any reason, she'd sentenced him to death down there, trapped away from help.

So she'd better come back, that was all there was to it.

At the top, the urge to look back, to reassure him was strong. But if she looked into those sad eyes it would feel like a last goodbye. Then she would never go. She would stay and hope for rescue, all the while knowing in her heart it wasn't coming.

Despite it straining every moral instinct she had, she walked away from him. For his sake, and for hers. Determined, powerful, and ready for whatever lay ahead in the looming dawn.

2

The birds collected around the body's head, and they didn't stir when Elle passed by on the opposite side of the road. She maintained her distance, and limited the frame of her gaze with a hand pressed to her forehead in a sort of salute. He lay face-up, blood pooled around his body at the point where Charlie must have stabbed him. She saw his black boots and Blue Öyster Cult T-shirt, and knew it was Dale.

Once she was past him, a desperate impulse made her turn and say his name. As if he might just be asleep. As if she was performing an act of due diligence. Of course he didn't answer, and if she was honest she was a little relieved he didn't. Still, a cold rod of unease settled on her neck and spine, and every so often she would fight against the urge to look back and lose.

There would be no getting over the horror of the past few weeks, even if she got off this bloody island. This was it now, for the rest of her life. An unwanted eyesore dropped onto the landscape of her existence. All she'd wanted was a holiday, and they had given her this…this war zone. For what? That was what she need to know. What possible cause was great enough to warrant putting them through this?

Another few hundred metres on, she found Dale's blue exercise book on the floor. It lay open at the side of the road, spine up, like someone had carried it this far and thrown it away. Gee, perhaps? How long would it last out in the elements? She didn't know if Dale had any family back in Newcastle, but taking the book with her, just in case, felt like the least she could do for him.

When she got close enough, she saw crimson finger smudges on the cover. She picked it up and opened it to the first page.

DALE'S ISLAND BOOK

She felt a tug inside her chest, the handwriting blocky and almost childish. The wind blew then, lifting the front page and fluttering the next few pages into view. Elle almost dropped the book. After the wind died down she stayed one of the inside pages with her palm and stared. The lines were filled with the work he'd been doing over the last three weeks – not writing, but triangles. Endless lines of triangles, formed by a Biro flick up and a Biro flick down, with the pre-printed line forming one continuous base. She turned the pages, and every page until just after halfway was the same. As if he had been transcribing some steady pulse freehand.

Perhaps if they had found this in the complex unguarded one afternoon, the contents might have been funny to some of them. And Elle, on her high horse, would have found a way to feel sorry for him. What sort of person tells everyone he is writing a novel about them, and pretends to take detailed notes, while actually just drawing…this? Poor guy, she'd have said

But out here she had no such sympathy.

Again she felt an urge to look back. But she didn't. Instead, she closed the book and threw it as far as she could.

3

Some time later, she came across a beach by the road. Actual black sand here, as well as the customary pebbles. Down by the water, Gee sat against a rock staring out to sea, her bright shirt stark against the nothing stretching out in every other direction. Elle had begun to understand why Charlie and Mai had turned back. Up ahead the road and desert stretched through emptiness all the way to the horizon; no boats sailed in the sea and no planes in the sky.

Elle stopped and watched Gee. Gee didn't move, and after a while Elle called her name, surprised she wasn't more scared, given her and Dale's alleged attempted mugging of Charlie and Mai. But she knew, didn't she? Even before she crossed the sand and saw that Gee wasn't really sitting but slouching. Her eyes were closed, and before Elle turned away in disgust, she saw that something ran down her chin, adding more colours to her shirt. There were flies too, but thankfully the birds hadn't found her yet.

Her first reaction had been to walk away, but she didn't go far. Once she'd got herself together, listened to the ocean and stared at her dusty trainers, she walked back tentatively, head down. Again, she didn't want to see the body. Didn't want to think about what had happened here. But she did want to see what lay beside Gee, on the sand, still a quarter full.

A plastic water bottle with the cap off lay perilously close to rolling downhill and risking spilling its precious contents. The back of her mouth began to hurt, and the dryness felt like it was stretching down her throat. In a different situation, she would never drink from something that not long before had been in the mouth of a dead person. But the journey ahead was still so long.

She knelt down, grabbed the bottle and fled with it. She opened her mouth, and greedily poured a little in. It was less than a second before she retched, the salt violent with her taste buds and the back of her throat. She spat. Retched again.

She'd drunk the sea. Water, water, everywhere, and worldly Gee, with all her mountain treks and adventures, had drunk the stuff like a hopeless, lost girl scout. Surely everyone knew you couldn't drink sea water? It overloaded your body with too much salt. You slipped into a coma. You died.

She emptied the bottle, considered dropping it, and instead took it with her. Just in case she came across some fresh water. She argued with herself about going back to Gee. Checking her pulse. In the end, she returned. But just touching her skin was enough to know.

4

Elle lost track of the miles. More than ten, but surely no more than twenty? Hunger and aches in her legs and back joined with her thirst to drum up useless panic in her. The worst of it, though, was the sun. It was almost two o'clock according to her watch, which may or may not have been keeping accurate time anymore, and there wasn't a chance in hell she was leaving without another skin cancer. The back of her hands, her arms, shoulders and neck, all felt hot to touch and buzzed in that telling way. Even her eyes, dry and blurry from the wind and grit, felt seared.

Her hair felt hot to the touch, the blood from the gash in her head was dry and sticky down the side of her face. It was funny to think, back home it was almost winter. Maybe there would be snow. How nice would it feel to bury her face in snow now? Shove her head into a mound of the stuff. She'd eat it, too. Gobble it like ice cream. Delicious.

'In the winter we will build a snowman,' she sang, and on hearing herself began to laugh hysterically.

At least she could laugh still. She hadn't lost it entirely, even if she didn't quite feel herself now. And, if it weren't for the circumstances and all the dead bodies she'd seen in the last twenty-four hours, she might wonder if her current mental state had something to do with Dr Lineker's red-and-white pills.

On an impulse she dragged herself down to the sea, took off her trainers and walked in fully clothed. After all, she was on holiday, wasn't she? The relief was immediate, and she emptied her lungs and sank to the stone-cold bottom.

Once out in the sun again her clothes soon dried, and she felt more like herself. She'd come too far to go back now, so she might as well push on. She wasn't physically capable of doing what she'd just done again today, and she had already resigned herself to sleeping the night out in the desert. May as well explore the rest of the island while she had the last of her strength.

That was when two things happened within ten minutes of each other, giving her additional shots of adrenaline that spurred her on. The first was a chocolate wrapper, a Wispa, caught in a crack beneath a rock by the road. Elle picked it up, looked inside and saw the faintest traces of melted chocolate. There had been Wispas at the complex. Which meant either the wind carried litter this far, or more likely, someone from the trial had come this way. She supposed it could have blown over from Gee and Dale. But she didn't want to believe that.

Perhaps someone else was out here. Watching her.

She didn't want to believe that either.

The island began to taper, and the sea was visible on both her left and right now. She saw no signs of life but for the odd staring goat, but gradually the belief that something lay at the very end of the island had hardened into a conviction.

Then the sea appeared ahead of her. Every bit of land left was visible, a tongue-shaped barren mass. She closed her eyes and stopped to compose herself.

The journey had been for nothing.

No. She refused to believe that. She couldn't be sure. Not completely. The road *had* to go somewhere? It just had to.

So she dragged herself onward. If there was nothing there, so be it. She still had the unpaved east coast to explore. Who knew what might be hiding that way? That was something to cling to, wasn't it?

Soon a long shadow appeared on the horizon. Another island, perhaps, or even the mainland. It was too far to swim to. Ten miles. Thirty? She couldn't tell. But it drove her on the last half mile or so.

Then the road ahead appeared to end at a cliff edge overlooking the southern ocean. Once closer though, Elle found the road began to descend between the cliffs. The slope increased, and Elle had to fight against gravity to stop herself running even faster, savouring the sudden shade between the two rock walls.

When she passed the edge of the right-hand cliff the land opened up. The shock of what she saw stopped her dead.

'Yes.'

Up ahead was a wall. It was almost identical in style and height to the one at the complex. This wall didn't curve though, instead it ran between the left-hand cliff and one much further to her right. Was it the entrance to another building?

Her breathing quickened, and her eyes brimmed with tears. She followed the road to a closed green gate in the middle of the wall. Someone might come out to her now, seeing her on a video surveillance system, perhaps. She walked by a large dark stain on the tarmac, a dried pool of something drawing flies. She couldn't engage with that now – it wasn't necessarily blood.

She stood before the gate, a chill descending her spine in spite of the sun. She waited, hand on her hip, fingers feeling the edge of the pepper spray still strapped to her jeans. When no one came, she walked over to a panel on the inside of the wall and pressed the call button. When nothing happened she pressed it again. And again. Elle gritted her teeth, and in the clutch of panic began to scan the gate and the wall for other possible ways in. She shoved the gate. This wasn't going to happen, not like this. She wasn't turning around now.

She marched up and down the wall, calling out. She tried unsuccessfully to throw the empty bottle she'd been carrying over the wall in the hope it might draw attention. Still nobody came. She rang the bell again. Kicked and kicked at the gate. Finally, she slumped down, legs crossed, palms pressed against her closed eyelids. She watched colourful shapes dance on the backs of her eyelids and after a while only the distant roar of the sea anchored her to reality.

But she refused to give up, even then. She followed the road back up the way she came. On the west coast a cliff stretched out into the ocean. To get around it, she would need to swim past a dangerous-looking clump of rocks jutting into huge waves, like the underbite of some enormous carnivore. She walked up to the cliff overlooking the wall, her calf muscles straining.

From here, she could see over the wall. A slender, modernist villa, with flat roofs, concrete pillars, and painted a brilliant white, looked out over the sea. The sun reflected in rows of glass panels. A grass lawn, potted palm trees and sculpted bushes decorated the empty front drive.

The cliff on the east coast looked more promising, and within ten minutes Elle managed to get beyond the wall along that ridge. The way down was too steep, though. She passed the side of the villa, and directly below her was the start of a beach, golden sand forming a perfect crescent around the place's rear wall. An infinity pool, rectangular and tinted emerald, poked out above the beach at the back of the property. Here the design most resembled the trial building, the two structures fraternal twins architecturally.

She clambered along until the cliff entered the sea below. And still there was no way down. Another twenty metres or so, and she reached the end. Her hair blew around her face. Over on the other side of the cliff, the sea below chopped at the rocks. On the inside of the cove, though, the water only lapped. With careful footsteps, she managed to descend a further ten feet, at which point a ledge hung out over the water. No other option remained but to climb back up and find some other way.

But there wasn't any other way, and given her exhaustion, and what was at stake, she really didn't have time to stand and think about it like she'd done those times with Gee and Dale. So before her doubt could kick in, she ran and jumped.

5

Her already sore eyes burned from the assault of waves. She stumbled out from the surf half-blind, falling to her knees onto hard rock. With nothing to dry her hands on, she only succeeded in further blurring her vision by trying to rub her eyes with the backs of her hands. But the pain and disorientation would pass quickly; what mattered was, she had done it. She had made it. It had taken her over nine hours and she must have walked twenty miles. But here she was.

She blinked and blinked, drawing deep breaths through salty lips.

'Elle?'

Quick footsteps approached her. She looked up and squinted, able to make out a shape approaching her across the sand. She reached down to her waist and felt the area around her hip. The pepper spray had gone.

'Elle, are you okay?'

The voice was male, and she recognised it immediately. A moment later she felt a towel around her shoulders, overly redolent with detergent. She grabbed the corner and wiped her eyes. She could see again. Closer to the water there was a clear line where the yellow sand ended and black rock began. Was the sand artificial?

Then she saw him, freshly shaved and looking much older now. He wore a crisp white shirt, open at the chest. He glowed with health, angelic, apparently untroubled by plane crashes and dangerous side-effects.

But of course, what did he have to worry about, here in the safety of this compound? Especially as he was holding a handgun. Noticing her looking at it, he glanced down and said, 'I... uh.' Then he just stopped. Like the need to explain himself had simply vanished upon reflection.

Ted looked down at her with a pout that veered close to regretful. 'Do you want to come inside? You look like you might need a drink.'

Chapter Sixteen

1

He directed her to a flight of stairs leading up from the beach, but remained behind her holding the gun. It made Elle nervous, so she asked him questions to give her an excuse to keep turning around to check where he was. He gave one-word answers, telling her to keep climbing upwards, even after they had arrived at the ground floor of the villa. Here a stretch of immaculate lawn was overlooked by huge windows running the length of the building's rear.

She didn't ask the questions she really wanted answers to. Like, why he was here? And what did he know? Or, why the hell was he carrying a gun?

Elle walked out onto an enormous patio. Plush white loungers and oversized candle lanterns surrounded the infinity pool she'd seen from the cliff. Two smaller lawns grew either side, around which were palm trees and other hardy-looking foliage. It was all so well kept that there had to be a staff on site to maintain it.

They entered the building through thick glass patio doors – bullet-proof would be how Elle might describe them, if she managed to get home. Given where she now was, and how hopeless it had all seemed just an hour before, she probably should have felt more optimistic about that prospect. Except he was still holding the gun, even though it was just the two of them.

Inside the air conditioning salved her skin. He encouraged her to sit down on one of the many pristine white sofas arranged in squares along the windows of the huge open-plan living room.

'I'm filthy, Ted,' she said. 'I'll ruin them.'

He waved his hand as if it was no big deal. 'After what you've been through, you need to rest. What would you like to drink?'

'Water, please.' She sat on a sofa facing the sea. She wanted to tell him about Benji, ask him to get help as soon as possible. But something held her back. She first wanted to understand what was happening here. Wanted to make sure she wasn't putting Benji in any more danger. Because if anything happened to her, he was done for.

Ted stepped behind a cream bar – everything here was either white, cream or grey – and opened and closed doors as though he didn't know where the glasses were kept. Eventually, a high-pressure tap whooshed on, and he brought over a tall glass of water.

'Do you want something stronger, too? A wine or a beer or...an explanation? I can see you want an explanation.' She took the glass from him and gulped greedily. Her regret was instant, as it felt like it was going to come straight back up. Ted stood so that the sofa to her left, positioned at a right angle to hers, was between them. He raised the gun a little and used it to scratch his hip. 'That's not going to be a problem, Elle. But I need to know some things, too. Why do you smell like kerosene? Did something happen? I thought I heard an explosion yesterday afternoon?'

Once she had control of her nausea, she took another, smaller sip, fighting the urge to down the entire thing. He was staring at her, waiting for an answer. He appeared nervous, and it was clearly important to him that she tell him what she knew. She had no idea why Ted was here and what role he played in all this, but she couldn't put that dark stain on the road outside out of her mind. It was possible that the answer to this question might be leverage. And leverage was a good thing in the face of a lethal weapon. He clearly didn't feel safe in her company, which implied he might know about the potential side-effects of the pills.

'There was an accident,' she said. 'At the complex. Now, can you tell me something? Have you been here the whole time? And where exactly is here? And please, tell me why you're still holding that gun?'

Her voice sounded so measured. She was pleased that her rising terror wasn't yet obvious.

He looked at the weapon again, smiled as if he hadn't even noticed he was holding it, and shifted his weight onto his other leg. Then his expression hardened, and he squinted at her like she was a particularly small line of print in a contract.

'You saw what happened, didn't you?' he said. 'You saw what Harrison did. And what that girl did to George. Dr Lineker, God rest his soul. Are you here alone? Did any of the others come with you?'

She waited, letting him know she intended to get answers first. Then she said, 'You know who I am. Where I'm from. Why I was selected to participate in this trial. So, Ted… Is that even your name? Don't you think we ought to just…get on an even footing first?'

He looked out the window and nodded. 'Sure. Let's trade, then. That seems fair. You tell me something, and I'll…tell you something.'

'Well…okay. But can you give me the basics first? Is your name Ted?'

He ran his tongue between his lower teeth and lip. 'No. My name is Alex Firkin.' He paused again, watching Elle's face closely. As if the name might provoke something in her. And it did, because in Dr Lineker's letter he'd referred to an Alex, hadn't he? 'Like…so what? You probably want to know… This place, this is mine.'

'The house?'

'And the island. And the complex where you were staying. Apollo Wellbeing is my company. Mine and George's.'

He stopped, his face asking whether she had enough. She looked around the room, at its glaring opulence.

'What do you *do*, though? Apollo Wellbeing can't be your only business.'

'Do I get a question?'

'Do you think I'm on an even footing?'

He looked out the window. 'I'm involved in… I own a lot of different companies. Some of them quite successful. I'm interested in exploring new solutions in health and, particular, mental wellbeing.'

His name, Alex Firkin, now glimmered from the sediment on the floor of her memory. That word. 'Solutions'. She'd heard that before. In promotional literature. In contract-change letters. In upbeat emails about corporate initiatives and pep-webinars. She might even have seen his inoffensively corporate face before, too, in those communications, freshly shaven like he was now. God, that was probably why she'd felt he'd looked so familiar at the start of the trial. It had been nothing to do with Winston.

'Is one of your companies called Core Solutions?'

He smiled. 'Yes, and you work for us, don't you? At one of our new sites, as a receptionist? Sorry, an administrator.'

She didn't correct him with her actual title – centre manager. 'That's right.'

'I provided the initial finance for Apollo, and Dr Lineker was in charge of research and development. And, of course, I provided the complex here for the trial.'

She asked, 'Where is here?'

'Still not my turn?'

'I want to understand what happened. Why were you posing as a participant on the trial?'

'There's not much to understand really. Dr Lineker made some wild promises, and our first few forays into this venture had yielded…let's say, *mixed* results. On the encouraging side of mixed, I'd add. But *he* was confident this time. He'd tinkered with the drug and, from a personal perspective, I wanted to see, first hand, why he was getting so excited. But I was also a covert observer, feeding back data into the trial, finding out how the drug worked on you all without any observation bias. But mainly I wanted to see my money at work.'

'Was Cluedo part of your…observations?'

'It provided some interesting data, I'll say that much.'

'So why did you leave the trial?'

'Well, obviously, after what happened between Harrison and Paul, and with George and Hallie, I couldn't in good conscience allow my staff to stay on the site. So I insisted that we come back here while I determined what assistance to seek. Arturo, our pilot, and Shannon, the steward, they were already staying here, but the place has ten bedrooms.' He looked away as if he were trying to be humble, but this only served to underline that he'd meant the remark as a brag.

'You thought it was dangerous, then. At the complex.'

A worried expression appeared on his face. 'My staff were being targeted. They were the focus of the discontent.'

'So you abandoned us?'

'No, once I'd decided on the best, safest approach, I organised a solution. Help was on the way.'

'I don't understand. It's been three days now. Harrison was already subdued when you ran. And we didn't know *what* happened with Dr Lineker. Why didn't you round up those responsible, get the plane ready, and send home those of us that hadn't hurt anyone? Why did you leave us?'

His face twitched, and he dodged eye contact. 'What was the explosion? Tell me that first.'

Elle took a breath and another sip of water. Her hands gripped the glass.

'It was the plane.' He closed his eyes in frustration, as though he'd already suspected this.

She relayed the story of the crash, the attempted escape, about the bodies she'd seen sprawled across the island, and watched the colour drain from his face as his mouth fell open.

'Oh...oh fucking hell.' He walked around to sit on the sofa he'd been hiding behind, which was positioned perpendicular to the windows overlooking the ocean. 'I sent them all home. Yesterday evening, when we found out the emergency assistance team were going to be delayed another day. Jess, Monique...they were getting paranoid, they kept thinking they were seeing people walking along the cliffs. I wanted to keep them safe.' He appeared to be telling himself this more than Elle. 'So my complex?'

'It's gone. We think Charlie was trying to fly over it...He got in a pissing contest with Harrison. He insisted he could fly the plane but...it crashed right through the building. Harrison, Becks, they were inside.'

'You said "we"?'

'Benji and me.'

'Is he okay?' He sat forward, sounding genuinely hopeful.

It didn't feel right to hold back anymore. Not when he was in a position to act and had clearly been distressed by what he'd heard. He might now want to salvage what he could from the situation.

'Okay, so Benji was with me outside the complex when the crash happened, but he was badly injured. I left him this morning – he can't walk and he's lost a lot of blood. But, if we can get help to him soon, I think he'll survive.'

'Oh, God. Why didn't you tell me?'

Her gaze crept to his gun briefly. 'I didn't…don't know what this is all about.'

'How long do we have?'

'I don't know. Can we get to him? Do you have a car or something here?'

He shook his head. 'There was never much need for cars here. Monique, Jess and Carl took the minibus to the airstrip with Arturo and Shannon. It's probably sitting at the airstrip. I had a motorbike, but it packed in on me last Christmas. I'd already sent the rest of the villa staff home by boat.'

'Are there any other boats?'

He slumped back and looked up at the ceiling. Scratched his forehead with the gun. 'Has Ricoh shown up yet?'

Her whole body tensed at the sound of his name. He'd deflected the question, too, and that unsettled her. Because if his priority wasn't saving Benji, what was it? 'Can we at least call someone to help him? Get an air ambulance over. And don't we need to report the crash? What if…what if someone has survived and they need help? What if someone's trapped under the rubble?'

'It's fine, Elle. It's under control. As I said, there are a team of specialists coming here to sort things out. They'll go straight to him, okay?'

'A team?'

'Yes. A corporate accident like this…it requires a team.'

'And they're coming now? Are the police coming?'

'It's been…a task to assemble them at short notice. It had never been my intention to leave you all there so long and there have been transport issues. But they will be here very soon. The next hour, maybe.'

Elle looked up at the room again, her head light and her eyes still sore. No paintings hung on the walls. No rugs warmed the polished-tile floor. There was a basketball on the patio outside, and what looked like an indoor putting green over in the corner. But mostly the place had a catalogue feel, like it was simply a fashion accessory rather than a home. Did Alex own other islands, perhaps? Other houses like this?

That word, 'team'. She didn't like it. Not the police. Not Interpol. Not the emergency services. A *team*.

How rich did you have to be to own an island with a house like this on it? Presumably rich enough to have people on standby to come and cover up your tracks if something went terribly wrong. If you'd perhaps made a little bet on a project that had turned out to be the worst sort of investment. A team. And who might be in that group of people? Lawyers and private security – Benji might have been right about that. But who else?

Loneliness, even greater than what she'd felt out in the desert, closed its jaws on her.

'Is there anyone else in the house?' Elle asked again.

He sat up straight. 'Is that your next question?'

Despite his apparent concern, his obvious inner torment, she still didn't trust him.

'No,' she said. 'No, if I have to sit here trusting that help really is on the way, then I want to know more. I want to know what the trial really was. I want my debriefing.'

2

Alex looked disappointed. 'You don't trust me?'

'You still have a gun and you haven't told me why. So no, I don't trust you.'

'Ah, right,' he said, looking at the gun like he'd grown a new limb. 'Well, hang on, can I get an answer, please? Ricoh, any sign of him?'

'He's dead, too.'

'The crash?'

She shook her head. 'My turn now. The trial. What were you studying?'

He narrowed his eyes. 'There's a certain amount of acceptance to this,' he held up the gun, 'that makes me wonder if you know already. I know a lot of theories were being bandied around during the trial. So let me ask you, Elle – what do *you* think the trial was about?'

'Benji is dying. Why are you…playing games? Can't you just tell me?'

'It's not a game. It's just…' He leaned forward on his knees. 'To understand what this trial is about, it will involve giving you insights about yourself that are quite sensitive, Elle. So I need to establish first how much you might already have come to understand, just through everything that's happened.'

She paused. He sounded genuine. Insights about herself, what did that mean?

'Fine,' she said. 'Well, what I think happened is, you gave us all a drug called Silver Bullet.'

He looked shocked, but then his face relaxed when it must have occurred to him that without anyone policing the complex, they would have had the freedom to find any of Dr Lineker's notes that Jess hadn't taken.

'I think there was never actually a placebo, we were all given the actual drug. And I don't know what the drug was meant to do, or why we were brought here to this island, but I suspect those two things might be related.' She lifted her head, but his face gave nothing away. 'I also know that you all ran off three days ago, and you didn't answer me just now when I rang your bell. *And* you're still holding a gun. So I think the drug had an unexpected side-effect that you believe has made us dangerous. Or at least, *might* make us dangerous in a way that you can't predict anymore.'

'A side-effect? Interesting.' He got up and stood at the window, looking out at the water.

'Lots of us had headaches after taking the pills. The ones with the most severe headaches experienced odd symptoms. Not feeling themselves. Complaining of excessive boredom, even though the place was kitted out with every kind of entertainment imaginable. Some people got excessively selfish. And then there was the aggression – charming, friendly people acting violently and showing no regret about what they'd done afterwards. I'm not an expert, but it was like the medication changed everyone.'

'I see,' he said.

'It happened slowly. The first week or so we were all friendly, hanging out and having a laugh, but then people began to change. The drugs made them more inward in some way. I even said to Benji...with Harrison, it was like the medication made him...psychopathic.'

Alex nodded, his lips pressed together in a non-committal line. 'So you think the medication somehow...did this unexpectedly?'

'Maybe. You know, surely? Did it? Or maybe you meant to bring about these traits?'

He shook his head. 'I've had experiences with psychopathy in my work, and I suppose traits like lack of empathy, fearlessness, blaming others would fit. Lots of glib and superficially charming individuals, too. Individuals willing to pursue their own goals at the expense of others. Lacking impulse control.' He smiled now. 'So your observations are interesting. Can you elaborate? We definitely didn't *intend* to bring about those traits.'

She told him about Hallie and Ricoh's symptoms. About the graffiti in her drawer. About Harrison's obsession with his money, and how he'd been after killing Paul.

'Then there was all this security footage Harrison found on the cameras that he insisted on showing to us,' she said. 'Stuff he'd retrieved. Like Becks's accident?'

He nodded for her to go on.

'She threw herself down the stairs. And the goat that died? Hallie broke its neck.'

'That's interesting. Harrison retrieved video footage from our system? He shouldn't have been able to do that.'

'You don't sound very surprised about what I just told you.'

'No, sorry. No. I'd already seen those things.'

'You'd seen them?'

'Yes, we were observing you all very closely. We had to, because whilst Dr Lineker was confident in the new batch of pills, not all of us were. Looking back, it was after that, when the cameras started playing up… That's when I should have called time on the whole trial, just to be safe. Easy to say in retrospect. If Paul couldn't fix an IT malfunction, that's when you know there's an issue. I actually joked that Harrison might have the skills to help us… Turns out he did, but instead he hacked in, did he?'

'Apparently Paul had been sloppy and didn't actually know what he was doing. Also your system wasn't malfunctioning. Paul lied to you.'

'Excuse me? That wasn't my understanding.'

'Was it your understanding that Paul was stealing from you?'

'What do you mean?'

'Is that your question, then? Will you answer mine next?'

'Sure, what was he stealing?'

'He was trying to steal Dr Lineker's drug to sell to a third party, we believe. He was blaming the cameras malfunctioning to cover up his theft.'

'That was Harrison, though.'

She told him about Harrison and Paul's agreement, about the video footage of Ricoh seeing Paul, and, because it felt good knowing more than him, she told him about them finding Ricoh's body at the foot of the cliff.

He fell silent, vanishing into an inner world of calculations while his nose wrinkled in a predatory snarl.

'You don't look that surprised,' Elle said.

After a little more contemplation, his face relaxed. 'Well, Paul was never content. I did my best for him – what can I say? If he really did that, it would…it puts a few other jigsaw pieces together, sadly.' He stood up and walked to the window. He shrugged, but she could tell this news had stung him. And it made sense enough for him to believe.

She finished her glass of water and without asking, Alex came over and took it away to be refilled.

'Was I right?' she said. 'About the side-effects? That's my question, by the way.' He didn't answer. She got to her feet now and walked over to the window, wanting to see his reaction. He returned with the glass and took up a position between her and the patio doors.

Her gaze wandered to the left of the cove. Further down at the end of the jutting cliff, she noticed a jetty poking out into the sea. Moored at the far end was a small yacht, about the size of Granny Alice's.

'You said you didn't have a boat.'

He looked out towards the jetty. 'Oh. No, I meant I did, but there's not enough petrol.'

That wasn't what he'd said. 'So if we go out there now the gauge will show it's empty?'

'Well, no, but there's not very much in there. Not enough to get to the other end of the island, I shouldn't think. Sorry.'

She still didn't believe him. 'You must have petrol here?'

'No. We used what petrol we had on the extra minibus runs to and from the centre.'

'Really? How did the housekeepers get to and from the compound?'

'The minibus is electric. Carl would drive them both down each morning. It needed very little petrol.' He was contradicting himself now. Did it use lots of petrol or not? 'Honestly, Elle, the best thing we can do for Benji is sit tight and wait for assistance to arrive. They'll take care of everything.' He held out his arm in the direction of where she'd been sitting before. 'Please take a seat. I think it's best we're sitting down for this. Like I said, it's sensitive and…'

With some reluctance, she did as he asked. He returned to his seat on the sofa, too, the gun still in his hand.

He stared at her, and smiled. 'Sorry, I just find it all fascinating. That you don't even know.'

'Know what?'

'What you are? Do you feel different from other people, Elle? Have you always felt other people just…aren't quite like you?'

She frowned at him. Of course she felt different from other

people – didn't everyone? Yes, she supposed she was a bit over-sensitive. She knew not many women would willingly choose to live with their parents as they approached their thirties. But not everyone had a mum like hers.

'I don't feel different. No.'

'Okay, well, listen. Here's the thing. Our trial, Capricorn, had a number of outcomes we wanted to measure. I wanted my money's worth, and our unique situation here enabled us to do a lot with a little. One of the primary outcome measures was the effectiveness of SB-14 – i.e. was Silver Bullet every-thing George said it was? But I'll get to that. The other measure of particular interest to me was just how effective the algorithm was which selected you all to be here. I mean, we already knew it was good. What we wanted to know was how specific it can get. Whether it can pick sewing needles from haystacks rather than knitting needles.'

'There was a selection algorithm?'

'Yes. We built it to detect certain patterns of online behaviour, latch on to that person, and sort of keep a check on them. See if the behaviour was consistent. Then, when it was 90 per cent certain that you fit very specific personality criteria, it sent you the advert for our trial.'

'What personality criteria?'

He smiled, and it was oddly warm. 'You really don't have a clue?'

'No. I don't have a clue.' She couldn't hide her irritation now. How had she ever thought this man reminded her of Winston? He had a child-like quality to him that was in no way endearing, one that only the most spoiled hadn't shed by their thirties. And without his beard now, the thickness of the facial skin and the roundness beneath his chin suggested he was in his mid-forties at least, if not older.

'Apollo Digital is a separate company of mine, and we've

been working on algorithms that can diagnose mental health conditions and personality types and disorders, exclusively based on online behaviour. One of many things we looked at, funnily enough, was the tricky little area of psychopathy, as well as some of the other so-called dark-triad traits. In particular, we don't know nearly enough about something often called adaptive psychopathy, which refers to people with psychopathic traits who don't end up in prison and can actually have a level of success in the real world. Virtually all the research has been done on prisoners. They're cheap. They're a captive cohort. They're bored. We thought a tool that could detect the non-criminal sort might be useful to researchers.'

Elle looked at him and swallowed hard. 'Sorry, your algorithm detects psychopaths?'

His eyes widened in mock outrage. He tutted. 'Some people say it's something you *have*, Elle, not something you are, don't you know?' Then he laughed. 'Anyway, it's more complicated than that. It's more about clusters of traits these days – but yes, essentially our algorithm found people high in psychopathic traits. And it could also do that in quite specific ways. It was really that specificity which we wanted to test. So psychopathy and violent behaviour do go hand in hand in the academic journals, but is that just because we mainly study prison populations, where the violence is more detectable? Supposedly those outside the prison system are less prone to violence.' He put his hand up to his mouth and spoke through the corner of it: 'Unless they're just exceptionally good at hiding it.' He laughed again. 'But our algorithm was so good, it was able to pick out those with psychopathic traits who were also less prone to violence. You all lacked a conscience, but you weren't supposed to be dangerous.'

Now it was Elle's turn to smile, although it was really more of a rictus. 'I'm not a psychopath.'

Alex nodded. 'Well, you likely didn't know.'

'No. No, I'm not. Are you saying…all of them?'

'Yes. Every one. High-functioning, but high in psychopathic traits, yes. I was interested to see if you'd become aware of your own situation when it was reflected back at you by the others. But no, you all remained oblivious. Because to you, this is your world. You don't believe there's anything wrong with you.'

'No.' She looked away from him, unable to meet his smug face. His stupid algorithm was useless. She wasn't high in psychopathic traits, she was the exact bloody opposite. How could they have possibly—?

'You made a mistake. You really did. I found the advert for the trial on my mum's computer.'

'No, the algorithm would have weeded your mum out by age.'

'But how? Because my mum lies about her age all the time. On Facebook, on dating websites. She thinks she's a teenager.'

He paused, and shook his head. 'It's too complicated to explain, but it doesn't matter. You filled in a number of questionnaires, too, don't forget.'

She looked back at him. 'No. Just one. One which—'

'No, there was more than one,' he said. 'Yes, there was some debate about overkill, but we agreed at least two. Besides, the algorithm is more sophisticated than just—' He broke eye contact with her now, his brow a valley of ridges. Sounding unsure, he added, 'It knows everything.'

'I lied on my questionnaire. I was drunk and wanted the money.'

Something moved near one of the pillars at the far end of the room. Elle caught it in her peripheral vision. She jerked her head towards the motion but the room was empty.

'I know what you're up to,' Alex said, smiling. 'Nice try. But anyway, what this means is that you did correctly identify psychopathic traits in your fellow participants, but that wasn't anything to do with the trial or side-effects. That was just them. It genuinely was, for a time, fascinating to watch. Especially Cluedo. Each of you seeking to impose dominance over the situation you were in, and each of you resisting the others. Harrison with his whole chill-guy persona. Charlie and Mai with their claims to expertise and insider knowledge. Becks with her attempts to make people feel sorry for her. Everyone was lying all the time. They were predating on you, you know? As I'm sure you were predating on them, although you're harder to read.'

'What do you mean?'

'They wanted you for something. And when they didn't they were stringing you on for their amusement. It's called duping delight, and those with psychopathy take great pleasure from elaborate deception. You know Harrison's not really a tech bro? He lives with his rich mum in Lymington and uses her money to fund fruitless get-rich-quick schemes and holidays. Charlie's lived with his parents his whole adult life, and Mai lives in a flat paid for by her family. Hallie lives with her brother, and he uses his contacts to get her paralegal jobs. And you…live with your mum. Parasitic behaviour is another trait, and everyone on the trial was looking for an opportunity to better their circumstances without having to work for it. They were either trying to sleep with you, laugh at you or gain your trust to exploit later. Did you get any investment opportunities? I got at least four in the last few weeks. Dale wanted me to co-publish his novel.'

All of it clicked in Elle's head. She was an idiot for not seeing it before. She'd been too involved in herself, ludicrously, to even notice the gaping chasm between her and the others.

'I mean, didn't you find it unusual that no one said that

they had signed up to the trial for the good of humanity?' Alex said. 'Do you know how peculiar that is? I asked each one of you about why you had agreed to participate, and every single answer was about the holiday or the money. I've worked around clinical trials my whole career, and the vast majority of participants do it out of the goodness of their hearts. Which, incidentally, is why trial recruitment in general is getting increasingly hard.'

'Is that why you offered such enormous incentives on this trial?'

'Oh, well, trying to get those high in psychopathic traits to give up their time voluntarily is impossible. But, luckily for us, you're all reward-motivated, and risk-seeking. So we set the bar high to make sure we had a good pool to choose from.'

'And did it work?'

'It was still hard. Initially we had selected twenty participants. Eight just didn't cooperate at various stages of the recruitment phase. One didn't show up at the airstrip.'

'Are you even allowed to offer rewards like that? We found something in Dr Lineker's notes…he said he didn't get ethical approval for this trial.'

'Ah. Well, I mean…look, he handled all that stuff. I had very little to do with it.' He studied her reaction, and his expression softened. 'This island is a disputed territory. I bought it from the Moroccans, but the Spanish still think it's theirs. They're both very keen for me to support their claim to it.'

'So it's *not* a Canary Island?'

'Not officially, but it might as well be. It's near enough and has the same geography. But my point is, this place is out of the way enough that we can sort of pick and choose which authority might support our decision to go alone at this early stage of product development. Now, I'm not saying that it was a research outcome or anything, but…the MHRA and the FDA…these bodies slow down medicine development and stifle innovation.'

'They stop drug companies poisoning the population,' Elle said. 'Stop them running trials where people die.'

'Of course, but some of these people are the worst kind of bureaucrats. Authorising copy after copy of drugs we already have while stifling anything truly new. What George claimed to have discovered was going to change the world, and for it to have sat unused while each round of tweaks went through years and years of approval – well, what about the ethics of that? I'd probably be dead before the drug ever got to market. Meanwhile…psychopaths, bloody cliché-spouting moral deserts, are —' His voice cracked, and he swallowed. His playful enthusiasm had drained away. 'Are free to destroy people's lives.'

He looked to his left, gazing out to sea.

Again, something moved in the corner of Elle's eye to her left, but when she looked back at the room, it was still empty. A trick of the light. That's what it had to be. 'Are you okay?' she said. 'Did something happen to you?'

'Look, you don't care. You can take the mask off now.' He pointed his gun at her, and Elle clenched her fists. He looked down, realised what he'd done, and put the gun hand back on the sofa at his side.

'I'm not what you think I am, Alex.' She worried about what was happening to him, the way he was talking and acting. He was working himself up to do something, possibly to her. She needed to keep him talking. Keep him calm and distracted. She tried to look around for an alternative exit. His 'team' really didn't fill her with hope.

'What was the drug, then?' she asked.

He shrugged, making a face as if she was a complete idiot. 'It was the cure, of course. It was a drug that enhanced the affective system, gave the conscienceless a conscience. And empathy. Remorse. Feelings of love and warmth for their fellow man. Basically, it's a drug to make you give a shit.'

Elle said nothing, trying to ignore the poison in that loaded *you*.

She tried to process the information he'd just given her.

Ricoh. Hallie. Whoever had written that message in her drawer.

They're taking our souls.

They hadn't lost their conscience. They'd never had one. But if you'd suddenly been given one, without knowing what was happening to you, might you feel unlike yourself? Inauthentic, even. Like some fundamental part of you, your *soul*, had been taken away.

Both of them had said they were feeling things they hadn't experienced before. Ricoh saying he was trapped in his own head, but that he wasn't himself. That made sense now. And Hallie insisting that Dr Lineker had put something terrible inside them. Because really, what would it be like, to have conducted yourself with no conscience all this time, and now suddenly, all at once, to feel remorse? All those transgressions collapsing on you at once. Suffocating you.

Isn't that how Hallie and Ricoh had seemed? Suffocated. And to suddenly feel fear, where perhaps you'd never felt fear before, like on a precipice. Might you climb to the top of a cliff to understand that, to test yourself? Might you swim out into the depths of the ocean and keep swimming?

'Let me ask you, Elle – did you feel any different?'

She raised her head and eventually shook it.

'No, that's the problem. It's been…inconsistent. George made some interesting strides, and he had my interest… He said if we generated some initial positive results, perhaps by being slightly maverick about it, we could bring in more investors and spread the risk of the costly research and development at a later stage. More money to run further trials and make the necessary changes to the drug that would deliver the results he had promised. He spoke positively about the tests he'd been performing in secret on a handful of his forensic patients. Said he'd really seen results.'

'Why?' Elle said.

'Why? Do you know how much psychopathy costs economies? What governments would pay? Jess did a fantastic analysis for us… Billions. The prison population alone has a far greater representation of psychopaths than the general population, just as a starter. And this isn't even including the damage done by *your* cohort – the adaptive, functional psychopaths. Just because you don't go to prison doesn't mean you don't do harm. In fact, it's long been suspected by some people, that the reason the world is so difficult to change, the reason we can't control climate change and stop injustice, is because psychopathy actually proves to be quite a useful trait in today's hyper-individualistic times. Quite a lot of the people at the top of society have psychopathy. Politicians. Lawyers. Accountants.'

'Business leaders.'

'Yes, exactly. And with my algorithm, companies could detect in-house psychopathy and offer solutions through occupational health.'

'Seriously?'

'And this would have been the start. Moral bio-enhancement is the future, Elle. It could be rolled out to the wider population. I mean, who doesn't secretly suspect that social media isn't at least exacerbating latent psychopathic traits, if not actually inducing psychopathy? The formal research hasn't been done, but we know it, don't we? Social media algorithms are designed to generate conflict because it generates more clicks. Fomenting the otherising of people who disagree with each other. Maybe it was before your time, Elle, but believe me when I say there was a time when people disagreed with each other, and it was fine. That was part of life.

'Anyway…you see, psychopathic traits turn up even in people who aren't clinically psychopathic. And, thinking even bigger, it's been shown…shown that our moral…our moral hardware is fit for small societies but not for this big globalised world with its problems like global warming and…and an expanding population. We have too much empathy for people we know and not enough for people we don't. It affects our moral judgements. It's going to kill us all.'

'I'm losing you. So empathy is…sorry, bad, too?'

'It can be, yes. At the global level. On tests people are more likely to bump someone up an organ waiting list if you tell them a sad story about their life, even if they know nothing about the person they're displacing. So maybe everyone, not just the psychopathic, could do with a little moral booster shot every so often. To keep the world from destroying itself.'

'Moral boosters for the world. Hmmm. That sounds… lucrative and not in *any* way dystopian,'

'Dystopian? You'd rather the world ended? Anyway, it's beside the point now. George's Silver Bullet didn't work, did it? I had high hopes, especially after some of the earlier testing we did had results, too.'

'Did you run tests on the island before? Were we not the first?'

'You were the first trial, the first we would use to build our case. But you weren't the first to test the drug. Thing is, although George was a good salesman, his results were never consistent – not enough to convince other investors without an interest in psychopathy. Every brain seemed to react differently in ways we didn't understand. The last set of tests we did here had four people for two weeks. And two of them seemed to improve their moral decision-making on the tests, the longer they remained on the drug – one more than the other. And they had slightly improved EEG readings too.'

'So the questions were testing moral decision-making?'

'Yes. The rest were logic puzzles thrown in to try and make sure you didn't guess what we were trying to measure.' He said this proudly, with the same smugness he'd shown when he'd told her about the number of bedrooms in the villa. Part of him was enjoying the chance to show off.

'What did the EEG do?'

'Hang on. It's surely my turn? Where did you find Ricoh's body, exactly?'

She told him, and he nodded. 'EEG?' she said.

'It's complicated, but George said you could detect psychopathology by measuring the brain waves when presented with…alarming or surprising stimuli. I've seen it in action, it's quite compelling.'

'And my brain did that?'

'Yes. Well, I mean…we never got to the point of analysing the results, so I haven't looked specifically. But we saw some earlier EEG results change. But as I said before, it wasn't compelling enough. But George argued me around, told me we needed more participants. He convinced me to run one larger, longer trial, and that he knew exactly what changes to make to the drug. And that from that we would have enough to present at conferences. So I did. Against my better instincts, I did. What can I say? I did tell you, I like a gamble.'

'But…but…didn't it cross any of your minds that having or not having a conscience is a pretty fundamental thing? That your entire…identity and personality might be wrapped up in that. You can't just flick that on and off like a switch.'

'And you know this, do you? Because in science we like to get evidence for such massive claims. But, no, I did wonder –

of course I wondered.' He leaned forward. 'I wanted to see it. Besides, we thought the benefits of conscience would overwhelm the negatives.'

Elle shook her head, the only outlet for the mounting rage she felt at the man's arrogance. How was it allowed, in this day of such extreme moral outrage, that a single man could have the power to run his own private experiments on a sort of whim? Or worse, because there might be money in it, or some extreme libertarian point to prove about government bureaucracy.

'So everything that happened here was for nothing? All these people are dead for no reason.'

He looked crestfallen. As though he'd momentarily forgotten everything, and that she had been very unkind in dragging it all back into the spotlight. 'It's not...not for nothing. I've learned so much that I can't begin to explain. I'm convinced now, there can't be a cure for this. George's heart was in the right place, but he was wrong. People like Harrison and Hallie, people who charm and steal and kill for their own ends, there is no fixing them. And there is no such thing as being a less dangerous, less violent, more functional psychopath. I really wanted to believe that there could be and maybe I did at one time. But now I know. There are those who get caught and those who don't. And that changes everything.'

Elle pushed her hands through her hair, unable to deal with the sharpness of his sanctimony. '*You* did this, though. Harrison, Hallie, Ricoh, Mai, Charlie...you said it, they were functional before. Going about their lives. *You* created this situation, put people with psychopathic traits together in an enclosed space, on a bloody island, gave them an unapproved experimental drug which potentially altered their entire personality—'

He shook his head. 'Maybe in Ricoh's case. A little in

Hallie's. But what they did, that was because of what was already there. The drug simply didn't do enough.'

'You have scientific evidence for this, then?'

Now he glared, a man resentful of his own trap. And she hated him. She hated what he was, what he stood for, the immovable object of extreme wealth and privilege. A man not used to hearing he was wrong, and who believed his fortune was earned. He might have a conscience, he might not. But what good was a conscience when you were so powerful that even your well-intentioned errors could destroy lives?

'Hallie didn't kill Dr Lineker.'

He looked disgusted. 'Of course she bloody did.'

'It was an accident. How do you think I found out about the drug? Dr Lineker left a letter to Jess, told her that he had… an aneurysm in his head. Told her about how he'd been cutting corners because at any moment he might die. And you can see it on the video footage, too. He collapsed on her and fell.'

'Rubbish. And…and…that doesn't even matter.' Again, she appeared to have stunned him. He was clearly piecing together what it all meant and how plausible her reasoning was.

At that moment another movement caught Elle's eye.

3

From behind a pillar, Hallie appeared. She stared at Elle, two fists held either end of what looked like a thick curtain tie. She brought a finger up to her lips and started to creep towards Alex from behind. Elle had no idea what to do, and could only stare while Hallie advanced on an oblivious Alex. She wore the same clothes she'd been wearing three days ago. They were soaked in blood. Her usually straight hair was wild and sun-frizzed. Her face twisted with pain at every step of progress she made.

Once behind Alex, she raised the cord above his head. And still Elle only stared. The gun was still next to Alex, his hand resting on its handle. She wasn't sure what his intentions were, or why Hallie was here now and why she was covered in blood. With no idea which side to choose, she became a paralysed spectator.

Hallie brought the cord down around Alex's neck and twisted it. In the same move she dropped behind the back of the sofa with the cord's end clutched over her shoulder. Alex's eyes bulged, his head pinned to the ridge of the sofa back. He dropped the gun, hands clutching at his throat. When he couldn't free himself, he tried pulling himself forward, but just as he managed to raise his head Hallie yanked him back. Then he tried to roll himself over the top of the sofa. But Hallie realised what he was doing, so stood up again and pushed him back down.

That was when he grabbed the gun from where it had fallen on the cushion. He lifted it up and fired it at her head. Elle screamed, covering her head as the gunshot reverberated around the room. Hallie ducked, and he lost his footing, falling back onto the sofa. Hallie wrapped the cord around his neck again, pulling tight. He choked and retched, unable to free himself, and his eyelids flickered. His eyes found Elle's, pleading with her to help. But she couldn't move. Didn't know who to trust. She was back in the hospital reception again, fire extinguisher in hand, unsure what to do. Alex twisted the gun into one of the rear cushions with his remaining strength. He was going to try and shoot Hallie through the sofa.

Elle felt a surge of bravery now, the gun and his gaze pointed away from her. She sprang up from her seat, reaching towards him and grabbing the weapon from his hand with surprising ease. He stared up at her, resignation in his bloodshot eyes.

'Hallie, let go,' she said. Hallie did no such thing. Feeling brave, Elle climbed over the sofa and said more firmly, 'Hallie, let him go.'

Elle had never held a gun before. The cool metal rested heavily in her hands. She raised it up, aiming at Hallie, who stared back dead-eyed. Shakily, Elle began to count down from three. On one Hallie let go, clearly sensing at the same moment Elle did that Elle meant to pull the trigger.

Alex coughed, sucking in air with a harrowing creak as he bent double over the sofa.

'Oh my God.' Elle tried to catch her breath. 'Oh my *God*.'

'Give me the gun,' Hallie said.

'No. Sit on the sofa next to him,' Elle said, still pointing the weapon towards her. Hallie got to her feet but didn't move. 'Please.'

4

Alex and Hallie sat at opposite ends of the sofa. Elle kept the gun aimed at Hallie, who at this point seemed the bigger threat. She sat on the edge of the marble coffee table at the centre of the sofa square.

'You know he shot me?' Hallie said. She lifted her top, revealing a gory wound seeping at the farthest edge of her stomach. She glared at him, and sounding no angrier than someone running a little late, she added, 'I'm going to die now.'

Alex pinned Hallie with a murderous expression. 'She killed George. I assumed she would kill me too.'

Hallie shook her head, 'I'm walking up to his gate, and he stone cold walks out with that gun, and I put up my hands to say 'Please help me', but instead he just shoots me. In cold blood.'

'She asked you for help and you shot her?'

'People with psychopathy, they play you for your sympathy, Elle. You have to be cold, too.'

'He'll shoot you, too, you know,' Hallie said. 'Why did you stop me dealing with him?'

'I'm not going to shoot you, Elle,' Alex said.

'No? Why'd you shoot me then, you shit-head? Fucking in agony here.'

'I thought you'd killed Dr Lineker. I only intended to incapacitate you.'

'I didn't kill him.'

'Well, I didn't know that. But Elle has convinced me otherwise now.'

Hallie screwed up her face in confusion. Elle retold the story she'd already told Alex; about the video footage Harrison had found, about the letter hidden in Dr Lineker's office that he'd written to Jess, explaining everything.

She shook her head, appraising the memory in the middle distance. 'He just fell on me and… I tried getting him off me. It was the gravity. It just pulled him over. He made this fucking terrible sound at the bottom, I think he hit the rail. It went through me. I've not felt anything like it. Like I'd fallen down there.'

'Where did you go afterwards?'

'I panicked. Those drugs were already messing with my head. Making everything…too emotional. I kept thinking about all these…things I've done. Like, this stupid old woman that I got fired at work. She should have retired years before, she was useless, but no one had the heart to do it. So I forced the issue by leaving some nasty porno in her drawer for the boss to find. I haven't thought about her in years, and all of a sudden I was sitting out on that bloody cliff thinking about how upset she must have been. Feeling bad about it. And I've never been scared of heights. Never. Yet all of a sudden my legs start shaking when I stand at the edge of a cliff.'

'You were probably one of the lucky ones the drug affected,' Alex said. 'You were feeling regret and fear the way most of us do.'

'Lucky ones?' She curled her lip at Alex. 'I heard what you said just now, telling her what the drug does. That you think me and her are psychos. But if anyone's a psycho, it's the person who makes a drug that makes people feel the way I was feeling.'

She turned back to Elle. 'I knew how it would look, me being out there with Dr Lineker when he fell. I knew the cameras might have made it look like I pushed him off. And fuck knows what godforsaken prison I'd end up in, so I grabbed some things from my room and got out of there. I wanted to go home and I was determined to do it my way. My brother's a barrister, he knows people. He could help me if I ended up on trial.

'But there's nothing fucking out there. I went across the desert so no one could track me, but there's nothing there. Nothing at all. I got lost, and I kept imagining being dead and no one would ever find me. Eventually I found a road, I don't know how long I'd been out there for. I heard an engine in the distance and followed it towards the airstrip. I saw the plane take off. I thought I'd been left behind so I started waving madly, but then it flew low, too low. I didn't see the crash but I heard it. Thank fuck I wasn't on board, I was so relieved. When I got to the airstrip I found Carl dead on the ground, all stabbed up. I didn't want to hang around, so I walked back the way I'd come, thinking the road wouldn't be there if it didn't go somewhere.'

'Didn't you see the minibus?' Elle said.

'Yeah, but I can't drive. Never bothered to learn. Anyway, I keep walking for what feels like forever until I pass Dale, and he's dead, so I carry on. When I turn up here hoping for help, *he* walks out and bloody shoots me.'

'I'm sorry,' Alex said.

'Then he drags me a few metres, don't know what he was doing, but I was pretending to be dead. And then he just gives up and walks off, and I'm lying there in the dust covered in blood. When I knew he'd gone, I got up and made my way down to the sea, swam around the rocks, nearly bloody drowned, but then I found a boathouse and a boat tucked away in the cove. I was going to take it off the island that night if I didn't die, but I went into the boathouse to hide and try and stop the bleeding. I must've passed out from the bullet wound because I only woke up this afternoon when I heard you two talking on the beach.

The three of them stared at each other.

'What are we going to do?' Elle said.

'You need to shoot him, and then we need to get in that boat and head towards whatever land is on the horizon. There's fuel in the boat, right? I heard him say that. And he was probably lying about there not being much. Were you lying?' She looked at Alex who answered with a glare.

'I can't shoot him, Hallie. He's not tried to—' Was she really going to say he hadn't tried to harm anyone? She couldn't in good faith, so instead said, 'I'm not shooting anyone if we all agree to leave here alive.'

'Elle, this fucker will kill us the moment he gets a chance. Weren't you listening to him? He was working himself up to do it. Asking how many people were left, where all the bodies were. This whole thing is on him now. Lineker's dead. Everyone else involved is dead. He's got his crew coming, right? What do you think they're going to do? If any of this gets out, he's done for.'

Elle didn't want to be swayed by Hallie. But didn't she have a point? Perhaps once Elle might not have believed a single person might wield the kind of power that could make something like this disappear. Not someone with legitimate, legal businesses anyway. Yet if places like this existed, secret islands with luxury mansions, was it so implausible that there might be teams of unsavoury people who, for big money, would come out to clean up messes like this for you? She surely had to err on the side of caution, get out of here before anyone else arrived, so the real authorities could get here as soon as possible.

'We need to go back for Benji before we leave,' Elle said.

Hallie shook her head. 'No. He's a part of this shit. He should go down with the rest of them. If he's not dead already.'

'He's not part of this. You're wrong.'

Elle knew it would take something extreme for her to actually fire the gun. But she took confidence in the fact she wasn't trying to make excuses now. Not for Hallie or for Alex. She wasn't trying to see where they were coming from. Understand their story. Empathy could be dangerous, that was what Alex had said.

'You want to risk using up the petrol on that?' Hallie said. 'If we go back, and he's dead, we're all stuck.'

'Does the boat need a key?' Elle asked Alex.

He rubbed his throat where a bright-red welt had formed. 'It's a push ignition. But you won't get there, she's right to worry.'

'I don't believe you.' She flicked the gun up once. 'Come on, let's go. We've wasted too much time already – we're going to help him.'

Hallie and Alex glanced at each other.

Elle raised her voice: 'Both of you. Now.' She took a

breath. And because she wasn't yet a monster, she added, 'Please.'

5

Alex and Hallie moved slowly up the main staircase, both emitting grunts through gritted teeth. How much of their pain was real and how much they were putting on was unclear, but she gave them the benefit of the doubt and felt cruel but in control. Elle kept her distance as they collected two suitcases from a walk-in cupboard upstairs. Downstairs again, she ordered them to collect food, water, and a large first-aid kit from beneath the kitchen sink.

'Let's go then,' she said, marching them out of the kitchen and back into the oversized living area through a large opening in the wall. Elle was about to pass through herself when she noticed an iPad lying on the table.

'Alex,' she said. He stopped and turned. 'Do you have Wi-Fi here?'

His stony expression didn't change, which told her all she needed to know. How could she not have thought of it before? This wasn't the trial complex. This place was fully connected – how else had he contacted his team?

'And a phone. You must have a phone.'

He continued to stare at her. 'I've already told you that a team is on its way.'

'I want to call the police myself. On the mainland. Get them to send help for Benji.'

'My team will sort all of that. If you put in a call now you might delay them.'

'I really doubt that. And the fact you're saying this makes me worry. It scares me actually, Alex.'

'What scares you?'

'I don't want to sound paranoid, although you can probably forgive me after all this, but as it stands the only people who know about what happened here now are me, Hallie, Benji and you. And you tried killing her, and you held a gun on me while I told you what you needed to know. So yeah, I'm worried your team is going to try and pull off a cover-up.'

'That's not true. My entire team know about this, right down to the housekeeping staff I sent back by boat. You're being paranoid. I think we're *all* being a bit paranoid.'

'Will you log me in to your iPad, please?'

'Elle, no. There are private documents on that—'

The gun had been down at her side, and now she raised it and pointed it at him. 'Just do it, Alex.'

The seriousness in his expression softened, not in a pleasant way, but the way a gambler's might after committing to his final bet, one that would cover all his losses. 'No,' he said, sounding scared but determined. 'Shoot me, if you want, but you're not messing this up, Elle.'

She stretched both arms to push the gun closer to him. She had to stand firm or the power dynamic would collapse. Her advantage would be lost.

'I'll count to three then,' she said. 'One…'

'For fuck's sake, Elle,' Hallie said, shaking her head. She walked towards Elle at speed. Elle turned the gun on her.

'Hallie, stand still.' Elle took a step back.

Still she kept coming, looking fearless and vaguely fed up. Elle raised the gun and fired it at the ceiling. Plaster and dust flew through air still reverberating with gunfire. Alex jumped, but Hallie barely blinked. She kept coming, and now Elle pointed the gun at her again and took another step back, her backside touching one of the chairs tucked beneath a glass-topped dining table. Hallie reached out, fearless, and grabbed the barrel of the gun in two hands and began to try to pull it from Elle's hands.

'Give it,' Hallie said.

Elle held firm, and Hallie began to pull harder, twisting a little now.

'Don't, Hallie.' The remaining assertiveness in her voice sounded brittle.

'Babe, you're not shooting anyone. Give me this.'

After a few more tugs, Elle's eyes welled up and blurred her vision. She couldn't do it. Hallie threw a punch at Elle's stomach. It wasn't hard, but it knocked her back. But she held on. She might not be able to shoot her but she'd be damned if she was giving Hallie—

Hallie threw another punch, a compact little rock striking just below Elle's ribs. She let go of the gun and fell back with the pain. She tried catching her breath and couldn't, watching with horror as Hallie stumbled back with the gun, right into Alex. He moved quickly, aiming a punch at Hallie as he tried to grab the gun from her hand.

The two of them wrestled, the gun between them. Hallie was small, but strong, and managed to turn the gun around and fire it. Alex cried out, agony choking his yell up into a scream. He dropped to his knees, but still held on to Hallie's hands with the gun clasped between them. Hallie tried firing the gun again, but Alex had used a finger to block the trigger. His face reddened, and he grunted while trying to wrench the weapon from her grip. She aimed a kick at his side, but stumbled. As she tried to steady herself, she let go of the gun.

Alex wasted no time. He grabbed the gun and fired once at her face. Blood spattered on the white surfaces. Hallie collapsed to the floor, turning as she did and landing on what remained of her face just a few feet from Elle's hand.

He took a moment to catch his breath. Then he raised the gun and shot Hallie once more in the back. She didn't move.

'You're all the same,' he said. 'That's the bloody truth of it.'

Elle tried to speak. To slow him down, but the pain in her abdomen didn't allow her to take a full breath. She had to move, though. She could hear hatred in his voice. If she ran now, perhaps if he was hurt she could get to the boat.

'I didn't know what to do before,' he said. 'I really didn't. I almost, *almost* believed you, you know. I said you were different before. That superficial charm you all have, only you came close to seeming genuine to me. And just now, you actually looked scared. I almost believed we . *had* made a mistake selecting you. But just now…you sat there watching her choke me. And then you stopped me shooting her, even though you knew what she'd done.'

Elle took in as much air as she could and forced it through her vocal cords, 'I saved you.'

He shook his head. 'No you didn't. You needed me to confirm about the boat key so you could escape. You needed me because I was useful.'

Elle shook her head, but he was looking down at his blood-soaked trousers now. She wanted to stall him, give herself enough time to make a run to the patio doors just behind her. If they were locked she was done for, but if they were open, it would be a straight line across the beach to the jetty.

She managed a slightly deeper breath, and said, 'What do you mean, we are all the same?'

He sneered. 'My wife was killed in a hit and run. We'd been married two years when this…man hit her with his car outside the school where she worked, and just drove off. It was the morning, and everyone assumed it was a joyriding kid or a drunk. But they traced the man to this suburb in Richmond. He was this comfortable, middle-class guy with a wife and two teenaged kids. The whole thing had been caught on CCTV, and…he owned up to it. Said my wife hadn't been looking where she was going, which was demonstrably false. But, he also admitted being late for a meeting, which was why he hadn't stopped and reported it. He swore he would have done eventually, he just hadn't got around to it. Can you believe that? Hadn't got around to it.'

'Are you saying…?'

'He went to prison, not for long, but I paid some people to get me answers. I needed to know how he could do something like that and apparently show no guilt or remorse, which he never once did in the whole ugly business. I wanted to know everything about him, and someone tried scoring him on the diagnostic tools for psychopathy on a hunch. He scored highly. I'd never really understood psychopathy before. I thought it was like Norman Bates in *Psycho*. I wanted to understand what this thing was, how I could stop it. How I could help and stop people like him just being out there in the world. Lots of people I talked to made it seem like an illness. So an illness might have a cure. That's what I thought.' He gave a bitter laugh. His hands holding the gun shaking. 'But there's always been differing opinions, Elle. And I told you, I wanted to believe the earnest, wide-eyed Dr Linekers of this world, but my head always said something different.'

He tried standing, winced, and crouched again. Blood was pooling around his shoe. When he'd regained his composure, he said, 'Do you know what they used to call psychopathy, Elle? They used to call it moral insanity. Which, after all this, I think is the most honest appraisal. People like George, they want a world where we're all broadly the same, and where having no conscience is like having a disease. They don't like the idea that if you have no conscience, you are fundamentally different. You can't be part of even the most basic social contract. You're parasites on it. Burrowing through your tunnels to get ahead in the world built by the rest of us. And all this talk of successful and unsuccessful psychopaths – there's just clever and not-clever. Ones that get caught and ones that don't. But I've seen enough here to know you're all the same in the way the rest of us are all the same. Under the right conditions, you're all monsters.'

'You *made* the conditions.' Elle's voice was barely a whisper.

'Well…no doubt this will take some clean-up. Likely we've violated Nuremberg, Europe, Helsinki…all the ethical policy agreements for human trials. But it was done with due diligence and a good heart. You know, some people think psychopathy isn't even a unitary concept. That it doesn't exist, even. Non-industrialised, indigenous tribes even have concepts for psychopathy. And do you know what *they* do with the morally insane? They take them out somewhere remote, and they never come back, Elle. Because maybe they see the wood for the trees, and that if we let you go about your business, it's at the expense of the rest of us.'

'Maybe what happened here is good, then? You've taken ten out of the population. Good job.'

'I don't feel bad, if that's what you're trying to do. Is it any different from dealing with a tick or a tapeworm?'

'I'm not a psychopath,' she said.

Smiling, he braced to stand once more. 'That's exactly what a psychopath would say.'

At his full height he tried to put some weight on the bleeding leg again. He cried out, stumbled forward and reached out with both hands to grab the kitchen island for support. Either through fear of setting it off, or because he lost his grip, the gun fell from his hand and struck his foot. It slid on the floor, closer to him still but within reach if Elle dived for it.

She didn't though. Instead, she got to her feet – her back,

her legs and the new pain in her stomach all raising their voices into an agonising cacophony. But she didn't stop to listen. She was at the patio door in a few steps, tugged the handle, tugged again, but it was stuck. She looked back, and Alex was bending over for the gun. She tugged again, a cry of frustration passing through her lips. It wouldn't come. It was locked.

'Elle, it's easier this way,' he said, 'My work does so much good in the world, and this accident would cast a shadow on it all. I'm sorry.'

The latch. She hadn't tried it. She pushed it up, and blessedly the thing lifted. With a pop of air the door slid to one side, just before a bullet hit the glass and it fractured into thousands of pieces while remaining in the frame.

He'd shot at her. He really meant to kill her.

She ran, out through the door and across the patio to the glass balustrade. She was still a floor above where she needed to be, so she straddled the glass and was in the process of bringing up her other leg when another bullet flew, obliterating the glass beneath her. She fell backwards, catching sight of Alex standing halfway out of the patio door with the gun raised.

Her thigh struck a glass-topped patio table, causing it to topple with her on it. Her head struck the concrete floor a moment before the table did the same and smashed. She tried to roll over and blacked out. Only for an instant, though, because pain from her thigh tore through her like a spear. She screamed. She tried to sit up, but her head hurt. Her hand reached down behind her, underneath her backside, and she half expected to find space where her leg should have been. Instead, she found a shard of glass embedded in her thigh. Who knew how deep, but her landing had further wedged it in. The sharp edge cut her fingers and she withdrew them. Had she been shot, too? She didn't know. Everywhere seemed to hurt equally.

Footsteps approached the balustrade above her. He was coming. With great effort she rolled onto her stomach and surveyed her options. More glass panels separated the beach from the patio here. In the far corner was a gap, the golden sand beyond it. But she would be out in the open there. A sitting duck. Was she any safer down here though?

Glass crunched beneath feet. He would be able to see her any second. He would shoot her again and it would be over. Would it hurt? Would it be like sleep, her thoughts spiralling down like so much water down a drain until oblivion?

No. She wasn't ready to die. Not here.

Beside her a triangular shard of glass from the table lay by her right hand. She picked it up and crawled to the foot of the wall. Glass fell into her hair and onto her skin from Alex's approach above.

It would hurt him. He would scream and cry out, and it would hurt her heart to hear it. But she couldn't hesitate. Not now. She got to one knee, tried to bend the other but couldn't, the pain too intense where the shard was stuck. So she used her hands, pushed up quickly against the tide of her agony.

His leg appeared high above her. She had one chance. She jumped up using her good leg, grabbed his ankle with both hands so her whole weight was held by his leg, and jammed the shard into his calf.

It was his turn to scream, and the gun fired, missing her. With her good leg she kicked against the wall, pulling him with her. She crashed to the floor, crying out, her chin striking the concrete after his leg struck the back of her head and knocked her to the floor. Her palm stung, and when she held it up a crescent-shaped line of blood began to seep. But there wasn't time for that, because Alex was somewhere nearby.

Elle looked back. He lay with his back against the rear wall, right arm outstretched. The gun was no longer in it. It lay halfway between them on the patio surrounded by broken glass.

He stared at her. She stared at the gun.

She spun around on her belly like a parachutist, crying out, and her hand landed on it first. His hand closed on hers. Their faces were inches apart. No one had ever truly looked at her with such blazing hatred before, but Alex's glare was carcinogenic. She yanked her hand away from him, and he yanked back with a hold on her wrist. But he was leaning forward, off balance, and her hands and lower arms were slick with blood, so with a spin of her body to the right, she was able to get free of him. She didn't stop though, and she kept rolling until she struck the glass barrier.

When she sat up he was crawling towards her, through the glass on his hands and knees. She held up the gun, having no idea how many rounds a model like this had. She had no idea – full stop – about bloody guns, having fired one only once at a holiday camp with Granny Alice in Spain.

'Okay, Elle,' Alex said. 'Well, this is the test then.' He got up on his knees, teeth bared, arms still reaching out to her. He was still trying to get to her. 'The real trial, if you like. If you're really not a psychopath, then—'

She fired the gun.

Chapter Seventeen

1

S he hadn't meant to fall asleep. But she opened her eyes to tall shadows and a lavender sky. And drying blood. She moved her injured leg and a fly took flight, landing on Alex's outstretched arm. He hadn't moved. She fought panic and nausea, winning, and with great care stood up and made her way to the nearest set of steps around the side of the building. She went back into the house, every step feeling like it was further opening the wound on her leg. Her legs still ached from walking all day, and like her arms, were covered in cuts. But they all appeared to be superficial. Her hip ached from where it had struck the table, and her back still complained from where the breeze block had hit her. But she was alive. And now she had to help Benji.

In a downstairs bathroom she touched the glass in her leg once more, but it hurt too much to pull out. Instead, she tied a towel around her leg as tightly as she could manage, with a hope she'd be at a hospital before the day was out. She searched downstairs for a landline, but only found a mobile phone, the keypad locked with a fingerprint lock and the battery almost down to nothing. She packed it with the iPad anyway, not sure if the latest phones allowed you to override the security for an emergency. She had no clue how to do this, but Benji might.

She dropped both the packed cases down to the ground level through the hole in the glass through which she'd pulled Alex. Elle half expected him to be gone when she looked down, but he was still there. She walked back around to collect the bags, began to drag them out towards the opening to the beach, and stopped.

If she didn't try, she might regret it. Distasteful as it was.

She retrieved the phone, sat down beside Alex, and lifted his hand and placed the thumb on the phone. The screen wobbled, claiming the print wasn't recognised. Using her fingers and spit, she tried wiping the blood and dirt from it. She pressed it again. No luck. The phone warned her this was her last try.

She was losing light, and every second counted for Benji. Still, she had to try. She got back to her feet, and with stuttering steps and breaths she went back up to the house and retrieved a tea towel wetted at one end. She returned again, head woozy, and wiped and dried the finger. Then she put it to the screen.

The phone locked her out. She took a long breath, wanting to smash the thing against the wall. But she didn't. Instead, she turned it off to save the battery, and walked out to the jetty.

2

The boat was slightly larger than Granny Alice's, and the interior was much more high end. The cockpit was teak-rendered, the controls in the helm finished in leather. She used the joystick function to ease it out of the jetty, and it handled better too. This stung. Granny Alice's life savings only afforded her a boat a third as nice as this one. How often had Alex even used it? It looked like a show boat.

A digital display showed a fuel gauge hovering just above the halfway line. At full speed Granny Alice's boat had been able to travel just under 100 miles on a full engine. At a lower speed, around 200. With half as much fuel in a slightly bigger boat, she conservatively used the same estimate. The island might be as long as twenty miles, and the complex was located maybe five or six miles along the south coast. That meant at full speed she had enough to get there and back. But if she took it easy, might she be able to get back and across to the other island?

If she went too slowly, though, it might be the difference between life and death. Especially if they planned to avoid encountering Alex's team. She supposed it all depended on the factors out of her control, like the efficiency of the boat, and how far that island was from here.

She'd searched for fuel in the shed before leaving, but found nothing. Really, it wasn't like her options were plentiful. She'd either make it, or stall in the middle of the ocean. Hopefully they'd be picked up before their supplies ran out.

Once out into deeper water, she began to pick up speed. She gave a final lookout in the direction of the island and brought the boat to a stop.

She kept staring. And staring.

Was this what Winston had meant about her? About burning in the fire of martyrdom. Was it a death wish to try and get back to the south coast?

Then again, what life would it really be, knowing she might have saved Benji? Forever tormented.

Elle pressed on, manoeuvring the boat starboard and back towards the complex.

3

After twenty minutes travelling at thirty miles an hour, the fuel gauge had dipped noticeably below the halfway point. She slowed the boat to save fuel. She stood at the helm and watched through the open sides for any signs of civilisation she'd missed on the unexplored east coast. She passed another caldera and jagged mountains, before something loomed into view that made her almost stop the boat.

A half-finished building stood at the top of a cliff inside a small cove. No wall surrounded it, yet it had the length and look of the trial complex. Scaffolding clung to the outside. A cement mixer sat in front of it near the edge.

Was this an abandoned version of the place they'd eventually built? Or had Alex planned to build more on the island? Perhaps to turn it into a destination for his moral bio-enhancement project.

Once she was as certain as she could be that there weren't any workers up there, she pressed on. Perhaps it was the painkillers she'd taken from the first-aid kit, but a numbness had overcome both her body and mind. It was almost pleasant, with the low sun and the sea spray. Her cuts, bruises and sunburn had all downed communications. The nausea she felt every time she pictured what had happened to Alex when the bullet struck his head was more ripple than wave.

It wasn't that psychopaths didn't feel, Winston had explained to her in that other life she'd once had. It's that they just feel things in a shallow way.

Maybe she was a psychopath after all? Or the trial had made her one.

She summoned the energy to give a short and bitter laugh. Not just at this idea, but having been here at all. Had none of them, not even Jess or Dr Lineker, suspected that Elle wasn't like the others? Or was there an element of self-fulfilling prophecy once a diagnosis had been made? Like the urban myths about patients faking mental illness and then never being able to convince professionals they'd lied.

Or perhaps the force of Alex's wealth, the glow of his powerful algorithm, made them sideline any professional doubts they had. Especially given that the others had clearly displayed psychopathic traits and behaviour. Superficial charm. Deceit. Lack of remorse.

The algorithm clearly worked.

Which did raise the question of how the algorithm had selected her. But of course, it never had. It had selected Mum. The advert had been on her computer. On her search engine. The thing had never shown up when Elle looked for it on her phone.

She smiled again, shook her head. Granny Alice had known, hadn't she?

Don't let her ruin you, she'd said. *Because she will if you let her.*

Her eyes welled with tears. Granny Alice felt close again now. Closer than at any point since she'd passed.

She'd known all along. Perhaps she knew the term 'psychopath', perhaps she didn't. But she'd known since Mum was a child.

All her selfish behaviour. Her manipulativeness. Her utter lack of guilt at all the things she'd put Elle through.

And now suddenly it made sense. What was wrong with Mum had a name. And if it had a name, it might mean something could change. If not for Mum now, then for Elle.

Because a psychopath couldn't help how they were. All this time she'd been hoping Mum might change. That if she just loved Mum enough, she might become a better person. And that one day Mum might release Elle by becoming more independent.

But Mum could never do change, could she? She would use Elle until she couldn't anymore. And then, like the men she saw, she would move on to someone else.

Despite the rage that had catapulted Elle here, she knew things would have gone back to normal once she was home. She would have told Mum she was leaving, and Mum would have quashed Elle's bravery.

Now she knew though: crocodile tears. Perhaps every one Mum had ever shed. And looking back now on those displays of despair, had there even been the faintest irritation glimmering in Mum's wet eyes?

Elle felt the unmeshing of mental nets now, so many that their contents might overwhelm her if she didn't lock herself down with some brutal mindfulness. Every explanation and story Mum had given her over the years was up for review now. All her supposed physical pains and confidence issues that had kept her out of regular work. Elle's vanished adopted cat, Lucky, whom Mum always hated. And Dad, who had died before she'd been born – or so Mum had told her. What did this mean?

It was too much, too much, too much. She needed to focus, focus, focus.

If Elle could get out of here, if she could get back home, everything *would* be different now. She could get away from Mum. She wouldn't think twice. She would have Benji in her corner. There would be fallout from the trial, yes, but she knew she had done nothing wrong. Or at least, nothing that hadn't been to save her own life.

All she needed to do now was get home.

4

When she rounded the corner of the island, the leather steering wheel opened the wound on her right hand. She didn't feel much, but worryingly that was an experience happening all over her body. The leg in which the glass was embedded had grown cold, similar to the sensation just before pins and needles set in.

Finding the location of the trial centre was easy enough, because the smoke from the plane crash still rose into the air in the ever-diminishing distance. Finally, she passed the cove at the back of the trial complex. She didn't look too closely, but made out the line of buoys and the stairs on the cliff. An odd, disorientating nostalgia drifted through her. Once past the cove, she slowed the boat and brought it closer to the shore.

The sun now hung just over the sea, and so it was hard to make out where on the slope down to the pebbled beach she had left Benji. She manoeuvred as close as she dared and stopped the boat, dropping anchor and standing on the platform at the back.

Waves nudged the boat, their lapping sounds all she could hear.

He should have heard her approach. He should have come down to the beach if he was awake.

'Benji!' Her shout seemed to die in the air in front of her.

Now fear and misery punctured the cocoon she'd been hiding inside. Her hopes began buckling beneath the weight of the silence and stillness. She was convinced now that he was gone. In fact, how stupid and naive she had been, hoping that he might have lived. How utterly bloody idiotic. And now she was likely dying of blood poisoning from an infection, when she could have made it back to a hospital on that island.

But yet again, even though it would have been beneficial to

her own survival to be that little bit selfish, that little bit *psychopathic*, she had come here to save someone else.

'Well,' she said. 'So be it. That's who I am.'

She closed her eyes and smiled. Listened.

A noise drew her attention to the shore.

What had it been? A goat's cry, perhaps. How very cruel would that be?

But this had been louder. A shout, maybe.

She squinted, scanning the slope and the beach. And then she saw movement. Halfway up. To the side of a large rock clump that might have been *their* rock clump. It was so far away really, but it was something. Enough to make her believe she *might* have heard someone shouting.

It would be a goat, though. Or a piece of detritus blowing across the slope.

But no…because what it was starting to look like to her, beyond doubt, was an outstretched arm, waving at her. Telling her this all might be fine after all. That they would go home together. That he would be by her side when she defied Mum. That the future she'd always wanted was just moments from starting. She closed her eyes. Could picture it all.

She had no idea what to do now. Whether she should swim the remaining distance to shore, or whether she needed to get the boat closer. Did she even have the strength left to make the swim? And if she ran it aground, she might damage their only way back. Presuming there was even fuel left to make the journey.

But all that could wait. Because now the pain was beginning to return, and it was angry and vengeful, and ready to take her over.

Elle sat down on the platform, her eyelids heavy. Just some time to compose herself was all she needed. A rest in the dying sunlight.

And despite the pain, the hope she had right now was bliss. And in the brief moment when it hadn't been there just now, she'd missed it. She'd missed it so much. So just for a few more moments, she wanted to enjoy it.

And she deserved that much, didn't she? To enjoy herself. After all, she was meant to be on holiday.

Acknowledgments

Randomised Clinical Trials are the gold standard of evidence for any treatment or therapy. They are marvellous things, and subject to all kinds of ethical and legal scrutiny for very good reasons. Inventing a trial like this, and finding ways for it to go wrong, involved a lot of research, and even then liberties were taken. All such liberties, errors, interpretations, misinterpretations, and misunderstandings are down to me entirely. I am very grateful for the inspiring writings of Ben Goldacre, Amanda Schaffer, Martha Stout, Kevin Dutton, Robert Hare, Kent Kiehl, Mary Turner Thomson, James Thomson, James H. Fallon, Hervey Cleckley, Abigail Marsh, Ashley Watts, Elvio Baccarini, Luca Malatesti, Mirko Daniel Garasic, Heidi L. Maibom, S. Lilienfield, M. Widows, and Jon Ronson. I'm also thankful for the conversations I've had with Elisabetta Sirgiovanni, Alex Finch, Jerome Arab, Tom Fairfield, Mark Bryant, and Katherine Wong. Also massive thanks to James Dillon-Godfray and London Oxford Airport for the insight into how the other half lives.

The Trial owes so much to my brilliant editor, Jennie Rothwell, and I'm incredibly grateful to her for both her faith in me and in helping bring this book into being. Thanks also to my hard-working agent, Joanna Swainson, who not only found me the perfect home at One More Chapter, but along with Jennie helped shape and better this novel in our mini writers' room. I am lucky to have both of you in my corner. Thanks also to Thérèse, Nicole, Caroline, and all the Hardman & Swainson team, and to Emma, Sara, Charlotte, Bethan, and all the One More Chapter team. Thank you to David Cox, Heather Critchlow, and Helen Brewster for comments on early drafts. Thanks to Ezra, Ed Davey, and Sam Leon for unrelated assistance in the between-novels times. Thanks to Cinema Under the Stairs, Botley football folk, the Mrs Barton's Mobile Plan chaps, and the Criminal Minds and Doomsday writing groups. Thanks to Mom, Dad, and the whole extended Masters clan—friends included (you know who you are, and thanks for still not trying to murder me). Finally, thank you most of all to Helen, Joe, and Alice, for being the absolute best.

ONE MORE CHAPTER

One More Chapter is an
award-winning global
division of HarperCollins.

Sign up to our newsletter to get our
latest eBook deals and stay up to date
with our weekly Book Club!
<u>Subscribe here.</u>

Meet the team at
<u>www.onemorechapter.com</u>

Follow us!

 @OneMoreChapter_
 @OneMoreChapter
 @onemorechapterhc

Do you write unputdownable fiction?
We love to hear from new voices.
Find out how to submit your novel at
<u>www.onemorechapter.com/submissions</u>